POISON

Also by Ashley Hodges Bazer

THE CROWN'S CALL SAGA

HERALDS OF THE CROWN
Poison
Fusion (available November 2014)
Reconciliation (available May 2015)

Asylum: The Circeae Tales

POISON

Heralds of the Crown
Book One

Ashley Hodges Bazer

Heralds of the Crown: Poison
by Ashley Hodges Bazer

© 2014 by Ashley Hodges Bazer

All rights reserved. No part of this book may be used or reproduced, graphic, electronic, or mechanical, including photocopying, recording, taping, or by any information storage retrieval system without the written permission of the author.

Published by Rising Press

Cover art by Bryan Hodges

This book is a work of fiction. People, places, events, and situations are creations of the author's imagination. Any resemblance to actual persons, living or dead, or historical events, is purely coincidental.

The Scripture quotation is taken from THE HOLY BIBLE, NEW INTERNATIONAL VERSION®, NIV®, Copyright © 1973, 1978, 1984, 2011 by Biblica, Inc.™ Used by permission. All rights reserved worldwide.

ISBN-13: 978-1-5009-0011-3
ISBN-10: 1-5009-0011-7

To my Gary.

Thank you for inspiring Gaultier,
through your strength,
your faith,
and your unending patience with
and love for me.

I love you.

"Sing the praises of the Lord, you his faithful people;
praise his holy name.
For his anger lasts only a moment,
but his favor lasts a lifetime;
weeping may stay for the night,
but rejoicing comes in the morning."
Psalm 30:4-5

It is a time of peace in the Circeae system. The Logia—gifted followers of the triune God, the Crown—lead the people in anticipation of the arrival of the Divine Warrior and the Ruler Prince. Yet challenge and struggle lurk in the shadows. The Strages, enemies of the Crown, are on the move, gathering strength and numbers. Their mission: to eliminate the Logia, discredit the Crown, and eradicate His name. They begin with a series of attacks on small Logia communities...

CHAPTER ONE

Atrum: 428 Coronus Tempus

Marcella wound the hair of one of the Logia between her fingers, yanked back his head, and savored the *shing* of the blade across her enemy's throat.

Pathetic and misguided. Only a fool would choose to place his faith in a passive, invisible deity like the Crown. As the deep red life spurted from the Logia's throat, the light in his eyes dimmed. She shoved the limp body away, ridding herself of the stench of the Creator King.

The tiny black coils emblazoned on her hands and arms burned with gratification. When she had claimed her first Logia kill, Lucian bestowed the marks of honor, as he had done with all his followers. At first, the pain had been overwhelming. But over the years, she grew to appreciate and understand it. To use it to her benefit.

Gazing across the tree-dotted landscape of Atrum, Marcella caught sight of her cohorts in the waning sunlight, each clad head to toe in black, like shadows. The small group of Strages had invaded the Logia camp swiftly and silently. The Logia in the communal area were first to be slaughtered—their screams barely in their throats before the sound was stolen with fierce slashing of metal against flesh.

Banshee and Madigan stomped through the graveyard of bloodied bodies, more than likely searching for any Logia who had survived the initial attack. Specter paused and knelt next to a female who had made the mistake of reaching for him, probably begging for mercy.

Weak. A small smile played on Marcella's lips as Specter stroked the woman's cheek, though he didn't need to touch her in order to kill her. Carnifex, their magnificent Strages god, had endowed him with the ability to take control of other people's nervous systems. The false sympathy upon Specter's darkened brow was evidence of his intent to toy with the wretched woman. Within seconds, her body went rigid, and Specter flashed Marcella a satisfied grin.

Banshee, her face hidden behind a painted black and white mask, gestured with the tip of her blade to a row of tents draped in heavy cloth. "Others wait inside."

Madigan plodded toward the structures. His blond hair caught in the breeze of the evening. He was young and thick in both wit and muscle. Still, he should have known better. The Strages were forbidden to enter the Logia homes, although the ancient rules seemed a little pointless now.

~Halt.~ Lucian's voice touched her ears, though the command was meant for Madigan. The boy stopped, and Marcella turned her attention to the one who had penetrated all their minds.

Their leader, Lucian Thaedrial, stood at the border of the camp, cloaked in thick black wool. The crisp cut of his jacket and trousers only added to his unusually tall height. He looked more appropriately dressed for a party, rather than a bloodbath. Yet his piercing eyes watched closely, despite the distance.

What does he see?

No doubt he'd witnessed the ferocious raid, executed with skill and precision. Perhaps he'd even taken notice of Marcella's victory over three Logia males and two females. If she could just earn an ounce of his pride. His approval...

Pressure built in Marcella's brain as Lucian's orders pressed into her thoughts. *~Bring the children to me.~*

~If there are none?~ Marcella asked.

A strident and painful roar seized her brain, inking out the scene before her. She never should have questioned Lucian. He saw all, he knew all. He was one with Carnifex, and worthy of her obedience. Her few words would cost her even more later.

Between Lucian's palms, a massive ball of green flame took shape. He launched the ball forward, and it arced through the treetops. Dangerous sparks and embers rained from above as branches exploded with fire. Although the flame spread like a true wildfire, it carried no heat. It was a toxin. During each of their crafting, the Strages had been taught how to offset the effects.

The glowing ball hit two tent structures toward the middle. Three small children darted from the collapsing fabric, only to be caught up in Madigan's waiting arms. With nothing more than a nod, Specter dropped the squirming nuisances into unconsciousness.

Marcella gripped the hilt of her sword as the green blaze enveloped the shelters. Her markings tingled with anticipation. Men, women, and children began to flee. But the Strages had been well-trained. Body after body fell, victims of Lucian's toxin, Specter's wrath, Banshee's screams, or Madigan's strength.

Marcella's gaze fell upon a man who shepherded a group of children and several women, including one holding an infant, toward a silvery spacecraft a short distance away. The ship was an older model and rather quaint. Despite its wear, it would serve the purpose of their escape, or at the very least add to their protection. She stalked toward them, slashing her blade to make a pathway through the greenery. She could almost taste the blood, making the craving more intense.

The man's eyes met hers and widened. He shouted at his flock and pushed the ones closest to him toward the ship. The fear in their faces reflected off the chrome hull in distorted alarm. Marcella reveled in it. The ramp of the ship fell against the ground with a puff of dust. Anxiety thudded through Marcella's chest. She wouldn't reach them in time, even if she ran.

She paused, focusing on the panic and horror emitted by the ones before her. As her eyes closed, a wellspring of fury burbled into her heart. Her empty fist clenched while her fingers coiled around her sword grip. She concentrated on the years of agony, torment, and terror under Lucian's leadership and used that to fuel her power. With a soft breath, she thrust a ring of dark energy from her body, wielding her most threatening weapon of supernatural force.

Emptiness overwhelmed her, taking her to her knees. Fire raged through her fingers as the markings absorbed the essence of death. She fought for breath and lifted her eyes to see every Logia near the ship crumple to the ground. Confident as she was in her skill, she knew Lucian would expect her to assess the remains. To make absolutely certain they were all dead. And her sword would be her insurance.

Pushing off the ground, Marcella darted toward the ship. The scattered bodies were indeed lifeless. More than likely, Lucian would scold her about the dead children, but she did what she had to do. Had the Logia escaped, word of the Strages would have spread. Trouble would rise for Lucian and his followers, even though Marcella knew Carnifex was far more powerful than the Crown.

A sharp cry directed Marcella's attention to the landing gear of the ship. "Shh. She'll hear you. It's all right, precious one," a woman's voice whispered.

She already has.

Marcella snaked toward the female's hiding place in silence. The cries continued, although muffled. The stabilizers would have been the perfect hiding place had the baby been quiet. But the noise, joined with the woman's tearful words of comfort, rang through the well above and echoed. She would be an easy kill.

Maybe Lucian will forgive her for slaying the children if she brought him the infant. Carrying it back would prove interesting, though. She'd never held one, and Lucian would want it unharmed.

As she drew closer, Marcella noticed the timbre of the female's voice had changed. No longer did the words lull and soothe. They were fevered. Pleading, but not with the infant. The woman was praying for protection from the Crown.

It will be a pleasure to help this poor creature understand she believes in a god who isn't strong enough to stand against Carnifex. Disappointment would fill the Logia's final moment.

Stepping around the stabilizers, Marcella opened her arms, as if presenting herself. "I found you," she taunted.

The woman screamed and clutched the baby to her chest. Frightened blue eyes stared at Marcella, tears cresting her eyelashes and spilling down her cheeks. "Please. Please let us go. The child...she's done nothing. She's innocent."

Innocent. You were innocent once.

The thought came from nowhere and splintered Marcella's concentration into disjointed confusion. She'd been Lucian's for as long as she could remember. He'd raised her. Crafted her. And soon, they would wed. Innocence had no part in her life.

"The child is Logia. That is enough." Marcella swept her sword in the air. The sound helped her refocus.

"But you..." the female held a trembling finger toward Marcella. "You're..."

"I'm what?"

Why am I engaging this woman in conversation? Lucian had given strict instructions not to speak to the Logia. The mission of the Strages was simply to rid the Circeae system of the followers of the Crown. To exalt Lucian. To bring Carnifex glory.

"The Crown calls you," the woman murmured.

A piercing light filled Marcella's vision, obliterating the ship and its stabilizers. She froze. Was this one of Lucian's punishments? Had he seen her talking with the Logia? No. Pain always accompanied Lucian's touch. There was no pain. This was different. This was...

Peace.

A soft cooing sound tugged at her attention. She lowered her eyes, and nestled in her arms, was a baby a bit older than the one the Logia woman held. This one smiled at her, a strand of her long brown hair wound about its chubby fist. His fist. Marcella smiled. Somehow, she knew the infant was a boy. Her boy. Her...son. She lifted a finger to touch the boy's cheek. She felt something for this little being. Something unfamiliar.

The light vanished, leaving Marcella feeling like her chest would cave in. Her arms were empty and aching. Her sword lay in the dirt at her feet.

Specter stood at her side. His hold throughout her body was undeniable. Marcella should have been able to counterbalance him, but he'd caught her off guard.

The Logia woman knelt before Madigan with her hands clasped together. Her head was angled upward as she stared past Madigan. She wasn't begging for mercy. She was praying to the Crown. Madigan silenced her tongue as he gripped her head and snapped her neck. Nausea rolled through Marcella's stomach, but whether it was in reaction to the woman's death or Specter's touch, she couldn't tell.

"Let me go." Marcella swatted at Specter.

He shook his head, his brows twitching in arrogant glee. "Lucian would like to speak with you."

Straight ahead, Banshee held the Logia woman's bawling child. A smirk sat upon her lips. Of course. She would deliver the child to Lucian and receive his praise instead of Marcella. Since Lucian had announced his intention to take Marcella as his bride, Banshee had spared no effort to hide her jealousy.

And any chance she could get to make Marcella look bad, she took.

Well, it won't happen again. Marcella's head swam as Specter hooked his arm through hers and led her back toward Lucian. She tugged her arm away.

I will not fail Carnifex. Nor will I fail Lucian.

◆

Pavana: 39 days later

Marcella launched her shield against the wall with an aggravated roar as she marched into the weapons room of Lucian's ship, the *Caedes*. Self-fury and leftover adrenaline propelled her into a brisk pace through the tiny armory.

She'd let the death of that female Logia get to her. Although weeks had passed, the woman lingered in Marcella's dreams. Marcella had even taken to carving her arms with a dagger to rid herself of the vision of cradling that baby. Her very own son. She stared down at her sword. The spotless metal shone back in her eyes, reflecting her failure.

The markings, cascading over her shoulders, up her neck, and across her forehead, itched with unrequited blood. They should be burning with glory and filling her with satisfaction. Or at the very least, provide distraction from thinking about what she had done. Instead, the uncomfortable tickling made her want to slash and shed her own skin. Again.

Fingers wound about her elbow, pulling her around. Lucian stared at her, his disgruntled eyes examining hers. Stormy anger had clouded over his normally handsome features, and his dark hair had shaken loose from its slicked-back style to dangle in long strings across his forehead. What once had been ice-blue eyes stared at her with colorless intensity. His lips pressed together in a dangerous calm while he inhaled slowly through his nose.

"You had four Logia on their knees, Marcella," he finally hissed.

What could she say? Something deep within her conscience had betrayed her and left her vulnerable.

"I know," she muttered.

Lucian whipped Marcella about in his arms. He held her back to him, and took control of her sword. The cold steel of the blade pressed into her neck while Lucian's hot breath breezed across her ear. "Why didn't you kill them?"

Marcella closed her eyes. The vision played through her thoughts once again. The Logia residents of Pavana hadn't suspected a thing. The invasion was swift, as usual, although the numbers weren't at all what Lucian had expected...and no children. Marcella had single-handedly rounded up three men and a woman. A few well-placed jabs with her sword immobilized them. Madigan positioned them for an execution-style death. But looking into the eyes of those Logia, while she should have been slitting their throats, she had returned to that alternate world where she held the child. Her child. And in that moment, everything felt peaceful and serene—a far cry from her reality. Her few seconds of hesitation allowed Specter to kill the Logia instead.

Lucian slanted the blade, nicking her skin. "Answer me."

"I saw something," she whispered quickly, feeling the sting of his anger as much as that of the blade. He would have executed her without a second thought had she ignored him.

Dropping the sword to his side, Lucian stepped around to face her. "Show me."

If Marcella shared the vision, punishment would follow. Lucian wouldn't understand. A baby? She barely understood it herself. "I—" she stared to protest.

His fingers slid behind her neck and pulled her into him. He pressed his forehead to hers. The strain in her head caused her knees to buckle, but Lucian held her with an unnatural strength. He searched her thoughts until he found the memory of the vision. His disapproval grounded her with surprising gravity.

"You want a child?" Lucian whispered, disgust saturating his tone.

Marcella answered with the only thing she could offer—the truth. "I've never given it much thought."

He withdrew from her, once again looking into her eyes. "You are mine, Marcella."

"I know," she murmured with a nod.

"You will not bear children. Do you understand?"

Of course, she understood. She had accepted her role...hadn't she? Lucian was her world. He was her life. Her everything.

"Yes, Lucian."

He watched her for a long moment before he caressed her cheek. His fingers trailed down to her shoulders, his grip changing from tenderness to violence. He forced her to her knees as ferocious, consuming energy crackled between his palms and her body. A constricting tightness emptied Marcella's lungs, leaving her gasping. Somehow, a whimper for mercy slipped from her mouth.

"Find pleasure in the pain, Marcella," Lucian instructed.

It was an old crafting drill. One that she had passed many times before. She should have been able to derive some delight in the agony he inflicted and return it to him. However, the skill escaped her at the moment. All she could focus on was the powerful torment.

Her head rolled back as she looked up at him. "Please," she managed.

Lucian released her and shoved her back on the floor. She gulped at the air, her chest heaving in desperate wheezes. He knelt at her side and twisted his fingers into her hair. "We have a problem, Marcella."

Tears of regret stung her eyes and darted down her cheeks as she edged toward him. It was a vain gesture, but all she had at the moment. She meant so very little to him. "Forgive me, Lucian. Please."

"I'm not in the business of forgiveness," Lucian said, an iciness magnifying his sudden distance. "I have not yet forgotten what happened on Atrum. You deliberately disobeyed me."

"I had to stop the Logia from escaping."

"You are not to use your powers in my presence!"

Instinct prodded Marcella to fight back, but with the trouble she already faced, it was best to keep quiet. She surrendered with a silent nod.

"You will pay for this and the other infractions. I cannot have my bride making me look the fool. I crafted you too early. You will have to be calibrated."

"Wh-what does that mean?"

"That means that you will be subject to Specter for twenty-four hours before I adjust your center. You'll discover new levels of pain." Lucian stroked her hair as he would a pet. "Far more than what you just experienced. I will have to break you."

Marcella closed her eyes, fear lodging itself in her throat. It was useless to plead with him. That would only lead to worse torture. *What's happening to me? I'm stronger than this.* She was Marcella, slayer of Logia. That vision had really affected her. Perhaps the calibration, as Lucian called it, would help her find her true path again.

Lucian crossed to the doorway and beckoned Specter. The black-haired Strages appeared immediately, followed by Madigan. Had they all been listening? They unquestionably enjoyed the show. Especially Banshee.

"Get up," Lucian ordered.

Pushing up from the floor, Marcella rose to her feet. She avoided any eye contact, shame weighing heavily on her shoulders. Specter and Madigan grabbed her arms, holding her firm. She had no fight left in her, though. Soon, Lucian would free her from the burden of the vision and return her to her former glory in Carnifex's name, no matter the cost. She'd surrendered to the idea, almost welcoming it. Lucian's gaze fell to Specter. "I want you to take her to the threshold and keep her there. She needs a good reminder of just how close she is to meeting her end."

Specter licked his lips and sneered at her. Regardless of her frame of mind, he always repulsed her.

"Once you have her under," Lucian continued, "I want you to inflame her markings. She has grown complacent."

Marcella bit her lower lip. Doubt stirred in the recesses of her heart. Somewhere deep inside, she heard the gentle cooing of the baby she envisioned in her arms. *Is there something beyond what I've treasured in Lucian?* Recollecting her encounters with the Logia, they each seemed to embody the same tranquility that had accompanied the vision. They radiated light. Goodness. They died without fear. Marcella only felt darkness and disgrace. Pain and anguish. It was all she'd ever known. And now, she would surely know more of it. And yet, her memory of the vision—and the feelings it awakened—remained.

Lucian pressed in close to her as the men tightened their grips. He brushed his lips along her cheek, then whispered, "I will not let you disappoint me again, Marcella."

"I won't," she murmured, attempting to mask her uncertainty.

With a nod, Lucian stormed past them, executing his dismissal at the same time. Madigan and Specter tugged on Marcella's arms, leading her out of the armory and toward the crafting chamber. A soft cry fell from her lips as she silently prayed.

Someone save me...

CHAPTER TWO

Caelum: 27 days later

The doors of the Caelum domicile stood before Marcella, protecting its residents from intruders. She had pleased Lucian in the days following her punishment. He had shattered her back as part of his calibration. It wasn't a full crafting, but it served its purpose. She had become used to the constant pain that now assailed her body. It motivated her.

The only real relief came when she wielded her sword to slaughter Logia. In those moments, she felt intense warmth that embraced her, calling to her from an unreachable realm. It didn't make any sense, but she attributed the serenity to the approval of Lucian's god Carnifex, pleased with the fulfillment of his wish to exterminate the Logia. Although no one else close to Lucian described such feelings. Lucian's expression had carried both suspicion and anger when Marcella had told him what came over her every time Logia fell dead at her feet. She stopped speaking of such things.

The current mission had led the Strages to Caelum, home to some of the most devout Logia. Lucian had his eye on a small domicile that housed orphan children. He'd told his five followers of an imminent battle with a particular Logia positioned to protect the faith. In preparation for this, they were to raid the domicile, kill the adult Logia, and return to Lucian with the children, as usual. Marcella found herself wondering if that was how she came to be in Lucian's custody.

The others explored the outer buildings, leaving Marcella to take on the chapel itself. Banshee gave strict instructions to report back before contacting Lucian. It was almost funny how poor Banshee fancied herself second-in-command. Marcella couldn't care less, though. She didn't want the responsibility of leadership. She was...content...under the wing of Lucian.

She pushed open the door to the nave and closed it behind her with a soft click. The silence shook her as she imagined a couple of elderly Logia, along with perhaps a female and several children cowering behind a bench. A twinge of pity entered her heart. *Shame, Marcella. Pity is weakness.* Lucian's words echoed in her head.

Her sword sang with metallic resonance as she withdrew it from the sheath. Lifting her chin, she started down the long center aisle. She couldn't straighten her posture completely, but she still stalked forward with confidence, holding her sword at her side. The powerful tip dragged along the stone floor, adding a menacing scraping sound and an occasional spark as her boots clipped along in a measured pace. The effect, undoubtedly, frightened those in hiding.

Lucian would have been proud.

Movement near the altar caught her eye. *So, that's where you're hiding.* Her lips curled into a smile. This would be all too easy.

A whisper of a vision robbed Marcella of breath. Blood dripping from her hands that reeked of death. It only lasted the length of a heartbeat before an icy metal blade snapped against her neck and refocused her attention. A brawny arm captured her, another hand shaking the sword from her grasp. She closed her eyes and gritted her teeth. Of course, she could easily call upon the powers of Carnifex to wrench this buffoon from her back, but she'd toy with him a bit first. Let him think he'd gained the upper hand.

"Delia, warn the others to stay away. The grounds are occupied with Strages," the man who held her ordered.

A slender wisp of a woman—Delia, as the man had called her—slipped out from behind the altar. Raging jealousy struck Marcella with a brutal backhand. Delia was beautiful. Stunning. Her hair, silky, shiny strands of pure onyx, flowed over an elegant white gown. Taking her down would have required no effort. That was usually the case with Logia women. They were weak and frail. Had to rely on the strength of men to protect them. It was pathetic, really.

"You send her to her death," Marcella murmured. "The others wait just outside."

The man chuckled, sounding more like a faint growl. "A common mistake, Strages. She is Logia. She only needs to think the thought, and the others understand."

Marcella blinked as another instantaneous vision broke in her mind. The blood on her hands glinted with regret as she stood before a brilliant light, too bright to look at. The sticky, dark red coated her hands, slowly seeping into the markings that were now part of her. A haunting wail surrounded her. She sank to her knees, only to find herself held fast by the strong arms.

"Carnifex," she whispered in an effort to gain strength from his name.

"Carnifex is an invented god. He isn't real," the man said.

Heat burbled through her veins. "Lies!"

The man released her, but held his sword angled toward her as he reached for hers. Soon, she found both tips aimed at her. With a smile, he said, "Your god has yet to save you."

"Am I your prisoner?" Marcella asked. Her eyes wandered to the attractive woman near the altar. Certainly, she could distract the man by mentally attacking this Delia. Would he sacrifice her to stop Marcella?

"I don't take prisoners," the man said, his gaze following Marcella's.

"Are you the leader, then?"

"You could say that. I am the athaer of the Caelum domicile."

Marcella locked her eyes on him. Diversion. If she wasn't obviously focused on Delia, he might not see the attack immediately. "What's an athaer?"

"It's a position of prominence within the Logia faith."

"Your name?"

He met her stare evenly, placing both swords on the bench next to him. "All right. I'll play along. I'm Jett. And you don't want to do what you're thinking of doing."

With a slow blink, Marcella flashed a firebomb of mental energy spurred with hatred and anger toward Delia. An instant later, Marcella stared up at the high ceiling of the chapel, struggling for breath. Jett squatted next to her, his mouth moving as he peered down, although no sound reached her ears. Delia's delicate face appeared next to his, a look of concern coloring her loveliness. Marcella wanted to hate her, but for some reason, she couldn't drum up the fire. Jett gripped the woman's hand, his thumb caressing her gently. There was some kind of relationship between them. Something tender. Gentle. Unashamed.

Jett's voice finally came through. "...you hear me?"

"I—"

"You are in the throne room of the Crown," Jett explained as he helped her sit up. "You can't hurt any Logia here. We are protected. Safe. Didn't your Strages friends tell you that?"

Clearly, Lucian and the others didn't tell her many things. She felt the man's warm hand take her own, his fingers brushing along the markings that marred her skin. "He's claimed you," Jett murmured.

Marcella snatched her hand away. "They are marks of honor."

Jett shook his head, sympathy in his eyes. "The Strages know nothing of honor. Those marks hurt you, don't they?"

She rubbed the back of her hand, cradling it to her. *How does he know?* Lucian had said that the Logia were devious, but beyond the woman back on Atrum, she'd never encountered one long enough to hold a conversation. She wasn't prepared for this.

"It's my burden," she whispered, humiliation scorching her cheeks.

Jett offered her a hand to pull her to her feet. Marcella simply stared at it. Delia stood slightly behind Jett, watching Marcella warily. Evidently, this female Logia wasn't as trusting as the man. Of course, Marcella had tried to attack her, so Delia couldn't be faulted for being careful. It was a foolish mistake Marcella wouldn't make again. She would simply have to lure the Logia outside.

Jett smiled knowingly, dropping his hand. "Not a chance...Marcella, isn't it?"

What's happening here? She knew the Logia were gifted, but he shouldn't have been able to pull her name out of thin air.

"How did you know that?" she asked.

"The Crown has whispered your name. But Marcella isn't your true name. It was a name given by someone false. Someone who uses you for dark purposes. The Crown has a different name chosen for you. The Eternal Companion—Whom you saw as a brilliant light—has shown you a different life. One with a child." Jett's warm brown eyes turned sad. "And He's also shown you the blood on your hands..."

Marcella shrank back, heat pulsing through her veins. She hid her face from him as her heartbeat pounded her ears. *How can he possibly know the things I see?* She had to get out of this place. She must leave before he—

"You were stolen," Delia murmured.

Stealing a glance toward her, Marcella couldn't suppress the disgust that had finally surfaced. "What?" she spat.

"A long time ago," Delia said, kneeling next to Marcella. She lifted a hand to Marcella's cheek, her soft fingers brushing along the black markings that trailed along her jaw line. "You do not belong to Thaed. You will soon be called to choose between him and your heart. It will tear you apart."

Marcella stared at Delia before she batted the woman's hand away. These people knew things they shouldn't. Their insight shook Marcella. "Who is this Thaed? I belong to Lucian Thaedrial. Why did you call him Thaed? How do you know about him?"

"You are easy to read," Jett murmured. "The Crown has granted us a connection."

"You're manipulating me."

Jett shared a silent exchange with Delia before looking back at Marcella. "We don't have to. Search your heart, Marcella. We are different from everything you know and everything you have been told. Since you've walked in here, you've been questioning. Even before you arrived today. When Logia fall at your hand, you feel relief from the pain Lucian has inflicted upon you. Do you know why?"

Marcella bowed her head, grasping for the comfort of pain. It meant Lucian—and Carnifex—still held her, still claimed her.

Jett's hand touched her hair, stroking it with warmth and kindness. "The relief comes from the brief encounter with the Crown as He gathers His children to take them home to Eternity. It is another one of His ways of calling to you."

"You lie," Marcella whispered.

"Do I?" Jett whispered back.

He took her fingers, angling them to fall into her line of sight. She watched as the black markings faded from the backs of her hands.

"I am not doing this," Jett said, watching in matched awe.

Marcella again jerked her hand away, holding it to her. Panic eroded any clarity she had started to feel. Once Lucian saw that the marks were no longer there, he would certainly be angry. He would know something had happened. "He will punish me," she cried.

"Stay here. Claim asylum among us," Delia said. "We will help you."

The woman spoke the impossible. The promise sounded inviting, but how could Marcella leave the only life she knew? Lucian had long ago convinced her that the Logia were evil. But looking into this beautiful woman's eyes and hearing the tenderness in the man's voice—they were far from evil. They seemed almost... like what love might look like. If there was love without pain.

"I can't," Marcella shook her head. "I—"

"She's not ready," Jett answered for her. "But you have many questions, don't you?"

A loud banging rattled the door and echoed through the chapel. Marcella whipped her gaze toward the door, knowing what awaited her. Banshee grew impatient. The Strages had more than likely found nothing and were ready to leave for home empty-handed. Unless Marcella had been victorious, in which case they would descend like ravenous birds of prey.

With a nod, Marcella dared to look back at Jett. "I'm afraid," she confessed in a whisper.

Jett smiled, compassion in his eyes. "You need not be. You are no longer alone." He pressed a miniscule link into her hand. "When you can find a few moments to yourself, and when you wish to talk, use this. It is secure. Delia and I will do our best to answer your questions. You are always welcome here, Marcella."

She blinked, squeezing the link in her fist. "Why are you being kind to me?"

"Because it's about time someone was," Jett said, glancing toward the door. "It's time for you to learn you have been set free. From darkness.

From death. The Crown calls you, Marcella. He has for a long time. He desires your heart. Don't deny Him any longer."

"We shouldn't allow her to return to them, Jett. They will know," Delia whispered as she gestured toward Marcella's hands. "The touch of the Crown is evident."

"It is not yet her time," Jett said, a trace of sorrow in his words. "The Crown will give her the strength she needs."

"Marcella!" Banshee's shrill bellow carried through the rafters of the chapel.

"The Strages come," Jett stood, pulling Delia up with him. "Forgive us, but we must retreat."

"One moment," Delia murmured. "The Crown desires to deliver you from your torment."

Delia knelt at her side, placing a hand between Marcella's shoulders. A penetrating warmth relaxed away the tension and pain that had built up over the last few months. Marcella closed her eyes as her back straightened of its own accord.

Jett smiled, taking Delia's hand to lift her once again from the floor. "Remember what has happened here, Marcella. You will be in our prayers."

Marcella pulled herself to her feet, using a nearby wooden bench for stability. The door blasted open with magnificent force, toppling sacred sculptures and other pieces of art from the half pillars that stood along the back wall of the chapel. As the dust settled, Banshee appeared with a cross look upon her face. She had taken to wearing a wispy red scarf around her neck, which now reminded Marcella of the blood in her vision. Marcella quickly spun around, expecting Jett and Delia to be within plain sight. They, however, had vanished completely.

"You kept me waiting," Banshee said, glaring at Marcella with resentment.

Marcella glanced down at the backs of her hands. Her fingers still carried the marks, but the areas between her knuckles and her wrists were now completely clear. She quickly hid her hands and the link by folding her arms over her chest. "The chapel is abandoned."

"Abandoned? Then what took so long?" Banshee questioned as Marcella crossed the center aisle toward the entrance. "What, were you praying?"

"I wanted to be thorough." Marcella strained to keep control of her emotions.

Banshee glared at her. The black and white paint on her face was unable to conceal her animosity toward Marcella. "Lucian grows impatient," she spat.

"Lucian will appreciate my attention to detail." Marcella walked coolly

HERALDS OF THE CROWN: POISON

past Banshee to exit the chapel.

She could feel Banshee's eyes boring into her back as she stepped into the sunlight. She tried to slump her posture to keep up the pretense. Banshee was suspicious as usual, and no doubt would poison Lucian's mind toward Marcella. *Well, Banshee can try.* Marcella would play the game as long as she could. But Jett and Delia's words were beginning to ring true. Another voice called to her. As she lifted her eyes toward the bright sun, she realized, as Delia had said, it would just be a matter of time before she would be forced to make the choice.

CHAPTER THREE

Crenet: 43 days later

"Gaultier Lassiter," the revered Athaer Castus said as he breezed down the long aisle of the vast chapel to greet Gaultier and his friends.

Gaultier was keenly aware of the clicking of his boots echoing off the stately stone walls and pillars of the nave. Although he was devoted to the Crown, it had been a number of years since he'd set foot in a Logia chapel.

Castus took Gaultier's hand in his own, embracing him with his opposite arm. "Son, it's been too long."

The older man looked the same as he had when Gaultier left years earlier—silver hair cropped close to his head that highlighted his merry, dancing eyes. His heavy maroon robes helped to hide any weight he might have put on in recent years, but they couldn't mask the evidence of a slight double chin. Regardless, he looked wonderful to Gaultier.

With a soft chuckle, Gaultier returned the affection, smiling at the athaer. "It is good to see you, Athaer Castus."

"I am grateful you could come." The athaer nodded with respect to Gaultier's two friends, Jax and Alton, who had accompanied him on this call and now stood behind him. "Let us retire to my office. We can make introductions there, and then I can bring you up to date."

"It's been a strenuous journey, Athaer. My men would appreciate food and rest," Gaultier said as he, Jax, and Alton followed Castus into the inner portion of the chapel.

The three had traveled directly from Serenata at the request of the athaer, not even stopping to top off fuel. While the ship had many amenities and comforts of home, the length of the flight had been draining. Even Gaultier felt worn down.

"I'm afraid that will have to wait, my son. My apologies," Castus looked back over his shoulder toward the men. "The athaer of Caelum is standing by to speak with you."

Gaultier shot a quick glance toward Alton. "He is here?"

"No. He cannot leave his domicile at this moment. But he has news of movement, just what we've been waiting for. The Dignitaries have asked me to advise you of your new mission. It's all rather urgent, otherwise I would welcome you with abundant hospitality. You know that." The athaer smiled, concern drawing his lips tight.

"We understand," Gaultier said on behalf of the men. He knew Jax and Alton would agree, regardless of the hunger in their bellies and the sleep in their eyes.

The work chamber behind the altar of the chapel was tidy and neat. Not only was it an office for the athaer and his assistants, but it acted as the library for the other Logia who resided and studied here. Tall bookcases formed the walls, holding ancient volumes of Logia history. Gaultier had spent many hours with his nose in these books. It was like coming home.

Athaer Castus gestured to several chairs in a ring near his desk. As the men took their seats, he activated a darkened glass monitor mounted on the wall. "Athaer Criswell, the crusaders are here," Castus stated.

The interior of the Caelum domicile materialized on the display. Gaultier watched as a young man stepped into view. He couldn't have been much older than Gaultier, perhaps even a few years younger. *Oh, I hope Castus isn't planning on chastising me for not pursuing a life as an athaer.* While he knew that the function of the athaers was important, Gaultier felt called to be a crusader for the Logia faith across the system, particularly as the threat grew. Their work on Serenata had reflected that most clearly. The unrest among the people of Bellemort had started to fester, but with outreach and prayer, Gaultier and his friends managed to settle them into a more amicable situation.

"Gentlemen," the man on the screen nodded. "I am Jett Criswell, athaer of the Caelum domicile."

Gaultier cleared his throat, gesturing first toward the brown-haired man at his right, then the blond one at his left. "This is Jax Tyler. Alton Dunning. I am Gaultier Lassiter. We hail from Serenata."

"You are all Logia?" Jett asked.

"No," Gaultier said. "Jax is Lumen."

"We are thankful for our Lumen brothers. You apprenticed under Athaer Castus?" Criswell asked, looking at Gaultier.

"Since my childhood."

"Excellent," Criswell smiled. "I've heard good things from Athaer Castus and Athaer Mersus about you. Tully was most grateful for what you did to support him in Bellemort. Your intercession made all the difference there. It is a pleasure to meet you. I only wish the circumstances were more agreeable."

"I'm afraid we are rather unaware of the circumstances," Gaultier said, eyeing Athaer Castus. "We only know we face a matter of great importance."

"I wasn't trying to conceal information, understand," Castus explained to Athaer Criswell. "I just told them what they needed to know at the time."

"Of course. That is appreciated," Criswell said. His attention turned to the men, his expression falling to a most somber air. "I've had contact with the Strages."

Alton shifted in his chair while Jax leaned forward. This is what they all had been waiting to hear. The Logia were aware the rise of the Strages was coming, but no one knew when exactly. The news was both frightening and exciting, as the trials ahead would be arduous, but it also meant the long awaited reign of the Ruler Prince was on the horizon. The Crown incarnate as a living, breathing man.

Gaultier frowned, staring at Criswell. "Are you certain?"

"Absolutely. A young female associated with the Strages entered the chapel here at the Caelum domicile a little over a month ago. I had to wait until I had approval from the Dignitaries before we could take action."

Gaultier shared a quick frown with Alton. "I don't understand. Domiciles are sacred grounds. Strages should not be allowed to enter."

Criswell nodded. "Correct, but the chapel is open to any who are seeking the Crown. This girl was conflicted. I asked her to remain in contact with me."

"We should warn the domiciles system-wide."

"I don't wish to stir up any hysteria, Gaultier," Criswell answered. "For the Strages, coming here to Caelum was a strategic move. I don't believe they are going to start randomly attacking domiciles. The sanctuaries remain sacred. No Strages can enter, unless invited in by one of us. But they are starting to initiate engagement. And this confirms our fear that this group committed the recent Logia murders."

"Have you at least alerted the councils?" Gaultier asked, looking between Castus and Criswell.

"Not yet," Criswell said, tapping his lips with his finger. "Under the advisement of the Dignitaries, we are to keep this on a need-to-know basis. They want confirmation and solid evidence before we make any announcements to the individual domiciles or their councils."

The two athaers went on to disclose the information they had on the Strages—a small, yet effective band led by one who called himself Thaed. The exact number of members was unknown, but it was thought to be less than ten. Gaultier had heard the news of the attacks on Atrum and Pavana, but the details of the brutality had been kept quiet until now.

"I fear we are seeing the initial stage of the formation of the Gathering," Castus said quietly.

Gaultier shook his head. "It is too soon."

"We thought the same," Criswell said. "But my contact with that young Strages woman revealed a timing we hadn't thought of."

"What do you mean?"

"The naming of the Protectors will happen within the year," Castus answered.

Gaultier glanced toward Alton, who released a slow steadying breath. The naming of the Protectors meant the Challenge would shortly follow—a deadly battle between the Logia and the Strages. The victor would lay claim to the system.

"'My trust and my hope dwell in the Crown,'" Gaultier murmured, quoting from the Creed, the Logia's holy book.

"Indeed," Criswell replied. "But on this side of Eternity, we must prepare for what lies ahead."

Gaultier nodded, leaning forward to settle his elbows on his knees. "Of course. What do you want us to do?"

"Observe," Athaer Castus said. "And if need be, hold them at bay with physical force."

It's to be a sacrifice, then. Just like the other Logia who had been unfortunate enough to find themselves in the presence of the Strages. The enemy of the Crown wouldn't fight fair, and as much as Gaultier wanted to place his hope in divine strength, he knew he alone was no match for the Strages. Still, he had a duty and service to fulfill in devotion to the Crown.

"I had a vision of a snowy, abandoned hillside," Criswell said.

Alton bent forward to whisper in Gaultier's ear, "Asper."

"I'm not sure what's involved, nor why my vision led me there, but the Dignitaries have determined you will be sent to Asper to monitor any movement. We believe the Strages are gathering in a forsaken location," Criswell explained. "There is good reason for you to be there."

Gaultier nodded, accepting the mission. "We have advanced surveillance gear onboard our ship. We like to keep our eyes open as we're traveling."

"The Dignitaries were wise to name you." Criswell smiled. "I understand that a base was established on Asper years ago. You should find a docking space for your ship, basic accommodations, a communications system, and more monitoring equipment. Athaer Castus has the direct coordinates. He will supply you with the provisions you require."

"We report directly to the Dignitaries, then?" Jax asked.

Criswell shook his head. "Report to me. I will then get the information to the Dignitaries as necessary."

ASHLEY HODGES BAZER

Athaer Castus looked at the men in the room. "It is rumored that Athaer Criswell and his wife Delia will be named Protectors."

Gaultier bowed his head toward Criswell, as did the others. It was a heavy responsibility Gaultier never desired. And although it was a great honor, it was also a great burden. He offered a silent prayer for Athaer Criswell. *My King, show favor on this man.*

"We'll leave immediately for Asper." Gaultier said, shifting to the edge of his seat.

Castus nodded and turned once more to Jett. "I will alert you when they launch."

"Thank you, Athaer. Gaultier, Jax, Alton, I hereby commission you in the name of the Crown to the previously stated duties on Asper." Criswell looked at each one in turn. "You are in our prayers and petitions. Go with the blessings of the Creator King, the hope of the Ruler Prince, and the discernment of the Eternal Companion. Crownspeed, my friends."

"Thank you. You are in our prayers as well, Athaer Criswell," Gaultier confirmed with a smile. "*Soli Deo Gloria.*"

Criswell smiled back. "*Soli Deo Gloria.*" The monitor faded to black as his end of the link terminated.

Gaultier rose, clasping his hands behind his back. "Athaer Castus, if you will direct us to the provisions..."

Castus lifted his gaze to Gaultier, a concerned frown lining his brow. "A moment, Gaultier. I'd like to speak with you. There's something you need to see."

Don't do this.

"Something, Athaer? Or someone?" Gaultier fought the scowl that threatened to spread across his face. He should have known that in coming back here, he'd have to face the past. *I don't care to see him.* "Now is not a good time."

"It's been too long, son," Castus urged.

"But the mission..." Gaultier met the athaer's pleading gaze.

Castus was right, of course.

"...will still be awaiting you after you speak with him," Athaer Castus answered with a reassuring smile, standing to join Gaultier. "It's time you both let go and move on."

Gaultier surrendered with a sigh. He jerked his head toward the door. "Jax, Alton, I'll join you shortly. There's someone I need to see."

CHAPTER FOUR

The large mansion seemed to sprawl across half of Tersus. The cold blue brick and slate that formed the outer wall blocked the sunlight, allowing the Strages a few shadows in which to slink. Tersus, being a moon of Crenet, was bathed in bright sunshine throughout the length of the day, but sleeping hours had set in. The streets were deserted, and all the heavy drapes in the windows of nearby homes were drawn. Of course, that didn't matter. The Strages knew how to get in and out without being seen. Lucian had trained them well. Madigan crushed the handle of the door to the servants' quarters, and everyone filed in.

The house was still. Silent. Lucian had told them at least two Logia families had taken up residence here. The place easily could have held many more than that. Marcella disguised her awe as they ascended from the servants' area into the main foyer. Grand chandeliers floated above a wide marble staircase that split in two halfway up. The floor, tiled in black and white, reminded her of a game board she'd seen in Lucian's chambers. The back wall consisted of tall windows, while three steps led to the front door. She'd never seen anything so exquisite. Even Lucian's magnificent fortress back on Venenum, where he had chosen to stay during this raid, couldn't compare. Everything was so dark there, while this place radiated with joy and life.

Taking the lead, Marcella withdrew her sword and silently directed Banshee and Specter toward one side of the staircase. She and Madigan would take the other. Banshee shot her a nasty look. Banshee undoubtedly thought she could handle the whole thing alone. And she probably could. But Marcella was in charge.

"Get going," she whispered, pointing again to the opposite staircase as she started up.

At the top of the stairs, four corridors split off into separate wings. Marcella watched across the way as Banshee took off down one wing. Specter glanced back toward Marcella with a shrug. She gave a nod, then

ASHLEY HODGES BAZER

lifted her chin, indicating they needed to get to work. If things weren't done correctly, the first victim could scream, which would alert the others. Speed was of the essence.

Madigan bounded down one of the wings, leaving Marcella to the other. She crept quickly along the wall, opening the first door she came across. Sunshine met her eyes, allowing her to scan the room with ease. Nothing. She dashed through, making sure no one was hiding in strategic places. Empty.

The next two rooms were empty as well. *Perhaps the entire mansion is abandoned.* Maybe the Logia caught word that the Strages were coming. Or Lucian's information could have been somehow skewed. Whoever had tipped him off would surely pay, if that was the case.

The last room along the hallway was smaller than the others. And dark. Full-length curtains covered the windows in deep shades of burgundy with elegant black swirls printed on the fabric. Marcella glanced down at her fingers. They bore the exact same pattern. Odd coincidence.

Her eyes fell upon a corner where a large ornate looking glass stood in a thick wooden frame, while the frame was supported in a stand. A second glass was mounted on the wall across from the mirror. A scraggly woman draped in black appeared through the glass. Marcella raised her sword. The woman did the same. Marcella bared her teeth in a menacing manner, as did the woman. And before long, Marcella realized the woman in the frame was she. *It's a reflecting glass.* She'd never seen such a thing before.

She sheathed her sword and crossed slowly to the standing mirror, completely entranced. Her fingers first touched the glass to make certain it wasn't a clever trick. As she stared at the woman, she was appalled by what she saw. She touched her reddish-brown hair, winding the long strands between her fingers. Haunted brown eyes stared back at her and examined the cruel black strokes that licked her neck, cheeks, and forehead. She thought of the ones that crawled up her arms and across her chest, down her back, and encircled her legs. Quickly, she tugged off one of the fingerless gloves she'd worn since meeting Jett on Caelum. The back of her hand was free and clear. The color of delicate porcelain.

Her breath caught in her throat. The marks were supposed to be badges of honor. Lucian had given her the first one as a child. The rest had come over time, each area receiving new marks with the numerous Logia kills she'd committed. She staggered back as the realization hit her, along with the memory of the vision she'd had at Caelum. They were blood marks.

Pushing back her sleeve, she scratched at her arm, trying to remove the marks. She shrieked as she rubbed, then clawed at her face. Finally, she collapsed before the mirror, sobbing. Her hair fell down around her

HERALDS OF THE CROWN: POISON

shoulders, and as she glanced up to her reflection, she saw just how hideous she was.

A golden light filled the mirror, surrounding her in warmth. As she watched the glass, the marks on her reflection faded. The woman before her glowed with confidence and security. She no longer appeared fearful or menacing. She carried an unidentifiable strength behind her gentleness. That was the woman Marcella wanted to be.

She crawled closer to the mirror, gripping its frame in her fists. As she touched it, the image disappeared, dissolving back into the cold darkness of the room and gruesome features of her face. With a cry, Marcella smacked the glass with her powerful fist. While it should have shattered, it remained intact.

"I don't understand," she murmured, uncertain of to whom she was speaking. She looked back at her fingers and thought of Jett's god. The Crown. Lucian's enemy. Jett had said the Crown had taken away the marks from her hands. That He'd given Jett her true name. The name he told her she would one day discover.

"I'm sorry," she whispered, glancing up. She wasn't sure why she looked up. It just seemed right that if a pure and true god existed, he would be above her. Unlike Carnifex, who came from the fiery underbelly of their home world of Venenum. *He isn't real,* Jett had said. But the Crown had to be real. Lucian wouldn't hate the deity so much if it were imaginary. Her meager prayer continued, "I don't know what is happening to me, but I need help."

She bowed her head only to see a dainty hand slide a book out from the bottom of the mirror. Marcella fell back in alarm. She hadn't known anyone was there.

"Who are you?" she hissed.

The hand pointed to the book, then opened toward her. Whoever it was intended for her to have the bound volume. She crept back toward the book, cradling it in her hands. The title read *The Creed.*

She stared at it for a long moment before looking up to see a beautiful young woman with blonde hair peering out at her from behind the mirror. "It is the Crown you seek," the woman whispered. "Those Scriptures will help you understand more about Him."

Marcella held the book to her chest. "I—"

The woman crawled out, moving closer to her. "Marcella. The Crown calls to you. Don't you hear Him?"

"You know my name," Marcella breathed...barely.

"My brother and I have spoken." The woman smiled.

"Your—"

With a nod, the woman took Marcella's hand. "Jett Criswell of Caelum.

He told me of you."

Marcella looked at her in awe. "Were you expecting me?"

"I knew you would come."

Snatching back her hand to rub her face, Marcella forced herself to inhale. "I cannot take this book. If I am found with it, they'll kill me."

"Hide it. Learn from it. Jett and Delia are longing to hear from you. To help you. Don't deny the Crown any longer, Marcella. Great things will come of your choice."

"What is your name?" Marcella asked softly.

"Elianna."

A delicate name for a delicate girl. Her hair, worn long and soft, tumbled over her arms in honey-blonde curls. She wore a simple gown, made from a light blue-gray satin. It matched her eyes perfectly. She looked like a crystal doll that could shatter at any moment. Marcella should have felt envy in staring at this beautiful creature, but only peace and love filled her heart.

"Elianna is a lovely name," Marcella whispered.

"Yours is, too." Elianna lifted her fingers to show Marcella. "The marks are fading even more."

Marcella gasped as she examined her fingers, now completely clear, just like her hands. She pushed up her sleeve again to see the markings fade away. Her eyes darted to the mirror. They still remained on her face.

"In time, Marcella," Elianna said, brushing back Marcella's hair in a maternal fashion, "you will be free from those markings. Your true beauty will be evident for all to see."

"I am—"

A piercing shriek resounded through the room. Marcella's hands instinctively flew to her ears as she recoiled back to the floor. Banshee stood in the doorway, her eyes furious and fuming.

"I knew it," she screeched in accusation. "You betray us."

"No." Marcella scrambled to hide the book within her jacket. She quickly got to her feet, glancing down at Elianna. "I—"

Elianna bowed her head and began to murmur a quiet prayer. Marcella lifted her eyes to Banshee, who now stalked to the center of the room.

"Take her life, Marcella." Banshee pointed a sharpened fingernail at Elianna.

"You are not leading this mission," Marcella said quietly.

Banshee planted herself directly in front of Marcella. She was indeed a tall woman, as Marcella, staring straight ahead, could only see her collarbone. Banshee angled her head to look down on Marcella.

The command was given slowly and full of grit. "I said, take her life."

Trembling, Marcella's fingers encircled the hilt of her sword. She knew what was expected of her. She knew if she committed the deed, Lucian would probably forgive her for the faded markings and restore them. But she also knew that something else—Someone else—called her heart.

The thought came to mind to use her sword against Banshee. The woman was a powerful warrior, and could easily best Marcella simply in strength. But she heard something say that Banshee's life was of worth. That she was loved, even if she denied the true Crown.

If she couldn't harm Banshee, she certainly couldn't harm Elianna.

Without making a move, Banshee opened her mouth and let out another cataclysmic scream. The glass on the wall shattered into jagged pieces. Marcella closed her eyes, but not before she saw Elianna's body go limp. It took all Marcella's strength to fight off Banshee's influence and not join Elianna.

"Lucian will be interested in my report." Banshee once more looked down at Marcella.

"I'm certain he will be," Marcella murmured, resisting the urge to drop down to check on Elianna.

Banshee suddenly gripped Marcella's throat, squeezing off her air. "You did this at Caelum, too, didn't you? You let the Logia go."

Marcella held her gaze, allowing Banshee the moment of triumph. She was done with the games. She was done with their Strages ways. She wanted nothing more to do with killing and maiming. And now, she would have to look for an opportunity to run. Preferably before returning to Lucian's influential presence.

"You will face Lucian. Don't keep us waiting. We launch in ten minutes. If you're not on board, I will send Specter and Madigan to fetch you, and I promise you, it won't be pleasant."

Banshee pushed Marcella away, dropping her to the ground. "If Lucian gives you a second chance, you'd best watch your back. I don't play fair."

Marcella cowered on the floor as Banshee spun around and stormed from the room. Once she was out of sight, Marcella allowed herself a choked sob before she crawled to Elianna and turned the beautiful girl onto her back. A crimson line of blood streamed from Elianna's ears and nose. Banshee had indeed committed lethal harm.

Elianna's eyes fluttered open, and a hint of a smile played on her lips. "Fear not, Marcella. I am prepared for this moment."

"I'm so sorry, Elianna," Marcella cried, taking the girl's hand. "Please tell me how I can make it right."

"Find your way to the Crown, Marcella," Elianna whispered, her words impeded with coughing. "Only He can give you the peace you desire."

She was dying. Marcella knew it, but she wasn't ready to let go. Not yet. Not after just finding this lovely creature. If Elianna died, then all the beauty in the system would surely fade away.

"The Logia can heal. Help me heal you," Marcella wept. "Tell me how."

Elianna smiled, her delicate fingers brushing against Marcella's cheek. "It is time for me to go home to Eternity. Do not mourn, for I rejoice as I enter the arms of my King." She coughed again, her eyes rolling back. "I only hope to see you there one day, Marcella."

Marcella gripped the woman's hand, tears falling freely from her eyes. She felt Elianna's strength fall away as the woman's soul slipped from her body. "No," Marcella cried, looking into Elianna's lifeless eyes.

Pulling Elianna close to her, she whispered, "Don't leave me alone in the dark."

She felt a hand stroking the back of her hair. Comforting words filled her mind, *You are never alone.* The Voice that spoke them was familiar, but at the same time unrecognizable. Marcella lifted her chin and glanced around the room.

Empty.

What do I do now? She could try to make an escape. Was she ready for that? Living in fear the rest of her days. Lucian knew her secrets. He would know where to look for her. And he wouldn't let her go without a fight. Betrayal was sure to make him angry. He would want to punish her.

Carefully, Marcella closed Elianna's eyes. She folded the woman's hands over her chest and gazed upon her beauty for another long moment. As Marcella started to rise, her gaze fell once more on the mirror. The marks that swirled over her forehead and along her jaw had disappeared.

"No," she said again, this time with panic. Undoubtedly, Banshee would inform Lucian of her disobedience. And Marcella might have been able to talk her way out of that, playing on Lucian's distrust of Banshee. But with the marks disappearing, Lucian would know something had occurred that was a complete affront to him. She had to find some way to mask her skin.

She looked about the room. If she had a writing instrument, she could draw the marks back onto her skin. It would require much detail and upkeep, but for the time being, that was the only option she could think of.

Ripping through the desk in the room, Marcella found nothing. She had ink and instruments at the fortress. But getting there... Getting past Lucian...

"Show me," Marcella now pled to the Crown. "Help me find a way to hide this."

She rushed into the closet and found a rack full of scarves. She pulled off several that matched the colors she normally wore—dark blues and black. She shoved them in her pocket and wrapped one around her throat. Running her fingers through her hair, she arranged a few shorter strands to lay flat over her forehead. Maybe Lucian wouldn't notice.

Opening a drawer, she found a dark pair of gloves. She tugged off the fingerless hand coverings she wore and exchanged them for full-fingered ones. They were thick, and if she had to use her sword, they would encumber her skill. But for now, they would do.

As she stepped from the closet, Marcella paused in front of the shattered mirror on the wall. It had been a few minutes since Banshee left the room. Specter was probably on his way to retrieve her. Banshee hungered to see Marcella suffer at Lucian's hand. She couldn't escape his wrath.

She wrenched a piece of the glass from the frame and slid it into her pocket along with the scarves. Not only could she use it when painting her face, but she would be able to see where the markings had faded. It may not be much, but it revealed her progress in the Crown.

Stepping once more to Elianna's body, Marcella glanced down. "Thank you," she murmured before dashing from the room. Procedure dictated Madigan would be along any moment to collect her body. When he didn't accompany them, Lucian demanded proof of the kill. Marcella certainly didn't want to see that. She would go on and board the ship. She'd be in trouble, regardless of her willingness to complete the mission, but she could read a few pages in the Creed before anyone else got on the ship. Perhaps she'd find some reassurance that would help her through the coming moments.

CHAPTER FIVE

When Velius stepped into the library, Gaultier tried to hide behind the cover of the Creed. Vel's gaze locked on him, though, and he had to lower the book. Out of respect—although it was not earned, but obliged—Gaultier rose.

"It's good to see you, Gaultier," Velius murmured, crossing to him.

"And you, Vel," Gaultier replied.

Gesturing to the chair, Velius invited Gaultier to sit. The silence between them tensed with discomfort. Gaultier gripped the book to his chest, using it as a shield. *Give me strength for this moment, my King.*

"I don't really know what to say." Velius clasped his hands in his lap.

"There's not much to say, is there?" Gaultier snapped. He closed his eyes, taking a breath. "I'm sorry. I promised myself I wouldn't do that."

"You're well within your rights to be angry with me."

"No. I am dedicated to the Crown, Vel. I cannot hold onto anger, or the repercussions will lead me to a place I don't wish to be." Gaultier stared at the man across from him. "I think you know that."

"I know," Velius whispered, bowing his head. "Gaultier, I am sorry for the things I did all those years ago."

"So you've said. Many times."

"And I've meant it every time," Velius said, looking back at him. "The reason I keep saying it is you won't release me from the burden."

"I'm not the One you should be looking to."

Velius stared at him for a moment before he said, "I've made my peace with the Crown."

"Then isn't that all that matters?"

"No." Velius shook his head. "Not when I see the hurt I've caused."

"I've gotten over it." Gaultier fingered the pages of the book.

"Have you? Or have you run away from it?" Velius asked.

The metallic taste of blood touched Gaultier's tongue as he chomped down on his lower lip. Velius had struck a nerve. Gaultier often thought about his motivations in leaving Kapelle. Castus had wanted him to follow a path, set by Gaultier's father, to become an elder, then an athaer, leading up to being named Protector. Instead, Gaultier chose to join his friends from the domicile in traveling the system as crusaders. They would go where they were needed in the name of the Crown. And that was one of the reasons they had come back to Kapelle when Athaer Criswell issued the call. No, that was the only reason. Gaultier would have preferred to stay far away from the domicile. Away from Velius.

"I'm following my calling," Gaultier insisted, talking around the question.

"That's not what I mean." Velius left his chair to kneel next to Gaultier. "I want resolution. Healing. Gaultier, please. You are all I have left here. And I am all you have."

"You made that choice, Velius. I have Castus. And Jax and Alton. I'm fine." Gaultier shifted to evade Velius's intense stare.

"I am on my knees, Gaultier."

Gaultier glanced down. Velius had remained at the domicile since the night he'd returned in a hysterical state. Years had passed, yet Gaultier could still see him shouting and screaming for Castus, his long, dark hair sticking out from his skull in wild tangles and dingy gray tatters hanging on his gaunt body.

He had changed so much since then. It seemed as though he had completely forsaken the Strages and taken up the mantle of the Logia, as he had been raised. In fact, he'd become an elder, focusing on his gift of restoration. Castus spoke nothing but praise when Velius's name had come up in his correspondence with Gaultier. And although Velius and Gaultier had had snippets of conversations via link over the years, this was the first heart-to-heart they'd had. And that was why Gaultier had avoided returning to Kapelle. He knew the instant he arrived, he'd be cornered.

"I..." Gaultier blew out a breath.

The only way to end this would be to release Velius. Which he could do...verbally. Whether or not he meant it, he didn't really know.

"Fine. I forgive you," he whispered.

Velius closed his eyes, took Gaultier's hand in his and pressed his cheek to it, just as Gaultier had watched him do with Castus long ago. "Thank you," Velius whispered back.

"I have much to do. I am going to Asper in just a few hours," Gaultier said, trying to find an excuse to rejoin his friends. "It's an assignment from Athaer Criswell of Caelum."

"He is a good man." Velius looked up at Gaultier. "Will you keep in touch with me?"

Just as I thought. It wasn't only forgiveness Velius was after. It was a

ASHLEY HODGES BAZER

relationship.

Gaultier nodded with a sigh. "Let us plan to have weekly visits via link. I will make an effort to do so."

Velius smiled. "That is more than I could ask."

"I would like to hear more about your journey, Vel," Gaultier said, eyeing the man before him. How he wished he could find a measure of trust. "I know you've worked hard."

"And I will be happy to share." Velius pulled back to stand. "I look forward to getting to know you again."

Gaultier rose, matching Velius's height. "And I you."

Velius extended his hand toward Gaultier. *Am I ready to do this?* Gaultier stared at the offered hand for a long moment before grasping it. Without thinking, Gaultier pulled himself close and embraced Vel. In an instant, he was transformed into the little boy who wandered into the domicile, lost, hurting, and alone. But in this one embrace, he'd come home. Years of pain melted away, freeing Gaultier and Velius both.

Gaultier pulled away, bowing his head. Emotion had weakened his resolve. "I must go."

Nodding, Velius stepped out of the way. "I wish you Crownspeed."

"Thank you." Gaultier crossed to the doorway. "We'll talk soon, Vel."

Before the man could say anything more, Gaultier left the library. He jogged into the chapel, looking up at the ornate altar.

"Why does it have to be so hard?" he whispered in prayer. "He should be the one person I can count on, and yet, there's such strain there..."

Gaultier knew the answer. He cared deeply for Velius. Looked up to him. Admired him. And when Velius made the choice to turn away from the Crown and the Logia, it had wounded Gaultier deeply. Add to that the Strages recklessness—wickedness—that led to the death of his parents, and it was no wonder Gaultier had trouble holding on. As a Logia, he couldn't entertain hatred, but the relationship with Velius certainly suffered. It was yet another reason Gaultier had rejected the idea of striving for the Protector role. His heart harbored feelings and issues that would only interfere with the purity and righteousness required to fill that position.

Gaultier spoke aloud to the Crown. "I no longer wish to feel this way. Take these burdens of anger, and mistrust, and doubt. I wipe the slate clean and vow to give Velius a chance. Please, my King, don't allow him to let me down again."

With that, Gaultier slipped from the chapel in search of Jax and Alton. As he had told Velius, there was much to be done before they took off for Asper. But now, his heart felt a little lighter. Something in him had changed. Despite his caution, trust in Velius sprouted, and Gaultier hoped in time, the friendship between them might blossom.

30

CHAPTER SIX

Venenum: 26 days later

Marcella slid her leather gloves onto her hands. Luckily, Banshee had left her alone since the encounter at the mansion nearly a month earlier.

Jett and Delia had also made contact several times. Jett reassured her she had nothing to do with Elianna's death, and he harbored no ill feelings toward her because of it. A solid friendship had developed between them, and both he and Delia urged Marcella to return to Caelum. Marcella couldn't deny the thought had crossed her mind on more than one occasion. She could not yet leave Lucian and the Strages, but she had to protect herself in some way.

During his teachings, Lucian had started to talk of the Gathering. Marcella shuddered at the thought. He described the Gathering as a select group chosen by himself and Carnifex. They were to be merciless and uncompromising as they sought converts to the Strages faith. They were also to issue the official Challenge of the Logia, battling against the Protectors. Victorious, the Strages would rid the system entirely of the Logia and any followers of the Crown.

Marcella's heart had changed. Anger, hatred, and fear had been her constant companions, but the Crown had taken all that away. The Creator King filled her with joy and light...and it became harder and harder to conceal it.

Grabbing a small well of ink and a fine writing brush, Marcella pulled out the shard of mirror she had taken from Elianna's home. Her fingers brushed along the copy of the Creed she kept hidden with the reflective glass. As much as she wanted to read its inspiring passages, she hadn't the time. Lucian had been away on a private mission, taking with him only Banshee. His sudden disappearance worried Marcella, and when she attempted to contact Jett and Delia, she received no response.

Upon Lucian and Banshee's return, Lucian commanded the Strages to join him for the evening meal. He had something to share. Marcella prayed that the meal wouldn't include a reprimand. Or worse.

Lucian had said nothing to her, apart from the instruction to meet later that night with the others. Banshee just smirked, lording over her the knowledge of what had occurred in Elianna's room. Marcella was certain, as they traveled, Banshee had told Lucian everything.

She had practiced touching up the markings while Lucian was away. Had he caught her, he would've more than likely tortured her before taking her life. He would have counted losing the markings betrayal of the worst kind. And he certainly wouldn't accept her pleas or excuses. The Crown calling to her in the midst of such malevolent chaos? It was preposterous. Delia often assured her that it was because the Crown had an important role for her. Lucian would balk at the thought.

Admiring her work in the mirror, she touched the tip of the tiny brush to one last spot under her left ear, dabbing the ink onto her skin in a delicate spiral. Ironic how the coveted markings were once beautiful in her eyes. Now, they were an anguished reminder of the lives she had stolen. She murmured a prayer of forgiveness. It had become her recent mantra. Yet, she hid behind the painted markings, unable to accept fully the gift of mercy and grace the Crown offered.

The hour grew late. Marcella packed up her inkwell, the brush, and the mirror in a folded square of cloth, and placed them atop the Creed in the back of the drawer of her little table. By now, the other Strages would be in the dining hall. Lucian would more than likely keep them waiting. It was done with purpose, to remind those under him he was in charge. Marcella had often been with him, making the ordered entrance only moments before he did. Tonight, however, Banshee had taken her place.

"'Fear not, for I am with you. Forever your King, always your Companion,'" Marcella murmured, reciting the words of comfort she had committed to memory from the Creed.

As she descended the darkened staircase, the whisperings of her comrades echoed from the dining hall. Her heart swelled as the idea of running to the docking bay and stealing a craft to travel back to Caelum overwhelmed her. The thought was nothing more than a simple hope, however. She didn't know the first thing about piloting.

Stepping into the dining hall, all eyes turned on her. Lucian stood at the head of the table, a look of fury reddening his features as his gaze fell on her. Within a heartbeat, he cast aside the evidence of anger, pasting on an apathetic expression. No one ever made Lucian wait. No one. Marcella would certainly be in trouble now.

"Glad you could join us, Marcella, dear. Take your seat, please," Lucian said, the tone in his words indicating an icy distance Marcella knew

HERALDS OF THE CROWN: POISON

she would regret.

Her usual seat was at Lucian's right hand. But she had guessed correctly. Banshee now sat there with a haughty smile curling her lips. She didn't wear the black and white face paint. A cruel, forgotten loveliness surrounded her delicate frame. The black robes and red scarves that normally accentuated her frightening strength and power were replaced with a simple satin sheath of slate gray. Pale blonde hair caressed her bare shoulders. Marcella could now see Banshee's markings stained her skin in alarming jagged lines like shattered glass. She felt pity for the woman.

As Marcella lowered into the only empty seat at the far end of the table, she dropped her eyes to avoid the glares from the others. Specter sat next to her, and she could sense him using his influence to infiltrate her body. He enjoyed using his abilities whenever the whim suited him. He'd often told Marcella he took particular delight in wrenching his associates into frenzied hysteria when they were in trouble with Lucian. It took some effort, but she held him off. Lucian had once taught her how to counterbalance the various powers of the Strages.

Lucian, dressed formally in a tailored jacket, reached down to lift his goblet from the table. He took a long, slow sip, another reminder that those under him awaited his every movement. Winding his arm about to rest the goblet close to his chest, he stared down at the Strages, his eyes finally landing on Marcella. She felt her cheeks blaze with heat. It wasn't an effect of Specter's touch, but of the discomfort she felt remaining in the company of this evil.

"As I said before we were rudely interrupted by childish insolence, which will not again be tolerated, I have brought you here tonight to share in a victory and to give you a taste of an upcoming ritual that will seal the fate of the Logia across the system. We will no longer be bound by the Challenge, for I have thwarted the Crown's plan to hold us in his grasp. Carnifex has overcome and will conquer not only the weak, pathetic Crown, but his servants as well."

The others applauded and cheered. Marcella knew she should. Her breath came faster as she clapped her hands together. The gloves muted the sound. As Lucian once more stared at her, she dropped her eyes to the empty plate before her.

"Release her, Specter," he demanded.

Right away, Marcella felt Specter withdraw from her. She lurched forward as relief clumsily spilled over her. Lucian, still holding his goblet, stalked slowly around the table and paused at her side. His presence was mentally and emotionally staggering.

She focused on the plate while Lucian trailed a single finger along her cheek with a sensual familiarity. "Take off the gloves," he commanded with

ASHLEY HODGES BAZER

a quiet sternness.

"I am cold," she whispered. *Please don't pursue this further.*

"I gave you an order, *pupa*," he said, using the pet name he called her long ago. Before he crafted her. His tone exposed his anger. He already knew the markings were gone.

Swallowing hard, she unbuckled the strap that wound about her wrist. She berated herself for not taking the time to ink her hands as well. But that wouldn't have mattered. Lucian had a way of seeing things beyond the normal eye. She was foolish for trying to hide from him.

He placed the goblet on the center of her plate, taking her bare hand between his. His fingers rubbed over the top of her fair skin, almost as if he grieved the loss of the markings. Releasing her, he stepped back and dipped his finger in the goblet. Stained red with his choice of drink, he ran his finger along her cheek a second time. Marcella closed her eyes. She knew the ink ran with the application of the liquid. Shame brought heat to her cheeks again, although an icy chill slithered across her back.

Lucian said nothing, but grasped his goblet and returned to the head of the table. As he passed Banshee, his hand swept tenderly through her hair. It was a motion intended to hurt Marcella. To drive a wedge of jealousy into her heart. Banshee had become Lucian's new queen. But funny enough, Marcella no longer cared.

"Bring in the prisoner, Madigan," Lucian ordered before taking another long draw from his goblet.

The door on the far end of the hall opened. Madigan dragged across the floor a man dressed in soiled brown rags. A head covering hid the man's face. His hands were tied behind him, but his legs kicked with resistance. The visible skin was a brutal purple, cut and scraped. He'd been beaten more than once.

"The Logia, on behalf of the Crown, are weeks away from naming their Protectors. Those who will accept our Challenge and battle us for rule over the system. As I stated earlier, I have thwarted such plans. For as the Logia elders deliberate over who is to be their Protector, Carnifex granted me foresight."

Lucian crossed to the man, now on his knees in front of Madigan. "Banshee and I returned to a location that should have brought this about months ago. However, folly and infidelity interfered with clear judgment," Lucian said, looking now at Marcella.

Her eyes darted to the door. How far could she make it before Specter's touch would boil her blood? Before Banshee's scream would liquefy her brain? Before Madigan would tackle her? Before Lucian would—

"Behold, I give you the Logia Protector, mighty and valiant and on his

HERALDS OF THE CROWN: POISON

knees in reverence to Carnifex's servant."

Lucian ripped off the head covering, revealing Jett. The beatings disfigured his face with swelling and bruising. Marcella's breath caught, but she tried to keep from revealing her guilt. Panic swam through her. If Jett was here, what had they done to Delia?

Fiery eyes shone beneath Jett's wild, unkempt hair. Despite the thick gag in his mouth, he disputed Lucian's claim that he was in any way submitting to a servant of Carnifex. Red streaks discolored the brown fabric across his chest. Wide gashes along his arms and neck remained open and raw.

"Raum Carrick joined us and lured the Logia out of the domicile. And through this, Raum has earned a place among us. The Logia was alone when we found him," Lucian answered Marcella's unspoken question. "But that matters not. He was the one we sought. Jett Criswell, hailed among the Logia as elder, teacher, priest, and Protector-elect.

"Pathetic." Lucian spat on Jett as he circled around him like a predatory animal. "If your beloved Crown cares for you so much, why has he not come to save you?"

Jett closed his eyes and bowed his head. Marcella joined him in silent prayer, but Lucian's severe slap cracking across Jett's jaw ripped her from the consoling sanctity. Jett toppled to the side with a whimper. Madigan, with ease, reached down to set Jett upright again.

"The death of the Protector must be carried out properly," Lucian said, meeting Marcella's disbelieving stare. "We travel to Oresed tonight. At the break of waking hours, in three days' time, the ritual will begin. The sacrifice of the Protector will be made at the Gateway Dome. This will end the Challenge, and as the Logia fall away, the Strages will rise."

Lucian stormed from Jett's side to Marcella. "To redeem yourself for your mistake, *pupa*, you will complete the ritual. The blood of the Protectors will stain your hands for the glory of Carnifex. You will be recrafted upon our return. Your calibration evidently wasn't enough. The pain of the markings will be restored with constant force, reminding you of your true servitude."

A choke-hold of terror and mortification snaked around Marcella's neck. Crafting was a painful process, both physically and mentally, involving the complete destruction of the Crown's creation and mending by the power of Carnifex. She had been fully crafted long ago as a child, and the memories were faint. But she had watched Banshee's recrafting years ago, which horrified her. Even Banshee's attack screams were more bearable than the ones she gave that night.

Marcella lifted her gaze to see Jett's mournful eyes pleading with her. The moment Delia had spoken of upon their meeting was at hand. She was

ASHLEY HODGES BAZER

now forced to choose between her heart and Lucian. But the choice was easy. Obvious.

"Specter, escort Marcella to the crafting chamber. I will personally dispense ten lashes, then you are to run her through basic drills until we are ready to depart." Lucian wound his hand into Marcella's hair. He then yanked her head back, forcing her to look up at him. His eyes were soulless, leaving Marcella feeling as though she were staring into the void of death. "You are mine, *pupa.* Never forget that."

CHAPTER SEVEN

Oresed: 3 days later

Exhaustion and agony ravished Marcella's body. Lucian's lashing sapped nearly every ounce of her strength. He had ordered the crafting drills only to put her in a state of absolute psychological weakness. And when the moment of the sacrificial ritual—Jett's execution—was to take place, he would fill her with enough energy to get her through. But how could she do such a terrible thing? Surely, it would seal her fate and isolate her from the Crown forever.

Specter's mental focus trained solely on her. He monitored her body's every movement. Lucian must have instructed him to do so, knowing how brutal the drills would be. What he wasn't counting on was the resentment that propelled Marcella to fully entrust her soul to the Crown. And in truth, while resentment played a part, it was the promise, the hope, that called to her. In her anguished despair, she prayed to the Crown for guidance.

Jett.

Of course. She had to get to Jett. He was being held in the cabin next to her. Marcella saw him as they brought her on board. He had been beaten, yet again, and caged like an animal, anchored to the far corner of the room.

The ship had landed less than an hour ago, with Lucian's private shuttle immediately behind, and all but Specter vacated to prepare the site for the ceremony. No doubt, they would return shortly. Whatever she was going to do would have to be quick.

Marcella moaned, hoping to lure Specter a little closer. Really, the distance didn't matter. She could have flattened him from anywhere within the ship. But she wanted to control the energy wave to prevent from hitting Jett. *Perhaps the Crown will protect him.*

Sure enough, Specter fell for it. As he leaned in toward her, she gripped his tunic and called upon her gift. His eyes went wide with surprise

ASHLEY HODGES BAZER

and alarm as his control lifted, slipping away into nothingness. The shockwave of force burst through him, rendering him unconscious. He collapsed on the floor next to her.

Taking a breath, she whispered a prayer of thanks and pushed herself up, fighting the pain that gripped her. Lucian was too confident to bind her. Or perhaps, for some reason, he still trusted her. She hoped he made the same blunder with Jett. It would take her too long to find a key, and if Lucian had gone that far, he'd probably have carried the key with him.

Creeping from the room, Marcella crossed to the cabin next to her. The door opened with ease. Cowered in the corner, just as she remembered, sat Jett. His expression was one of peace, and as Marcella moved closer, she heard him praying quietly.

His faith astounded her.

Before she said a word, he opened her eyes and looked at her. "My friend," he murmured with a relieved smile.

She fell against the bars of his cage, reaching for him. The thought of Jett's kind, lovely wife came to mind. "Delia?"

"She's safe," Jett answered. "We knew they were coming. I was the only one to remain, for we were given glimpses of this moment."

So Jett had stayed behind on purpose? That was beyond comprehension. Surely, he had to know he would face death at Lucian's hand.

"You chose to sacrifice yourself?" Marcella asked.

Jett smiled despite the cuts on his cheek, shaking his head. "This moment is not about me, Marcella. This moment is about you. Your choice."

She shirked back, dropping her gaze to the floor. "I am not that important," she stammered in a whisper.

"Oh, but you are." Jett moved closer to take her hand. "Marcella, every one of the Crown's children is special to Him. He loves you as though you were the only one. You are not alone."

Marcella bowed her head, fighting back tears. *Not now.* She couldn't risk emotion taking over now.

Jett's fingers caressed her hand tenderly. "He's washed you clean, Marcella. The Crown has taken away your past and entrusted you to make a good choice for your future."

"Lucian will kill me," she whispered.

"If he does not, he will kill me," Jett answered. "I am prepared to face that. Are you?"

Marcella stared at him in awe, silence settling upon her shoulders. How had it come to this? She had once been reconciled to a life of slaying and maiming. She was comfortable and...well, content. She was revered.

But a question was injected into her heart. A single question that wielded far more power than her physical strength and mental abilities combined.

At once, she knew what to do. Her fingers fumbled with the lock of the cage. Grasping it tightly, she channeled the same energy she had used against Specter to plow through the metal, deconstructing its cellular configuration to turn it into metallic dust. She glanced up at Jett, who now returned her gaze with astonishment.

"Go," she whispered.

"No. I will not leave you." Jett climbed out from behind the bars. "We face them together."

Marcella glanced over her shoulder toward the door. Nervousness began to devour the peace she felt with Jett. "I'll find my way. The Logia need their Protector."

Jett bowed his head in humility. "I have not yet been named, Marcella."

"You will be," she murmured. "And Delia..."

A glowing smile touched Jett's lips. "She will be touched by your sacrifice."

Closing her eyes, Marcella nodded. She realized despite her effort to deny herself the desire, she longed for someone in her life to care for her as Jett cared for Delia. Their love for each other would make facing Lucian worthwhile. Not to mention the reward of Eternity as she approached the Crown.

"Before you go," Marcella started, turning to him. "I wish to..."

Jett must have understood without her saying it aloud. He gripped her hand, bowing his head once again. "Then pray with me," he said.

Marcella assumed the prayerful stance, repeating Jett's words when he paused to allow her to do so. "Creator King, Ruler Prince, and Eternal Companion, You are the saving grace that rules my heart. I give my being for Your service and Your care, regardless of the circumstances that may come my way. I pledge my temporal devotion and beg You to embrace my eternal soul. Forever a servant and follower of the Crown, I place my life in Your hands and trust You with all I have. *Soli Deo Gloria,* always and forever, may it be so. *Assentior.*"

Jett looked upon her with joyous pride. "My sister in the Crown," he said, wrapping his arms around her.

Marcella allowed his grainy tunic to dry her tears. She clung to him, savoring his acceptance and love. This was what she had been searching for. It was a shame that in the few hours that she had left of her life, she found it. But now, she was promised Eternity, surrounded with such love and peace.

"You should go," she whispered in Jett's ear.

"Hold fast to the Crown, Marcella. He will protect and keep you." Jett locked his eyes on hers. "I pray you will make an escape, and when you do, find the Logia. They will help you. Crownspeed, sister."

"Crownspeed," she mumbled, watching as Jett bolted quickly from the cabin. He moved with grace, strength, and speed, regardless of his injuries.

She crawled back to her cabin, unable to find steady footing. She feared what was to come. Imagining the look in Lucian's eyes rattled her. Alone, she would not have the courage to face him. But as Jett said, she was no longer alone. The Crown resided in her heart and strengthened her soul.

Specter began to stir. Marcella returned to her reclined position on the cushioned bench. Lucian would easily deduce she had been the one to release Jett, but perhaps she could buy her friend a little more time to flee by concealing the signs of his breakout.

My King, I beg You to place a shield over Jett, my...brother...in You. How strange, but wonderful, to think those words. *Help him to find means of escape. Deliver him safely back to the Logia...and to Delia. And give me the strength I'll need to face Lucian.*

<hr>

Marcella closed her eyes to slits and went limp when she heard footsteps entering the ship. From the gait, she knew it was Madigan. He'd probably been sent to fetch the prisoner. That meant that the Strages were ready to begin the ritual. For close to an hour, she'd been praying for Jett and listening for sounds of struggle. She hoped he'd gotten away.

Madigan pounded on the door before busting it wide open, revealing the stout, tow-headed boy. So young. Lucian had chosen him for his might. Madigan was just a child, a Logia they had discovered on one of their raids. Lucian crafted him, easily manipulating him to serve the Strages. The boy never questioned Lucian and followed him blindly.

"Specter, Thaed is ready for—"

As his eyes took in the scene, he stopped. Marcella could tell he was processing what to do. He moved to Specter's side, touching his shoulder.

"You asleep?"

Specter groaned and lifted a hand to his head. He glanced toward Madigan before leaping to his feet. Marcella squeezed her eyes closed as Specter's fists curled around her tunic and pulled her off the bench. "What did you do?" he demanded, shaking Marcella.

She didn't have to feign weakness or injury. The crafting drills had ensured that. With a cry, she grasped Specter's wrists, holding on as he jammed her against the bulkhead.

"You toyed with my head! What did you do?" he asked again.

HERALDS OF THE CROWN: POISON

"I—"

Madigan gestured over his shoulder. "Um, Thaed is waiting."

Specter threw Marcella to the ground. He too knew better than to keep Lucian waiting long. Why did Madigan refer to Lucian as Thaed? Before Marcella could ask, Specter kicked her in the ribs. Her body curled in on itself as she clawed the floor and gasped for breath.

"Did he send you to get the prisoner?" Specter asked Madigan.

"Yes."

"Then do it. I'll bring the girl."

Marcella closed her eyes again. *Please, Madigan. Please don't leave me alone with Specter.* Her heartbeat began to pulse with adrenaline and panic. She couldn't get enough breath... She...

Glancing up toward Specter, Marcella realized he was getting his revenge. Without her knowing, he had taken control of her body. Habit lured her to turn to the darker ways to block him, but Jett's reminder that she wasn't alone once again rang in her ears. A whisper of a Logia prayer slipped from her mouth, and an instant later, Specter's grip fell away.

In anger, he grabbed a fistful of her hair and pulled her to her feet. "We will let Thaed deal with you."

"Lucian!" Marcella cried, her hands trying to help her head find relief.

"Thaed is his name now. Carnifex has manifested himself in Lucian. We now serve a living, vengeful god."

So it was true. Somewhere inside her, she had hoped her observations and instincts were wrong. That Lucian was just going through a phase in his faith and that he would eventually come around to seeing the error of his ways. Perhaps even live in peace with the Logia. Specter's statement confirmed her misjudgment.

"He is Carnifex?" she asked.

Specter laughed. "He has birthed a new vision of what the Strages will be. All will soon bow at the names of Thaed and Carnifex and pledge their loyalty to us."

"Perhaps in fear, but not in devotion," Marcella murmured.

"And so it appears you will be the first to discover what happens to those who refuse," Specter said, his hand squeezing the back of Marcella's neck to push her into the corridor.

Madigan stood in the hall, a worried look in his eyes. "He's gone," he mumbled, uncertainty gushing from him.

Specter's gaze once again fell on Marcella. "Madigan, report to Thaed immediately. Apprise him of the situation—"

"What situation, Specter?"

Lucian appeared at the end of the short corridor, staring at the three of them. Behind him, Banshee filtered in. Madigan bowed before Lucian as

Specter shoved Marcella forward.

"Tell Thaed what you've done."

Marcella whimpered at the force, stumbling toward Lucian. She caught herself and took a couple of calming breaths before she lifted her eyes to his face. He raised an eyebrow as his foot tapped a pattern of impatience. He didn't appreciate the games.

"I let him go," she whispered.

"You did what?" Thaed asked, taking a single step toward her. His head tilted as his expression darkened.

Marcella straightened, an inner peace overtaking the pounding in her heart. "I let him go," she professed with an air of confidence.

"You let him go?" Thaed repeated.

"It wasn't right, Lucian."

"You let him go?" he asked again. His words were slow, thick with anger.

"I had to."

"You had to." Thaed echoed with a tone of accusation as he crossed within inches of Marcella. He hadn't been this close to her since before she'd met Jett back on Caelum. Waves of anger rolled off him, palpable with heat. "You had to release the Logia I took captive to help us fulfill our plan and end their despicable religion?"

Marcella stepped back, dropping her eyes. "Y-your plan is wrong."

Thaed stared at her, then looked about the rest of the Strages before his glare returned to her. "Say it, Marcella."

She leveled her gaze to his. "I'm leaving, Lucian."

"Say it."

Peace filled Marcella completely, removing all traces of the trembling that had started when Lucian had first confronted her. "I renounce your ways. I am done."

"Say. It."

Supernatural confidence took control. Marcella lifted her chin as she spoke the words of ultimate commitment. "I have given my life to the Crown."

The ship fell to a deep silence and grew very still. Lucian took a slow, measured breath before his fingers snaked into Marcella's hair. He drew her close to him, his hand resting tenderly along her cheek. Marcella closed her eyes, old feelings of desire and longing creeping into her heart. But she now knew Lucian couldn't fill her the way she truly desired. He couldn't love her. She held her breath, waiting for the moment of finality. Lucian was only a heartbeat away from killing her.

Instead, he stepped back and whispered his realization, "You know the prisoner." His hand remained on her cheek as he stared into her eyes.

"He is a friend," she admitted, fighting shame with her knowledge of the Crown.

His thumb caressed her cheek with a false tenderness. "It wasn't just a mere encounter."

"No," Marcella said softly. "We spoke often following that day."

"Your betrayal knows no bounds," Lucian said at a level meant only for her to hear. His fingers now stroked her hair. "You were to be my bride and my queen."

Marcella met his gaze, shaking her head slightly. "I am not sorry. The true King has earned my devotion."

The anguish Lucian displayed was only a disguise for his anger. Faint ripples of fury passed over his face. In his eyes, Marcella could see a nightmarish evil beyond what she'd ever seen before. It unnerved her. Slowly, his hand dropped to his side as he stared at her.

A single nod gave the order for the Strages to attack.

Specter, the closest to her, bent her arm behind her as Banshee approached with a lethal smile. As Lucian's new second-in-command, she was entitled to first blood. Sharp claws scraped along Marcella's cheek, eliciting a pained scream from her. Specter held her firmly as Banshee backhanded her. The talons encircled Marcella's throat, digging deeply into her skin.

Having the upper hand, Specter wrenched her other arm from its socket. She tried to cry out, but Banshee's grip choked off her air. Specter held her arm as he jammed his elbow into her dislocated shoulder. Madigan's meaty fingers wrapped around her knees and knocked them together in overwhelming agony. Specter yanked back on her arm, and she felt something snap. Nausea crashed through her stomach as her arm gave. She spun in Specter's grasp. His sinister smile met her pleading gaze before he slapped her hard, sending her into Madigan's clutches.

The boy's ominous grin frightened her. He secured his hand against the back of her neck and smashed her head into the wall of the corridor. He whirled her around and did the same on the other side before he threw her to the floor.

She cringed, trying to get her arms to cooperate to cover herself, but they wouldn't obey. Specter's polished boot stepped on her hair as she tried to lift her head. He stared down at her, while Madigan slashed her arms with tiny flicks of a dagger.

"Enough," Lucian said, having watched the attack from his casual stance against the wall.

Beaten and bloodied, Marcella lay on the floor, whimpering, "Lucian..."

The Strages moved back, allowing Lucian to step within her sight. "I am Thaed, high cleric and father of the Strages, and a servant of Carnifex who now resides within me. You will bow before me." He bent low to examine her eyes. "What do you have to say for yourself now, Marcella?"

"N-never will I bow before you, Lucian." Marcella lifted her head with a hint of a smile. "*Soli Deo G-gloria.*"

Thaed's face, red with rage, turned sad for one instant. He eased a sharp instrument from his sleeve and knelt down over Marcella. She had little fight left, but he instructed Specter and Madigan to hold her. She watched in horror as Lucian tore the neckline of her tunic.

"The Strages will always blaze in your heart," he muttered, scrawling the blade against her skin. She screamed and writhed in pain while he carved something deep into her chest. "You are marked for me. Should you live through this and encounter Logia, you shall surely know. It will pain you to be near them."

Marcella cried as the men released her. She wanted to roll onto her side, to shield herself in some way, but any control she had over her arms resulted in excruciating pain. The Strages had done their job well.

"Pathetic." Lucian shook his head, looking toward Banshee. "Give me the emulsion."

Banshee handed him a glass vial full of bright red liquid. Madigan and Specter again took hold of her and lifted her from the floor. They dragged her back into the cabin and shoved her onto the bench. She slid limply to the side, unable to withstand any further torture. Madigan grabbed her hair and tugged her back into a sitting position, allowing Thaed to force the liquid into her mouth. It tasted bitterly acidic, burning as it traveled down her throat.

"You will not be allowed to sing the Crown's praises, nor tell anyone what has happened here," Thaed said, gripping Marcella's jaw closed so that she had to swallow the mixture.

Marcella sputtered and gurgled as the liquid wrenched her voice from her. Thaed held her firmly until she went limp under his grip. Through all this, he had yet to take her life from her. And with the numbers he had slain, it made no sense as to why he would keep her alive. The answer had to lie with the Crown.

Thaed patted Marcella's cheek to get her attention. "Your god has left you here, Marcella. Do you still believe in him?" he asked in a taunting tone.

She couldn't voice her answer, but she nodded through her tears. Now more than ever. Her conversations with Jett, Delia, and Elianna resounded in her mind. The Crown indeed called to her. He had a plan for her. He would see her through this.

"Then we'll see if your precious Crown can find you in oblivion," Thaed hissed.

He pressed his palm to Marcella's forehead and muttered an intense, sinister curse. Her vision spun the room, the eyes of the observing Strages swirling into shadowy clouds. The blinding darkness enveloped her consciousness, taking her far away. As the black void washed over her, all traces of awareness and sensation vanished.

CHAPTER EIGHT

Asper: the next day

"We've lost signal. Again," Jax said as he stepped into the small living quarters they all shared.

Living quarters was putting it nicely. The space, carved into the side of the mountain, smelled of dirt. While it provided some respite from the terrible climate of Asper, the room was always cold. Even though they had a heater, it couldn't warm the space properly. Planks of wood and sheets of netted orange plastic held the packed soil in place. Gaultier couldn't even stand at his full height.

The base, as Jett had called it, consisted of this little room, a corner of which served as a dining area, and a wide corridor that led to an equipment room, where they did most of their observation. The installed monitoring devices proved to be much more comprehensive than the ones on Gaultier's ship. Whoever had created this operation knew what they were doing. But it would have been nice if they had considered those of greater height and found a way to better generate heat.

A second corridor split off from the observation room, leading to the docking area. Somehow, they had managed to squeeze Gaultier's ship, the *Midnight Sun*, in there. It wasn't a large ship by any means, but just as with the rest of the base, everything seemed to be cut small.

"That's the third time we've lost it today," Alton said from his relaxed position on his cot. "It has to be that nasty storm out there."

"Yeah, earlier, I picked up a transmission of some sort. When I started to check it out, everything went down. I've been trying to get it back for the last hour or so, but no response," Jax replied.

Gaultier rose with a sigh, winding his chunky gray scarf over his stooped shoulders. "I'll go check on it."

"You sure, man?"

With a nod, Gaultier rubbed his hands together and breathed into

HERALDS OF THE CROWN: POISON

them to warm his fingers before getting back into the required ensemble of heavy outer gear. "Yeah. I want to know what that transmission was."

"Take the rope," Alton suggested. "The wind is blowing too hard."

"Night is coming on, too. You'd better hurry, or you won't make it back," Jax added.

"I'll make it back. Just have some coffee brewing, okay?" Gaultier smiled at his friends as he shrugged a quilted coat over his body.

Alton stepped in front of him to help him with the fasteners. The provided coats were certainly warm, but they were bulky and hindered most movement. Still, Gaultier wouldn't dare brave a venture outdoors without one.

"What kind of adjustment do you think it needs?" he asked over Alton.

Jax rubbed his chin. "I can tell you via link after you get the snow dusted off. I think we're going to need a, oh, probably close to a forty-degree tilt, angled toward Aevum, which should be due north this time of day."

Gaultier nodded, patting his coat. Alton reached into the pocket and produced a pair of gloves. He helped Gaultier ease his fingers into the thick leather before tucking the extended cuffs into the sleeves of the coat. Gaultier grinned. "I'm glad all the fine-tune equipment is in here. I couldn't press a button with these things if I had to."

Alton chuckled, spinning Gaultier around. Gaultier trudged out of the room, followed by Alton, while Jax returned to the observation room. Another short corridor, lined with cables and wires, led to the entrance of the bunker, protecting the small base from the outside with an oval-shaped metal door. Gaultier didn't relish the idea of going out again today, but it was necessary, especially with the news of a transmission.

Lifting a wide helmet, Alton placed it on Gaultier's shoulders and strapped it to the coat. "Check link," Gaultier murmured.

"Loud and clear," Jax responded in his ear. "Coordinates transmitting...now."

Gaultier blinked as red letters and numbers popped into view on the helmet's visor. "You know, Jax, I don't think I need this right now."

"Mandatory, buddy. You know that."

Gaultier sighed. He meant to disable the coordinates readout in his helmet earlier. The information was intended to be helpful, but it just got in the way of his sight.

"You're really worried about the rules out here, Jax? I thought I was in charge of this mission, anyway."

"Fine." The lettering disappeared. "But if we lose you, it's your own fault."

"I'll have the rope."

"All the same."

Gaultier glanced down to see Alton laughing. He popped his friend in the chest as he brushed past him. With all the padding around his arm, Alton probably didn't feel a thing.

Alton fed the rope into Gaultier's gloved hands before securing it around his waist. One of the structure's wooden support beams served as the rope's anchor. The men used the rope only when the weather was really severe. If they couldn't make it back on their own, the others could pull them in. Low-tech retrieval system.

Giving his friend a nod to signal him to open the door, Gaultier sighed again. Alton pressed his weight against the door before unlatching the four locks that held the door to its frame. With tremendous effort, he stepped back, holding the door so that it wouldn't blow inward. He couldn't stop the snow from whipping in, though. Gaultier moved forward, out into the bitter cold. The door behind him slammed closed.

The wind thrashed around him, whistling shrill tones through his helmet. "You still got me, Jax?"

Static nipped at Jax's connection. "...stly. Get ba... ...oon as you ca..."

"Great," Gaultier muttered. He was pretty much on his own now.

He pressed into the snow and wind, thankful for the protective glass that shielded his face from the cold. The receiver was only a five-minute walk from the bunker, but with the harsh weather, it took closer to fifteen. Gusts of wind threw Gaultier to the ground more than once. Each time, he pushed himself back up, brushed himself off, and continued on. The snowdrifts created large banks he had to walk around, adding more time to the walk. He grumbled under his breath.

"...ah...?"

"Can't hear you, Jax. You're breaking up," he said, finally catching a glimpse of the receiver.

As he approached, he noticed quite a bit of damage to the antenna and receiver dish. The box holding the rest of the equipment looked as if it had been tampered with—dented and smashed in.

"If you can read me, we've got a problem out here, guys. Someone has been here."

Gaultier knelt down, his glove-thickened fingers fumbling with the tiny lock on the box. "Blast," he whispered, before raising his voice for the link to pick up, "I'm not going to be able to get into this tonight, guys."

He stood to examine the antenna and dish. Both appeared to be pretty beat up, too. Strange. Asper was, for the most part, unexplored. His small group had been out here for just over four weeks and had seen no one. They'd only received trace signals of spacecraft passing overhead. And this damage looked intentional. Not like some random wild animal searching for a meal.

The cold started to wear on him. It was time to head back. They might even have to scrap the mission at this point. Jett, Castus, and the other Logia elders wouldn't be pleased, but they'd have to deal with it. No matter what they may have prophesied, the Strages or the so-called Gathering—or whatever they were going by—was not happening out here. Gaultier wondered if the Strages even existed, despite Jett's claims that he'd encountered them. The only other faction he'd ever heard of that opposed the Logia teachings was the Crepusculum. And they mostly kept to themselves.

As Gaultier turned to start the trek back to the bunker, a fierce flurry of wind and ice caught him square in the chest and knocked him back. With a groan, he lifted his helmeted head, then dropped it on the ground. He landed atop of an outcropping of rock and the jagged edges jammed into his spine, despite the padding. He closed his eyes for a moment, knowing full well how dangerous that was out here in the cold. A single minute of rest could turn into overexposure, hypothermia, or even result in not waking up.

"...ual...?" he heard along with a loud pop and more crackling static.

"Yeah, I'm here. I'm heading back," he murmured as he opened his eyes again.

A large branch from a treetop above plummeted toward him. He tried to roll out of its way, but one of the limbs smacked against his helmet, shattering the glass. Brutal cold lashed against his skin with the glass as the link fizzled out completely.

"Blast!" Gaultier cursed aloud. He tugged the helmet off his head, chunks of glass falling onto the snow.

He jerked a glove from his hand and felt around in his pocket for the spare knitted hat he'd taken to wearing when inside. Tugging it over his long hair, he then jammed his fingers back into the glove. He'd have to get back to the bunker quickly. His face was already frozen, and he didn't know the extent of his injuries, although he could feel the sting of several cuts.

Abandoning the helmet, he gripped the rope and gave a light tug before pulling hard on it. He was thankful for the guide at this point. Stumbling into the blinding snow, he headed back to the bunker.

The banks had altered slightly. Gaultier wound around them, but stopped short when he saw what appeared to be a human hand sticking out from one of them.

"By the Crown," he whispered, rubbing his eyes with his gloves to make certain the cold wasn't just playing tricks on him.

He clambered up the drift, brushing away snow from the hand. He noticed a tinge of blue to the exposed skin. Uncertain of what he'd find, he kept digging. The wind didn't help, as it continued to fill in the gaps he'd dug.

The rope around his waist tugged on him and dragged him back down the bank. He regained his footing, then jerked hard on the rope. Hopefully, Alton got the message. Moving quickly, he climbed back up the bank and continued brushing away the snow.

He slid his gloves along the arm, working through the snow to get to whatever body might be buried under the drift. Carefully, he hooked his arm along the person's shoulders and reeled back. As the body wrenched free from the snow, he tumbled backward down the bank. With another loud curse, he jumped to his feet and dusted off the snow.

A woman hung halfway out of the drift, her brown hair matted with snow and ice. She wore a blood-stained white tunic that blended in with the surroundings, and it certainly wasn't enough to protect her. The blue continued throughout her skin, and Gaultier couldn't tell if she was even alive. He dashed back up the drift, ripping off his gloves.

"Miss? Miss, can you hear me?" he asked, touching her ice-covered cheek. Her face held a multitude of bruises and cuts. In fact, her body was beaten beyond what anyone could probably stand.

Oh, by the Crown, she's still breathing. Barely, but she was still taking in air. He planted himself in the snow and quickly unfastened his coat. He ducked out of it, wriggled it through the rope, and wrapped it around her. He then adjusted the rope around his waist, lifted her into his arms and yanked on the now taut line. *Come on, Alton. Reel us in.*

The rope jerked him forward, but he caught himself. Shifting the woman slightly, he anchored back against the rope and started to walk toward the bunker. It was cold indeed, but he didn't have too much further to go. Besides, he couldn't just leave the girl there to die.

As the bunker came into view, Gaultier tugged on the rope repeatedly, hoping to get Alton's attention and assistance. "Alton!" he called out, but the wind carried his voice to the treetops. Finally, he reached the bunker and kicked on the door. It opened, allowing Gaultier and his new companion to stumble into the semi-warmth of the bunker.

"What the...?" Alton started as Gaultier set the woman down in the corridor.

"We have to get her warm. Grab my cot, and take it to the observation room."

"Why?"

"It's the warmest room we have. Move, Alton!" he ordered, examining the frozen woman.

Alton darted back toward the living quarters. Gaultier patted the girl's cheek again. "Come on. Can you hear me?"

No response.

HERALDS OF THE CROWN: POISON

He grabbed her wrist and felt for a pulse. It was faint, but he could feel it.

"Jax! I need a warming blanket. Quickly!" Gaultier called out as Alton stepped over them to set up the cot in the equipment room.

"Still got no signal," Jax said, sauntering into the corridor with a white corded blanket. He stopped short when he saw Gaultier kneeling over the beaten, unconscious woman.

"Yeah, it's a little beyond repair right now," Gaultier mumbled. "We're scrapping the mission."

"Who is that?" Jax gestured with the blanket toward the female.

"Don't know," Gaultier said, edging his arms under her to move her into the observation room. "Bring the blanket and follow me."

He settled her carefully on the cot and situated the blanket over her. Jax activated the blanket's warming cycle. Alton leaned against the wall, staring down at the girl. Gaultier sat back on his heels.

"How long before we can be out of here?"

"Won't take long to shut everything down. It's just a matter of packing our personals and starting up the *Sun*," Jax answered quietly.

"Good. I want to give her a chance to wake up. Maybe she can answer a few questions I have."

"We can get you cleaned up in the meantime," Alton said.

"I don't care about my—"

"You've got cuts that need tending to. And look at your hands."

"He's right, G," Jax said.

Gaultier glanced down. His hands carried deeply embedded fragments of rope fibers. His palms blazed with rope burns. His knuckles and fingertips were nipped with frostbite. He hadn't even noticed, but now that the injuries were pointed out, everything started to hurt.

"All right, surgery time. While Alton is working, Jax, I want you to contact Jett and Castus. Tell them we're en route back to Kapelle, then go ahead and shut everything down. Except our heat. And proceed with preflight checks. As soon as she's awake, I want to get us out of here," Gaultier said.

"She may not wake up, G," Alton murmured, stepping closer to her. "She's been beaten up, and she's definitely been exposed to the cold for too long. And here..." He pointed to her forehead. "She was hit with something. Hard."

"Somebody brought her here to die," Jax whispered.

"Then we can't let her. Alton, give me your kit. I'll work on my hands. You watch over her," Gaultier said. "No woman should ever be treated like this."

Alton unzipped a small black bag and placed it on a table near Gaultier before he knelt at the female's side. "She needs a restorer, G. I can't do much for her."

"Do what you can," Gaultier insisted. "She might know who—or what—went after our equipment out there."

CHAPTER NINE

She opened one eye to a dim interior. Multicolored dots of light lined one of the walls. The makeshift bed under her was efficient, not meant for long, hard sleeping. She tried to sit up, but her body wouldn't work with her. Wide layers of cloth bandage wrapped her right arm from her wrist to her shoulder. It was bound to her middle with more cloth. A stiff splint held her left arm in place. Lighter gauze covered one eye, and she could feel other bandages along her face.

A man appeared in the doorway. Broad-chested and muscular, he cut off any chance of escape. Not that she could move if she wanted to. His clothing was non-distinct—a black tunic and matching trousers. A thick gray scarf wound about his throat. Wild, dark curls danced across his shoulders as he stared at her with black eyes.

"You're awake," he said plainly, his voice husky.

She started to say, "Yes," but no sound came from her throat. She tried again, but nothing. Instinct raised a hand to her throat, but with her movement restrained, she could only look up at him in panic.

"It's all right." He stepped into the tiny room. "You're safe. Can you not speak?"

She shook her head, attempting to make any kind of sound, but still, she could not.

He knelt on the floor next to her, placing his hands on either side of her face to study her non-bandaged eye. "Might be a result of your injuries." He dropped his hands and sat back on his heels. "Let me tell you what I know. I'll ask you some yes or no questions, and you can just nod or shake your head. All right?"

She nodded.

"I found you outside, which is odd because we're on a pretty remote planet in-system. You were nearly frozen to death, but you somehow survived. From what we can tell, you were beaten rather violently, and then hit over the head. We tried to care for your injuries the best we could. I imagine you have a pretty nasty headache, though, don't you?"

Nod.

"Do you know what happened?"

Shake.

The man frowned and bowed his head. "I had hoped you could tell me." He glanced back up at her. "You must be scared, huh?"

Nod.

"Do you remember anything? Any little detail?"

Shake.

"How about your name? Where you're from?"

She thought for a moment. *Easy question. Come on. What's my name?* Her eyes widened as she realized she had no answer for him.

He understood. She saw the flicker of worry cross his face before he regained control. "All right," he murmured, gently touching her shoulder. "It's okay. I know people who can help you. They're just..." He blew out a breath. "Just far away."

She glanced down at her body, fighting back tears of fright. Struggling desperately to remember something—anything—she clenched her fists and squeezed her eyes closed. A darkened void was all that met her.

"Hey, it's okay." The man placed his strong hand along her face again. "We're going to help you. I am Gaultier Lassiter. I'm here with two friends, Jax Tyler and Alton Dunning. I'll introduce them to you in a little while. They're getting things ready for takeoff."

She let out a sigh, trying to allow herself to trust the man before her. He seemed friendly enough. And so far, he hadn't taken advantage of her lack of memory.

"Are you willing to travel with us?"

With her only other option being to stay in this cavernous place, she nodded quickly. Gaultier shifted slightly, lifting a blanket from near her feet. "Are you warm enough?" he asked.

Shake. She was freezing.

"I wondered." He situated the blanket over her. After he examined some sort of control, he adjusted its knob. At once, she felt comforting warmth flow from the blanket. "Alton said you were too hot, but I thought you might have been feverish."

She shivered, wincing as the slight movement started a chain reaction of throbbing throughout her body. Gaultier placed his hand on her shoulder, his expression turning sympathetic. "Hold on. We're going to get you to a restorer."

A restorer? She had no idea what that meant. But it sounded like this man wished to help her.

"You're going to need a name. At least something I can call you so you

HERALDS OF THE CROWN: POISON

know that I'm talking to you." He smiled softly at her, a single finger brushing back a strand of hair from her forehead. "Cora?"

She shook her head with a frown.

"Hmm." He looked up, plucking another name from nowhere. "Sprilla?"

She stared at him with a raised eyebrow, which caused him to laugh.

"Sorry," he chuckled. He closed his eyes, bowing his head for a long moment. He almost seemed to be caught in prayer. As he resurfaced, he smiled at her. "All right, since the Crown obviously showed you favor out there in the cold, how about Hanileh? Where I come from, it means *grace of the Crown* and *little one.*"

With a smile and a nod, she looked into his eyes. He smiled back and leaned over her to remove the gauze from her eye. "Hanileh," Gaultier said softly. "It suits you perfectly."

"We're ready to go, G!" a voice called through the cave.

Gaultier tossed a quick glance over his shoulder before looking back at her. "Are you ready?"

Hanileh nodded as a shiver of uncertainty ran through her. Gaultier dabbed at her eye with the gauze. "I'm going to ask Alton to help me. I don't think you should try walk yet. We'll carry the cot onto the *Sun*—that's my ship, the *Midnight Sun*—and get you settled into a comfortable bunk. Should make traveling back to Kapelle a little easier. And we'll help you. You're not alone," he murmured as he stood and stepped back, offering another smile of encouragement. "I'll be right back."

Watching him go, Hanileh turned her eyes to the ceiling. How could she not know who she was? And how in the system had she ended up here with this Gaultier person, beaten and broken? Gritting her teeth, she blinked as hot tears pierced her eyes. She just wanted to go home. But she had no clue where home was...

———————◆———————

Gaultier slipped into his cabin where Hanileh slept. Before departing Asper, he and Alton had emptied out one of the *Sun's* storage compartments and placed her cot inside. He just didn't have the heart to make her endure the trip back to Kapelle on that cot, so he settled her in his cabin. If he needed sleep, he'd use the cot.

Leaning against the wall, he watched Alton skillfully tend her injuries. As he looked at the girl, he tried to get a reading or sense of her, but nothing came to mind. Later, when he could be alone with her, and she was a little stronger, he might try to fuse with her. She was beautiful, despite the cuts and bruises along her face. Gaultier found himself getting angry at whoever had harmed this delicate creature.

"How is she?" he asked of his friend.

"The same." Alton snipped the end of a bandage before pressing it to the wrapped portion of her arm. "But no signs of infection, so that's good news."

Gaultier's eyes turned to Alton, fighting the hesitance to ask his next question. "Have you tried a restoration?"

Alton had recently discovered he bore the Logia gift of restoration. It was quite by accident. He'd been Lumen all his life, pledged to defend the Logia and the Crown, but never believed he held Logia powers. During a rowdy game of tossball, Jax's toe caught in a hole, and he went down on his arm. Alton, having gone through a couple years of medical study, examined it. As he did so, he murmured a prayer of guidance. He received guidance, all right. He'd been granted a precious gift. Jax's arm was immediately healed.

"No," was Alton's firm reply. "I'm not ready yet."

"All right. I understand," Gaultier said.

The discovery had been something of a shock. Alton wanted to find out more about his gift, and focus on Logia study for a while before he began using the gift. He didn't wish to abuse it. This spurred a wide debate through those belonging to the Kapelle domicile. Gaultier supported his friend, though.

Alton gestured for Gaultier to draw closer. "Did you notice this?" he asked, peeling back Hanileh's blood-soaked tunic from her shoulder.

A strange symbol had been deeply cut into her skin. Gaultier immediately recognized it. The Strages. Jett had disclosed it in one of their recent link conversations.

"I didn't see it before," Alton said, glancing up at him. "But once I got it cleaned up, the symbol was clear. She's marked, G."

Gaultier stared at the symbol for a long while before lifting his eyes to Hanileh's motionless face. He'd just stumbled across this girl, and now they were all wrapped up in a crazy intrigue that could prove dangerous. Yes, she was injured and frightened, but she couldn't be evil. He'd heard the Crown Himself reveal her name to him. So who exactly was she?

◆

"Hanileh, we've arrived at Kapelle," Gaultier said, stepping into the tight cabin.

She hadn't slept much. Her mind was too busy trying to pull the tiniest strand of memory from within. Even a slight fragment would have been something. It disturbed her that she found nothing. Nothing.

During their two-day flight, she'd met Alton and Jax. Alton took care of the cuts on her arms and face. And with Gaultier's assistance, he redressed the cloth bandages and made sure she was comfortable. Jax gave her detailed information on the ship, which meant nothing to her, but she enjoyed his excited chatter. Gaultier remained close, reading to her from the Creed. The passages gave her some peace about her situation.

"How are those legs feeling?" Gaultier asked with a smile. "Ready to give it a go?"

Hanileh nodded. *Anything to get up and out of this bed.*

Gaultier anchored his strong arm under her and helped her to sit. She closed her eyes as the room spun. She had indeed been lying down too long. As gravity took hold in the different position, she felt aches and pains in multiple places.

"Take your time," Gaultier said gently. His arm remained along her back, an ever-present reminder of his kindness and support. Someday, when she could, she would have to ask him why he was being so kind to her. A complete stranger.

"My friends are waiting in the domicile to meet you and to help you."

Hanileh frowned. She'd already met the two men on board. Since she couldn't ask the question, she cocked her head in hopes he'd understand.

"No, not Jax and Alton." He smiled. "They'll meet up with us in a bit. They're going to shut down the ship and advise our friends on what to unload."

Ah. With a slow nod, Hanileh glanced down at her useless arms. An insufferable heat flushed through her cheeks and ears. *I can't move. Why is this happening?*

Gaultier's hand brushed along her back. "We'll take care of that. The domicile has a restorer. Let's get you on your feet."

His arms encircled her as she shifted her weight forward. The ache in her knees turned to fire, but Gaultier held her firmly. "It's okay," he whispered. "You're doing great."

Her first step was wobbly and clumsy, but with a few more, she regained full command of her stride. Gaultier stayed close, though. At the ramp of the ship, Hanileh's self-consciousness kicked in. Her stomach fluttered, yet she forced her lips into a small smile as she met Gaultier's gaze. His return smile filled her with confidence and warmth.

"I've asked Athaer Castus to have Velius meet us in the consultation room adjacent to the docking bay. Velius is a Logia restorer. You will find him to be wise and gentle." Gaultier looked down. "He's my...well, let's just say I've known him for a long time."

Hanileh blinked. *Tell me more. Please.* She wanted to know more about Gaultier. There was something he wasn't saying about Velius. He did speak of the Kapelle domicile with great respect and affection. She could tell he looked to Castus as a father figure. If he had parents, he hadn't spoken of them. And of course, she couldn't ask.

Navigating the ramp wasn't easy. The angle added extra pressure to her knees. She clenched her teeth and tried to focus on breathing. Toward the bottom, she noticed Gaultier mostly carried her. He was gentlemanly enough not to mention it, though.

"The consultation room is across the bay. I can take you the rest of the way if you wish," he offered.

She shook her head. She might not have known much about herself, but she knew that she wasn't a weakling. Resolve and pure stubbornness took control as Hanileh resumed walking on the flat surface of the docking bay floor. An amused smile touched Gaultier's lips.

"You are determined, aren't you?"

Hanileh pushed a provoked breath through her nose, causing Gaultier to chuckle.

"Well, you don't have to be rude about it," he laughed.

As promised, the consultation room was just beyond the exit of the docking bay. A man stood at the door, waiting for them.

"Gaultier," he said, bowing his head in respect.

"Velius," Gaultier greeted him.

Hanileh could sense a slight tension between the two. Her mind wandered as she tried to figure out the connection, but Gaultier cleared his throat, bringing her attention back to the moment.

"This is Hanileh."

The man, who resembled Gaultier, smiled at her, extending his hand in welcome. As she looked closer, she noticed Velius and Gaultier shared many similar features, only where Gaultier wore his hair long about his shoulders, Velius's was trim and neat. *Old friend,* Hanileh thought as she looked at Gaultier in question. *Or relative?*

"She cannot speak, and she has no memory of what happened to her," Gaultier explained to Velius. "As you can see, someone went to great lengths to hurt her."

"Then it's quite possible she brings danger with her." Velius's tone and expression reprimanded Gaultier.

"It's possible, but it's our duty to help," Gaultier said in polite argument.

"If it can be done without compromise." Velius opened the door to the consultation room. He looked at Gaultier. "Stay with us."

"I am to report to Athaers Castus and Criswell upon arrival."

"They will both understand."

Gaultier stared hard at Velius for a moment before he gestured for

HERALDS OF THE CROWN: POISON

Hanileh to enter the room. He followed closely behind and waited near her as Velius closed the door behind them. Velius crossed into the open room, taking a chair from its place near the wall.

"Tell her to sit," Velius said.

"She understands us, Vel." Gaultier gestured for Hanileh to take the seat. "She just can't talk."

"Once she regains control of her arms, perhaps she'll be able to write and tell us what she knows." Velius waited for Hanileh to sit before he began to remove the bandages. "Did Alton not attempt a restoration?"

"He doesn't feel he's ready. I don't wish to push him."

"A gift is a gift. It's not a matter of developing it."

"Let's not talk about this right now, all right?" Gaultier smiled gently at Hanileh. "I imagine our guest is frightened enough."

Hanileh watched the two men in awe. How similar they were, yet so different. Gaultier's eyes held a deep compassion and kindness she didn't see in Velius. But she trusted Gaultier. He would not mislead her or harm her.

Velius examined her carefully. When he brushed against her right shoulder, the pain stole her breath. As she gasped, Gaultier stepped closer, his hands reaching for her in a protective manner.

"Dislocated shoulder," Velius stated.

"Be careful," Gaultier whispered. "She's been through enough."

"Are you going to let me do this?" Velius looked up at Gaultier.

Hanileh bit her lip to edge away the rising tears in her eyes. Yes, her injuries were painful, but the friction between the two men disturbed her. The flight had been so peaceful and calm, but here, where it should be serene, there was unspoken violence and anger.

Gaultier touched Hanileh's hair, stepping back to give Velius space. The man resumed his examination, studying Hanileh's cuts and bruises. She winced as he touched her left shoulder. He carefully situated her tunic, staring at the deep wound on her chest. His eyes lifted to meet hers, a look of recognition in his expression.

"On second thought, Gaultier, perhaps you should run along to report to the athaers." Velius covered the wound with her tunic once again. "This will be an easy mending."

"Restoration," Gaultier corrected, angling his head as he watched Velius. Hanileh sensed some mistrust on his part.

"Old habit," Velius muttered, looking into Hanileh's eyes. "She will be fine. I will bring her into the chapel when we are finished here."

Hanileh glanced beyond Velius to Gaultier. She didn't want to be left alone with this stranger, and Gaultier obviously didn't want to leave her alone with him, either.

"She will be fine, Gaultier," Velius repeated. "I've done this once or twice, you know."

Gaultier nodded, his eyes shifting to Hanileh's. He gave her an encouraging smile. "I'll see you in just a few moments, all right? You're in good hands here."

Swallowing hard, Hanileh lowered her gaze. Velius touched her arm gently, craning his neck to make eye contact. The smile on his lips charmed her. She didn't realize how enraptured she was with him until she heard the door click. Gaultier had slipped out without her noticing.

Velius's hand traveled down her arm to take her hand. "Let's get you healed up, shall we?"

Hanileh nodded, keeping a watchful gaze on him.

"Some of this, I can take care of in the old-fashioned way," Velius said, his other hand moving to her broken shoulder. "Close your eyes, and take a deep breath."

Doing as he instructed, Hanileh shut her eyes. As she filled her lungs, Velius's grip tightened, and with a sudden movement, snapped her shoulder back into place. Hanileh gasped as the shock and pain set in.

"Hold on," Velius whispered into her ear.

A warmth filled Hanileh, starting in her shoulder. Velius murmured prayerful words, his hands resting lightly over each of her injuries. The throbbing eased up, melting her muscles into working order. The gentle heat worked through her and erased the pain completely. She began to feel relaxed and very sleepy.

"Stay with me." Velius chuckled softly.

Hanileh forced her eyes open, looking at the man kneeling in front of her. He reminded her so much of Gaultier. She wished she could find the key to the mystery.

"Try to move your arms. Just go slowly, and don't get discouraged if they don't respond right away."

Taking another breath, Hanileh glanced down at her arm as she tried to move it. No response. She furrowed her brow, looking back at Velius.

"Nothing?"

She shook her head.

Velius frowned. "And I can't get that wound on your chest to heal, either."

He splayed his hand against her chest and closed his eyes. He spoke quietly, the tone of his prayer changing to a more commanding timbre. Hanileh's air choked off, leaving her wide-eyed and panicked. Velius's eyes rolled back in his head as he muttered words that made no sense to Hanileh. She tried to pull away, wanting nothing more than to breathe. Within seconds, Velius withdrew his hand, leaving Hanileh doubled over and panting.

But she could move. Without pain. The deep cuts on her chest remained, however.

Velius stood and turned away from her. His shoulders were slumped, and he said nothing for a few moments. Before long, he spun back around. Hanileh noticed a trail of blood from his nose. He'd wiped it away, but a slight trace lingered along his lip.

"I must return you to Gaultier," Velius said, his voice rough with an unknown anguish.

Hanileh bowed her head in thanks, hoping Velius understood. She wasn't certain what had occurred while he restored her, but whatever it was had pained him. Certainly that wasn't the way of the Logia. At least not the Logia Gaultier had spoken of as they traveled. Perhaps Gaultier could explain.

She stepped toward the door, waiting for Velius to lead the way. He dabbed at his nose with his fingers before brushing past her. His posture had changed. He now seemed to carry the weight of shame on his shoulders. Nevertheless, he opened the door, offering his hand to Hanileh to escort her into the chapel.

CHAPTER TEN

The chapel was breathtaking. Earlier, Gaultier explained that Kapelle, on the planet Crenet, was the home and headquarters of the Logia faith.

Caelum, in the Aevum rotation, was the second largest. Regiam, also on Crenet, was considered the royal city. It would be where the Ruler Prince, when He appeared, would establish His reign of the Circeae system. Gaultier spoke of that moment with heartfelt reverence. Hanileh found herself hoping she would see that happen within her lifetime.

She'd never seen an interior as spacious and open as the chapel. Impressive arches, far above them, held the ceiling in place. The curves dove down to form massive pillars. Each pillar carried a delicate metal railing that spiraled around it. White candles lined the railing, warm orange flames dancing with joy and radiating a gentle light throughout the sitting area. Attractive burgundy pillows cushioned long wooden benches.

At the far end of the chapel, the grand altar caught her eye. The symbols of the Logia and the Crown were built into the wall, wood and metal set into the stone. Hanileh recognized the Creator King, the Ruler Prince, and the Eternal Companion, thanks to Gaultier's readings and words as they flew to Kapelle. She resisted the urge to run to the altar to touch the symbols.

Velius walked only a step or two ahead of her. He yanked her forward, giving her no time to stop and look, which is what she really wanted to do. Substantial sculptures and paintings along the outer walls begged to be admired. She would have to wait, though.

Jax and Alton sat on a bench near the altar, deep in conversation. Gaultier spoke with a man in deep dark red robes at the end of the center aisle. Hanileh rushed past Velius to Gaultier, unable to hide her excitement. In light of the glorious building, she'd nearly forgotten about the healing.

Gaultier greeted her with a broad smile. "You look like you're feeling much better."

Lifting her eyes to the ceiling, Hanileh nodded. She opened her hands and spun around in the splendor.

"It's beautiful, huh?" Gaultier said, joining in her appreciation.

It's amazing! She gave another eager nod, smiling at him.

Gaultier chuckled softly, glancing beyond her to Velius. "Thank you."

The man in the robes stared at Velius through narrowed eyes. His mouth formed a straight line of displeasure. Hanileh stepped a bit closer to Gaultier.

"I couldn't..." Velius gestured toward his slumped left shoulder. "I couldn't heal the cuts on her chest. They..."

"They bear the stain of the Strages," the robed man finished for him.

Velius bowed his head, wringing his hands. Dark circles clung to his eyes. Hanileh felt sorry for him. Gaultier's gaze darted between the three of them.

The robed man said to Velius, "Perhaps you should go rest, son." A hint of reproof tinged his words.

Velius only nodded before turning to step away. Gaultier slipped a protective arm around Hanileh, watching Velius for a moment. He then looked at the robed man. "Athaer Castus, this is Hanileh."

Castus eyed her in silence. He then gave her a courteous smile and offered her a hand of welcome. "It is a pleasure to meet you, Hanileh. You are welcome among us. I am sorry to hear of your difficulties, but perhaps we will be able to help you find some answers."

She smiled, warmed by this man's friendliness. She nodded her thanks, wishing she could express herself through other means.

Gaultier dropped his arm from her back. "The athaer and I have some business to attend. Jax, Alton, would you mind showing Hanileh around?"

Jax stood, followed by Alton. "Sure, G," Jax said.

"Will you be all right?" Gaultier asked her quietly.

She nodded, assuring him with another smile. There was much to do and see. And although she felt safe and comfortable in Gaultier's presence, she trusted the two other men who accompanied him.

Gaultier patted her arm gently, his eyes zeroing in on his friend. "Alton, you might want to look at that injury. She could probably use a pressure bandage or something."

"We'll take care of her, Gaultier. It's okay." Alton grinned.

With fingers lingering on Hanileh's arm, Gaultier stepped away to join Castus in crossing the altar. Hanileh turned, still astounded by the beauty and grandeur of the chapel. As she started back down the aisle, a painful fire ripped through her, stripping her of strength and breath. Alton caught her before she hit the floor, but his touch sizzled with heat. A panicked cry lodged in her throat, but no sound came out.

"G!" Jax shouted. His word echoed through the rafters of the chapel.

ASHLEY HODGES BAZER

Gaultier was at her side in no time. The pain dissipated as quickly as it came on, leaving her panting and worn. His hands held her head as he stared into her eyes. "Are you all right?"

Hanileh nodded. She felt fine now. In an instant, her strength had returned. She no longer hurt. It was unexplainable.

Gaultier glanced up, then back to her. "I'll be just a few moments. Alton and Jax will help get you settled, all right? They'll take you onto the resting quarters."

Again, she nodded. He helped her to her feet, smiling with his gentle kindness. Jax offered his arm, but she waved him off. She was fine. Really.

Gaultier stepped away as Alton led them further into the chapel. Just a few feet away, however, the roaring, vicious pain returned, centering in her chest. Her knees could no longer support her, and she struggled to breathe.

He must have been watching that time. He was next to her within a heartbeat, before anyone could alert him. And once more, in his presence, she recovered to a state of complete clarity.

Allowing Hanileh to rest against his chest, Gaultier encircled her with his arms. "I don't understand," he murmured.

"I think I might," Castus said. "Leave her. Step away again."

Gaultier glanced down at her, patting her shoulder. "It'll be all right."

She sat on the floor, watching him go. Only ten feet away, the pain began to throb again. She struggled for breath, but none came. Looking up at the high, vaulted ceiling, she tried to fight it, but her own strength wasn't enough. She collapsed to the side, the cool stone floor her only relief.

Gaultier ran back to her, and just as before, everything changed. She could breathe, the pain subsided. His strong arms cradled her and returned her to a sitting position. They both looked to the athaer in question.

"You are her shield, Gaultier."

"Her what?" he asked, sounding puzzled.

"Whatever it is that causes her to suffer, you shield her from it. I'd venture to say it has something to do with the injury that remains. When you are near, she is fine. Strong. When you are separated, she diminishes to that sickly state."

"That's impossible," Gaultier murmured, his gaze falling to her once again. "Shielding happens between those who have known each other a long time. We just met. I don't even know her, really."

She blinked, uncertain herself. How could such a thing be?

"We must find the source of her suffering," the Logia athaer declared. "But in the meantime, you must remain close to her."

Gaultier held Hanileh in his arms, and she leaned against him. *Odd, being thrown together like this.* As he had said, she knew so little about him. She knew even less about herself. Perhaps there was a larger plan at work here. But for now, she would continue to trust in Gaultier and his ways, as long as he stayed close and kept the pain away.

◆

Gaultier extinguished the candle on the table next to Hanileh, softly wishing her a peaceful night's rest. He stroked her hair, his fingers lingering along her delicate cheekbone. Such mystery wrapped up in this girl. Yet it seemed so right, having her with him.

With a sigh, he stepped away to join Athaer Castus at the table a few feet away. Castus watched him. "You're tired, Gaultier."

"It's been a long few days, Avner." In this informal setting, Gaultier finally felt like he could be himself. A talk with his old friend would help. Confiding in Castus was always great therapy.

"It's been a long few weeks. I am sorry your mission proved fruitless."

"Did it?" Gaultier glanced over his shoulder toward Hanileh.

"Indeed," Castus said, pouring a mug of coffee for Gaultier, and then for himself. "I am concerned for all of us involved with this girl."

"She's harmless," Gaultier said. "It is the ones who hurt her we should be worried about."

"She brings with her the touch of the Strages."

Gaultier frowned, looking at Castus. "The Crown gave me her name, Avner. She belongs to Him. What exactly do you mean by that—the touch of the Strages?"

"Velius could not heal her. He relieved her pain, but something blocked his power. A mighty demon wages war inside her. It lured Velius into performing a Strages mending. In turn, I fear the mending fed the demon."

"With regard to this shield idea, I don't understand that in particular. I left Hanileh alone with Velius, and she was fine."

Castus didn't have to answer. Gaultier understood. He bowed his head, squeezing his eyes closed. Just as he feared. Velius was backsliding into the comfort of his old ways, abandoning the Logia path for the more easily accessible Strages one.

"It's not his fault, Gaultier. His time with the Strages weakened him. It was too much to think that he could handle encountering them so soon."

"Soon? It's been close to ten years now. Shouldn't he be stronger?"

"Darkness runs deep, Gaultier."

"Are you going to send him away?"

"I don't wish to," Castus answered quickly. "I will work with him personally. I can already tell he has entered repentance. It's now a matter of helping him understand he is forgiven. And just as important, that he needs

ASHLEY HODGES BAZER

to forgive himself."

Gaultier nodded, rubbing his hand over his stubbly chin. "I had hoped he'd progressed."

"Your brother is a lot like you, Gaultier. He wants so badly to do the right thing. And although he is older, he desires to please you, to gain your approval. He could tell this girl means a lot to you."

"So he jeopardized his soul to heal her?"

Castus tipped his head, a puzzled frown lining his eyes. "I cannot second guess the Crown, son. I do know He is at work in this, one way or another. Perhaps He is bringing about truths we cannot deny."

"I've put too much hope and trust into our relationship to just give up on Velius. I promised I wouldn't," Gaultier said. "I ask you don't, either."

"As I told you before, I will do what I can. The rest is up to him."

Gaultier lifted the mug to his lips. "And what of Hanileh? What have you decided about her?"

"She will not survive among us without your presence." Castus gazed across the room to where Hanileh lay. "Are you planning to stay?"

"There is much more work to be done, Avner. Jett has other monitoring sites he wishes us to check out."

"Mm." Castus's brow dipped into a slight frown. "You haven't heard. He and Delia are to be named Protectors next week."

Gaultier stared down at the dark liquid in his mug. His stomach tightened, as did his throat. *You didn't want that life, remember?*

"I am glad for them," he said.

"It should have been you."

"No. The Queen of Sagesse has chosen correctly."

"Your father groomed you—"

"And that's a responsibility I could not take on," Gaultier interrupted. He was being rude, but this was a touchy subject with him. "Velius never forgave me."

"Which is why he turned from the Logia."

"Only part of the reason," Gaultier replied. "It was much more complicated than just that."

"Well, let's get back to the issue of Hanileh," Castus said, relieving Gaultier of the subject. "I am unable to help her. The wound on her chest— the symbol of the Strages. Someone of great strength and power marked her for a reason that is beyond me. The stain runs deep, though. I'd venture to say whoever did that also took her voice and her memory. They wanted to keep her quiet."

"Terrible," Gaultier said. He'd thought the same thing, but he'd not given voice to the theory. Hearing someone else say it only solidified the horror.

"I suggest you take her to Sagesse. Jett and Delia are already wrapped up in preparing for the ceremony and settling into their roles as Protectors, otherwise I would ask them. But the Queen should be able to help somehow. Perhaps she will even be able to restore Hanileh," Castus said.

"The Pathway to Sagesse will be accessible?"

"For those approved by the Council. I will petition them on your behalf."

"And another athaer will take over Caelum?"

"Something else for Jett to worry about following the ceremony. He had asked me if you might be willing." Castus smiled.

Gaultier shook his head, hiding his face with his mug. He lowered it after a long sip. "I don't feel called to the position of athaer."

"It's a shame," Castus answered. "You'd make an excellent one."

With a sigh, Gaultier again glanced back toward Hanileh. "So the Challenge is upon us?"

Castus frowned, taking his mug into his hands. "I don't believe so. Not yet. Everyone expects the events to fall back to back. I speculate there will be many years between the naming of the Protectors and the actual Challenge. And I don't foresee the Challenge to immediately produce the Divinum Bellator. Things will progress gradually," Castus paused to drink from his cup, "and I don't believe we will see it in our lifetimes."

"What happens to Nyssa?" Gaultier asked quietly. He probably shouldn't have spoken the Queen's name, but it seemed appropriate in the moment. Her given name was a secret entrusted only to Dignitaries and athaers, much like that of the Ruler Prince. Gaultier's father had told him the Queen's name once long ago.

Castus didn't bat an eye. "Her role is complete. She has lived in dedicated service to the Crown, and once the ceremony is finished and the Logia have left the palace, she will join the Crown in Eternity."

"She will die alone?"

"No, Gaultier," Castus answered with a smile. "She will not die at all. She will be spared from such a human event."

"That would be something to see."

"Indeed. But no one will. It will only happen once everyone has left Sagesse. The entire star cluster will vanish."

"*Soli Deo Gloria*," Gaultier murmured.

"And at that point, who could deny the existence of the Crown?" Castus lifted his mug in cheers.

Gaultier's mug met the athaer's, but not with the joy Castus displayed. Gaultier's thoughts were wrapped up in the days to come. The Crown's plan was in full swing, and Gaultier would give everything he could to defend it. He prayed Hanileh wasn't going to be a stumbling block.

CHAPTER ELEVEN

The library was a welcome respite following a restless night. Gaultier sat at a table, stifling a yawn as he flipped through one of his favorite books. He rubbed his back, shifting uncomfortably in his chair. Under the advice of Athaer Castus, he'd spent the night on a palette next to Hanileh's bed. At least she slept well. The floor had not been as kind to Gaultier.

Hanileh looked completely different than the woman Gaultier had rescued just days ago. She'd showered and changed into fresh clothing supplied by some of the women of the domicile. Gaultier found himself staring at her lovely, delicate face. Inquisitive brown eyes peered out from her soft auburn hair which had been swept back and secured with a ribbon that matched the maroon pinafore she wore. The pristine white blouse complemented the modest dress in its Logia colors. She was...dazzling.

Catching his stare, Hanileh met him with a shy smile. The tinge of color that lit her cheeks only added to her charm. Gaultier smiled back and returned his eyes to his book. Before long, he lifted his gaze to see if she was still looking at him. She was.

With a soft chuckle, Gaultier closed his book. He folded his hands atop its cover and leaned forward. How he wished she could talk, or at least communicate in some form. He popped his hand against the book as the idea struck him.

"Let's try something," he said to her.

He stood, crossing to Athaer Castus's desk. Removing a writing utensil and a notebook of paper, he dashed back to Hanileh's side. "Velius suggested perhaps you could write and tell us what you know. Want to try?"

Hanileh's face lit up as she nodded. Perhaps she did know where she came from. Who she was. Any detail would help them get closer to finding answers.

She snatched the pad and the pencil from him, setting to work. He watched over her shoulder as she wrote. The letters were perfect in form, but the words were nothing more than gibberish. Gaultier hoped perhaps it was a foreign language.

"What does this mean, Hanileh?" he asked, pointing at one of the words.

She gripped the pencil tightly, looking up at him with tears in her eyes. With a shake of her head, he understood she couldn't write. Just like she couldn't talk. Something prevented her from doing so. Castus's words came to mind—a demon waging war inside her.

Gaultier caressed her cheek gently. "It's okay. It's not your fault. We're going to find the answers. I promise."

With another encouraging smile, he picked up his book from the table to return it to its shelf. He then selected one of the copies of the Creed and opened it to one of its reassuring passages. Leaning against the bookshelf, he murmured a soft prayer before reading the words. The Crown's presence filled him with tranquility. He just needed to trust.

His eyes flickered over the top of the book. Hanileh, still at the table, wrote furiously, her hand scrawling across the page with skill. Had his prayer helped her in some way?

He folded the book and placed it back on the shelf before moving back to Hanileh's side. Instead of words on the paper, he saw a fantastic drawing of the Kapelle domicile. Immediately, he recognized images of himself, Hanileh, Jax, Alton, Castus, and Velius. She was an amazing artist, especially to have completed such a meticulous sketch within just a few moments.

Placing the pencil aside, Hanileh sat back and stared at her work. Gaultier placed a hand on her back to commend her, but his eyes were drawn to the page. The renderings began to move, mimicking the scene from the day prior. Castus sending Velius to rest. Hanileh walking away with Jax and Alton, then collapsing. Gaultier at her side.

As the page settled back into frozen detail, Gaultier stared at Hanileh in breathless disbelief. "How did you do that?"

Hanileh looked back at him with uncertainty and fright.

He scrambled to turn to a fresh page. Grabbing the pencil, he put it back in her hand. "Try another. Don't think. Just let it flow."

Hanileh frowned, shaking her head. She pushed the pencil toward him.

Gaultier's fingers encircled her hand positioning it on the paper. "It's all right, Hanileh. This is a gift. Use it. Perhaps you will see something that brings back your memory."

She again shook her head, bowing her head and closing her eyes.

"Hanileh, trust in the Crown," he murmured, touching her shoulder. "I'm not going to let anything happen to you. I'm here."

Allowing his hand to rest on her back, he watched as Hanileh struggled in her own battle. But after a few moments, she leaned forward and set to work once again. This time, the Caelum chapel was the backdrop. A woman of Hanileh's height and structure entered the modest building, sword drawn. She resembled Hanileh, but wild, black markings disfigured her face. Her image stole through the chapel, only to be stopped by a drawing that looked exactly like Jett Criswell. Before long, a third drawing, this one with Delia's attractive features, joined the others. As the scene played out, Jett and Delia disappeared, only to be replaced with a vicious, frightening image of a tall woman, half of her face hidden behind dark shading.

"Who is this?" Gaultier demanded, pointing to the other woman.

Hanileh could only shake her head, the tears rising in her eyes again.

"Is this you?" He pointed to the first woman with the markings.

She shrugged, her eyes wide with terror.

"And those others were Jett and Delia Criswell. Did you know them? Did you attack them?" His questions fired as quickly as they came to mind.

Hanileh jolted from her chair, hurling the pencil across the room. She retreated to a corner of the library, hiding her face from him. He'd hurt her feelings and probably scared her. Scolding himself, he grabbed the notebook and tucked it under his arm before he picked up the pencil and approached her.

"Hanileh, I'm sorry. I've just...I've never seen anything like this," Gaultier said, taking her elbow to pull her attention back to him. "Please forgive me for questioning you. I don't mean to accuse you."

She sniffled, turning toward him a little. He could tell she so badly wished to say something. Her expression showed frustration and anger, but not toward him.

"I know," he murmured, his arm enfolding her. "But we're going to figure this out. I think we need to share these drawings with Athaer Castus. Perhaps he can shed some light on what's happening here."

Hanileh nodded, resting her head against his shoulder. He stroked her hair, holding her close to reassure her yet again. Another prayer slipped from his lips. "My King, we are uncertain and conflicted. Hanileh is precious in Your sight, as are all Your children. Guide her. Protect her. And help me to know what to do for her." Even in just the few short days he'd known her, he already couldn't stand to see her come to harm. And if her past held such darkness, would he be able to fight it?

◆

Castus stared at the sketch, watching as the two scenes unfolded on the pages. He was better than Gaultier at masking his concern, although Gaultier could sense it. The athaer lowered the pad to his lap, looking at

Hanileh.

"She tried to write, but nothing comprehensible came out," Gaultier explained. "And then, just moments later, she did this." He gestured to the notebook.

"I think we have our first glimpse of the Strages," Castus said. "Jett told us of this attack, but he didn't mention Hanileh. Do you believe this is her?"

"It looks a lot like her." Gaultier glanced toward Hanileh.

She bowed her head, fidgeting with her skirts. Gaultier reached out to take her hand and gave her a smile of encouragement.

"Do you think you could draw more?" Castus asked Hanileh.

She shrugged, her eyes falling to the notebook.

"Would you try, Hanileh?" Gaultier took the paper from Castus and offered it and the pencil to her.

As the men watched, Hanileh sketched the base on Asper. The scene between Gaultier and Hanileh took shape. She flipped the page and sketched their arrival at Kapelle. Velius greeted them and led them into the consultation room. The drawn image of Gaultier left the room, as he had in reality, and a darker expression took over Velius's sketched features.

"The mending," Castus whispered in awe. "We have proof."

Gaultier gritted his teeth. He wanted to have more faith in his brother, but the evidence was before him. He couldn't deny Velius was unable to sever himself completely from the Strages, although he lived under the guise of a Logia.

As if entranced, Hanileh flipped page after page, her sketches now turning to portraits. She drew a woman of great beauty, marred with jagged lines all over her body. On the same page, the face was transformed with black shading. The other pages were drawings of men—a young light-haired boy of brawny stature and a wiry man with slick, dark hair in elegant dress. Hanileh then closed her eyes and drew a final portrait. This one evidently frightened her. She struggled with it. Gaultier could tell she wanted to stop, but forced herself to keep going.

As she finished, she slumped back against the bench, exhausted. Gaultier took the notebook from her, passing it to Castus. As the athaer flipped through the pages, Gaultier took in each picture. Castus stopped at the last one. The sketched man was attractive, in an almost enticing way. Black hair cloaked his head, and his eyes seemed to look through the beholder. Determination set his jaw, and a callous, cruel expression settled on his features. Hanileh hid her eyes.

"You have quite a gift, young lady," Castus whispered.

"Who are they?" Gaultier asked.

"They are the Strages, Gaultier." Castus looked again at each page. "We must consult with the Queen and the Protectors immediately."

"By link?"

Castus shook his head. "No, you must go to Sagesse."

"You will not join us?"

"I cannot leave the domicile, Gaultier. There are those here who need me."

The athaer spoke of Velius. "You will help him?"

"As I promised before, I will do what I can. With evidence of the mending, it is more than likely the Council will expel him," Castus said. "I am sorry."

Hanileh straightened in her seat, a heavy frown lining her lips. She shook her head, gripping Gaultier's hand.

"What?" He wasn't in the mood to play a guessing game right now.

Hanileh reached for the notebook. Castus placed it in her hands. She turned back to the page of the mending, pointing to it repeatedly.

"What is it, young one?" Castus asked.

"I think she's showing that despite the mending, he did restore her. He tried, anyway. She's taking the blame herself."

Hanileh nodded, pointing to Gaultier.

"I wish it worked that way, young one. But as Logia, we are responsible for our choices," Castus said. "Velius did not have to give in to his old ways."

Hanileh looked at Gaultier, many questions in her eyes.

"It's a story for another time." His gaze lingered on the sketch.

"Not only did Velius slip into the Strages mending, but he hurt you, which probably contributed to his craving for the darker ways," Castus said.

"He hurt you?" Gaultier grabbed the notebook.

Hanileh shook her head, again pointing to the page. Gaultier watched as Velius used physical force to pop Hanileh's shoulder back into place. He closed his eyes after watching the distress and pain fill Hanileh's sketched face. He felt Hanileh pat his hand to get his attention.

"It is against the ways of the Logia to hurt any living creature, Hanileh. Regardless of the intentions or results," Gaultier murmured.

She snatched the notebook from him, jabbing the paper.

"Exceptions have been made, but they must be excused by the Council," Castus said. "With the mending that followed, it is blatant disregard of Logia belief."

Hanileh dropped the notebook to her lap, slapping her hands against it. With her lips pressed together, she rocked back in her seat and aimed her attention at a far corner of the study. Gaultier took one of her hands in his. "There are other issues here you don't know anything about. Velius's past has been...questionable."

She gestured toward herself, then pointed to the scene she drew of the

Caelum chapel.

"We don't know enough about this to make a conclusion, Hanileh," Gaultier said. "We know nothing of your past, and I'm not about to pass judgment based on a drawing."

Nothing about Hanileh demonstrated the evil of the Strages. How she could know such intricacies of the evil faction was indeed puzzling, but Gaultier simply could not, would not, believe she was involved with them.

"Which is why we must seek the counsel of the Queen of Sagesse," Castus added. "She will be able to help."

"I'll link Jax and Alton and tell them to prepare to launch," Gaultier murmured. "The sooner we find the answers, the better."

CHAPTER TWELVE

Sagesse: 2 days later

The palace at Sagesse was completely decked out with decorative banners and flowers for the ceremony. Without the extras, the palace itself was stunning. The adornment made it that much more picturesque. Ancient stonework gave the walls an ivory hue. Paired with the scarlet color of the Logia and the gold of the Crown, it glimmered with inviting warmth.

Gaultier insisted Hanileh stay close to him. Alton requested attending the ceremony, while Jax volunteered to remain with the ship. It wasn't that Jax didn't wish to see the important naming ceremony, but he knew it meant much more to Alton, because of his Logia connection.

Hanileh had given Gaultier a puzzled look when he and Alton spoke about seeing the Queen. He had to explain that while the Queen was held in high regard, she lived alone at the palace. The Queen watched and waited, acting as interim Protector until the official naming occurred. Her solitude allowed her to live in constant communication with the Crown until He spoke the names of the Protectors to her. The ceremony was considered a holy event that would herald in the possibility of the Challenge and would bring about the time of the Divine Warrior. This had to occur before the Ruler Prince would establish His rule among His people, as foretold by the Creed.

The great hall was packed. With the exception of a center aisle, padded chairs took up every inch of the floor, and every seat was filled. Ushers directed Gaultier to the balcony. He had found two seats together, although they were at the highest point. Regardless of the honor of attending, it would be difficult to see the ceremony.

As Gaultier helped Hanileh into her seat, fanfare trumpeters filtered into the smaller balconies on either side of the great hall. Their trumpets bore the crest of the Queen on burgundy banners. Together, the musicians

HERALDS OF THE CROWN: POISON

lifted their instruments and sounded the call to introduce those involved in the ceremony. From the first note, the crowd fell into a hushed, reverent silence, all eyes turning to the altar at the far end of the hall.

Four young female Logia traipsed lightly down the center aisle, solemn looks on their faces as they bore long golden rods with delicate flames at the tips. As they walked, they lit the candelabras affixed to some of the chairs. They crossed to the altar, lighting the candles on either side. Gaultier glanced over to see a riveted Hanileh

"Are you all right?" he whispered, taking her hand.

She nodded, a smile touching her lips. She must have been fascinated by the beauty of the moment and completely taken in. Gaultier settled back in his seat, curling his fingers around Hanileh's.

More Logia officials and elders walked the aisle, taking their seats in the first few rows. Finally, the trumpet song changed to a more regal sound. The entire audience stood, bowing their heads as the Queen entered and took her throne. Hanileh's grip tightened with excitement as she watched. Gaultier couldn't help but smile.

One of the Dignitaries, Athaer Erste stood at the center of the altar, ready to address the crowd. He lifted a hand and lowered it slowly, inviting the audience to sit. After a few seconds of rustling, Erste began, "Honored guests of her royal majesty the Queen of Sagesse, I greet you on behalf of the Queen and welcome you to the Naming of the Protectors. It is indeed a bittersweet moment, as we entrust the security of Logia faith to the custody of two people and their family to come. We rejoice with them, as the honor is tremendous. Yet we grieve, as we know the burden is great. I cannot think of two who deserve the honor more than Athaer Jett Criswell of Caelum, and his dedicated wife, Delia."

The trumpets blasted again. This time, only the Queen rose as the two Protectors-elect walked down the aisle. When Jett and Delia reached the bottom step of the altar, they paused, their eyes on the Queen. Gaultier held his breath as the Queen lifted her chin, looking first at Jett, then at Delia. The Queen bowed low before the Protectors, speaking the ancient words, "I believe these two, Jett and Delia Criswell, are worthy to face the vows of the Protectors."

A group of eleven elders, the rest of the revered Dignitaries, rose from the first row on both sides. Erste crossed the altar to join them. Four Dignitaries carried heavy crimson robes, while the others approached Jett and Delia. The men displayed the robes as the elders began running the Criswells through the Declaration of Vows. Gaultier mouthed each question, remembering when his father ran him through the drill.

"Jett Criswell, do you vow to uphold the Logia faith in everything you do? In your choices? In your thoughts? In your words? In your actions?"

75

Erste asked.

"I do," Jett answered solemnly.

A second elder repeated the question for Delia. She answered with a gentleness that made Gaultier smile. Although he'd never met her, he had heard Jett speak of her on more than one occasion. Gaultier admired the woman.

Another of Jett's elders stepped forward. "Take the next step."

Jett took Delia's hand, and together, they ascended the first of the steps toward the altar. The elder asked, "Jett Criswell, do you vow to regard the Crown with the respect and esteem He deserves? To always place Him above everything in your life, including your own personal needs? To honor Him before you honor your loved ones?"

"I do." Jett glanced toward Delia.

Gaultier sighed. He'd always found that vow to be ridiculous. As a dedicated Logia, that pledge was already expected. Those who loved the Crown had no reason to put anything before Him. Gaultier's eyes flitted toward Hanileh as Delia answered the vow. Hanileh was enthralled.

The third of Jett's elders stepped forward. "Take the next step."

The Protectors moved to the second step, and awaited the third vow. The elder looked at Jett. "Jett Criswell, do you vow to teach your children and your children's children the ways of the Crown? To hand down the Logia faith and keep the torch forever lit in His name?"

"I do."

Delia answered in kind after her third elder repeated the question. Gaultier's eyes wandered to the Queen, still on her knees before Jett and Delia. He always found it intriguing that royalty would humble themselves in such a way, but that was the call of the Crown. Nyssa's role as Queen was to uphold the faith until the Naming of the Protectors. At that time, no one really knew what to expect. She must have been feeling all kinds of uneasiness.

"Take the next step."

Jett and Delia moved to the third step. Jett helped Delia to her knees before he knelt next to her. Both bowed their heads and waited.

"Jett Criswell," the last elder started, his voice powered with great authority, "do you vow to lay down your life in the name of the Logia, should the Crown call you to do so? Defending Him and your fellow Logia with your very last breath?"

Jett hesitated for an instant. Gaultier was probably the only one to notice. Sure, any Logia would be proud to die a martyr, but making a verbal promise before the Crown, the Queen, and other esteemed members of the faith was daunting. The only moment it might have been tougher to answer that question would have been at the wrong end of a sword.

HERALDS OF THE CROWN: POISON

"I do," Jett whispered.

When Delia's last elder posed the question, she responded in the same manner. With the vows complete, the Queen rose slowly, touching the heads of both Jett and Delia. Her hands splayed upon them, she looked to the elders holding the robes. "I now find these two, Jett and Delia Criswell, worthy to bear the responsibility, the honor, and the Name of Protector."

The Dignitaries proceeded up the steps. All of them took hold of the robes as they settled them upon Jett's and Delia's shoulders. The Queen stepped in front of Jett. "Jett Criswell, you have taken the vows and through them, made your declaration. You have been found worthy. I must ask you, do you accept the call of the Crown in receiving the name Protector?"

"With honor, your Majesty," Jett answered.

"Delia Criswell," the Queen said, moving to Delia, "your husband has accepted the name Protector. That in itself is enough, however, the Crown has seen it fit to give you the choice as well. You have taken the vows and through them, made your declaration. You have been found worthy. I must ask you, do you accept the call of the Crown in receiving the name Protector?"

Delia reached out and gripped Jett's hand. "I stand with my husband, your Majesty. I accept the call."

"Take the final step," the Queen commanded.

Jett rose, his movement hampered slightly by the weighty robe. He extended his other hand to Delia and helped her to her feet. Together, they ascended the final step, now on the same level with the Queen. The Dignitaries lined the bottom step, lowering to one knee.

"Fellow Logia and followers of the Crown, today is a historic day," the Queen said, addressing her people. "Your long-awaited Protectors have been named in these before you, Jett and Delia Criswell. They have made their declarations through the vows of the Crown. They have been found worthy. I now present them to you and ask you to answer by the sign of *assentior*. Do you accept them?"

In unified song, the crowd rose and spoke, "*Assentior*." Gaultier once more looked at Hanileh. Tears filled her eyes on different terms this time. He could tell she wanted with all her heart to join in the agreeing pledge. She opened her mouth a few times, as if she were trying to speak. He hadn't seen her do that since he'd rescued her.

The Queen took Jett and Delia's hands in her own, lifting them high. "Then in the name of the Creator King, the Ruler Prince, and the Eternal Companion, I give you the Protectors, Jett and Delia Criswell."

Applause and cheering roared through the crowd. Jett stepped closer to Delia as the Queen withdrew to her throne to allow them the moment. They glanced at each other as the cheering continued, and the trumpets joined in the celebratory throng. Jett and Delia waved, bowing their heads in humble gratitude.

Gaultier took Hanileh's hand. "We should head downstairs if we hope to catch Jett and Delia."

They slipped from their seats and into the hallway that led to the staircase. An usher stopped them. "Excuse me, may I help you?"

"We must speak with the Protectors," Gaultier said.

"I'm afraid that is impossible. Their period of seclusion begins once they leave here, and they are moments from being escorted to the docking bay. Athaer..." The usher paused, an embarrassed smile touching his lips. "Excuse me. Protector Criswell insisted they head for their new residence on Maeror immediately."

"Maeror?" Gaultier asked. "Why Maeror?"

"I am not privy to such information, sir. I am a mere servant of the Queen and the Crown."

Gaultier rubbed his hand over his chin. "Of course. May we speak with the Queen?"

"I imagine she will tied up for a while following the ceremony," the usher answered. "The Dignitaries are to meet with her."

"I just need a moment."

"Wait here. I'll see what I can do."

As the usher walked away, Gaultier smiled at Hanileh. He then turned his eyes to admire a large hanging tapestry. "I imagine the Queen is overwhelmed with all this pomp. She usually lives here alone," he explained. "Not even a servant to care for her, with the exception of those who deliver supplies as needed. It's a lonely life, but —"

Hanileh had disappeared.

Blast.

Gaultier bounded down the stairs, chasing after her. "Hey, wait! We're supposed to stay here!" he called.

At the bottom of the grand staircase, Hanileh took off down the corridor. Gaultier scrambled to follow, realizing just how slick the polished marble could be. And how very fast Hanileh was!

"Hanileh!"

She ran smack into a contingent of guards, who escorted the Queen from the great hall to her chambers. The Queen spun around, surprise lighting her face, as the girl bowled through her guards.

Gaultier skidded to a halt, watching as Hanileh, her expression contorted and twisted in pain, gripped her chest and fell to the ground. Two of the guards grabbed her arms as another drew his sword and held it to her throat threateningly.

"Who are you?" he demanded.

Taking his cue, Gaultier crossed to them, his hands raised. "Please, your Majesty, allow me to explain." He bowed low before the Queen.

As he moved closer, Hanileh seemed to gain strength and feistiness. She yanked her arms from the guards and turned to the Queen with a pleading expression.

"What is it, little one?" the Queen asked, taking Hanileh's hands in her own.

Gaultier answered, "She is unable to speak."

"Who are you?" The guard with the sword flicked the tip of his blade toward Gaultier, obviously determined to arrest someone in this episode.

Gaultier lifted his hands again in submission. "I am Gaultier Lassiter. I represent Athaer Castus of Kapelle. This is Hanileh, and we came in hope Queen Nyssa might be able to provide some answers." Again, Gaultier shouldn't have spoken her given name, but it was certain to grab the Queen's attention.

The Queen stared at Hanileh, then at Gaultier. Turning to the guard nearest her, she said, "Tell the Dignitaries our meeting has been delayed. This is far more urgent."

◆

"Castus will be going before the Council of Elders tonight," the gravelly voice said, appearing in Velius's doorway.

Velius stared at his reflection in the mirror, his peripheral vision catching the source of the voice as the man shimmered into existence behind him. It was how Raum came to him. Velius wasn't sure how Raum was able to accomplish such a thing, flickering in from one place or another. Nor did he understand how Raum was able to bypass the law that Strages could not enter the Logia domicile. But he didn't question it. Raum and his master carried far more power than he could ever dream of wielding. Perhaps that was part of the allure.

"I know." Velius smoothed a wrinkle from his Logia robe. "There is nothing I can do."

"There is, in fact, something you can do," Raum said, pushing off the doorjamb to cross the room to Velius. "He must be stopped."

"Castus is a friend," Velius murmured. Convincing himself of this required more and more effort. "He's done much for me. And a lot for my brother."

"Much more for your brother." Raum's eyes examined the meager room before they caught Velius's gaze again. "Must I remind you?"

"Don't play on jealousy. I will not give in on account of something so petty."

Raum moved to Velius's side. "This is our moment, Vel. Thaed has spoken to it and orders you to follow through. You get me to Castus, I kill him, and you are named athaer."

Velius stared at Raum. "There are others in line before me."

Raum shook his head. "It has been arranged, Vel."

"Thaed does not order me to kill Castus personally?"

Raum grinned. "You desire it, don't you?"

Velius closed his eyes. As much as he didn't wish to admit it, he did desire to be the one to take Castus's life. He'd fawned over Gaultier their entire lives, even allowing Gaultier to shirk the responsibilities their father had hoped to see him take on—the role of Protector—to pursue crusades in the name of the Logia. Gaultier had earned hero status, leaving behind his older brother, who'd done nothing more than care too much. And although Castus was more than likely innocent, not knowing he'd placed Velius aside, it would give Velius great pleasure to see the athaer meet his end.

Raum paced the tiny room, scuffling his feet on the stones. "His blood cannot be found on your hands. Neither the Council nor Gaultier can find you to be at fault. Lead me to him, and I will take care of it."

"Why does Thaed wish to see me named athaer?"

The sinister smile returned to Raum's face. "Friends in high places, Vel. It gets him one step closer to the Protectors."

"The Protectors will soon be in place. Why not just issue the Challenge?"

"That would be following rules. Thaed doesn't do rules. He doesn't have to. His authority matches, no, exceeds that of the Crown." Raum's fingers toyed with the blade of his dagger. "The Challenge is ludicrous."

"Castus will soon enter the sanctuary for morning prayers."

"Then we must reach him in the chapel. Before he sets foot in the safety of the sanctuary."

Velius smiled, his hands disappearing into the arms of his robes. "How dramatic it would be to take him at the entrance..."

"It is done." Raum smiled in agreement. "Lead the way."

CHAPTER THIRTEEN

The Queen's reception chamber in the north tower was modest, yet elegant. Long wide drapes of burgundy sectioned off part of the room. The guards escorted them into the room and stood by, swords drawn. Gaultier sat next to Hanileh on a velvet couch. It wasn't at all comfortable. People weren't meant to be comfortable here.

The Queen waved the guards out of the room. "Leave us."

The guards were reluctant to leave, but a stern look from the Queen finally sent them away. Once they were gone, she glanced toward Gaultier and Hanileh. "Give me just a moment," she said, unclasping the opulent robes from her shoulders.

She shrugged the heavy burgundy material from her body, revealing a snug white tunic and black leggings. The sparkling diamond tiara was placed aside on a nearby table. Grasping her long ebony curls in her hand, she wound a cord about them, taming them back into a thick tail.

"Much better." She smiled, crossing to a chair near Gaultier and Hanileh.

"Your Majesty," Gaultier said, rising as she came closer.

"No," the Queen said. "Please, call me Nyssa since you already know my name. And please drop the formalities. I am not this fancy, elegant woman everyone thinks me to be."

"Your position is respected," Gaultier explained.

"My position is eliminated," Nyssa countered. "The Protectors now command respect. I am nothing more than your sister in the faith."

"I am honored, nevertheless." Gaultier bowed his head.

"All right, get it out of your system," Nyssa said, causing Hanileh to grin from ear to ear.

"I apologize in keeping the elders waiting."

"They can wait." Nyssa glanced toward the doors. "I know my fate. I don't need them to explain it to me."

"You aren't pleased to join the Crown?"

"Don't misunderstand me," Nyssa said. "It is every Logia's joy to meet the Crown in Eternity. I just had hoped to have the chance to live a little first."

Gaultier nodded. He related all too well to Nyssa's plight. That was yet another reason he had chosen to avoid the title of athaer.

"Why are you here?" Nyssa asked, suddenly changing the subject.

Gaultier smiled to Hanileh before opening the satchel he'd brought with them. He removed the notebook of drawings and placed it on his lap. "Before I show you this, I want to give you a little background."

He told the story of how he'd first encountered Hanileh and of their journey back to the Kapelle domicile. He also relayed Castus's thoughts and the symbol of the Strages Hanileh carried.

"May I see it?" Nyssa asked.

Hanileh pulled her tunic down from her left shoulder, revealing the tender scar tissue that started to cover the deep gashes. Nyssa gasped softly. "Who did that to you?"

"That's the thing. She doesn't remember. She has no memory at all."

Nyssa rose, leaning in toward Hanileh. "May I?" she asked, holding out her hand.

Hanileh nodded, staring at the Queen. As Nyssa touched her forehead, Hanileh closed her eyes. Nyssa did the same.

Gaultier held his breath. *Oh, please let Nyssa discover something. To draw out some memory or information of any sort.*

After a moment, though, Nyssa withdrew her hand, shaking her head. "I'm getting nothing."

"We experienced the same." Gaultier lifted the notebook and offered it to Nyssa. "But then she drew these."

Nyssa lowered to her seat, slowly viewing each of the sketches. Her face remained calm and expressionless until she saw the final picture. Fright flickered across her features, lighting her green eyes with apprehension. "He..."

"Castus said he is the leader of the Strages."

"Yes," Nyssa whispered. "Very dangerous."

"We just want to understand why she is seeing these things. And this gift—no one has heard of it. Drawings that animate themselves?"

"It is unique," Nyssa said, closing the notebook. She looked at Hanileh. "They are images of the past, no?"

Hanileh shrugged, reaching for the sketches. She opened it to the scenes she remembered and nodded. Flipping the pages to the drawing of the Caelum chapel, she pointed first to the paper, then to her head, shaking it.

"You don't remember this?" Nyssa asked.

HERALDS OF THE CROWN: POISON

Hanileh again shook her head.

"Have you tried to draw other scenes? Or perhaps the future?"

Hanileh glanced at Gaultier.

"She hasn't drawn anything since these," Gaultier said, gesturing to the notebook.

"Try," Nyssa insisted, rising to fetch a writing utensil from the table that held the tiara. She placed the pencil in Hanileh's fingers while Gaultier opened the paper pad to a fresh page and rested it in Hanileh's lap.

Hanileh frowned, looking between Gaultier and the Queen. Gaultier understood. They were expecting too much. Just as he and Castus had done in the study. They pushed her too fast.

"Just close your eyes and draw what you feel, Hanileh," Gaultier said before looking at Nyssa. "May I help you hang your robes?"

Nyssa took the hint and returned to her seat. "There is no use. They will be gone within days, no doubt."

Hanileh did as Gaultier suggested, settling back against the couch and closing her eyes. Before long, the scratching of the pencil filled the void of conversation. Gaultier watched as the great hall took shape on the page, the ceremony recreated in animated drawings. It was a magnificent recreation, but not what Nyssa had asked for.

Smiling proudly, Hanileh held up the notebook. It was no wonder she'd drawn the scene. She had so enjoyed the ceremony and the pageantry.

"It's beautiful, Hanileh," Gaultier murmured.

"Close your eyes and try again," Nyssa said. "Try to find images of the future."

Hanileh sniffed, furrowing her brows together. She pressed the pencil to the page, and Gaultier could tell that she was concentrating, but nothing came.

Gaultier looked at Nyssa. "I don't think her gift includes prophecy."

"Something, little one. Anything. Please try," Nyssa encouraged.

Closing her eyes, Hanileh set back to work. Gaultier shook his head, rising to his feet in order to pace. This was pointless and a waste of time. They had other things to worry about. But before long, he heard the pencil scratching again. Hanileh was deeply entranced in what she was drawing.

Gaultier slipped behind her as she finished. The scene was the Kapelle sanctuary. A woman resembling Hanileh knelt on the steps of the altar, a blanket clenched in her hands. Distress and devastation was evident on her face. Two men stood with their backs turned in private conversation. The mood of the scene was heavy and oppressive.

"What is this?" he asked, looking at her.

Hanileh stared at the page. She shrugged, blinking rapidly. Her finger pressed to the blanket before she cradled her arms in front of her.

"A baby?" Nyssa said.

Hanileh answered with a nod, and then another shrug. She apparently had no idea why she'd drawn that scene. It meant nothing to her, even though the woman looked like her. Perhaps that was just part of the drawing talent—the subjects resembled their artist.

"Queen Nyssa, can you help us? Do you understand any of this?" Gaultier asked, sitting next to Hanileh again.

"I must admit, I am as mystified as you are." Nyssa stared at the freshly drawn scene.

Hanileh flipped the page, apparently inspired. She drew a magnificent dome with a beautiful mountain range as its backdrop. A wide river snaked around the base of the dome, and an enormous clock spanned the height and width of one of the mountains. Near the clock, she sketched what appeared to be a domicile built into part of the mountain. A tall, slender figure stood at the entrance.

As Hanileh completed the drawing, the figure looked out at them. Hanileh gasped, while Queen Nyssa fell back in the seat next to her, breathless.

"What was that?" Gaultier asked, looking at the figure. Yes, it was an odd looking person, but nothing that elicited the fright he saw in the Queen's face.

"I was afraid of this." Nyssa closed her eyes.

Hanileh looked up at her, blinking in question. She was as clueless as Gaultier.

"Afraid of what?" he asked on both their behalf.

"I know where we must go to seek the answers," Nyssa whispered.

"Where?"

"Do you have your own ship?"

"Yes."

"Prepare it. We leave within the hour."

"Where are we going?"

"We travel the Pathways to Oresed."

"Oresed?" Gaultier questioned. Nyssa must have lost it. Oresed was untouched. Unexplored. Some even said abandoned. No one went to Oresed for any reason. "What's on Oresed?"

"The Continuum."

Gaultier raised a hand to rub his forehead. "I'm confused."

"It's a long story," Nyssa said. "I can tell you more as we travel. The Continuum consists of five beings who were once one with the Crown, entrusted with great powers. They grew jealous and split from the Crown. They live in hiding in the Horologium mountain range on Oresed. They will help us."

"This is madness," Gaultier said, shaking his head. "I don't wish to engage betrayers of the Crown."

"You've exhausted your efforts among us. No one here can help you." Nyssa pointed to Hanileh's drawing. "We are being led there."

"They are evil," Gaultier argued, eyeing the picture.

"Yes, they are. And this little one is being held in the grasp of evil. Don't you sense it? It's what blocks her voice and her memory." Nyssa stared at Gaultier. "The Continuum is the source of evil, Gaultier. They will be able to help her."

"Evil only does harm," Gaultier murmured.

Nyssa shook her head. "They will listen to me."

"You are coming with us? Are you able to do so?"

"I must. I am the only one they will recognize."

"But—"

"It is decided. Prepare your ship," the Queen demanded.

"I haven't decided that we are going."

"I have," Nyssa said, rising. "And you are under my authority."

"Should we not at least consult the Crown?"

"You forget, I am a conduit. The Crown has already told me to go. To seek this. It is His will. And you are falling into your role. Trust Him."

Gaultier stared at her, then nodded. She was right. He had to acquiesce to her judgment. He nudged Hanileh. "Let's go. We need to tell Jax and Alton, then report back to Athaer Castus."

"I will meet you in the docking bay in fifteen minutes," Nyssa said.

Gaultier shook his head. "It will take longer than that for us to refuel and get the *Sun* ready for liftoff."

"I wish to see those ship preparations happen," Nyssa answered. "Gaultier, grant me this. And allow me the adventure."

Gaultier had nearly forgotten she'd never experienced much of anything, even tasks as menial as refueling a ship. He bowed his head as he stood. "We will wait for you, then," he replied, taking Hanileh's hand.

CHAPTER FOURTEEN

"**I** can't believe you did that, Hanileh," Gaultier said, half-scolding, half-praising. "Those guards might have killed you."

Hanileh shrugged with a smile as they stepped up the ramp of the *Midnight Sun*. She seemed pretty pleased with herself. Still, Gaultier was in charge of this mission, and she would have to listen to him. He told her as much, and she took his hand, pressing it to her cheek with a regretful gaze. He couldn't help but smile.

"It's okay. Just let me handle things, all right?"

She nodded, still holding his hand. Alton appeared at the top of the ramp with Jax next to him. Gaultier squeezed Hanileh's hand with a smile, looking up toward his friends.

"The Queen is on her way. She rides with us."

A miserable look of grief lined Alton's face. "Gaultier," he whispered.

"What is it?" Gaultier released Hanileh's hand to rush up the ramp.

Alton and Jax stepped back allowing him to enter. Hanileh followed, standing just behind Gaultier. Alton ran his fingers over his face, rubbing his mouth before he dropped his hand to speak.

"Jax just got word from Almus on Kapelle. Athaer Castus was found dead on the steps leading into the sanctuary early this morning, just before prayers."

Gaultier's heart sank. He leaned against the table in the main cabin. Castus hadn't been sick when they left. He was— Gaultier closed his eyes, already knowing the answer to his question.

"How?" he managed.

"Multiple stab wounds," Jax whispered.

The news was too much. Gaultier gripped the table, now relying fully on its strength to hold him up. Castus, his friend, his surrogate father, had been brutally murdered.

Hanileh's tender hands touched his back. Gaultier shook his head. "I'm sorry, Hanileh. I must return to Kapelle. We cannot go to Oresed."

HERALDS OF THE CROWN: POISON

Her touch remained. He got the sense she didn't care about her troubles right now. She was worried about him. She cared only for him. It was a bright point among such heavy sorrow.

"It's worse, G," Alton said in a solemn whisper. "Velius has been named athaer."

"What?" Gaultier straightened, staring at his friends.

"The Council of Elders issued the official word."

"There were others...Almus..." Gaultier started. Almus had assisted Castus for as long as Gaultier could remember. Even Gaultier himself was in line before Velius. Not that he wanted the role, but Velius wasn't prepared. Especially with his recent slip up.

"The word came down from the Council, G," Jax said. "It went to domiciles system-wide."

Gaultier lowered into a chair. "You know how this looks?"

"Like Velius killed Castus and threatened the Council?" Alton asked. "Yeah. But the Council also disclosed information on the investigation. Castus was killed by an intruder. There were witnesses who encountered Velius on the domicile grounds near the time of Castus's murder. He was nowhere near the scene."

Gaultier dropped his head into his hands. It made no sense. "Once the Queen boards, alert her to the complication, then get us in the air. Set course for Kapelle. I...need some time."

"We are not going to Kapelle," Nyssa said, appearing at the entrance to the ship. "We go to Oresed as planned. I am sorry, Gaultier, but this burden is not yours to bear. The Council of Elders will deal with things."

Gaultier looked at her. Ire began to eat at him. "You don't understand. You've been locked away in this palace all your life. The athaer is an important role, not to be taken lightly, or casually granted to a reckless, irresponsible—"

The Queen cleared her throat, cutting him off before he said too many careless things about Velius. "Gentlemen, ready the ship and get us in the air. And show Hanileh what you're doing. I would like a word with Gaultier alone."

"She cannot leave my side," Gaultier muttered. Hanileh probably would have been fine, being just a few feet away, but he didn't want her to go. "Whatever connection we have, I am her shield. Athaer Castus—" Emotion choked him as he spoke of his friend.

"Fine. Hanileh, stay," she said, waving the others away. She then knelt next to Gaultier. "I know you, although you don't know me. Castus, Jett...and your father...all spoke highly of you. They told me you were as faithful as they come, that you were strong and secure in the Crown. That you lived by the rule that the Crown is on His throne, mighty and powerful, handling all situations, large or small."

Gaultier closed his eyes, nodding. That was indeed how he felt. He never doubted the Crown. Not once.

"Then you must believe He has the situation at Kapelle under control without you. Your duty is here and now. Your responsibility is to this young woman He has placed in your path. He wants you to help her," Nyssa said, her words full of conviction. "Kapelle, Velius—these are things out of your control, even if you were there in the midst of them. Trust the Crown to take care of such things. He has a reason."

"You're right," Gaultier murmured. In his grief, he'd overlooked his beliefs.

"Now, you are granted some time to yourself. I will direct the gentlemen in the cockpit. Allow the grief to come. Grieve your loss, but never lose sight that Castus is Home. He is celebrating, as should we." Nyssa smiled. " I shall soon join him. I would like to hope no one wishes me away from the embrace of the Crown."

Gaultier bowed his head, again closing his eyes. Imagined visions of Castus enjoying the promises of Eternity brought a soft smile to his lips. Before long, he heard the door to the cockpit open and close. Alton disappeared into his cabin. A blanket settled around Gaultier's shoulders as Hanileh took a seat next to him. She slipped her hand atop his and rested her head against his arm.

How nice it was to have a comforting presence. Someone to listen. Someone who wouldn't break the silence with shoulds and shouldn'ts. Someone who just sat near him to let him know he wasn't alone in this.

"Thank you," he whispered.

Hanileh patted his hand and squeezed his fingers. He responded in kind. "Tell me Velius didn't kill him," he said, glancing down at her.

With a helpless look, frustration in her eyes, Hanileh shrugged. She, of course, couldn't tell him anything.

"He is my brother, Hanileh. A reformed Strages. You are familiar with them, are you not?"

Hanileh blinked, then shook her head. She pointed to him and shrugged again. She apparently didn't understand much of anything that was going on.

"You are familiar with the Crown," Gaultier said. In their time together, he'd read her several passages that spoke of the Crown's love.

She held up three fingers.

"Yes, that's right. The Creator King, the Ruler Prince, and the Eternal Companion. Together, they form the Crown. They are each separate, yet they are one. He has always been. He will always be. Nothing created Him," Gaultier explained. "Followers of the Crown are called Lumen. Some have gifts that can only be explained as a touch of the Crown. We are called Logia."

Hanileh gestured to the cockpit, then to Gaultier. He nodded. "Jax is Lumen, while Alton and myself are Logia. Alton is gifted with restoration, the ability to physically heal. I am gifted with strength, knowledge, and other abilities that call me to be a leader.

"The Crepusculum are the dark equivalent to the Lumen. They oppose the Crown and support the efforts of the Strages. They don't know they are toying with very dangerous things.

"The Strages, well, they can only be described as wicked. They count themselves as enemies of the Crown, and they acknowledge their powers are rooted in evil. They are bent on destroying the Logia."

Hanileh's hand slowly fell on her chest, a look of heartache on her face. Gaultier nodded again. "You now understand our concern, Hanileh. But nothing I've seen in you has shown the characteristics of the Strages. The Crown gave me your name. You do not belong to them.

"As I was saying, my brother Velius—my parents raised us as Logia. My father believed I would one day be named Protector. Velius, being older, courted jealousy and resentment. It was only a matter of time before he fell. The Crepusculum took him in, preying on his hurt. They won him over and introduced him to the Strages. Even though he didn't have a hand in it, his so-called friends took the lives of our parents.

"Many Logia don't believe the Strages exist. I've seen them first hand." Gaultier stared at the floor, remembering the horrific night only a few short years ago. He blinked, looking back up at her. "Although it was catastrophic, it led Velius back to the faith. He joined me at Kapelle and learned from Athaer Castus. He discovered his gift of restoration, and he made great strides. Until he met you."

Hanileh released the breath she had been holding. Her shoulders drooped, and her whole countenance seemed to wilt.

"You're not responsible for him slipping. I'm not saying that," Gaultier reassured her. "He is responsible. You were just the catalyst who revealed the Strages's hold runs deep. And that's why I fear he had a hand in Castus's death. A little taste of something leads to a much stronger craving."

Placing her hand upon his once more, Hanileh scooted a bit closer. She resumed her position of comfort, half embracing him.

"You understand me so well, Hanileh," Gaultier murmured. "I wish I could understand you."

As they sat together, the lights on the ship dimmed. The normally smooth-sailing craft convulsed violently. Gaultier secured his grip around Hanileh.

"We have entered the aperture of the Pathway," he said, holding her close. Only seconds later, the lights returned to their full glow, and the Queen emerged from the cockpit.

"We approach Oresed," she announced.

"Explain more about this Continuum," Gaultier said, releasing Hanileh to gesture to the seat across from them.

Nyssa lowered into it, leaning on the table. "Long ago, the Crown entrusted a few of His created beings with five attributes—Time, Space, Soul, Breath, and Silence. They acted as agents for Him, and all was well. However, Time began to plant seeds of unrest among his brothers. And at the Gateway Dome on Oresed, the Continuum declared their independence from the Crown. They turned their backs, leaving the Crown in an oppressive sorrow. He has since sought reconciliation, but the Continuum are stubborn, believing they are righteous and blameless. Legend says evil was birthed at the site, manifested into a being who will strive to bring an end to the Crown."

"So why are we seeking their help?" Gaultier asked, glancing at Hanileh.

"Because through Hanileh's drawing, the Crown directed me to them. Yet another attempt to bring them back into the fold."

Gaultier shook his head. "This is foolishness. I've never heard of such thing."

"That's because the stories have fallen to legend, given no credence among the Logia." Nyssa bowed her head, her voice lowering, "Just as I will."

Hanileh reached across the table to nudge the Queen. Nyssa smiled sadly at her. "It's all right. I have accepted it. I just pray when the Challenge is issued, the Logia will not suffer the same fate. It will be a sad day, should that happen."

Gaultier took a breath. "We won't let it happen. You named two very capable and commendable Protectors."

"They won't face the Challenge alone," Nyssa stated. "They will have assistance."

"You intend to name more Protectors?"

"No. The mantle will fall to their household. It will be many years yet before the Challenge is issued."

Gaultier chuckled, shaking his head. "Avner was right."

"About?"

"He said neither he nor I would see the Challenge in our lifetimes."

Hanileh lowered her eyes, her fingers seeking his. Gaultier realized she was worried about him. He looked at her, then at the Queen, whose expression also showed distress.

"And Castus was killed..." Gaultier said, recognizing their concern.

"Nothing's going to happen to me. I promise."

The Queen lowered her eyes. "I'm glad to see your faith return with full force. Just don't drop your guard, Gaultier. We live in uncertain times. Stone we once stood upon has turned to sand."

"Then we find a foothold on a Solid Rock, my lady," Gaultier said. "The Crown."

Jax peered out from behind the entrance to the cockpit. "We're in orbit around Oresed, my lady," he said to the Queen.

"Excellent," she said, rising. "Hanileh, would you excuse us, please? I would like Gaultier to pilot us the rest of the way."

Gaultier glanced up at the Queen. "Jax is our lead—"

"Yes," Nyssa interrupted with a stern look. "But you are called to this."

Gaultier nodded slowly, patting Hanileh's arm as he stood. "Move over there," he commanded gently, pointing toward the rows of seats along either side of the bulkhead. "And put the safety harness on. Who knows what we may be facing here."

Following the Queen, Gaultier entered the cockpit. Jax slipped out of the pilot's seat, switching places with him. Looking back over his shoulder, Gaultier said, "Keep an eye on her. Let me know if she needs me."

"She'll be fine, G," Jax murmured, closing the door behind him.

CHAPTER FIFTEEN

Nyssa placed a hand on Gaultier's shoulder as she lowered into the chair next to him. "You care a great deal about a girl you know so little of."

"She needs me." Gaultier scanned his readouts to dismiss the comment.

"I think there's more to it than that."

"She's the only thing I'm in control of right now," he admitted, glancing sideways at the Queen. "I can't fix the issue with Velius, nor can I help Castus..."

"You are not in control of her, Gaultier."

"That's not exactly what I meant." Gaultier rubbed his hand over his brow. "She is in my charge. My responsibility. I can keep her safe, protected. And maybe I can help her figure out this conundrum."

Nyssa chuckled softly, turning her attention to the viewport.

"What?" Gaultier asked, trying to keep the aggravation from his tone.

"It's just amusing how humans think they can manipulate or affect circumstances."

Gaultier glanced at her. "Are you not human?"

"I told you, I am a conduit." Nyssa turned to face him. "But that has little significance in this matter. You need to learn to trust the Crown."

"I do trust the Crown," Gaultier responded stubbornly.

"To a certain extent, perhaps. And you've been faithful in your duty to Him. But you've never really gone out on a limb for Him. You've stayed in comfortable surroundings—"

"I spent a month on Asper—"

"I'm not talking about physical surroundings, Gaultier." Nyssa's gaze locked on his. "I'm talking about denying the call to leadership within the faith."

"I've led Jax and Alton—"

"As a small band of crusaders. You could do, be, so much more, Gaultier."

92

"I never felt the call to walk the Protector path."

"You're lying. To me and to yourself."

Gaultier bowed his head, speaking softly, "Things changed, Nyssa..."

"When your parents were killed. I know. But the Crown provided support that would have elevated you—"

"I didn't want to be elevated!" Gaultier turned his eyes to her. "I didn't want to have to be the one to judge Velius, to put him in his place."

Nyssa sat back in her chair, once more looking out the viewport. "He has long come between you and the Crown."

"Do we really have to discuss this?" Gaultier whispered. "I thought we were here to help Hanileh."

With a knowing smile, Nyssa glanced back toward Gaultier. "It's all about the bigger picture, Gaultier. Remember that. You may think you are helping her, when it is really she who is helping you."

"I suppose you find that amusing as well."

"Interesting, really. The Crown's ways are mysterious and wonderful."

"*Soli Deo Gloria*," Gaultier murmured as he dropped from Oresed's orbit to break atmosphere. "Where are we heading?"

"We're breaking their rules," Nyssa said. "They wish for us to locate the Gateway Dome and pass over. That way, they can claim a soul."

Gaultier shook his head. This whole thing sounded so wrong. Dirty. Sacrilegious. How he ended up in the midst of it, he would probably spend the rest of his days wondering.

Nyssa continued, "The Dome is a place of abandonment and overwhelming sorrow. I am sparing you from facing that, not to mention the arduous journey from the Dome to the Horologium Range."

"Do you want me to thank you?" Gaultier asked, raising an eyebrow.

"Just do what I say. Once I see the clock, I'll be able to direct you to the cave that leads to their lair."

"And what will they say, since we're breaking their rules? Will they even bother to help us?"

"I will ensure they do," Nyssa said quietly.

Below the ship sprawled a lush green valley that rolled into staggered rows of purple rock. Deep gray clouds settled over the range, limiting visibility. Gaultier frowned, flipping on extra sensors to keep from crashing into the stony crags.

"They know we're coming," she whispered. "Hence the clouds."

"Well, if they operate time and space, I would think so."

"The Pathway's disruption did it." Nyssa shifted in her seat. "I had cloaked us."

Gaultier frowned, part of him wanting to ask a million questions, but another part of him really not wanting to know. This was beyond his

ASHLEY HODGES BAZER

teachings, beyond his beliefs. But as Nyssa said, the Crown's ways were both mysterious and wonderful.

"Tell me where to go."

Nyssa straightened in her chair, pointing across Gaultier's line of sight. "There. The clock."

Gaultier blinked in disbelief as he saw an expansive circle formed by sizeable numbers in an ornate scrolled pattern. They jutted out from the mountainside, proud and frightening in their size, yet undeniably beautiful. At the center of the circle, three thick shafts of gold spanned from a mounted cylinder. One moved faster than the others, ticking off seconds in the hour. Never in his life had he seen anything so magnificent.

"How did they—"

"It's an affront, Gaultier. A visible mockery built over many years of boredom and despair." Nyssa shook her head, staring at the clock. "The Creator King weeps."

Gaultier lowered his eyes, terrified in hearing the Crown was disheartened. What would that mean for His people? Surely the Continuum didn't hold power over the Crown...

Nyssa smiled. "He weeps for them, Gaultier, out of compassion. Yes, they hurt Him, but He is the Victor. He will make things right through the Divinum Bellator and the Ruler Prince. The Bellator will reconcile the Continuum to the Crown, while the Ruler Prince will reign over death and put an end to the evil in this system. You know all this."

"I didn't realize the passages about the Bellator referred to reconciliation with the Continuum, though. As far as I knew, those beings were just..."

"Legend," Nyssa said softly.

"Yes."

"Scholars have identified them differently. But if you go back with the knowledge you now have, you will see it."

Gaultier pulled back on the throttle as they closed in on the clock. "If we survive this," he said.

"You will." Nyssa pointed to the mouth of a cave between two numbers toward the bottom of the clock. "Dock there."

Gaultier angled the *Sun's* thrusters to direct the ship toward the cave. "I'm going to alert Jax and Alton to gear up."

"No need," Nyssa said quietly.

"We'll need weapons..."

She shook her head. "Leave it all behind. Trust me, Gaultier. Trust the Crown."

Gaultier frowned again as the stone cavern swallowed the ship in its black jaws. "I do trust you. And the Crown." He carefully settled the ship on the ground, muttering, "It's the Continuum I don't trust."

Nyssa was out of her seat and exiting the cockpit before Gaultier even started to shut down the ship. She hadn't mentioned how close the supposed lair was, or how long she intended for them to stay, but he figured it might be best to leave the *Sun* in standby mode. As he reached across the console, the whole ship powered down on its own.

"Hey! A little warning, next time, G!" Jax called from the main cabin.

"I didn't do it!" Gaultier shouted back, fumbling under his seat for the emergency hand torch.

A beam of light sliced clumsily through the darkness, refracting off the viewport. "You okay, G?" Alton asked.

"Yeah," Gaultier said as he secured his hand torch. "A little disgruntled with our hosts, but I'm okay."

He joined the others in the cabin and moved immediately to Hanileh's side. She blinked in response to the bright shaft of lights, but didn't seem to be too shaken by the darkness. Still, she stepped close to him, gripping the side of his tunic in her fist.

"It's all right, Hanileh." Gaultier smiled in the shadows. It was good to be needed. "I'm here."

"We best be on our way," Nyssa urged, gesturing toward the exit.

Alton and Jax crossed the cabin to open the ramp. Nyssa descended into the inky darkness. Jax murmured to Gaultier as they passed, "Should we grab something?"

"The Queen says no. No weapons."

"They would do you no good," Nyssa said from the bottom of the ramp.

The belly of the cave held an eerie blue glow. As they stepped from the ship, the hand torches clicked off. Gaultier fiddled with the switch on his, but to no avail. Something else was in charge here, and whatever it was wanted the small group to know it.

Gaultier edged toward the blue glow. He nearly plummeted off a steep precipice, but thankfully Hanileh was watching and pulled him back. The rock floor gave way to a vast room, swathed in the dim blue light. In the center of the opening, a grand stalagmite rose proudly from the ground, spinning an orb of energy above it. The source of the blue light.

"What's that about?" Gaultier asked, gesturing to the orb.

"This marks the entrance to their lair. Very few have been here, and even fewer have left," Nyssa murmured. "Legend says if you capture the orb, you maintain control over the Continuum. What they don't tell you is that anyone who tries is immediately incinerated."

"It's the source of their power?" Jax asked. "They must be crazy to leave it so accessible."

"It's not accessible. Nor is it the true source of what power they claim to have. It's a lure and a lie. It's nothing more than a weapon." Nyssa crossed beyond Gaultier to a set of stone steps crudely cut into the rock. The steps led to the ground level of the room.

Gaultier hesitated, gripping Hanileh's hand. He watched as Nyssa descended the stairs, his eyes darting between her and the globe above. As she neared the stalagmite, the energy around the orb crackled violently. Nyssa lifted her hand to touch the pillar. A slab of the wide stone shifted, then slid to the side.

Nyssa glanced back over her shoulder. "Are you coming, Gaultier?" she asked.

For the first time, doubt about Nyssa crept into Gaultier's thoughts. *What if she is one of them? Leading us here for adverse purposes?* He closed his eyes a breathed a prayer of guidance.

Trust.

Reassurance washed over him almost immediately. He looked down, once again meeting Nyssa's gaze. "*Soli Deo Gloria,*" she whispered, although he heard it clearly in his ear.

Gripping Hanileh's hand, he led Jax and Alton down the stairs to Nyssa's side. She tilted her head, looking at him. "Faith, Gaultier," she reminded him. "The King is with us."

Another set of stairs awaited them within the stalagmite. Nyssa started down, followed by the others. Gaultier went before Hanileh, ready to protect her if necessary. Of course, he wasn't sure what he'd do if he had to go up against supernatural beings, but he held onto Nyssa's words. *The King is with us.*

A brighter blue light pierced the darkness around them. Nyssa lifted her chin, walking briskly down a hallway that seemed to take them deeper into the underground. Hanileh wound her fingers around Gaultier's tunic, hiding behind him. He nodded toward Jax and Alton, indicating they should keep up with Nyssa. He paused, though, to speak with Hanileh for a moment.

"Are you all right?" Gaultier asked, turning toward her.

She nodded, but terror filled her eyes.

"It's okay to be afraid. This is strange to me, too, but I'm choosing to trust the Crown. 'In times of uncertainty, I will carry you,' He says." Gaultier murmured.

Hanileh gestured to her throat, then to her head, shaking it with a frown.

Stepping closer, Gaultier placed a hand alongside her cheek and looked into her eyes. "We've come this far, Hanileh. Let's get the answers we seek. You are a child of the Crown. That alone makes this worthwhile."

Hanileh crumpled against him, her head on his chest. He wrapped his arms around her, holding her close to him. "We'll trust together, all right?" he whispered.

She nodded, still clinging to him. Running his hand over her hair, he pulled back and smiled into her nervous gaze. "Come on." He took her hand as he led her down the hallway to catch up with Nyssa and the others.

The long corridor flared out, widening into a deep mouth of rock. As Gaultier and Hanileh joined the others, rocks materialized to cover their entrance. Gaultier looked to Nyssa, who crossed into the new room with confidence.

"Show yourself," she called out, "in the name of the Crown."

"He bears no authority here," five voices spoke in chorus, echoing off the walls.

Hanileh edged closer to Gaultier. He put an arm around her waist, drawing her near. Jax and Alton glanced at each other. Gaultier knew they regretted leaving their weapons behind.

"I said show yourself!" Nyssa demanded.

Slinking from behind clusters of rock, three beings emerged. They were extraordinarily tall. How they had hidden from view, Gaultier wasn't sure. Wisps of white hair shone against their translucent skin, which was covered with leather and beads. The sight of them was disconcerting. These were beings created by the Crown?

Hanileh gasped behind Gaultier. He turned quickly to see a fourth being towering over them. The man's fingers settled upon Hanileh's shoulders, easing her from Gaultier's grasp. Hanileh's expression revealed panic.

"You shouldn't have come, Nyssa," the being said. Gaultier heard him, yet he hadn't moved his mouth.

"I couldn't send them on their own."

"Wise," the being murmured, turning Hanileh in his grasp to examine her. "My brothers are hungry."

Nyssa stalked across the room, taking Hanileh's hand to pull her away from the being. The Queen returned Hanileh to Gaultier, then stood between them and the Continuum. "You know the Crown is displeased."

"And we care not!" the being stated, his voice raised. "Your efforts to reconcile us are futile."

"I am not here to reconcile you with the Crown. That duty belongs to someone else."

"The Divinum Bellator will fail," the being spat.

"Don't be so certain," Nyssa answered. "But I am not here to discuss that with you. We are in need of your assistance."

"Why not petition your precious Crown?"

97

ASHLEY HODGES BAZER

"There are things going on here He will not touch."

"Cannot touch," the being interjected.

"Will not. Not yet. It's not yet His time." Nyssa gestured to Hanileh. "She has been marked by the Strages."

"And what do you expect us to do about it?"

Nyssa sighed, glancing over her shoulder toward the other beings. They had crept toward the group during the exchange. Gaultier pulled Hanileh closer, now joining Alton and Jax in their lack-of-weapons regret. Although he could tell Nyssa was right. No weapon would keep them safe against these beings.

"You will restore her," Nyssa answered.

"There is a price."

"This will serve as atonement."

"We atone for nothing."

"Let's not get into this now, Time."

The being, Time, shifted, appearing even taller than he was. He glared at Hanileh. "We get her gifts and power."

"This is not a negotiation. You restore her. Now." Nyssa looked between Time and the others. "And if she is harmed in any way, there will be no opportunity for reconciliation."

Time stalked toward Nyssa. "You don't understand. We don't want reconciliation."

Nyssa held her ground, not even so much as flinching as the tall being approached her. "Ternion comes."

Her words stiffened Time in a halt. He lifted his eyes to his brothers, and they seemed to share a silent conversation. Gaultier watched their faces, catching expressions that showed argument and eventually, agreement. Time relaxed his posture, returning his gaze to Nyssa.

"You wish for her to speak?"

Nyssa extended her arm to Hanileh. Gaultier could feel Hanileh tremble. He bolstered her with as an encouraging smile as he could muster. "It's all right," he whispered, passing her onto to Nyssa.

"Breath can find her voice, but we do not do this here," Time said, his long fingers encircling Hanileh's wrist. He pulled her past the group to lead them further into the room.

"And we will not enter your prison," Nyssa argued.

"It is not a prison. It's a collection. Think of it as a museum." Time stood, holding the petrified Hanileh. "And if you don't follow our rules, it will result in a fractured soul."

"What is he talking about?" Gaultier whispered to Nyssa.

"They collect bodies and souls, Gaultier. Soul," Nyssa pointed to one of the three, "is the keeper of the shards. He is a master of illusion, but all he really possesses is fractured souls. The shards contain those pieces."

"And the bodies?" Alton asked.

"They are entombed in ice. Those who have ventured this far to obtain answers."

"Like us?" Jax's eyes widened in distress.

"I told you, you are safe with me here," Nyssa said. "I speak for the Crown."

"Why do we have to go in there?" Gaultier murmured.

"It is where Silence resides."

By the Crown...

Gaultier started toward Time and Hanileh, only to have Nyssa stop him. "It's not what you think, Gaultier. They are not going to kill her, but Silence has to be involved in this. They must combine their powers in order to restore Hanileh."

"This is insanity."

"There are things far more terrible and wonderful than this, Gaultier. You know the Crown's ways are not our ways."

Gaultier leaned in toward her. "That name you gave Time. What was that?"

"Not one to be taken lightly." Nyssa lowered her eyes for a moment before lifting them to the rock ceiling above. "It is the precious name of the Ruler Prince. You are the first to have heard it."

Time waited near a rock wall, his brothers having joined him. Their eyes were all on Hanileh. Gaultier fought the urge to sweep to her side and ward off the evil beings. If nothing else, he just wanted to comfort her.

Nyssa walked toward the Continuum, the men behind her. As they came near, the rock wall dissipated, revealing a darkened chamber. At the center, a stone slab welled up from the floor. Time guided Hanileh to the slab and gestured for her to lie down.

"It's all right, Hanileh," Nyssa said. "They will not harm you."

Gaultier stepped toward the slab, but Nyssa held up her arm to keep him back. "They can do this without you."

"I want her to know I will not allow anything to happen to her."

A collective chuckle rose from the Continuum. Nyssa shook her head. "It wouldn't matter, Gaultier. If they chose to do something to her, you could not stop them."

Gaultier looked beyond Nyssa toward Hanileh. While the beings took their places around Hanileh, she locked onto his gaze. The fifth being, Silence, skulked from the shadows, trailing his fingers along the table as he stared down at Hanileh. How Gaultier wished he could take her place.

CHAPTER SIXTEEN

Hanileh stared into Breath's eyes as the other members of the Continuum took their stations at her hands and feet. She was grateful for Gaultier's presence, but fear still held her in its grip.

Queen Nyssa spoke with regal measure, "Be gentle with the girl. Remember she is only human."

"Leave us to our work, Nyssa," Soul snarled, gripping Hanileh's hand.

Breaking her concentration, Hanileh's gaze flickered toward Gaultier. A look of concern lined his face. As always, he was flanked by Jax and Alton. He looked as uneasy as she felt.

The cold grasps of the Continuum wound around her wrists and her ankles. She stiffened as Breath turned her head to look at him again. "Relax, child," he said. "We will find your voice."

His hand slid down to her neck, his bony fingers splaying over her skin. The Continuum began to hum with low, guttural sounds. Hanileh wasn't sure what was happening, but slowly, her breath began to leave her. As the fingers squeezed around her throat, her upper body tightened in panic. She tugged on her limbs, trying to break free from the ones holding her, but they proved much stronger.

Opening her mouth, Hanileh gasped for air. Her eyes flew to Gaultier. Jax and Alton restrained him at the order of the Queen. He shouted at her, "She can't breathe!"

The Queen stepped forward. "He's right."

Hanileh squirmed and struggled, but no relief came. The fingers tightened even more. Her end was coming. With a final effort, she arched her back and cried out.

She...cried out.

The Continuum released her. She lay on the stone table, her chest heaving with much needed air. When she finally caught her breath, she looked up at Breath.

"Th-thank you," she whispered.

The being nodded once and stepped aside. Gaultier pulled away from his friends and moved to Hanileh's side. "Are you all right?" he asked.

She nodded, smiling softly at him. "I can speak again."

"But still no memory?"

She shook her head.

Gaultier looked up at the Continuum with a frown. "I almost hesitate to ask." He touched her neck tenderly.

"I'm fine. A little shaken, but okay."

He nodded, rising up to address the Continuum. "Her memory."

Soul changed places with Breath. "Can be recovered."

Time raised his hand. "For a cost."

Silence murmured something to Space, who in turn lifted his chin to pipe in, "They still owe us for her voice."

"I've already spoken on this," Nyssa said.

"What do you desire?" Gaultier asked, overriding Nyssa's statement.

Nyssa shot a deadly look at Gaultier. "We do not bargain."

Hanileh bit her lower lip as she reached for Gaultier's hand. He took hold of her fingers with a gentle squeeze. "Please don't fight over me," she whispered.

Space spoke once again for Silence. "Our collection is not yet complete. We lack a Logia."

Gaultier started to respond, but the Queen interrupted. "And you shall still. As I said, the Crown does not recognize your authority and therefore, no bargains shall be agreed upon. You help this girl as your deference and atonement to the Crown."

Time stared at Silence, who nodded once. Another silent exchange happened between them. Time lifted his chin and bowed yieldingly to the Queen. The Continuum returned to their places, with Soul at Hanileh's head.

Gaultier squeezed her fingers reassuringly before placing them in Breath's hands. He stepped back behind the Queen, but kept his eyes on Hanileh.

Sharp, pointy fingernails scratched over her forehead as Soul slid his palm into place. The Continuum pinned Hanileh to the table as shockwaves of pain radiated through her head. She could hear her newly restored voice echoing screams off the cut stone walls. Flashes of memories slammed into her mind, tearing her apart mentally. Haunting visions of nightmarish scenes cut into her heart. No, it couldn't be...

An image of a handsome man blazed in the center of the maddening whirlwind. The man she'd drawn. The one who frightened her and worried Nyssa. In an instant, Hanileh saw a child being snatched away and raised in shadow. Horrifying murders and blood of the Crown's children being spilt.

Black lines squiggled through her skin, tracing evidence of evil through her. She cried out time and again, begging for the torture to end.

She opened her eyes to see Gaultier hollering something. The Queen pulled back on his shoulder and delivered him to Jax and Alton's grasps. Soul lifted his hand from her in a grand gesture. She felt a sensation, like falling from a great height. A vacuum of silence erupted into a chaotic roar of upset, raised voices. She whimpered as she returned to reality, with a new, frightening set of memories.

Hanileh...no...Marcella, as her memories told her, stared at the ceiling. How evil she had been. Blindly evil. Her actions and judgments were staggering. The Continuum stepped away and left her alone with her thoughts.

Gaultier moved into her line of sight. She closed her eyes again. If he knew, he would surely reject her. That would be unbearable.

"Are you all right?" he asked gently.

"No," she whispered as he sat next to her on the cold stone table.

"Care to tell me about it?"

"I haven't the nerve." Marcella returned her gaze to the ceiling. "How could it be?" she asked, more of the Crown than anyone.

Gaultier pushed her hair back from her face. "It's the past, Hanileh."

"I'm not Hanileh."

"Then tell me your name."

"Mar—" Her tongue stumbled over the name. "Marcella."

"Marcella." Gaultier repeated with a gentle smile. "Beautiful. Just like you."

"It is an evil name bestowed to represent the terrible things I once did." Her eyes quickly raced over her arms to see if the markings had returned as well.

Taking her hands in his, Gaultier said softly, "I have the ability to share thoughts and memories with another person. The Logia call it fusion. Will you allow me to see what it is that haunts you?"

Marcella pressed her lips together and gave a single nod of consent. She stiffened as Gaultier's warm fingers caressed her cheek and settled behind her ear. His presence grew closer as he slipped into her mind. She couldn't hide now. Her memories filtered into his.

He took a deep breath as he withdrew, looking down at her. "I can see why you are upset."

Marcella turned her chin, feeling the full brunt of his rejection. Gaultier's hand slid along her face and drew her attention back to him. "You're not that person, Hanileh. You made the choice before your memory was taken. I saw it. You changed of your own volition," he said with hopeful encouragement.

"I don't want to be Marcella."

"You're not," he reassured, helping her to sit up. "I told you, when we first met, the Crown spoke your name to me. He told me to call you Hanileh. You belong to Him. But now, He's allowing you to make another choice. Do you wish to return to that path, now that you know who you were? Or do you wish to follow the new one given to you? I can assure you, you won't be alone should you choose the new path." He smiled at her, taking her hand in his.

Marcella stared at the gentle man before her. She'd never known such tenderness. He embraced her, regardless of what she had done. As she stared into his eyes, she saw no sign of rejection.

"I choose the new path, Gaultier."

He smiled again, his fingers brushing along her shoulder. "Look."

The brutal mark of the Strages on her chest faded into her skin. Lucian's grasp was no more. The Crown accepted her, and she was indeed transformed.

"We should get going, G," Jax said, glancing at the backs of the Continuum who now blocked the exit.

"Yes, now that this business has concluded, we must consult with the Dignitaries to discuss our next actions," Nyssa said.

"Nyssa," Time said, turning back to face the small group, "this service doesn't come free."

Nyssa folded her arms over her chest, staring at Time. "Enough. I've already told you this is a way to atone—"

"And I've already told you, we have no interest in atoning," Time answered flatly. "Particularly with Him."

"We owe you nothing."

"You owe us everything."

Lifting her chin, Nyssa spoke in a regal tone. "These are children of the Crown. They are under His protection. You will not touch them."

Time's eyes bore into each of them one at a time. It was as if he was memorizing their very souls. His gaze came to rest on Nyssa, transforming into a smirk.

"You think you can stop us?" he challenged.

"I just did," Nyssa answered. "The Crown is being merciful, Time. I would not test the limits of His grace."

The Queen turned to Gaultier. "You and your friends take the girl out of here. I will follow."

Gaultier nodded, helping Hanileh to her feet. Jax and Alton took the lead, moving beyond Queen Nyssa toward the Continuum. Time and the others stood unmoving.

"Let them pass," Nyssa insisted.

"Would the Crown lower Himself to defend his children?" Time asked mockingly as his fingers slipped along Gaultier's shoulder.

"He won't have to. I have the authority to stop you. But if that was not the case, yes, He would."

"It's been so long since we've seen Him." Time stared into Gaultier's eyes.

Gaultier was mesmerized, his gaze locked onto the being. The other members of the Continuum stepped closer. Hanileh started to reach for Gaultier's hand, but Soul blocked her, gripping her arm with supernatural strength. She whimpered as she heard Breath whisper to Space, "One for each of us."

"Enough!" Nyssa cried in a voice not her own. Hanileh wondered if she had just heard the voice of the Crown.

The command carried enough weight to cause the Continuum to shirk back and slink away from the small group. Time still held Gaultier, but with a stern look from the Queen, the being roughly released him. Gaultier stumbled back into Jax.

"You okay, man?" Jax asked softly.

Gaultier groaned. "Fine," he said, shrugging off his friend. He dropped his eyes to the floor, taking Hanileh's arm. "Come on."

They passed through the lair, their gait purposeful and determined. Hanileh held fast to Gaultier, glancing back once or twice to make sure Nyssa was with them. The Continuum also followed, but with slower, measured steps.

"Nyssa," Time called out.

"It is done, Time," Nyssa responded. "*Soli Deo Gloria.*"

"*Gloriam nostrum et nostris tantum,*" Time responded.

Gaultier halted in his steps, closing his eyes. Hanileh glanced back toward the Continuum. "What did he say?" she asked of Gaultier in a whisper.

"'The glory is ours and ours alone,'" Gaultier whispered back. "It is abject blasphemy."

"How wrong you are," Nyssa said to Time, shaking her head sadly. "The Day of Reconciliation is coming. Be wary."

"I order every day, Nyssa," Time argued. "The Day of Reconciliation is in my hand."

"He really believes he rules over the Crown," Alton whispered to Gaultier.

"You only think so," Nyssa answered. "Continue in your delusion, then. You shall soon see." She shepherded everyone toward the exit. "Come. It is time for us to leave."

"Nyssa!" Time shouted as Nyssa shuffled the group out of the lair and up the tight staircase.

With a supernatural voice that shook the rock walls, Nyssa pointed at Time. "*Mihi vindictam. Orate unciam invenio gratiam tui.*"

Gaultier yanked on Hanileh's hand, pulling her up the stairs behind him. "Come on," he urged.

"But Nyssa..."

"She will come," he answered.

"Gaul—" Hanileh said, pulling back as she saw rocks falling at Nyssa's feet.

"Now, Hanileh!"

Gaultier dragged her through the cave and back toward the *Midnight Sun.* Before they reached the ship, he ordered, "Jax, get the *Sun* running. Alton, I want you standing by the ramp to help Nyssa."

They clambered up the ramp. Jax took off for the cockpit. Gaultier pointed to the row of seats along the wall. "Strap in," he said to Hanileh.

"I don't understand," Hanileh murmured, moving to the seats.

"We're in the midst of an ancient argument between the Crown and the Continuum, Hanileh," Gaultier said as Alton took up his position by the ramp. "Nyssa is as she said—a conduit. She is relaying a message from the Crown Himself. She said vengeance belongs to the Crown and the Continuum should pray for a measure of grace. Once she leaves, we will be met with great resistance on the part of the Continuum."

Gaultier opened up a compartment, withdrawing a small case. "I'm heading down to the engine room. Alert me when Nyssa's on board." Pointing toward Hanileh, he again said, "Strap in."

Hanileh settled back in her seat, slipping the mesh harness around her shoulders and attaching the waist belt. She watched as Gaultier disappeared down a hatch that led to the engine. She wished she could go with him.

Alton offered her a small nervous smile. "It will be okay."

"Yeah," she said, leaning her head back against the bulkhead. Nothing had been okay for a long time. The only thing that felt okay was being with Gaultier. But even that had led to a variety of troubles. She began to wonder if anything would ever be okay again...or if Alton's words were just another empty platitude.

Nyssa marched aboard the ramp, her eyes on Hanileh. "Where is Gaultier?"

"He went below." Alton raised and secured the ramp.

"I must speak with him," Nyssa said, stumbling toward the table at the center of the cabin.

Alton bolted to her side. "My lady, may I help you?"

She waved him off, her unsteady legs carrying her toward Jax's cabin. "Fetch Gaultier."

ASHLEY HODGES BAZER

"On my way," Alton said, dashing for the ladder. He called out as he ran across the cabin, "G!"

The Queen, now gripping the wall, looked at Hanileh. Something about Nyssa had changed. Her face bore the strain of conflict, and her eyes carried an unknown sorrow. Hanileh wanted to move to her side, but at the same time, she was too terrified to move.

"Hanileh," Nyssa breathed, "you will make things right. Never forget that."

Hanileh gripped the arms of her seat, shrinking back into the chair as Gaultier leapt up from the engine room ladder. The Queen disappeared into Jax's cabin, followed by Gaultier. Hanileh stared at the door, wondering what Nyssa might have meant. She had many questions, but now was not the time. She would just have to wait and trust in the Crown.

CHAPTER SEVENTEEN

Gaultier helped Nyssa to Jax's bunk. He knelt at her side, holding her hand in his. She had aged beyond her years, every moment draining decades of life from her. "Nyssa, tell me what to do...how to help you." Gaultier said quietly, trying to mask his shock as he looked into the Queen's sunken eyes.

Nyssa gasped for breath, reaching toward him. "Time...has...claimed me," she said. "Nothing can be done."

"That can't be!" Gaultier cried. "You serve the Crown. You belong to Him."

"The Crown will use this, Gaultier," the Queen said softly. She then emphasized her words with what little strength she had. "He has a plan, and His authority reigns over the Continuum's misguided powers." Her voice dropped again. "They are always listening, Gaultier..."

"You're slipping away." Gaultier said through clenched jaws.

"Protect Hanileh. Keep her from seeing me. Within the hour, I will look like a long-decayed corpse, and I will no longer be able to communicate."

"Can we not help you? Petition the Crown? Something? Anything?"

"Gaultier, the Crown does not always see it fit to answer our prayers in the way we want Him to, but His answers are always the best for His Kingdom. Trust Him in this."

"I can't..."

Nyssa began to cry. "I need you to. I cannot do this alone. I am frightened."

Gaultier stared at the withered Queen, his heart failing him. "I will be strong for you, my Queen," he whispered.

"Be strong for her, Gaultier," Nyssa said. "Hanileh needs you."

"I will see her through this."

"Beyond this. The Crown has chosen you for her. Care for her. Protect her. Love her."

Gaultier bowed his head. Really, this was not something he wished to discuss with the dying Queen, not when there were much more important things to talk about. But somehow, she read feelings that had already started to grow.

"That will require little effort," Gaultier answered.

"Because it is right," the Queen's gaunt face tightened with a smile. "With you, she will bring forth the Divinum Bellator. Everything we have waited for is falling into place."

"The Divine Warrior?" he asked. The Divine Warrior was a long-anticipated being within the faith that would carry special gifting from the Crown. Once the Challenge was issued, the Divine Warrior would triumph over death, leading the way for the Ruler Prince to establish His throne over the system.

"You have tried to escape your calling, Gaultier," Nyssa said. "But you have long known you are important to the Crown's plan. He has placed you in this situation in this very time to do magnificent things for His glory."

"My son, then?" he asked, a sense of disbelief mingling with long-forgotten and ill-placed joy.

Nyssa went rigid, a look of agony writhing along her features. She gripped Gaultier's hand as her spine arched in the struggle. After a moment of utter helplessness, Nyssa fell back on the bed, gasping for breath. "Your son will free me," she murmured. "My role in this is not yet complete."

"What do we need to do, Nyssa?"

"Return me to Sagesse, but do not place me where everyone would expect a Queen to reside. Marauders and fortune seekers will attempt to find me in the Throne Room. I wish to rest in my chambers at the base of the north tower."

"Your words are my duty, my Queen. I serve you for the Crown."

"Your ship will have access to the Pathways to and from Sagesse. Share this with no one, Gaultier. Speculations will be made, but the Crown will guide your son. The Strages seek every opportunity to frustrate the Crown's will, and we must keep them from discovering too much."

Gaultier glanced over his shoulder, thinking of Hanileh. She had been in the grasp of the Strages—even counted herself as one of them. The Crown had transformed her, but Velius had made similar claims and struggled constantly in his identity.

"She may question and doubt herself, but be assured the Crown has spoken her name. She belongs to Him," Nyssa said, answering Gaultier's unspoken uncertainty. "And you."

"When will this happen, Nyssa?"

"Soon." The Queen's withered hand released Gaultier as her body stiffened into complete immobility. She struggled to tell Gaultier more.

HERALDS OF THE CROWN: POISON

"You...may be called...to agonizing sacrifice. But...always...trust..."

Her eyes closed, and her voice faltered into a final gurgle. Gaultier stared as her shriveled skin grayed into a leathery, lifeless sheath. He gripped her wrist, surprised by the faint, slow beat that still pulsed through her veins. Murmuring a soft prayer, he shook open a blanket at the foot of Jax's bunk and settled it atop the Queen's motionless body.

"*Soli Deo Gloria*," he whispered, jarred by his last few moments with Nyssa.

◆

Gaultier stepped from Jax's cabin, his eyes meeting Hanileh's. She dropped her gaze to stare at the blank page before her. Something was wrong, that much was plain. Unfamiliar distress clung to Gaultier's features, and Alton had been darting in and out of the room since they'd left Oresed. Now they had returned to the Palace of Sagesse, and Alton had disappeared into Jax's cabin once more.

"Hanileh, I need you to go to my quarters and stay there until I come for you," Gaultier said before calling Jax to join him.

"But—" she started.

"Don't argue with me, please. Obey my order."

Jax stepped from the cockpit. "I'm keeping the *Sun* on standby," he said, "in case we need to get out of here quickly."

"Good thinking," Gaultier said, turning back to Hanileh. "Please. Get going."

"I am afraid to be alone," she whispered.

Gaultier directed Jax toward the cabin where Nyssa waited. He then stepped close to Hanileh, taking her hand. He placed a small link into her palm. "You're not alone. Never alone."

"Is Nyssa ill?"

A frown darkened his already solemn expression as he lowered into a seat next to her. "I don't know how to answer that," he said quietly.

Hanileh's fingers gripped her drawing pencil and set to work. Before long, the image of Nyssa, decked in her full regalia, appeared. She lay on her back on a wide stone dais, one arm crossed over the other. Hanileh sat back and watched as the beauty of the Queen dissipated into wrinkles and age spots. In the sketch, Nyssa opened her eyes, revealing deep, black pits.

Flicking the pencil from her fingers, Hanileh turned to Gaultier in horror. He clasped his hands together and leaned against the table, squeezing his eyes closed.

"He won't take her life. He can't. He doesn't have the authority."

"Who?" Hanileh asked, glancing at the door of the cabin. "What are you talking about?"

"Time of the Continuum has claimed the Queen, Hanileh. As payment for services rendered."

"What services?" The realization struck Hanileh. *Oh, no. No. Not me.* "My voice? My memory?"

Gaultier nodded, blowing out a breath as he pushed off the table into a nervous pace.

"They can have them back. Don't let them do this!"

"It's too late. She paid the price—"

"No!"

"—and it's done."

Hanileh leapt to her feet in the direction of the cabin. "I won't let her do this!"

Gaultier followed, wrapping Hanileh into an embrace. "We don't have a choice, Hanileh."

"I'm not worth the sacrifice!"

Gripping both sides of her face, Gaultier looked into Hanileh's eyes. "I don't ever want to hear you talk like that again. You are a daughter of the King."

"I have the blood of the Logia on my hands." Hanileh pulled away, turning from him as hot tears stung her eyes.

Gaultier placed a tender hand on her shoulder, easing her back to face him. He took her hands into his, holding them up before her. "They've been washed clean. You are redeemed. Remember?

"This was Nyssa's choice. She came with us to act as an intercessor. If it weren't for her, one of us—you, me, Jax, Alton—would have had to make the sacrifice. Nyssa will be freed when the Divine Warrior comes to face Death. The Crown will protect her during this time. We must believe that."

"What has he done to her?" Hanileh asked.

"He's taken years. It's the only thing he has within his power. Silence was not allowed to touch her, so Nyssa is still alive. She has yet to fulfill her role in this, Hanileh, otherwise the Crown would take her. At least, that's what she's told me."

Hanileh covered her face with her hands. It was all so overwhelming. The way her past crashed into the present... She hated herself. She hated who she had been when she was in league with Lucian. And she wondered how she would retain what she had become with Gaultier, especially in light of the pain she had caused.

And when she would have to stand on her own.

Gaultier pulled her close to him, holding her against his chest. "The Crown Himself saved you, Hanileh. I believe that. He has a purpose for you beyond what we can see. Don't allow the lies of the enemy to penetrate

HERALDS OF THE CROWN: POISON

your heart."

"I'm worried that when we part ways, the lines will blur, and—"

Withdrawing from her, Gaultier held her shoulders and looked into her eyes. "Wait. Who said anything about parting ways?"

"I can't expect you to care for me forever, Gaultier."

A hint of light fell from his eyes. She had wounded him. "I just—" she said, stumbling between recovery and apology.

"We didn't meet by accident. It wasn't a happy coincidence." Gaultier stared into her eyes, brushing her hair back from her face. "I knew that from the start. Didn't you?"

He leaned in, placing a tender kiss on her lips. Hanileh nearly forgot to breathe, until he pulled back, holding her gaze.

"How can you—" she started in a whisper.

Shaking his head, Gaultier squeezed her hands in his. "Don't ask me how I can love you. It's all very sudden. All I know is that I do. I can't explain it. But I've never been more certain of anything in my life, aside from my service to and love for the Crown."

"It seems so natural." Hanileh looked back at him. "But is it true love? Or is it just circumstantial?"

"You're over-analyzing it, Hanileh," Gaultier answered with a gentle smile. "Gifts of the Crown are beautiful, honest, and not to be questioned." His hand caressed her cheek. "You are my gift. I believe it."

"And you are mine." Hanileh turned slightly to kiss Gaultier's wrist.

"Let us return Nyssa to her home. That is her request. She also asked you not see her. She doesn't want to frighten you unnecessarily. Once she is settled, we will travel back to Kapelle."

"Why Kapelle?"

"I need to report back to Cas—" Gaultier paused, lowering his eyes for a moment. Grief was still fresh for him. "I mean, Velius. And Jett. He needs to know what's happened to Nyssa."

◆

Hanileh peered around the entrance to the great hall, watching as the men carried Queen Nyssa across its vast floor. Gaultier had given her strict instructions to stay on the ship, but she didn't want to be that far from him. And as much as she hated to admit it, curiosity got the best of her. She wanted to see what had happened to Nyssa.

Gaultier, bearing Nyssa in his arms, stepped through a draped doorway on the far side of the hall. Hanileh had a good idea of where they were taking Nyssa. The same place she had first greeted them only days earlier. It felt like months ago. After he disappeared from view, Hanileh scuttled

ASHLEY HODGES BAZER

through the room, trying hard to focus on the door ahead. The room dwarfed her, making her feel dizzy and afraid. During the ceremony, it had been full of people. But now that it was empty, the void threatened to consume her.

On the far side of the door, Hanileh plastered herself to the wall to catch her breath. The flood of relief stopped short, though. The men had paused in the middle of the corridor. If Gaultier saw her, he'd surely send her back, and she couldn't bear to cross that big room again. A nearby container, wide enough to bear a potted tree, would make a great hiding spot. She dashed for it and ducked down next to the ceramic pot.

Hanileh recognized the hallway. It was indeed where she and Gaultier had first encountered the Queen. The familiar staircase stood at the end of the hall, curling upward toward the top of the tower, but also splitting off in the direction of the upper levels of the great hall. Alton and Jax opened a set of doors, allowing Gaultier to enter with Nyssa before disappearing with them.

With caution, Hanileh stepped out from behind the tree and made her way down the corridor. Anxiety slithered over her skin with the unsettling stillness that dwelt throughout the palace. Her imagination began to get the best of her, causing her to spin around to see if some invisible being had followed her from the great hall.

She backed down the corridor, examining every crevice and corner for justification of her paranoia. A wall stopped her from moving any further, taking both her breath and a tiny scream of fright. The wall grew arms that wrapped around her. She whirled around quickly, finding Gaultier's anxious gaze looking down at her.

"I told you to stay on the *Sun*."

"I didn't—"

"It's all right," Gaultier's expression softened into a gentle smile. "I feel like you should be here for some reason."

He reached for Hanileh's hand, leading her toward the room where they had delivered Nyssa. Alton and Jax situated the room, pulling all the furniture against the walls. The sitting area where she had demonstrated her sketching ability to Nyssa was no more. Against the far wall, between two marble pillars, a wide cushioned bench had been placed upon a platform, now serving as a bed for Nyssa's body. Thick burgundy drapes hanging from the pillars cast heavy shadows over her.

"Is she—?"

"No. She's very much alive," Gaultier answered, stepping behind Hanileh, his hand still attached to hers. "She is aware of everything going on around her. And she's aware she is doomed to this prison until the Divine Warrior arrives."

HERALDS OF THE CROWN: POISON

Hanileh turned in toward Gaultier, lifting her eyes to him. "It is my fault she suffers."

"No, Hanileh."

"Had I not questioned Lucian—"

"Then you would have remained in his power and service." Gaultier gripped her hands tightly. "Hanileh, the Crown has ordered this. Long before any of us were even born. While this astounds all of us, it is not a surprise to Him. I told you, it was no accident you came to me. You must not allow guilt and fear to stir up questions of what might have been. Live in the moment, and give it over to the Crown."

Hanileh took a breath, hoping to gain even an ounce of Gaultier's strength and wisdom. She nodded before turning back to face the Queen.

"She'll need her robes," Hanileh said, crossing the room to where the pile of ornate robes awaited.

The men followed her as she gathered the heavy fabric in her arms and moved toward Nyssa. Hanileh stared for a long moment at the once beautiful Queen. She looked as if she had been deceased for eons.

Gaultier paused next to Hanileh, glancing between her and Nyssa. "Why does she need her robes, Hanileh?" he asked softly.

"The picture I drew. She wore the robes," Hanileh answered, her eyes still on Nyssa. She tore her gaze away to look up at Gaultier. "And those who will come to release her will have a greater sense of respect when they see her in her full regalia."

Gaultier nodded, directing Jax and Alton to assist. Together, they carefully dressed Nyssa. Hanileh stood straight, her eyes staring at the wall ahead of her for a moment. Of course. Turning quickly, Hanileh descended the steps, heading for a small table along the wall.

"Hanileh?" Gaultier asked.

"Her tiara," Hanileh responded, lifting the glittering piece.

Exercising great care, Hanileh walked back to the Queen. She placed the tiara upon Nyssa's head, situating the now gray hair around it. For a moment, Hanileh allowed her gaze to linger upon the terrifying visage that once held such loveliness and life.

"Thank you," she heard Nyssa whisper in an imperceptible breath.

A flash of an image pierced Hanileh's thoughts. Space enabling Time to extend his grasp across star systems, and the other Continuum brothers, standing behind them to receive the souls of those he chose. Nyssa showed her their proximity to her put them at risk. Time still felt cheated, and were he to find a loophole, he would take them all in a heartbeat.

"We must go." Hanileh stumbled back down the stairs of the dais.

Gaultier sailed to her side, placing a strong arm around her waist. "What is it?"

113

"The Continuum. Nyssa is trying to protect us. They are searching for us."

Jax ran ahead as Alton adjusted a couple other pieces in the room. Gaultier gave a deep nod of respect toward Nyssa before guiding Hanileh from the room. She squinted as they ran back through the great hall, relying on Gaultier to get her to the other side. She could hear him murmuring prayer after prayer—protection over them, Nyssa, and the awaiting domicile at Kapelle.

The *Sun* was a welcome sight. Gaultier delivered Hanileh to a seat and waited for Alton to get on board. As he secured the ramp, he ordered Alton to run down to the engine room to scramble their output codes.

"We need to get out of the Pathway as quickly as possible. The disruption is how the Continuum can track us," Gaultier added. "After you get us encrypted, I want you to strap in."

Alton nodded, his eyes falling on Hanileh as he passed her to go down to the engine room. Gaultier dropped into a seat next to her, pulling the harness over her shoulders. "I need to help Jax with navigation. Once we're in the clear, I'll let you know. But for now, try to get a little rest."

Dread threatened to keep her from doing as Gaultier instructed. She shifted in the seat, trying to find the right spot. It wasn't the chair below her that made her uncomfortable, though. The past few days had started to catch up with her, and it was all just too much to deal with.

He lifted his hand to her cheek, brushing a loose strand of hair back over her ear. Gently angling her head toward his, he placed a tender kiss on her forehead. "It's going to be all right. I promise," he whispered before withdrawing to the cockpit.

Chapter Eighteen

Hanileh stirred as Gaultier slipped a blanket over her shoulders. She met his gaze with a smile and whispered, "Thank you."

He gave a quick nod, a gentle smile playing on his lips. As she rested her head against the back of the chair, Gaultier slid into the open seat at the table with Jax and Alton. She probably should have tried to settle back to sleep, but she couldn't help listening in on the men's conversation.

"I altered our course slightly. We only have another few hours," Gaultier said.

"You'd think with all we went through, she'd at least have given us a Pathway to get back to Kapelle," Jax mumbled.

"She went through a lot, too," Alton reminded his friend. "She paid a steep price."

"Nyssa made quite the sacrifice, yes, but it wasn't against her nature to do so. Let's be thankful, and say no more of it," Gaultier said. "Besides, she provided a Pathway from Sagesse to Tripudio."

"So what's the plan now, G?" Alton lifted a mug to his lips.

"We go back to Kapelle, maybe base there for a while."

"Tell him," Jax said, his eyes on Alton.

"Tell me what?" Gaultier looked first at Jax, then to Alton, who shook his head in Jax's direction. "What's going on?"

Hanileh sat up a bit and pulled the blanket around her, watching the men as she listened closely. *Jax and Alton have been keeping something from Gaultier?* Her time of silence had taught her to hear beyond the obvious. She caught the slight sense of panic in Gaultier's voice, as well as the regret in Alton's.

"We're not going to stay at Kapelle with you, G," Alton said, lowering the cup to the table. "I'm going home to Marita. And Jax has had a request from a crusader on Pavana."

Gaultier pushed back from the table, turning his back to all of them. Hanileh wished she could see his face. He'd been through a lot, too, and he

ASHLEY HODGES BAZER

was hurting. It took all her strength to stay in her seat and not rush to comfort him.

"Have I done something?" Gaultier's voice was husky.

"No, G," Jax answered. "Your priorities have changed. And so have ours."

"And with Velius in control of Kapelle, he's going to want you close," Alton said. "I imagine he'll appoint you as an elder. Your crusading days are over."

Gaultier glanced over his shoulder toward Hanileh and ran a hand over his face. She held his gaze, hoping she communicated some sort of reassurance. He shook his head before turning back to his friends.

"I have every intention of confronting Velius about Castus's murder when we arrive. If he asks me to be an elder, I plan to tell him no."

"You've never been able to tell Velius no, G," Jax scoffed, rocking back in his chair.

"More importantly, you've never been able to deny the Crown," Alton stated. "He's leading you to a different path. He's leading all of us to different paths."

Leaning heavily on the chair before him, Gaultier blew out a heavy breath. "How is it that you're able to see that and I'm not?"

"Like I said, your priorities have changed," Jax said, his eyes darting quickly toward Hanileh.

She dropped her gaze to her lap, sinking back in her chair. *Have I become a distraction to Gaultier?* She never wished to come between him and the Crown. Perhaps the Strages had accomplished just what they sought to do through her, regardless of her willingness to participate. Curling in on herself, Hanileh covered her face with her hands.

Gaultier's gentle fingers covered hers and pulled them down as he knelt next to Hanileh. "Don't let Jax rattle you, Hanileh. That's just how he is. Alton is right. The Crown is leading us to different callings. And He brought you into my life with a greater purpose in mind than we might ever know this side of Eternity." He leaned up and pressed a kiss to her forehead. "I wouldn't change a thing."

Rising, Gaultier turned back to Alton and Jax. "So it must be," he said. "I will petition the elders to provide transportation, unless you want me to alter course again."

Jax cracked a grin. "Not necessary. I'm catching up with my new crew in Kapelle."

"And Marita already has plans to meet me at the domicile," Alton murmured.

"I didn't realize when the domicile paired us up that saying goodbye would be quite this hard," Gaultier said softly.

"It's not goodbye, G," Jax said. "Don't get all melodramatic."

"We're still friends. Good friends." Alton smiled. "We'll always be there for you."

"Then I have one request before you go." Gaultier lowered his voice to a whisper. He spoke so quietly Hanileh couldn't make out what he was saying. She frowned, shifting slightly to a more comfortable position.

The three men glanced over at her, smiled all at once, then turned back to their little circle. Whatever they were planning apparently didn't include her. Hanileh crossed her arms over her middle, feeling a serious pout coming on. *Well, that's just fine.* She was the outsider, after all. And she had broken up this little group. *I guess I owe them this moment.*

◆

Gaultier had remained close to Hanileh for the duration of the flight. As they approached Crenet, Jax excused himself to take control of the ship. Alton slipped away to gather his things, leaving the two in awkward silence. Hanileh lowered the blanket to her lap, sneaking a glance toward Gaultier.

His eyes met hers.

"You have something to say?" he asked gently.

Hanileh nodded. It was almost funny how in tune he was with her. She'd tried to mask her concern, but evidently, she hadn't.

"I don't want to interfere in your life, Gaultier." She bowed her head. "I don't want to come between you and your friends. I've already taken so much from you."

Reaching across, Gaultier eased his hand against her cheek, pulling her attention back to him. He stared into her eyes for a long moment before he spoke. "You've taken nothing I haven't freely given. I believe the Crown has orchestrated everything we've experienced, Hanileh. And that includes you."

His fingers slid down her arm to take her hand in his. He focused on their hands, then looked back up at her. "He brought you to me. To teach me..." He squeezed her hand as he once again dropped his eyes. "To teach me how to love and trust again."

"How can I—"

Gaultier shook his head. "You don't have to do a thing. That's the amazing part," he said, smiling up at her. "And I'd like to hope the Crown brought me to you for similar reasons."

Hanileh stared at him. Again, it was as if he had sensed what was in her heart. With Gaultier, she felt safe, confident, and peaceful. Things her recently-recovered memories didn't seem to contain. He had become her shelter, and in that, she had fallen in love with him.

ASHLEY HODGES BAZER

"When we arrive at the domicile, I have some business to attend with my brother. After that, one of the Logia elders will marry us. I've asked Alton and Jax to stay long enough to participate." He frowned the length of a heartbeat before an expression of anticipation transformed his face into that of a hopeful little boy.

"Will you have me, Hanileh?"

He was serious? He wanted to forever be bound to the monster she was? The murderous, vile creature that wreaked evil as if it were child's play? The deluge of memories overwhelmed her, reminding her of the terrible marks that had once stained her body.

"No more," Gaultier whispered, looking into her eyes. "You are not that person any longer. Hanileh, Nyssa told me we were intended for each other. Trust in what the Crown is doing here."

Could she? Could she let go of her past and embrace a future with Gaultier?

Hanileh pressed her lips together, choosing to believe his words. Choosing to trust, just as he implored her to do. She had found comfort and security in Gaultier, as well as companionship and what she believed was love. They could have a fresh start. Together. One in the Crown.

"Yes, Gaultier. I will have you, if you will have me."

Gaultier chuckled, pulling her close. "That's the reason I asked, Hanileh. Of course."

◆

"Gaultier is coming home," Velius said in the stillness of his chambers. Raum was there, waiting. Listening.

"Thaed wants the girl." Raum's usual graveled tone grated in Velius's ears. "He said it didn't matter if she was dead or alive, but I think part of him wants her alive so that he can toy with her a little longer."

Velius moved into the room, slipping the heavy athaer robes from his shoulders. He didn't know how to respond to Raum. There was something about Hanileh. Something Velius found attractive. The linked message he'd received from Gaultier indicated she was now able to speak. Velius had hoped upon their return, he'd be able to spend some time with Hanileh. To learn more about her, and to show his interest. Hearing Thaed wanted her dead shook him to his core.

"They have a past, you know," Raum said, stepping from the shadows into view.

"I know." Velius caught Raum's gaze in the mirror of his wardrobe as he hung the robes.

"You like her." A sneer accompanied the taunt.

"I've entertained the notion," Velius said, hoping to dismiss the comment.

"Thaed won't let you have her." Raum leaned against the wall next to Velius. "She was supposed to be his."

Velius shook his head, crossing the room to fetch a drink. He poured himself a tall glass of a golden brown liqueur, then downed it. He slammed the glass on the table and looked at Raum.

"I don't want her."

The sneer returned. "Then you are lying to yourself."

"Did you come here for something?"

"You're in Thaed's service now, remember? The athaer thing is a nice ploy, but you have his work to do."

Velius's fingers danced over the glass canister. "What does he bid?"

"We all will get what we want," Raum replied, a teasing lilt in his words. "Well, maybe not entirely what we—"

"What does he bid?" Velius asked again, raising his voice.

"Word had it Gaultier is taken with Thaed's toy. That your brother now feels something akin to your own desires. If that's the case, he'll want to protect her from thugs like me."

"And Thaed." Velius eyed the canister.

Raum cleared his throat. "I'd watch what you say, Vel. He hears more than you think."

"Go on."

"Convince Gaultier to attempt a permanent fusion with her."

Velius gasped, staring at Raum. "You speak the impossible."

"The Divinum Bellator is rumored to be able to do it. A few slick words here and there, paired with his overgrown ego, and you could easily convince him."

Dropping his gaze to the floor, Velius lost himself in thought. *The Divinum Bellator?* Had Gaultier such importance he was now believed to be the Divine Warrior of the Crown? Velius tried to imagine what he'd say to his brother to persuade him to do something so against the Crown. Permanent fusion had been banned by the Logia after several couples died in their attempts to create an enduring bond between them. Gaultier would no doubt balk at the idea. What Raum considered ego, Gaultier considered humility.

Raum stepped close to Velius, lowering his voice to a tone of conspiracy. "Play on his mistrust, Vel. Make him feel guilty. He'll buy into it. All you have to do is get both Gaultier and the girl into a trance-like state. Then I'll come to help you. We'll kill Gaultier, and take the girl to Thaed."

Velius's jaw fell open.

"Don't deny you want him dead. He'd be out of the way. No more competition. No more being bested by him. It would be over, and you'd have the relief you seek."

"I don't want to be the one to take his life," Velius whispered.

"You're such a coward, Velius," Raum muttered. "Of course, I'll do it."

"And Hanileh..."

"If you follow through with this, perhaps Thaed will show you a little favor before he kills her...if you catch my drift." Raum nudged Velius with his elbow.

Velius shrugged off Raum and walked a few steps to gain a little distance. "I want more than just a fleeting physical connection with her."

"Thaed has unfinished business with her, Vel. You're in love with a dead woman."

"I'm not in love," Velius snapped.

Raum stepped to him, gripping his tunic to pull him close. "Then make it happen. Bring her to Thaed and give him reason to reward you."

Velius closed his eyes, sinking into Raum's grip. "I will consider it."

Raum shoved him away, and Velius fell to the floor. "Make. It. Happen," Raum said again as he shimmered into non-existence.

Velius flopped back onto the cold tile and stared at the ceiling. "Did You intend for my life to be nothing but conflict?" he asked of the Crown. Or of Carnifex. He was no longer certain of his standing with either deity. "I've done all You have asked, yet both sides torment me. And what would happen if I renounce both? If I were to shun You, as You have done to me?"

His thoughts turned to the Crown. He chuckled mockingly. "Yet Your darling Gaultier has it all. He walks in the Light. He is upheld in the eyes of all Logia. And he has encountered the most beautiful, engaging woman. Help me save her. Help me find a way to keep her from Thaed."

He tucked his legs under him, kneeling in reverence to lift his earnest petition to the King. "And help her to open her heart to me. I don't claim to know what love is, but I know I feel something special for her. Help me to show it, and make her receptive. *Soli*—"

A coughing spell overwhelmed Velius before he could speak the final words of his prayer. Odd. He rose, moving once again to fill his glass. The liquid burned going down his throat, but eased the sudden tickle that tormented him. He shook his head and cleared his throat. He then lifted the glass and threw it against the wall.

CHAPTER NINETEEN

Crenet: 3 days later

Gaultier barged into the sanctuary, scanning the darkened room for his brother. He probably should have been more reverent, but anger tainted his judgment. The sanctuary was the most sacred place in the domicile. Before the domicile was built, the Logia had blessed the grounds. He prayed for forgiveness and understanding from the Crown.

Velius knelt at the altar. With clenched fists, Gaultier stalked toward him, interrupting his murmured prayers. "Tell me you had nothing to do with it."

"Welcome home, Gaultier," Velius said in an even tone. He didn't bother to look at Gaultier. He remained in his prayerful stance. "You must be exhausted after such a harrowing journey."

Gaultier drew his sword, the tip aimed at Velius's neck. "Tell me, here before the Crown, you had nothing to do with Castus's murder."

Cocking his head slightly, Velius stared at the blade as his hands raised in surrender. "Violence is not permitted in the domicile, Gaultier. Particularly in the sanctuary."

"With every evasion of my accusation, you admit your guilt," Gaultier stated, his brows furrowing in frustration.

"There is no blood on my hands, brother." Velius met Gaultier's glare.

"Did you arrange it?" he pushed, jabbing the sword closer to Velius.

"Why would I do such a thing?"

"You were named athaer, Velius. With others in line before you."

Velius chuckled, rolling back on his heels. "What, did you want the job?"

Gaultier dropped his hand to his side, allowing his sword to rest against his leg. His shoulders slumped as his chin fell against his chest. "Quit playing with me, Vel. Give me an honest answer."

He heard the satin swish of Velius's robes as his brother stood and moved to his side. Velius took the sword from Gaultier's hand and replaced it in the sheath. "You've been through much in the past few weeks, Gaultier. The loss of your friend, especially upon returning to his former home, weighs heavily upon you."

"It goes beyond that, Velius," Gaultier admitted, closing his eyes.

"The Queen?"

"...is at rest," he answered quietly, "until she is released by the Divine Warrior."

"And Hanileh?"

Gaultier lifted his chin, looking at Velius. "We are to be married."

An expression of shock followed by a wide, insincere smile spread across Velius's mouth. "Congratulations, my brother."

"You're not truly pleased," Gaultier said, narrowing his eyes.

Velius shook his head. "On the contrary, I am very happy for you."

"Then what was that look about?"

Velius blinked, shrugging his shoulders. "I, uh...well, it's a little sudden, don't you think?"

"She's been a constant in my life for many weeks now, Velius."

"You've only known her as Hanileh, but she has this other facet to her neither of you knew anything about."

"Her past matters not," Gaultier answered. "She has chosen a life in the Crown."

Velius pointed at him. "Then I ask you remember that when thinking of me."

Gaultier dropped his gaze to the floor, took a deep breath, and released it. "You're right. I am sorry."

Velius waved off his apology. "Think nothing of it."

"No. I was wrong," Gaultier continued, making eye contact with Velius. "You've made a commitment to a different life, and I should have recognized that. My distrust was ill-founded. Please forgive me, Velius."

"Already forgotten, my brother."

"I hate to ask you a favor after I insulted you so deeply," Gaultier said, "but I had hoped you would officiate our wedding."

"It would be my honor." Velius extended his hand to shake Gaultier's.

Gaultier gripped the offered hand, stepping into his embrace. Something felt unsettled between them, but Gaultier chided himself for again having a lack of trust in his brother. How long would he harbor old feelings against Velius? If Gaultier truly believed as he said he did, he knew the Crown had forgiven Velius long ago. He could not elevate himself to a loftier position of judgment than that of his King. He would have to let it go.

As Velius pulled away, he eyed Gaultier. "I know you are concerned for Hanileh's well-being."

"In light of those who hurt her as they did for no apparent reason, yes, I am," Gaultier answered.

"Her enemies are...how shall I put this?" Velius's gaze flickered to his open palms. He clasped them together once more as he looked at Gaultier. "The Strages are everywhere, my brother. If they have named her a target, then she is in trouble, no matter where she may be."

"I intend to protect her, Vel. I won't allow them near her again."

"There may be more you could do than just a physical protection, Gaultier. Thaed and his band know how to infiltrate minds. They could attack her mentally as well."

Gaultier bowed his head. He'd thought about that, but the only way he could protect Hanileh from a mental attack would be to fuse with her.

"I've done some research, Gaultier. The Council of Elders has debated on several occasions whether or not you are the Divinum Bellator. Or if you have some sort of connection to him. Think about it. You've befriended the Queen. You've encountered the Continuum. It's everything the prophecies say."

"I'm not the Divine Warrior," Gaultier denied. "I couldn't even cut it as a Protector or an athaer."

"It's in our lineage, Gaultier. Father's journals—"

"No." Gaultier lifted a pointed finger to Velius's face. "Don't bring him into this. I don't want to hear about him from you."

Velius bowed his head. "And the distrust continues..."

"What does any of this have to do with Hanileh?" Gaultier said, ignoring Velius's comment.

"I believe you could permanently fuse with her."

Gaultier stared at Velius for a breathless moment. "That's...that's crazy."

"Think about it, Gaultier. Intimacy beyond what any of us could conceive. You would truly be one with her in the name of the Crown. It wouldn't just be a ritual acknowledged on paper, but an actual binding, a fusing, of two souls."

Gaultier again dropped his gaze to the floor. "It took me years of working with Castus to master my control over fusion, Vel. And it's hard enough to endure just a few moments."

"I've found a way, Gaultier. I can help you. Let this be my wedding gift to you both."

With wary eyes, Gaultier glanced at his brother. "Your words sound dangerously close to Strages doctrine."

"And yours sound full of suspicion," Velius countered. He opened his hands, gesturing to the room around them. "May I remind you I stand in the presence of the Creator King?"

ASHLEY HODGES BAZER

Torn in internal debate, Gaultier's eyes drifted beyond Velius to look at the small altar. The symbol of the Crown crested proudly from the wall. He murmured a silent prayer. *Guide me, my King. I don't know what to do.*

"If it doesn't work, Gaultier, then it's not meant to be. But what harm could come from attempting such a thing?" Velius said gently.

"Your persistence won't lead me into temptation, Velius," Gaultier whispered.

"And what if it's the will of the Crown?" Velius whispered back. "What if He's offering you a precious gift, and you are turning it down?"

"My gift is Hanileh."

"And mine is to offer you a way to protect her," Velius said. "Surely you don't wish to see her in the hands of the Continuum, drained of life like the Queen, or mutilated beyond recognition by Thaed...do you?"

With a heavy sigh, Gaultier nodded slowly. "All right. I'll agree to try."

Velius smiled, gripping Gaultier's shoulder. "Then fetch your bride. I'll call together the present Council members for the ceremony and meet you in the chapel at the top of the hour. We will attempt the fusion in a private ceremony following the wedding."

Gaultier stared at the altar as Velius made a hasty exit. "Tell me I made the right decision," he whispered to the Crown. "And if I haven't, have mercy on us all."

———————◆———————

Gaultier led Hanileh down the long aisle of the chapel. Gentle candlelight swathed the altar in a warm radiance. Near the altar, Velius awaited, the Creed in his hand, with Jax and Alton standing on either side of him. Gathered in the first two rows were Almus and three elders, as well as several Logia and Lumen. Gaultier's friends were well represented.

As they walked, Hanileh thought about whom she might ask to attend such a precious moment. She never wished to encounter any one of the Strages again, particularly Lucian. Her final moments with him spun nightmares, even during the waking hours. As the memories slipped into her mind, she stumbled a bit.

Gripping her arm, Gaultier glanced at her, a worried look on his face. His eyes asked silently if she was okay. She gave a little nod and turned her focus back toward their destination. Once the marriage was pronounced, she could forget her past—forget Lucian—and look forward to a new beginning with Gaultier. A new life. He would save her from her own dark self.

Gaultier paused, gently pulling her to a halt. "Talk to me, Hanileh," he whispered softly.

She looked at him, blinking quickly. Everyone was watching. Waiting. Apparently, Gaultier didn't care. He took both her hands in his and studied her eyes.

"You're thinking of Lucian," Gaultier whispered.

Hanileh took a breath. She hated to admit it, but she also wanted to be completely honest with her husband-to-be. Besides, he'd fused with her last night to help eliminate some of the frightening dreams. His close presence had been a comfort, and they both had clung to each other as the connection dissipated. He had later said he could sense some of her thoughts—a residual effect from the mental union.

"I just want to marry you, Gaultier. I want to..." She paused, finding her own words ironic. "I want to forget."

A regretful smile touched his lips as he lifted a hand to stroke her hair. "I cannot take away those memories, Hanileh. We paid dearly for them. And I cannot take away the pain and fear that accompany them. The only One who can is the Crown."

"I know that." Hanileh bowed her head.

"I can only promise I will love you each and every day. I will protect you, defend you, care for you, and lift you before the Crown, trusting in Him to make me fit for doing all those things." Gaultier's smile eased into a serious, pleading look. "But only one of us—him or me—can stand at that altar."

"I don't want him, Gaultier," Hanileh said, meeting his gaze.

"Then let him go. He can no longer touch you. And I will make blasted sure he can no longer hurt you." He leaned in to whisper in her ear. "You don't have to be afraid anymore."

She smiled at him as he pulled away. "You said you cannot take away my fear."

Gaultier nodded, lifting an eyebrow. "And I cannot. I can give you a life in which you won't have to live in fear." He gestured toward the end of the aisle. "Now, would you like to continue?"

Her smile beamed brighter. Gaultier's reassurance filled her heart, confirming she was indeed making the right choice. She would move forward, leaving behind Marcella and all the Strages life encompassed, dedicating herself, heart and soul, to serving the Crown with the man now at her side. And by his word, Lucian would never again hurt her.

Velius received the couple with a warm smile and gestured for them to stand on the step below him. He looked over them to address the small crowd. "My friends, we come together today to celebrate the union of two lives. Two children of the King who wish to join in sacred matrimony. Does anyone object?"

Hanileh bowed her head as the chapel grew silent. From deep within,

ASHLEY HODGES BAZER

she could hear Marcella screaming, terrified of what Lucian might think. *He will punish you! Do you want to be recrafted?* she shouted at Hanileh.

Gritting her teeth, Hanileh looked up at Gaultier's questioning face. She forced a smile to her lips. He squeezed her hand.

"With no objections, let us continue on to the marriage pledge. Jax, Alton, do you have the wedding bands?"

Both Jax and Alton moved to hand off the golden rings. Alton offered the thick, wide one to Hanileh. "Place the ring on Gaultier's finger, and recite the pledge," Velius instructed.

As she held the ring between her fingers, she felt herself begin to tremble. Fighting back the nerves, Hanileh took Gaultier's hand in her own and slid the ring onto the appropriate finger. He lifted his other hand to hers, holding them steady for her as she spoke.

"Gaultier Lassiter," she started, gripping his hands tightly, "in the name of the Crown, I, Hanileh, pledge myself to you, mind, body, and soul."

She had learned the recitation quickly, and had had no trouble with it, but for some reason, her mind decided to go blank. She could see Lucian's taunting face lurking over her. Every cell in her body burned with a fierce tingling.

"Hanileh," Gaultier whispered. "It's not real. This," he shook her hands, "this is real. Hold onto the Crown. Hold onto me."

She took a steadying breath and continued, ignoring the tortured cries from her past self. "For the King created me for you. The Prince rules my heart and my judgment. And the Companion has brought us together."

"That's it, my love," Gaultier murmured in encouragement. She could sense him enveloping her, closing out the frightening influences.

"Of my own will, may it align with that of the Crown, I promise to care for you, walk with you, stand with you, and love you for the rest of my days. I am yours, Gaultier," she finished, looking him full in the face.

Gaultier smiled proudly, taking the second, smaller ring from Jax. "Hanileh, in the name of the Crown, I, Gaultier Lassiter, pledge myself to you, mind, body, and soul. For the King created me for you. The Prince rules my heart and my judgment. And the Companion has brought us together."

He stepped closer to her, his hand trailing along her neck. He lowered his voice, reciting the pledge at a level only she and Velius might hear. "Of my own will, may it align with that of the Crown, I promise to care for you, walk with you, stand with you, and love you for the rest of my days. I am yours, Hanileh."

Velius opened his arms, gesturing to the Logia in the pews. "By the sign of *assentior,* let us show our blessing upon this couple."

Hanileh leaned into Gaultier as the crowd all spoke, "*Assentior,*" in unison. Gaultier wrapped his arms around her, murmuring quiet comfort in her ear.

Velius announced, "In the Logia tradition, this man has taken this woman into not only his life, but into his heart as well. It is my honor to present Gaultier and Hanileh Lassiter, now one in the eyes of the Crown. Many blessings, my children."

The audience stood, offering applause and proud smiles. Gaultier kept his arm around Hanileh, shaking first Velius's hand, then those of his friends. As everyone started to go about their way, Gaultier shared a glance with Velius.

Velius nodded, jerking his head toward the sanctuary.

Hanileh watched, her eyes darting between the two brothers. "What's going on?" she whispered to Gaultier.

"Velius has a theory," Gaultier whispered back. "He believes I can fuse permanently to you."

Hanileh blinked in confusion. "So you'd..."

"...be able to know what you're feeling, thinking, experiencing. All the time."

Dropping her eyes to the floor, Hanileh frowned. It was hard enough inviting Gaultier in the first time. Revealing her darkest secrets. The evil she harbored within her. And again when he attempted to soothe her nightmares. Having him as a constant...

"Hanileh, it's a protective measure," Gaultier said. "It's not for me to judge you. And I'm nervous about the idea myself."

"You are?" she asked.

"I've never tested the limits of my gift, but it certainly doesn't sound like something the Crown would grant. We are each His own separate creation, even those bound in marriage." Gaultier kissed her hand. "My ability to fuse, in itself, is an invasion."

"No, Gaultier," Hanileh said, happy to be able to offer some reassurance herself. "It's an amazing gift that allows you to help others."

"I don't know that I will be able to handle a permanent connection," he confessed. "I've read of others who have attempted such a thing, and it either drove them mad or killed them."

Hanileh stared at him. He wasn't going to risk his life in order to permanently fuse with her. She wouldn't allow it.

"According to the Creed, only one being will successfully carry out such a thing. The Divinum Bellator."

"The Divine Warrior," Hanileh breathed, proud she retained some of the information she'd read over the last few months.

"Yes. Velius believes..." Gaultier shook his head, scoffing at the idea. "Velius believes I might be him. Or at least have some connection to him."

ASHLEY HODGES BAZER

"Are you?" she asked, her eyes focused intently on him now.

Gaultier furrowed his brow. "I don't think so, Hanileh. Nyssa told me my son would be... But no one really knows. Not until after the Gathering has come and issued the Challenge."

Hanileh closed her eyes. She didn't want to face any of this. It was too much to handle. She just wanted a quiet life with her husband, and someday, children.

"Come. Velius wishes to attempt this in his quarters. He doesn't want the elders to know."

"Doesn't that tell you something, Gaultier?"

"He's my brother, Hanileh. And the athaer of Kapelle. He won't steer us wrong. I've struggled with my trust in him, but I'm choosing to believe the Crown has led him to this. If not, what's the worst that could happen?"

Hanileh followed her groom with reluctance. The worst that could happen? *You could either go mad or be killed...*

CHAPTER TWENTY

Gaultier led Hanileh into Velius's quarters, just across from the sanctuary. The rooms were modest compared to the other residences of the domicile. Still, from what Hanileh could see, the area was tastefully decorated and rather peaceful with its candlelit aura.

Velius swept in from his sleeping room. He'd removed his official athaer robes, donning instead a casual dark tunic and matching pants. "Where would you be most comfortable, Gaultier?"

Gaultier glanced over his shoulder toward the sofa. "I will need to maintain physical contact with Hanileh."

"And I will need both of you to enter a state of slumber."

Panic lit a fire under Hanileh. If they were both unconscious, anything could happen without their knowledge.

"Gaultier," she said, grabbing his arm.

"It's all right, my love," Gaultier whispered before looking back at his brother. "May we use your bed?"

"Gaultier," Hanileh repeated, this time with urgency. *Something here isn't right. How can you be so blind to it?* "Have you at least told Jax or Alton?"

Gaultier gripped her hand, pulling her into him. "They didn't need to know. Trust me." He kissed her forehead. "I am choosing to have faith in Velius. And the Crown."

Velius gestured for them to follow. Gaultier positioned his arm at the small of Hanileh's back and eased her into the sleeping room. She disagreed with this entire venture, but she didn't wish to interfere in his bond with Velius. The strain between them remained constant, and Gaultier was doing all he could to hold onto the frayed strands of their brotherhood.

At the edge of the bed, Gaultier kissed both of Hanileh's hands before looking into her eyes. "I love you. And I am doing this because I love you. I cannot risk losing you." He leaned into her, pressing his forehead to hers. "The Crown is with us, Hanileh."

ASHLEY HODGES BAZER

Guiding her way, Gaultier seated her on the bed and instructed her to lie back. With her eyes on Velius, Hanileh did as her new husband told her. Velius offered her a reassuring smile, and took a knee next to her while Gaultier stepped around the bed to the other side.

"You have undoubtedly seen some dark things in your time, haven't you, Hanileh?"

"I have." She searched Velius's eyes for a sense of honor and worth.

"And those things are all coming into play right in this moment. The Strages. The Queen. The Continuum."

She nodded, unable to speak.

The bed under her rocked slightly. Gaultier's hand grasped hers as he settled next to her. Velius continued to hold her attention, though.

"Let me assure you," Velius started, touching her arm. He paused, dropping his eyes to where his hand rested upon her skin. He seemed lost for a moment before he snapped back into focus. "This is a gift," he breathed.

"Position her, Gaultier," Velius ordered with a complete about-face, pushing away from the bed to rise to his full height. "I will put her under when you are ready."

"Put me under?" Hanileh asked, her eyes darting between the brothers.

Gaultier's hand slid across her cheek, holding her gaze to his. "Velius is going to help you go to sleep. Then I will fuse with you and he will do the rest."

"But I—"

"Close your eyes, Hanileh," Gaultier whispered, his forehead once again resting against hers.

She swallowed hard, allowing her eyes to fall shut. The frightening feelings crept along her body in the form of nervous tremors. Gaultier kept his hand on her cheek, and she could feel his breath upon her lips.

"I am ready," Gaultier murmured.

Slight pressure touched the base of her skull, and before long, Hanileh escaped reality and landed in a quiet dream. She walked through the halls of the domicile, feeling as though she was searching for something very important. Looking down at her arms, she knew she should have been carrying something. *Someone, perhaps?*

In the distance, a baby cried.

Urgency propelled Hanileh to the sanctuary. But when she entered, the sanctuary was no more. It was, instead, a private residence. She spun around. The baby's cry, while getting further and further away, grew louder along with the pounding of her heart.

Dashing across the hall, she threw wide the door and ran in to the room. She immediately recognized it as Velius's quarters. Carefully, she crept along, no longer hearing the baby. Peering around the corner, she saw herself and Gaultier, stretched out on Velius's bed. Velius paced the length of the room, while a man dressed in black leaned against the wall near Gaultier.

"Let me do it, Vel," the man said. "Let me slit his throat."

Velius's expression revealed great pain. He paused, looking at the bed, then at the man. He shook his head. "I can't. I already went too far when I put him under. I just pray he'll survive that mental attack."

"Survive? Our purpose in this is his death."

"I can't do it." Closing his eyes, Velius dropped his chin to his chest. "I hope he won't know it was me."

"He doesn't trust you, anyway." The man pushed off the wall to circle around Velius. "You had to fight him to get them here."

"But he's here now." Velius stared at his brother.

"You think one measly display of trust is a life changing event?"

Velius's eyes flitted toward Hanileh. He crossed to her side of the bed, lifting a strand of her hair into his fingers. "And I can't let her go," he murmured.

"She is married to your enemy."

"Gaultier is not my enemy," Velius argued, looking to the other man, still holding Hanileh's hair.

"And she belongs to your master."

"Thaed is not my master," Velius whispered. His words sounded like he was trying to convince himself of that.

The man slammed against Velius, kicking the bed as he did so. In a heartbeat, Hanileh's awareness snapped from her position in the doorframe into an abrupt freefall. She screamed just before she hit the ground, opening her eyes to the mottled ceiling above her.

Velius sat next to her, brushing her hair back from her face. "It's all right," he murmured in a lulling tone. "Calm down."

"The man..." Hanileh blurted as she tried to sit up. She looked about the room, her eyes frantically searching the shadows.

"What man?" he asked, pressing back on her shoulder.

"He wanted to kill Gaultier."

Velius smiled, stroking her hair. "You're suffering an ill-effect of the unsuccessful fusing, my dear. You just had a nightmare."

"No," Hanileh said, again looking around. "No, it was real."

"Hanileh, I've been watching over you the entire time. You've been asleep for close to an hour. I attempted to make Gaultier's fusing a permanent bond," Velius dropped his gaze to the bed, "but I couldn't do it."

"I never had any sense of Gaultier."

Taking Hanileh's hand, Velius squeezed it gently. "He tried," he said softly, "but something kept him from fusing."

Hanileh glanced down at her hand as Velius began to caress her arm.

"Did you fight him, Hanileh?" Velius asked with underlying accusation in his tone.

"No, I—"

"Because I fear now he's injured. He hasn't woken up."

Hanileh pulled her hand from Velius and rolled over to shake her husband awake. "Gaultier? Gaultier, can you hear me?"

Velius's arms collapsed around her, pulling her off Gaultier and the bed. He held her, whispering into her ear. "It's all right, Hanileh. He just needs time. Give him time."

She struggled against Velius, crying as she fought to get back to Gaultier. As Velius's words sunk in, she fell back against him, using him as her strength. Time. Time had claimed Nyssa. Had the Continuum finally caught up with them? No. No...she did this. Marcella.

Velius's fingers brushed through Hanileh's hair as he enveloped her. "It's okay," he murmured again.

"Did I really do that to him?" she whimpered.

"Yes." Velius avoided her eyes. "But he knew the potential consequences of trying such a thing, Hanileh."

An anguished wail tore from deep within her, driving her to her knees. She never wished to hurt Gaultier. This whole thing was a mistake.

Velius sat with her on the floor, shushing her and cooing calming words. His fingers settled along her jaw, and he angled her face toward his. For the first time, she noticed a long scar trailing over his left eye. He drew her toward him, his lips brushing first along her cheek, then aiming toward her mouth.

Horrified, Hanileh pushed him away, scrambling back along the floor. She shook her head, trying to find her breath. "Wh-what—"

His eyes dead on her, Velius's comforting expression darkened with rejection and anger. Before she could move from the floor, Velius's hands were at her throat, pinning her against the bed. The same familiar pressure pressed into her mind, clouding her thought and reason. Silence boomed in her ears as the world around her fell to blackness.

"Hanileh?"

She awakened with a start to Gaultier's concerned, but relieved smile. He bent down to kiss her forehead, then looked back at someone across the room.

"She's all right," he said. "She's awake."

He lodged an arm under her, helping her to sit up. Her head felt heavy and groggy, like she'd been asleep for days. Gripping onto him, she asked, "Where are we?" Her voice was unexpectedly hoarse.

"In Velius's room. The fusion didn't work," Gaultier murmured with a hint of sorrow.

Velius stepped close with a glass full of water. "You must have suffered some pretty severe nightmares, Hanileh."

Gaultier took the glass and offered it to Hanileh. She stared up at Velius, trying to discern reality from dream. He smiled at her, his eyes full of warmth and invitation. No scar. He wasn't the same man who moments ago—or at least what felt like moments ago—attacked her.

She rested her head on Gaultier's shoulder, ignoring the water. "I want to leave here, Gaultier."

"Velius has arranged for us to stay here at Kapelle for a few days while we decide where we would like to go," Gaultier said, stroking her hair. "Take a drink, Hanileh. You'll feel better."

She took the glass, surprised by how shaky she was. The water sloshed out onto her chest before she landed the edge of the glass in her mouth. Gaultier gripped the glass to steady it for her as she took a long sip. He pulled it away and handed it to Velius, allowing Hanileh to once again rest her head upon his shoulder.

"I think it will just take some rest, Gaultier," Velius said, standing at her side, holding the glass between his hands.

"Yes," Gaultier answered. "Thank you for what you did, Vel."

"What he did?" Hanileh asked. She couldn't shake the sense of horror that had accompanied the events of the last hour. The strange man in black who had wanted to kill Gaultier. Velius making an advance toward her, then attacking her. And the confusion that blurred all of it.

"We nearly lost you, Hanileh," Gaultier explained, craning his neck to look into her eyes. "When I woke up, you were seizing something fierce."

Velius knelt at the bedside. "After Gaultier attempted to fuse, I put him under to make an effort at the permanent bond. I failed—"

"You didn't fail, Vel. It wasn't meant to be," Gaultier murmured.

"—and you suffered for it. Gaultier woke up with no problem—"

"You told the man you had attacked him mentally. And you told me Gaultier was hurt because I had resisted him." Hanileh pulled herself closer to Gaultier.

Velius shared a look of concern with Gaultier. "No, my dear. I never would do something like that. You must have been dreaming."

"You tried to...to kiss..." Hanileh trailed off, too upset by the memory of him coming onto her.

"Hanileh, I just performed your wedding ceremony to my brother," Velius stated, obviously taken aback by what she was saying.

Gaultier's hand trailed down her hair. "Those effects can mess with your mind, Hanileh. When I woke up, I felt strange, too. But it was just in my head. You'll understand when your head clears a bit."

Hanileh closed her eyes, leaning against Gaultier. She prayed the memories of the last little while were just imagined. They carried the same undertones of fright and pain as her memories of Marcella, and those most certainly were real.

"Take her to your quarters, Gaultier. Let her rest," Velius instructed. "Tomorrow, I will check her out. Make sure she can separate the nightmare from the truth."

"Thank you, Velius," Gaultier said. "We owe you a great deal."

Hanileh couldn't stop the whimper of doubt and grief that slipped from her lips. Gaultier pulled her closer, shushing her again. He shifted a bit, then rose, lifting her along with him. She crumpled into him, surrendering to the hope he would once again save her from the darkness within.

CHAPTER TWENTY ONE

Gaultier delivered a steamy mug of tea to Hanileh's awaiting hands as he joined her in the courtyard. He smiled down at her and touched her cheek with a single finger. "Feeling better, my love?"

"Confused, still," Hanileh admitted, taking a much-needed sip of the tea. It warmed her inside and out. "I want to contact Jett and Delia."

"We cannot. I tried when we returned from Sagesse. As Protectors, they are engaged in a period of seclusion that lasts for years. It's a time for them to learn discipline and focus on what is ahead. Besides, Velius has nothing but the best intentions for us, Hanileh."

She held the mug between her hands, resting it against her chin. "Tell me more about your relationship with him, Gaultier."

Caught mid-sip, Gaultier shrugged before he placed his mug on the table next to him. "There's not much to tell, really."

"Because the last time you talked about him with me, you were dead certain he had killed Castus."

Gaultier leaned back in his chair, blowing out a breath. "People change," he whispered.

"What happened between you?"

Bowing his head, Gaultier leaned forward on his knees. He clasped his hands together and stared at the floor. "I wish I could say we were close, but Velius always kept a careful distance between us. When my father started focusing attention on my Logia training, Velius became bitterly jealous. Instead of telling my father, he turned away. He began to run with a different crowd. And one night..."

Hanileh held her breath as she watched Gaultier close his eyes, slipping into the sea of memories.

"One night, he welcomed evil into our lives. We had returned home to Pavana from a lengthy time here on Kapelle. I was in my room on the upper level, and I heard my mother's screams. My father shouting. And then, everything fell silent. I don't even know how long I stood there, staring at

135

my door. I knew what awaited me on the other side.

"Castus came for me. He said he had had a vision, but he couldn't get there to keep the event from happening. He came to take me back to the Kapelle domicile, but I wasn't allowed to go down through the kitchen.

"I always wondered how they were killed. Did they suffer?" Gaultier looked up at Hanileh. "And even though Velius denied it, did he have a hand in it? Did hatred drive him that crazy?"

Hanileh lowered her mug to her lap and wrapped one arm about herself to ward off the sudden chill. She knew Velius was dangerous, but she didn't realize how much so.

"How old were you?" she whispered.

"Fifteen. Velius is five years older than me. Not long after that, Velius came to Castus, begging forgiveness and mercy. Castus gave him a place here. I avoided him for nearly two years until I left for crusading.

"Castus was the one who tried to settle things between us. He told me Velius had changed. Part of me wanted to hold onto that hurt and anger, but as a Logia, I knew I shouldn't. So I chose to embrace my brother. He was all I had left."

"Do you think he killed Castus?" Hanileh asked.

"No," Gaultier said, looking at his hands. "No, the Council would have discovered that by now. Any athaer candidate must go through a rigorous series of questioning. They are examined thoroughly. Almus showed me the results, and Velius passed."

"This fusing—" Hanileh started.

"I shouldn't have allowed it, Hanileh. I made a mistake, and I am sorry."

"I think it revealed a complexity about Velius that perhaps we don't even know the extent of, Gaultier."

"You believe the Logia Council of Elders of the Kapelle domicile to be wrong?"

Hanileh sank back in her chair, stung by Gaultier's disbelief in her. Gaultier sighed again, took her hand, and kissed her fingertips. "I'm sorry, my love. I am conflicted. Share with me your thoughts."

"I think Velius might prove stronger than he appears. I think he's adept at deception and manipulation. And I think he's got you exactly where he wants you."

"Forgive me, Hanileh, but I've known him a whole lot longer than you have."

"While that is true, I have seen facets of him he hides from you. I was in his hands when he performed the Strages mending. And while it's all still a little blurry, I am most certain he plotted with someone during the attempted fusion. He nearly allowed that stranger to take your life. And then, while you were still unconscious, he tried to take advantage of me."

"He would never go that far, Hanileh," Gaultier whispered.

Hanileh shook off Gaultier's grip, rising. Her tea mug clattered on the flagstones of the courtyard. "Why won't you believe me?"

Gaultier joined her in standing. "Because I don't want to think my brother is capable of such foul deeds."

"He had a hand in your parents' murders, Gaultier!"

"He's all I have left!"

Hanileh stared at him, falling back a few steps. "Is he?"

"I didn't mean that, Hanileh..." Gaultier said, reaching for her hand.

She pulled her arms into her, turning away. Gaultier's hesitant touch trailed along her shoulders. She closed her eyes as he pulled her into him.

"If Velius is capable of such things," Gaultier whispered in her ear, "then that means I am as well. And I cannot bear that."

Hanileh rested her head to his. "We are all capable of such things, Gaultier. It is the path we choose to follow that matters."

Gaultier met her with a long moment of silence. She turned in his arms, looking up into his eyes. "I am in no position to judge your brother, in light of the terrible things I once did—"

"You didn't know any better. And you've repented—"

"—but I am telling you the truth. Something about this whole thing doesn't feel right to me."

Gaultier pushed her hair back from her face. "I am sorry for not listening to you."

Hanileh pressed against his hand, closing her eyes. "Your path is far different from mine or Velius's. I almost understand his envy."

"Don't say that." Gaultier drew her close again. "I think it best we establish our lives away from the domicile, Hanileh."

"I agree," Hanileh answered, leaning into her husband. "Away from Velius."

◆

"You don't have to go, Gaultier. There is a place here for you," Velius said. "Always."

Gaultier hefted a crate into his arms. "We don't feel like you are making us leave, Vel." He carted the box up the ramp of the *Sun*.

"Then why are you going?" Velius asked, having followed Gautier into the craft.

Leaning on the stack of crates, Gaultier looked at his brother. "Hanileh and I need to find our identities apart from Kapelle. We need to find out who we are as a couple."

ASHLEY HODGES BAZER

"You're forsaking the Logia?" Velius asked.

"Don't be ridiculous," Gaultier said, returning to the task of preparing the ship.

Velius blocked his way to the ramp. "Tell me what this is about then, Gaultier."

"I've told you, Vel. Hanileh and I need some time. Just us."

"There's more to it than that."

Gaultier sighed, stepping back. "She's struggling, Vel. She hasn't told me, but I can tell. She is haunted by her past, and she doesn't trust the future. I want to help her. I want her to know not only my love, but the love of the Crown."

"And by leaving here, a place dedicated to such love, you think you might help her?"

"No," Gaultier answered. "But the Crown will."

"Gaultier..."

"Velius." Gaultier moved the crate on the top to a locker. "Unless you give me an order as the athaer of Kapelle, my wife and I are going."

"I just think it's a mistake," Velius said.

"I will stay in contact with you. And we will visit regularly."

"You're leaving a life of safety and security..."

Gaultier shook his head. "No. I'm finding that safety and security in the Crown instead of the domicile. I'm providing that for my wife, and if the Crown wills it, my children."

"You're shirking your responsibility to the Logia."

"Would you stop throwing that in my face?" Gaultier said, exasperation getting the best of him. "My responsibility to the Logia is undefined."

"Undefined? In line to be Protector? Asked to be an athaer?"

Gaultier blew out a breath, placing his palm flat on the stack of crates. "Hear me now, none of those came to pass because it was not the will of the Creator King."

"Are you certain, Gaultier? Or have you just denied Him?"

"You know what? This is why I'm leaving, Vel." Gaultier grabbed another crate to move it into a locker. "I am tired of having this argument with you."

Velius watched silently for a few moments before he nodded. "All right, Gaultier. Consider it dropped. I wish you the best in your new life."

Gaultier looked up at his older brother. The man seemed sincere in his goodbye. Extending his hand toward Velius, Gaultier gripped the offered fingers.

"Thank you," he murmured.

"Just be sure to stay in touch," Velius said. "I imagine you will soon require guidance and support, and I wish to be there for you."

With a silent nod, Gaultier's eyes followed his brother as he turned and left the ship. Gaultier wasn't sure what Velius meant by that last remark, but he tried not to think too much on it. Besides, there was a lot of work to do before he and Hanileh could lift off. He resumed placing the crates in the storage lockers.

◆

Serenata: 427 CT

The move had been good for them. Hanileh felt closer to Gaultier, and he indicated he felt closer to her as well. Serenata was beautiful. Gaultier had found a lovely home that looked out over a body of water. Beyond the water, tall, purple mountains hemmed them in. Hanileh was safe at last.

She sat on the soft white sofa, gazing out the large picture windows that formed the back wall of their home. Flying creatures spun lazy circles in the air before diving to touch the water. The movements were almost...hypnotizing.

Leaning against the fluffy cushions, Hanileh rested her head along the back of the couch, her eyes still drawn to the birds. Happiness and peace filled her heart. Deep within her, new life stirred. Gaultier's son. It was a secret she had kept from him for far too long, but she had been uncertain of what was to come. Tonight, though, she would tell him.

She smiled to herself as she thought of his reaction. He would be elated.

Won't he?

Doubt crept back into her thoughts. Gaultier had proved his love for her time and time again. Surely he would want a child.

But Lucian never did.

She squeezed her eyes closed, trying to blot that thought from her mind. Why, in the middle of this wonderful moment, would Lucian slip into her mind?

The birds. The birds could provide the distraction she needed.

"'Open your eyes and take delight in the Crown's creation,'" Hanileh murmured to herself.

Blindness met her as she tried to find the birds. Paralysis froze her limbs into place, reeling her backward into an altered state of consciousness. She could sense Thaed's presence, locking her into a prison of memories. She opened her eyes to see the dining hall of Thaed's fortress on Venenum. Where he had first confronted her about forsaking the Strages.

His fingers slithered along her shoulders, causing her to stiffen.

"So you defied me," Thaed said. "Again."

"I didn't defy you."

Thaed's intense stare appeared before her. "You speak. I commanded you not to say another word."

"You robbed me of my voice," Hanileh said. "And my memory."

His caress shifted to her cheek. "I took nothing from you that didn't belong to me."

Hanileh pulled away, then stared at him. "You did not own me."

"Oh, but I did." In a sudden movement, Thaed gripped the arms of her chair, his face close to hers. "And I still do."

He pressed his hand against her chest, just under her shoulder. Pain seared through her, forcing her to fall back in the chair. Thaed yanked her forward, depositing her on the floor at his feet. As she looked down, she saw the symbol he had carved into her, the one that had disappeared at the hands of the Continuum. Her skin and the mark now crackled with throbbing electricity, red and blue at the same time.

Releasing her, Thaed stepped back and started to circle around her. "You thought you were strong. You thought the Logia would save you. But look at you, Marcella. Weak, and on your knees, begging me for mercy."

"I'm not—"

The electricity sizzled from the mark to envelop her body. She cowered as whimpers escaped her lips. If it were only her, she could handle the pain. But she had to think of the baby.

"Please..."

"What was that?" Thaed turned his head and bent his ear forward.

"Please!" Hanileh cried out.

Instantly, the torture stopped. Hanileh slumped down, trying to catch her breath. Thaed's fingers slinked through her hair, sending shivers down her spine. Long ago, that kind of affection from him would have thrilled her. But now, it made her sick.

"Tell me, Marcella, did you leave me because I could not give you a child?" Thaed's fingernails scratched lightly along her neck.

"You would not," she murmured, staring into the past. "But we agreed to that, and I accepted it. No, Lucian, I left because both of us changed."

He gripped her neck and positioned her head to look at him. "You changed."

"What is it you want? Did you bring me here to torture me? To kill me? Then do it. Do it and be done," Hanileh said, her words far braver than she felt.

Thaed smiled, leaving his fingers entangled in her hair as he walked back in front of her. "Oh, no, Marcella. I intend to do far worse to you than kill you."

Her thoughts flickered to the life inside her. He wouldn't...

Thaed's smile widened. He stepped back and stared at her. "You're free to go."

"What are you going to do, Lucian?"

"He will be mine," Thaed started with a chuckle. "Just as your vision during your time with the Continuum suggested."

Hanileh's head swam with confusion. How could he have known about that? She had to get home to Gaultier. To tell him. To—

"Goodbye, Marcella," Thaed whispered as blackness cracked around her.

She blinked her eyes, trying to focus on her surroundings. By the Crown, she was still on the sofa. She lifted her hand to her forehead as she glanced around. Gaultier's high-backed leather chair. The overstuffed loveseat exploding with pillows. The extraordinary view from the window that held miles upon miles of water and lush landscape. The birds had disappeared, though.

"Gaultier?" she called, gripping the cushion below her.

"What is it, Hanileh?" he called back, stepping from the cooking area. He wiped his hands on a small, white towel and tossed it over his shoulder.

Relief washed through her as she looked upon his handsome face. He must have known something was wrong. He darted to her side and took her into his arms.

"You look shaken, love. What is it?"

"Lu-Lucian..." Hanileh cried against his shoulder.

"What about him?" Gaultier paused a moment. When she didn't answer, he said, "Hanileh, tell me."

Hanileh looked up into his loving, concerned eyes. There was nothing she could hide from him. Why she had kept the news of the child a secret for so long...

"You are going to be a father, Gaultier."

A broad grin of disbelief prefaced the nervous chuckle that escaped from Gaultier. "I am?"

Hanileh nodded, her eyes darting out to the water once more. Gaultier shifted to catch her gaze. "Then why are you distraught, my love?" he asked, his hand sliding along her cheek to draw her attention back to him. "What does...he...have to do with this?"

Pressing into his touch, Hanileh closed her eyes and bowed her head. "Lucian came to me in a vision."

"When?" Gaultier demanded. His amazed joy at the news of his child whipped into a serious anger at the news of his enemy's contact.

"Just moments ago."

"Here?"

Hanileh nodded before Gaultier pulled her into his arms. Cradling her close, he murmured, "What did he want?"

"He wants our child," Hanileh whispered before collapsing against him in tears.

Gaultier kissed the top of her head, whispering reassurances to her. "I won't allow anything to happen to the baby, Hanileh. Nor to you. You know that."

"He is powerful, Gaultier." She withdrew from him, glancing down to where the symbol had reappeared under her tunic. Her fingers fell to her chest. "He made the mark return."

Carefully, Gaultier peeled back the neckline to expose her shoulder. Her skin was clear. No mark.

"Not as powerful as the Crown." Gaultier took her hand in his. "And it is to Him you belong."

Hanileh closed her eyes and returned to her husband's arms. *I belong to the Crown*, she reminded herself, using Gaultier's words. *Not Lucian. Not Lucian.*

"'Fear not, for the Crown walks with you,'" Gaultier murmured one of his favorite passages from the Creed as he stroked her hair. "'The King protects His people, loves His subjects, and cares for His children. His sword is mighty, and His shield defends even the lowliest of His own.' Hold to your faith, my love."

CHAPTER TWENTY TWO

"She was really shaken, Vel," Gaultier said into the vid-link. "Lucian's hold still runs deep."

"No, Gaultier, he no longer holds her. He's just..." Velius sighed softly. "He's more powerful than we'd like to think."

"He's a coward. He operates in devious, insignificant ways that, after a point, begin to surmount to formidable evil."

"Such is the way of the enemy," Velius said. "The baby is not hurt? Hanileh?"

"No. They are both healthy and doing well." Gaultier rose, rubbing a hand over his chin. "I'm going to be a father, Vel. In just a few months. Am I ready to handle this?"

"Handle the parenting part? Or the keeping the child safe part?"

"Both," Gaultier admitted, leaning on the desk as he looked at his brother for reassurance.

"You'll do an admirable job, Gaultier. You always have."

"I feel so helpless against this Thaed character." Gaultier hung his head. "He touches her in ways I am unable to defend."

Velius paused in silence for a long moment. "I think it might be time for you and Hanileh to return to Kapelle."

"We can't do that," Gaultier protested. "We've not been away all that long."

"Gaultier, your child has great potential. The Council is anticipating a son, which they are eager to greet."

"You mean examine."

"To some degree." Velius rocked back in his chair, steepling his fingers together. "Your child might be the savior the Logia have been waiting for."

"Not the Ruler Prince," Gaultier murmured.

"No, not the Prince, but the Divinum Bellator. You've avoided responsibility to the faith for long enough, Gaultier. It's time you accepted your role in the bigger picture."

ASHLEY HODGES BAZER

Gaultier sank down in his chair with an exhausted breath. He didn't want to get into this with Velius again, so he swallowed his pride. "And retreating to the shelter of the Logia is accepting responsibility?"

"No. First of all, you would not be retreating anywhere. I am bestowing you with the title and responsibilities of Logia elder. You'll be rejoining the brotherhood that carries the banner of our Crown. A brotherhood that will protect and defend your family, just as you wish to do." Velius's voice flickered with a tinge of anger as he crossed his arms over his chest. "Secondly, and you know how I feel about this, Gaultier—you have denied your part in this for far too long. You are important to the Crown. He wants to use you, and you refuse."

"This again. I don't refuse—"

"You do. You refused the possibility of becoming Protector, and you refused the idea of becoming an athaer. Even now, the Crown stands before you with a glorious gift, and you refuse to see the child might be something extraordinary."

Gaultier leaned back and gazed over the screen of the vid-link. He'd heard this from his brother for years, but now it was starting to sink in. *Is Velius right? Have I been denying the Crown all along?*

"Let us help you, Gaultier," Velius murmured. "You don't have to go it alone."

"If we do this, Hanileh will think we perceive Thaed as a threat."

"He is a threat. All the more reason to return to the safety of the domicile." Velius shifted forward, staring at his brother through the screen. "Are you willing to lose your wife and child, Gaultier? Because of your false sense of humility or your over-inflated sense of pride?"

"You're being unfair."

"You are making this about you, Gaultier. And it's not at all about you. It's about the Crown. Just like Alton and his gifting."

"Totally different circumstances—"

"You've got to let go of yourself in order to save your child."

Gaultier ran his hand over his face once more. "You see more fault in me than I do."

"That's why I am the athaer." Velius smiled. "Instrument of the Crown for purposes of refining."

"Thorn in my side," Gaultier muttered. "All right. We will return to Kapelle. I'd like to speak with the Council upon our arrival."

"I'll make the arrangements," Velius promised. "You're doing the right thing."

"We'll see." Gaultier tapped his fingers on the desk. "I covet your prayers in this."

"You already have them. I look forward to seeing you, my brother."

HERALDS OF THE CROWN: POISON

"And I you. *Soli Deo Gloria*," Gaultier answered before he terminated the link. He sat back in his chair and lifted his eyes to the ceiling. "Show me Your hand, my King. Guide my path, for I feel lost."

------◆------

Crenet: 2 weeks later

Velius stood from his place in the Council chamber, calling the meeting to order. The Council members fell silent and took their seats. Gaultier watched in silence before catching Almus's gaze. He gave the older man a respectful nod, and Almus responded in kind.

"Friends," Velius said in greeting, "thank you for convening today. We welcome back our brother, Gaultier, and his wife, Hanileh. Which brings me to the reason we have gathered. Hanileh is with child."

Murmurs stirred throughout the Council members. It was news they all had awaited, although no one had known when it would be delivered. Almus rose, lifting a hand to request the floor.

Velius gestured for the older man to speak.

Almus met the eyes of each of the Council members as he spoke. "We all know the lineage of the Lassiters holds great promise for the Logia faith. I have spent some time with both Gaultier and Hanileh, and I fully believe the child she bears will be the Divinum Bellator."

Gaultier bowed his head. *Guide me, My King. I need you in this.* He never liked the attention that walked hand-in-hand with his family's position. Castus had once mentioned he should get used to it, but he never had.

"We must do everything within our power to protect not only this child, but Hanileh and Gaultier as well," Almus continued. "The Crown has given me a thought to increase their security, but it must be brought before the Council for vote."

"What is your idea, Almus?" Velius asked.

"Again, let me say the Crown Himself spoke this idea to me. He wishes for us to relocate the sanctuary. To wall off and bless a portion of the chapel to serve as the sanctuary."

More murmurings. Gaultier looked up, his eyes on Almus.

"The current sanctuary will then become Gaultier and Hanileh's quarters. It is sacred ground, so no evil shall defile it. They will be at the heart of the domicile, which will provide even further protection."

Gaultier couldn't believe his ears. Their living in the sanctuary would defile it. What was Almus thinking?

"Let me stop you there, Almus," Velius said. "I speak for the majority of the Council when I say that is a bad idea."

Ostium, a highly respected Lumen, stood, looking at Velius. "I respectfully disagree, Athaer. I think most of us are in accord with Almus. If the Crown Himself spoke the solution—"

"Ludicrous. We are talking about upending a consecrated domicile—"

"We are talking about protecting the future of the Logia faith, Athaer," Almus argued. "The domicile may be consecrated, but it is just a building. It's not the Crown."

Velius's eyes passed over his Council. "Then let's put it to a vote. All those who wish to relocate the sanctuary, by sign of *assentior...*"

Before Velius could get the words from his mouth, twelve men spoke in unison, "*Assentior.*"

Both Almus and Ostium returned to their seats. Velius's eyes narrowed. Gaultier focused on his brother, praying Velius wouldn't lash out because of the dissension. Instead, Velius lifted his chin. "Then so be it. Almus, you are responsible for the project. Choose your committee, and proceed."

"Thank you, Athaer," Almus said, bowing his head.

"If there is no further business, you are dismissed."

The men rustled about as Velius made a hasty exit. Gaultier smiled and shook hands as a few Council members approached him. His thoughts were on his brother, though. As much as he wanted to trust Velius, something kept him on his guard.

CHAPTER TWENTY THREE

Crenet: 426 CT

"Thaed demands we bring him the child."

Velius startled from his prayers as Raum materialized next to him. He hadn't seen nor heard from the Strages in months. Beyond that, the foul being shouldn't have been able to enter the sanctuary, the sacred heart of the domicile.

"Go away," Velius mumbled.

"Perhaps you didn't hear me," Raum said as a mental force pressed in around Velius's skull. "I said, Thaed demands we bring him the child."

"What child?" Velius cringed as the pain continued.

"The baby. The focus of Logia attention. The one they proclaim to be the Divine Warrior."

The pressure released, causing Velius to rock forward toward the floor. He took a few calming breaths before he straightened up, staring at Raum.

"He is Gaultier's son. And he's only a few days old. I cannot allow that."

Raum leaned closer to Velius, his fearsome black eyes blazing with fury. "I can do this without you, but it will cost you dearly."

The pain ripped through Velius's head again, flashing a ghoulish vision of blood and terror. He saw the residential corridor—overturned furniture and shredded wallpaper. Logia after Logia heaped on the floor in pools of red. Hanileh clutching a baby's blanket, a broadsword springing up from the center of her back. Gaultier sprawled across a table with Raum's dagger proudly protruding from his chest. The fleeting cry of Karaine as Raum carried the baby away, leaving behind the bloodbath.

"I still don't get why you care for Gaultier so deeply," Raum said as the vision faded. "He is the heart of your hatred."

Placing a hand on the floor, Velius propped himself up, again trying to

ASHLEY HODGES BAZER

catch his breath. "He is my brother," he whispered.

"He should have died along with your parents. They cared nothing for you, and neither does he."

Velius closed his eyes, trying to avoid the crushing despair that came with Raum's taunting. "Why do you need my help? You've already found a way to penetrate the sanctuary."

"This isn't the sanctuary, and you know it. You switched things around. This may be where you pretend to worship your precious Crown, but the ground isn't sacred. Gaultier and his family reside in that spot now."

"How did you know that?" Velius asked.

"I know a lot, Vel. Things you have no clue about." Raum scratched his neck with the tip of his dagger. "I need a way in."

"And if I allow you access to the sacred grounds...?"

"Then I take the child and deliver him to Thaed. From there, Thaed has a plan. He doesn't intend to kill the child, but he does plan to use him against the Crown."

"Where will he take him?"

"You can't know that. I'm not even allowed to know that. If Gaultier were to fuse with you, he would know the location and be able to thwart Thaed's plan. No, Thaed was very precise in how this was all to go down."

"What do I get from the bargain?"

Raum chuckled. "There is no bargain, Vel. You do as Thaed tells you."

"There's more." Velius eyed the evil man who knelt next to him.

"Of course, there's more. After the child is discovered missing, you must send away Gaultier and Hanileh. If allowed to remain in their quarters, Gaultier's abilities might pick up on a trail. Tell them you are doing it for their protection. When they return, move them to different quarters. Thaed will then take care of his unfinished business with Hanileh and end her life."

"I can't do it, Raum," Velius murmured.

"Then I must follow through with my orders. But before I do, Thaed wished for me to give you this." Raum pulled a leather-bound book from his layers of black clothing. "He thinks you need a reminder of your station."

Velius took the book, gently running his fingers over the black and gold cover. "What is it?" he asked.

"Open it," Raum urged.

Carefully, Velius cracked open the book. His eyes were drawn to the blank pages. He quickly flipped through, his frustration growing as each page proved empty.

"What is this?" he said, allowing his annoyance to taint his tone.

"Touch the page, Velius."

Placing one hand under the spine, Velius rested his other on the open leafs. Electricity began to crackle through him as Thaed's message came through. Overwhelmed by the power, hatred, and anger that suddenly slammed into his brain, Velius staggered backward, clutching the book. He couldn't drop it now if he tried. Thaed channeled through it, punishing Velius for his hesitance.

When relief finally came, Velius opened his eyes. He wasn't sure when or how it happened, but he now sat in a heap, leaning against the wall with his legs sprawled out before him. The book remained in his lap, but the pages now contained Velius's handwriting with the words, *Gloriam et potestatem Carnifex*, in various sizes all over. He knew what it meant, and it fed him with courage and pride. A frightening new power dwelt deep within.

Raum squatted in front of him, cocking his head with an odd little smile. "You belong to Thaed. In this moment, you will find the confidence you will need to proceed. Now, are you going to let me in?"

"I—"

"Recite the words, Vel. It will give you the answer you seek."

"*Gloriam et potestatem Carnifex*," Velius whispered, his fingers trailing over the words on the page. "Glory and power to Carnifex. The Crown must be defeated."

"And we can do that by securing the child for Thaed."

"Tonight. After they put Karaine to bed."

"Karaine. Such a common name."

"It was our father's name. Gaultier wished to honor him. The boy carries with him great hope for the Logia."

"And that is why he must be raised Strages. All I need is your permission to enter the room, Vel. The formal words of the Logia athaer of the Kapelle domicile. I will decide when."

Velius pulled the open book to his chest. "Raum Carrick, as athaer of the Kapelle domicile, I hereby grant you permission to enter the private residence of Gaultier Lassiter and his family. The grounds are sacred, formerly blessed as the sanctuary. You have a standing invitation to cross onto the grounds without repercussion."

"It is done." Raum faded away with a malevolent sneer.

Cradling the book, Velius rocked back and forth, repeating, "*Gloriam et potestatem Carnifex*." His loyalty would surely earn him favor in the eyes of Carnifex. And Thaed would praise him, perhaps even welcome him as a member of the Gathering.

───────◆───────

Hanileh hummed a soft, quiet lullaby as she held Karaine close to her. He had just nodded off, and his peaceful little face brought a proud smile to

Hanileh's lips. She couldn't imagine anything more beautiful, any gift more valuable. The Crown had indeed blessed her with tremendous treasure.

She pulled him even closer to kiss his tiny cheek as she rose from the rocking chair. Karaine flinched ever so slightly, and Hanileh soothed him with a gentle, "Shh." Drawing her fingers across his forehead, she swept back the wispy strands of dark baby hair. Precious.

The cradle waited just across the wide bedroom. Hanileh crossed to it, nestling Karaine amidst the cozy blankets. She carefully situated them around the baby before stepping back to admire him once again.

"You will do great things, little one," she whispered. "You're going to change the system."

Taking a deep breath to ease her body and mind, Hanileh joined Gaultier in the living area. Although it was later in the evening, he'd been working on some correspondence. He'd just shared with her an update passed down by Almus from Jett and Delia. Their son, Griffin, had recently celebrated eighteen months, and Delia soon expected a second child. It was wonderful news, of course, but Hanileh couldn't help but feel pity for the Criswells. As the Protectors, they were facing a potentially hazardous situation, and bringing children into it seemed selfish and irresponsible. *How soon they might have to say goodbye...*

A fleeting shadow caught her eye as she turned toward the archway leading into the living area. A chill tingled up her spine and down her arms. She spun around slowly, taking in the room. Nothing was out of place, yet she couldn't shake the unsettled feeling.

Oh, I'm just being silly. A nervous mother. Karaine will be fine.

She'd be in the next room and would certainly hear him cry should he awaken. Besides, they were in the safest place they could possibly be. Gaultier would reassure her, perhaps even gently chide her for being so edgy.

She shook her head and chuckled at herself as she slipped from the bedroom. Gaultier glanced up from his desk, angling his head toward her. "What's so funny?"

"I'm imagining things. I just put Karaine down, and thought I saw something in the room."

Rising, Gaultier opened his arms to her. "It's sleep deprivation, love. Not to mention the weight of the new responsibility."

Hanileh smiled as his embrace settled around her. He led her to a nearby sofa and sat with her. She leaned against his broad chest and closed her eyes. A nap would ease the tension she felt. Even if it was just for a few moments.

The chill snaked around her again, lurking with unwelcome apprehension. She pushed away from Gaultier, glancing toward the

HERALDS OF THE CROWN: POISON

bedroom. Something wasn't right.

"Would you feel better if we checked on him?"

Hanileh nodded, already on her feet. "I just—"

"It's all right, Hanileh." Gaultier smiled. "You don't have to explain it to me."

She brushed past him and walked hurriedly back to the bedroom. Gaultier followed closely, raising the lights a little to allow for better vision. When she reached the cradle, the world around her skidded to a halt.

The cradle was empty.

"No," she whispered, peeling back the blankets to make certain Karaine hadn't wriggled under them.

"Hanileh?" Gaultier asked, moving to her side.

"No! Gaultier, he's..."

Gaultier's eyes went wide with alarm as Hanileh yanked the blankets out of the cradle. She looked under and around it, searching for any sign of the baby. Finally, she toppled the piece, crying in frustration and despair.

Wrapping her tightly in his arms, Gaultier held her close. She screamed and sobbed against his shoulder. The pain was more than she could bear.

"Hanileh, calm down. I need you to answer me very carefully," Gaultier said, his tone almost patronizing.

"We have to find him!" she cried.

His hands settled on both sides of her face, drawing her attention to his own. "Hanileh, listen to me. Answer me. You placed Karaine in the cradle, right?"

She pulled away from him, her grief changing to abject surprise. "You think I did this?"

"No. No, of course not," Gaultier said, gripping her hands as tears began to stream from his eyes. He choked on his own breath. "You were only alone with me for a few seconds..."

"That shadow," Hanileh gasped, her eyes darting about the room. "I saw something, Gaultier. Someone. Someone was here with me!"

"Thaed?" Gaultier asked, shaking his head. "Impossible. We're on sacred ground."

Hanileh tossed her head back and wailed with anguish. How could this have happened? They had been so careful. The Council of Elders placed them in this room to protect the baby whom they believed was the Divine Warrior. But beyond that, he was their son. Their gift from the Crown. And now...

Hanileh ran through the room, snatching the decorative tapestries from their hanging positions in an effort to reveal any possible hiding places. She overturned furniture, plowed through piles of their belongings, and yanked open drawers. In the midst of her frantic and futile search, Gaultier's strong hands settled on her shoulders and whirled her around.

Guiding her eyes back to his once again, Gaultier shook his head. "We don't have time for this, Hanileh. We have to find him. I have to alert Velius and the Council. I want you to stay here. Do you understand me? Stay. Here."

"I can't—" she started.

"Fix the cradle. Straighten things up. The Council and Velius will wish to investigate, I am certain." Gaultier jumped to his feet, pulling Hanileh with him. "I will not grieve him until we know more, nor will I allow you to do so. I need you to be strong."

"Gaultier—"

"Hanileh, I know. I am not asking you to do this. I am ordering you. Stay here. I will only be a moment before I return with someone."

Gaultier whisked away, leaving Hanileh to stare at the heap of light blue blankets strewn across the floor. She fought back a sob as she stepped to the cradle to set it upright. Shock started to play in her mind, numbing her to her actions. With diligence, she folded the blankets and placed them back in the cradle.

CHAPTER TWENTY FOUR

"What is it? What's going on?" Velius pulled a robe around his body as he stepped from his quarters.

Almus kept his arm around Gaultier's shoulders. "You're needed, Athaer. Gaultier and Hanileh's child—"

"Something has happened to Karaine!" Gaultier cried. "He was there one moment, and gone the next."

"No," Velius whispered. "Where is Hanileh?"

Ostium stood at Almus's side. "She is in their quarters. Janua is with her."

Velius shook his head. "She shouldn't be there. It only serves to hurt her even more."

"We have to find him, Vel," Gaultier said, urgency rising with each passing moment. "He might still be on grounds."

Almus lowered his eyes. "He's not, my friend."

"You don't know that," Gaultier argued. "He—"

"Gaultier, I know. I had a sense of the child. Something I established shortly after he was born." Almus glanced at Velius. "I had a feeling something like this might happen."

"Then do you know what happened?" Velius asked.

Almus released a troubled sigh. "No. Regrettably, I let my guard down tonight."

"I have to go. I have to find him." Gaultier pressed his hands to his head.

"Not in this state, my friend," Ostium said. "You're not going anywhere."

"On the contrary," Velius said, "I think you and Hanileh should return to Serenata while we investigate."

"Serenata?" Gaultier said in disbelief.

"Hanileh needs you, Gaultier. You need her." Velius looked at Ostium. "Send Cordus with them. He can pilot the shuttle."

153

"I'm not leaving, Vel!"

Velius stepped close to Gaultier, looking him in the eye. "I am giving you an order as athaer of Kapelle. Look after your family, and let us do our job. We will find Karaine."

"Serenata is too far away," Gaultier choked out.

"Then seek solace in the Sunlight Gardens on Ossia. Ostium, fetch Cordus and meet Gaultier in the docking bay. Almus, please escort him there. I will link Janua and have him deliver Hanileh while I gather a crew to investigate. After you see them off, join me in their quarters," Velius ordered.

Ostium marched away. Almus squeezed Gaultier's shoulder in reassurance. "Come, Gaultier."

Velius lifted a hand, stopping Almus and Gaultier. "A moment with my brother, please, Almus?"

The older man frowned, stepping away. Gaultier stared after him until Velius moved into his line of sight.

"We will find Karaine," Velius promised. "Focus your energies on Hanileh. Don't let her slip. This could be a very dangerous time for both of you."

"I am at a loss, Vel," Gaultier admitted, tears stinging his eyes.

"We will cover you both in prayer. And rest assured, we will get to the bottom of this."

Gaultier nodded, too weak with emotion to resist his brother's insistence that they leave the grounds. He just wanted to get away from the hurt, the worry, and the fear. He wanted to find the place of trust again, but his faith in the Crown was now shaken.

Velius patted Gaultier on the back, guiding him to Almus. "Once they are on board, I want you to call together Lumen and Logia alike to pray around the clock for the Lassiters," he instructed the older man.

"I'd like to help with the investigation," Almus offered. "I might be able to pick up on something no one else would."

Heat spiced Velius's tone as he reiterated his order. "I've given you your assignment. Please see it through."

"Yes, Athaer," Almus murmured.

"Safe travels, Gaultier." Velius turned and moved down the hall. Gaultier watched as his brother lifted a link to his lips.

"Come, Gaultier," Almus urged again.

"What do I do, Almus?" Gaultier dabbed his eyes with the backs of his wrists to stop the escaping tears.

"Go with Hanileh. The further you are from here, the safer you are. I will alert Jax and Alton for you."

"But Karaine—"

HERALDS OF THE CROWN: POISON

"I know. I am greatly concerned Velius will not allow me to assist in the investigation. I fear something is amiss." Almus paused, looking at Gaultier. "You need to stay alive for your son, Gaultier."

"I feel so helpless."

"I know. But we must allow the Crown to be our help in these times. He is working, even if we don't see or feel it."

Gaultier nodded, rubbing his forehead.

"I hate to see you go, son," Almus said. "I fear for all our safety under Velius's authority. But I trust the Crown. Perhaps he is removing you from the domicile in order to protect you."

"Velius—"

"—has given me cause to be suspicious. Even in his goodbye to you, Gaultier. He couldn't bring himself to say 'Crownspeed.' I will be watching him. And asking a lot of questions."

Emotion finally took complete hold over Gaultier. Almus pulled him into an embrace, murmuring a prayer of strength over him. After a few moments, Gaultier composed himself once again, and they continued onto the docking bay in silence.

Hanileh greeted him with a worn, questioning expression, but he hadn't the energy to battle with her over Velius's decision. They were both in need of healing, and neither one would be able to help the other. Perhaps they would find the Crown in the Gardens.

Almus moved to Hanileh's side, whispering into her ear. She looked up at the older man with a tearful gaze and nodded. Almus squeezed her close to him, then gestured for Gaultier to join them.

"May the peace of the Creator King wash over you," Almus spoke the blessing over them. "Find comfort in His Word, solace in His arms, and tranquility in His love."

Cordus appeared at the top of the ramp. "The *Sun* is ready for flight," he said before disappearing again.

Almus nodded, patting both Gaultier and Hanileh on the back. "Crownspeed, both of you."

Gaultier took Hanileh's hand and led her up the ramp. As they entered the cabin, she pulled her hand away and chose a chair. Gaultier closed his eyes and murmured a meek prayer as he lowered into the seat next to her. He offered his hand to her. She turned away, crossing her arms over her chest.

Leaning back in the chair, Gaultier shuddered. Misery was a cold companion.

◆

Gaultier held Hanileh as they stepped into the space Velius used as an office. When Velius became athaer, he moved the office from the open study to a private room close to the entrance of the chapel. As they entered, Gaultier glanced at the strong doors of the chapel. He had expected to see signs of forced entry, but the doors showed no evidence.

Velius, seated behind the desk that separated the room in half, lifted a hand in greeting, then directed Gaultier and Hanileh to sit. He continued to scribble furiously in what appeared to be a journal. Gaultier nodded with a frown as he eased Hanileh toward a pair of chairs along the wall of the office. Surely Velius understood the gravity and urgency of the situation.

Hanileh stared past him to Velius. "He's not doing anything?" she asked, tears mixed with anger.

"Calm, Hanileh. We must not let fear motivate us," Gaultier answered.

"But he's just—"

"Making notes of the avenues I have already pursued," Velius replied, steepling his hands as he looked toward them. "If we chase our own tails, we will get nowhere."

"My apologies on behalf of my wife, Velius," Gaultier explained. "We've gotten very little sleep the last few days."

"Understandable, my brother. I, myself, have not been able to rest."

"We've been gone four days. Have you any news?" Hanileh trembled, but Gaultier couldn't tell if her shakiness was from fear or anger.

Velius shook his head, lowering his eyes to the desk. "I'm sorry. There have been no leads."

"Someone had to see something," Gaultier said. "It was not yet sleeping hours when Karaine went missing."

"Hanileh, how long were you away from him?" Velius asked.

Gaultier felt such deep pity for his wife. He'd watched her spiral from an elated new mother to a devastated, wounded soul. Not that he could blame her. He also fought the whirlpool of sorrow and despair that sucked him downward. Most difficult of all, though, was the ever-growing strain and distance between them.

"I've told you, I was away for only seconds," Hanileh snapped.

"She put him in his cradle, but as soon as she joined me in the living area, she felt a need to check on him," Gaultier said. "When she returned to our sleeping area, he was no longer there."

Hanileh bowed her head as a sob escaped her lips. Gaultier stepped closer to her, placing a comforting hand on her shoulder as he looked at his brother.

"Please, Vel, give us some hope."

Velius leaned heavily on his arms over the desk. "I—"

At that moment, Almus stole into the office, followed by Ostium, a young Lumen boy, and several members of the Council of Elders. Almus stared at Gaultier with an expression of sympathy. "I'm glad you're here, Gaultier."

Hanileh stood, hiding behind Gaultier. He knew she was fearful the elder had bad news. Gaultier's hand grasped hers as he asked, "What is it, Almus?"

"An emergency injunction." Almus stepped toward Velius, opening his hands in question. "Anything you wish to tell us, Velius?"

Velius rose, staring down the elder. "I don't know what you're talking about."

"Your arrogance will be your downfall, Velius." Almus shook his head. "I can't believe you thought you'd get away with this."

"Get away with what, Almus?" Gaultier asked, his eyes darting between his brother and the older man.

Almus turned to Gaultier, the sympathetic look returning to his eyes. "I'm sorry, Gaultier. He was afraid to come forward before now."

"I don't follow," Gaultier urged. "Please tell us."

Almus gestured toward the Lumen boy. "Vitni walked the halls of the domicile a couple of nights ago. He saw what he described as a dark being skulking around the secured areas of the domicile."

"A dark being?" Gaultier stepped forward.

"He was dressed all in black," Vitni said. The boy trembled.

"You can't judge someone based on the way they are dressed."

"It was more than that, sir," the boy replied. "The man had the markings of the Strages. Black brandings all over his skin. And his presence...it was like a-a-a void."

Vitni's description was all too familiar. Gaultier glanced toward Velius, who had bowed his head in silence. *No. This can't be true.* His brother hadn't betrayed him...again...had he?

"Th-the man—did he have a scar over his—" Gaultier started, a single finger brushing along his forehead.

"—left eye. Yes," Vitni confirmed.

Gaultier pressed his eyes shut. Raum Carrick. The same one who had romanced Velius into the arms of the Strages. The one who had taken his actions too far, resulting in the death of his parents. Evidently, Raum's hold on his brother ran deep. Gaultier almost had convinced himself Velius had changed. He chided himself for being so trusting.

"You did this?" Hanileh closed in on Velius. "You took Karaine?"

"No," Velius said quietly.

"Hanileh," Gaultier placed his arm between Hanileh and Velius, looking back to the group of elders. "Draugas, would you please escort my wife to our quarters?

ASHLEY HODGES BAZER

As the man stepped forward, Hanileh swatted at Gaultier. "No. I will not be sent away again. That's exactly what he wants. I must know what happened here. Did you kill him, Velius?"

"You don't understand," Velius said, again in a soft tone.

"Explain it," Almus answered.

Velius glanced up, looking first at the Council, then toward Hanileh. He would not make eye contact with Gaultier.

"The child is safe."

Gaultier clenched his fists, calling upon the strength of the Crown to resist pounding his brother. "Where is he?"

"You will not see him again," Velius answered coolly.

"What did you do with him?" Hanileh asked, a sense of horror in her words.

"He is the Divinum Bellator," Almus said. "No doubt the Strages are doing all they can to dispose of him."

Hanileh collapsed against Gaultier. "Lucian has him," she whispered in tears. "I knew he would find a way."

"The child is safe," Velius repeated. "You have my assurances no harm will befall him."

"Your assurances amount to nothing," Gaultier spat. "How could you do this, Velius? The Logia trusted you. I...trusted you."

Velius finally met Gaultier's eyes. "This is far beyond you, Gaultier."

Almus moved closer to Velius. "The Council demands you come with us immediately. You stand before us under intense scrutiny. And understand that your position as athaer is at great risk."

Bowing his head again, Velius clasped his hands before him. "*Gloriam et potestatem Carnifex.* The Crown shall be defeated."

"Arrest him." Almus stepped aside as the Council members made their move.

Hanileh bolted past Gaultier with a wounded scream, launching a full physical assault on Velius. Velius protected himself by grasping Hanileh's hands. From behind, Gaultier grabbed her and wrenched her from Velius. She fought him until the anguish ripped through her, overwhelming her with grief. Gaultier eased her to the floor, sitting with her as Ostium and the Council took Velius into custody.

Gaultier looked up to see Almus in the doorway. "We will keep him in the seclusion chamber under full guard. The Council convenes this evening and will likely strip Velius of his title. I shall assume the role of interim athaer until the Council names another," the elder said.

With a nod, Gaultier said, "Thank you. I would like some time alone with him. I will get the answers we seek."

Almus lifted his chin. "I am sorry, Gaultier, but I cannot permit you to

HERALDS OF THE CROWN: POISON

face him alone. If he is of the mind to take Karaine, then it wouldn't bother him to hurt or kill you. We cannot take that chance. I will be with you."

"I don't wish to put you in peril."

"It is my choice, Gaultier. I stand with you willingly, and I will protect you with my life."

Gaultier rested his head against Hanileh's. "Again, I thank you. I trust he was telling the truth about the child being safe?"

"If the child is in Strages hands, he will never be safe."

Hanileh whimpered.

Gaultier stroked her hair to soothe her. "We will find him, Almus. We must."

"I will meet you at the seclusion chamber in ten minutes," Almus said, his avoidance of confirmation striking Gaultier with doubt.

As the elder left the room, Gaultier held Hanileh close. "It will be all right, Hanileh. I promise."

"Lucian has Karaine. How can it be all right?" Hanileh cried.

Gaultier swallowed hard. "I will speak with Velius and—"

"You can't," Hanileh looked up at him, fear in her eyes. "You can't fuse with him. He will destroy you."

"That is why Almus will be there, Hanileh. He will not allow Velius to go too far." Gaultier brushed her hair back from her shoulder and whispered, "I will do what I have to in order to find our son."

"I want to be with you."

"No, Hanileh. I want you to go to our quarters and get some rest. I will ask Sopor to help you."

"I don't want to sleep, Gaultier."

"You need to," Gaultier insisted. "I need you to be strong."

Hanileh dropped her chin to her chest, her shoulder slumping. "Velius robbed me of more than just my son."

"Much more," Gaultier agreed. "But we will regain all we have lost with just a little bit of faith."

Forcing a reassuring smile to his lips, he gripped Hanileh's hand and stood. "Come. I don't wish to keep Almus waiting."

Hanileh rose, gesturing toward Velius's journal. "He said he made notes of the avenues he pursued."

Gaultier crossed to the desk, lifting up the journal to look more closely at it. The open pages contained only the words, *Gloriam et potestatem Carnifex*, written repeatedly in various sized letters. Every inch of the pages contained ink. As Gaultier flipped through, he saw page after page of the same thing. His breath caught as he realized the madness that had completely devoured his brother.

Lifting his gaze, he saw Hanileh with her hand over her mouth. She

159

had seen the pages. Gaultier closed the journal and tucked it under his arm.

"The Council will need this," he murmured softly as he returned to her side.

"I'm frightened," Hanileh whispered.

"'I shall lift my eyes and hold fast to Your promises, for You are the Redeemer of my heart. I place my sins before You, and You graciously cast them aside. My cares and burdens weigh on Your shoulders, as You remove them from mine. A King, a Father, a Brother, a Champion, You are all these and more,'" Gaultier whispered the verses he'd been studying with Hanileh.

"I am well aware of what the verses say, Gaultier," Hanileh shook her head. "They're just words. They do us no good. Lucian will take Karaine as his own. He will craft him and raise him as a Strages, just like he did with me."

"They are not just words," Gaultier said. "They are promises. Powerful. True. Let us commit our son to the Crown, and ask for His sovereign protection over him until we find him."

"Gaultier..."

"We serve a mighty Crown, Hanileh. I am choosing to trust Him. And I ask you—as my wife—to do the same."

Hanileh stared at him for a long moment. "I don't know if I can," she admitted in a hushed tone.

"Try, Hanileh. He once saved you. Marcella. Remember that."

Gaultier took a knee, bowing his head as he began to pray for Karaine. He scolded himself for not doing so sooner, but he believed the Crown already knew the matters that weighed upon his heart. The Crown knew how precious Karaine was, not only to them as parents, but to the system as the Divinum Bellator. Surely the Crown would protect His own Divine Warrior.

Before long, Hanileh joined him, gripping his hand as her weepy petitions aligned with his whispered ones. They prayed together for some time before Gaultier lifted a song of praise. Following the worshipful moment, he requested strength and wisdom in confronting Velius. Hanileh's passionate pleas touched him.

He lifted his chin, pressing a kiss to Hanileh's forehead. "I will escort you back to our quarters, then I'll send for Sopor."

"I love you, Gaultier," she whispered, linking her hand with his. It was the first sign of affection he'd seen from her since Karaine's disappearance.

"And I you, Hanileh," he said, pulling her close. "Our love is going to get us through."

CHAPTER TWENTY FIVE

Gaultier stared at the door that separated him from Velius. It took great effort to reign in the anger that raged through him. If he were not Logia, he'd more than likely walk into the seclusion room and throttle his brother. But he owed compassion and understanding to the man on the other side of that door. Just as the Creator King had granted Gaultier.

Almus placed a hand on his shoulder. "Focus on righteousness, my son. I am with you, as is the Crown."

Gaultier nodded, bracing himself as Almus unlocked the door. The heavy plank swung open. Velius sat in the center of the room on a simple wooden chair, stripped of his athaer robes. He wore only a plain gray tunic and black pants. He lifted his gaze to Gaultier, no hint of remorse or guilt on his face. Just a placid, unruffled expression.

Almus gestured for Gaultier to enter. After a moment of silent standoff with Velius, Gaultier stepped into the room. Almus followed, closing the door behind them. Gaultier took a calming breath. *Grant me wisdom and patience, my King.*

"Velius," Gaultier started.

"Gaultier." Velius smiled like a predatory animal playing with its next meal.

"You sent us away for four days."

"I had to shake you off the trail."

"Tell me this isn't true," Gaultier whispered, hoping his brother would say the whole thing was nothing more than a distasteful joke.

Velius tipped back in the chair and gripped its legs as he stared at Gaultier. "You are weak in your faith, my brother."

"We're not here to talk about me."

"I can offer you power like you've never known."

"This is not the place, Velius."

"Join us. Forsake the Crown and His diluted authority. I can show you the way to the true master."

"Enough!" Gaultier roared. "I will not bend, nor will I relent. You sit at the center of a Logia domicile and have the gall to try to sway me from the Crown? You will tell me what you and your friends did with my son."

Velius glanced toward Almus. "Get rid of the puppet."

"Almus is here to protect me."

"He can't protect you from me should I choose to unleash upon you."

"What's stopping you?"

Velius grinned. "The game is afoot in other locations."

Gaultier charged toward Velius, gripping his tunic in his fists. "What are you talking about?"

"You left someone very precious to you in a most vulnerable situation." Velius chuckled.

"Hanileh." Gaultier spun out of the room, rushing past Almus. "Lock him up, and wait for me outside," he ordered the older man.

Almus nodded, slipping out of the room behind Gaultier. Velius's laughter trailed on his heels. At this point, it would take every ounce of control not to obliterate his brother. Control beyond Gaultier's capacity.

◆

Hanileh slumped back against the satiny pillows on the bed. She stared at the ceiling above, praying for some form of clarity. Since she discovered Karaine missing, her only thought had been finding him. Gaultier assured her everyone who resided at the domicile had been interviewed. The Logia searched, sought, and retraced every step. And now, she had full confirmation her precious boy was in the hands of a terrible enemy.

A soft rapping on the door alerted her to Sopor's arrival. She lifted her head from the pillows. "Come in."

The gentle young man slipped inside, offering a soft, sympathetic smile. He'd been at the domicile for close to five years and had attended Gaultier and Hanileh's wedding. On several occasions, he had shared intense, private conversations with Gaultier, and the two had become close friends.

"Good afternoon, Madam Lassiter," he said in greeting.

Hanileh smoothed the blanket under her. "Sopor, I've told you, please call me Hanileh."

"My apologies, miss. I am not used to such informal interaction." Sopor stepped close to the bed with his head bowed. "Gaultier asked me to help you find rest."

"Yes, thank you. Although there is so much to be done," Hanileh said, her eyes again finding the ceiling.

"You will only be met with frustration and difficulty if you are not properly rested. I understand why you are feeling so distressed, but certainly a good, solid sleep will help you."

"Thank you, Sopor," Hanileh smiled, touching Sopor's hand. "You may begin."

Sopor slid his hand from hers as he sat on the bed next to her. His fingers gently brushed her hair back from her forehead, then pressed his palm to her brow.

"Just relax," he said softly.

Hanileh closed her eyes as a tingling sensation nibbled at her toes and up her legs. The tension eased from her muscles, lulling her into a state of supernatural peacefulness. As her own prayers mingled with Sopor's, she felt the presence of the Crown ebbing further and further away from her. It was puzzling, but she was so sleepy...

"Marcella..."

Alertness snapped back to her in an instant. Her limbs felt weighted down. She was on her feet, but unable to move. Although her eyes remained closed, she could see Lucian standing before her as if in a dream. He sauntered toward her, extending a graceful hand.

"I hold your life," he said, pointing to his palm, "right here."

"Release me," Hanileh demanded.

Thaed's amused expression drained to one of intense hatred. "I have everything I need from you. Your child is mine. Long ago, when I took you, I thought I could master your soul. You see, I knew you would be the one to birth the Divine Warrior. I crafted you, raised you, prepared you for our marriage bed."

"You didn't want a child."

"I made you think that as a means of control. I was going to be the father of the Crown's Divine Warrior. Talk about irony. The one who is to put death in its place, fathered by evil itself! But you allowed the Crown to interfere. You invited Him in. And for a time, you eluded me. Your shield hid you well.

"Now, I have a foothold. I've found a new way to ruin the Crown's plan. Karaine will serve Carnifex through me. He will be crafted and raised Strages. Death and destruction will conquer the Logia. And you will only impede my strategy. There is no reason to keep you alive any longer."

Hanileh felt her body weaken as her heartbeat slowed to an unnatural rate. She staggered toward Thaed, fighting to remain strong. "Please, Lucian..."

He pulled her close, and whirled her around to stand behind her. His arms snaked around her middle and her shoulders. "Referring to me by my old name will not conjure any memories or stir any sympathy for you," he breathed into her ear. "You will die by my hands, but I will show you mercy by making it easy on you."

"Lucian," Hanileh whimpered.

"Shh," he cooed, jerking her closer to him.

Her head rolled back onto his shoulder, and she looked up into his eyes. He trailed a single finger along her neck before he pressed his hand to her chest. Every cell in her lungs constricted as he robbed her of breath.

"Don't fight it," Thaed said, shifting her in his arms to lay her on the imagined ground.

Despite his words, Hanileh's body instinctively resisted his attack, but he was in full control. Relief eluded her. Release slipped away. He said he would show mercy, yet the fire in her chest that demanded air was relentless. The pulse in her veins beat more and more slowly while Thaed pressed a kiss to her lips. As he pulled back, her life drained away. Consciousness faded into nothingness.

A brilliant light tore through the darkness, liberating Hanileh's awareness from the void. Gaultier's presence banished the oppressive ambiance, filling her at once with his love and the Crown's restoration. Thaed was no more.

"Come on, Hanileh, open your eyes," Gaultier pleaded.

Her eyelids fluttered open to her husband's concerned expression staring down at her. His worry gave way to relief as he pulled her close. "*Soli Deo Gloria!*"

"What happened?" She glanced about the room.

Gaultier placed a hand to the side of her face, blocking her view. "No, I don't want you to see anything. Almus is on his way, along with several other members of the Council."

"I don't understand," Hanileh said, staring up at Gaultier.

Gaultier dropped his eyes to the side. "Sopor is dead."

Hanileh wriggled in Gaultier's strong grip. "What? How?"

Frowning, Gaultier shook his head. "I don't know, Hanileh. When I came in, he had his hands on you, and you weren't breathing. Sopor was so intently focused he didn't even acknowledge my presence. I touched his shoulder, and he fell to the floor. I couldn't wake you..." He trailed off, emotion filling his eyes with tears.

"Lucian was here," she whispered.

"I know." Gaultier lifted his gaze briefly before returning his attention to her. "We have a big problem, Hanileh. Bigger than we thought."

"He confirmed he has Karaine. He told me."

Gaultier nodded, holding her close. "And he won't hesitate to kill you. I will get Karaine's location from Velius. We will fight this, and we will bring our son home."

"The things he told me, Gaultier...he said he knew I would be the one

HERALDS OF THE CROWN: POISON

to birth the Divine Warrior. That was why he...took me."

"From your parents?"

Hanileh shrugged. "He didn't specify, but I would assume so."

Gaultier squeezed his eyes closed. "He must be stopped."

"Karaine is supposed to be the one to do just that," Hanileh said. "Do you suppose the Crown intends for him to do so from within Lucian's circle?"

Gaultier stared at her. "Hear this now. I will not leave our son in the clutches of the Strages. The Crown would not ask us to make such a sacrifice."

With a nod, Hanileh collapsed against him. The physical strain of her near-death wore on her in the form of amplified exhaustion. Gaultier shifted her slightly, working her into his arms. "Keep your eyes closed. I'm taking you to a place you can rest."

"Lucian will find me," Hanileh whispered.

"Then he will find me as well." Gaultier touched her forehead with his own. "And he will not slip away from me this time."

◆

Gaultier stormed into the seclusion chamber, his eyes boring into Velius. The madman smirked from his chair in the middle of the room. Stalking toward him, Gaultier gripped his tunic and jerked Velius from the chair.

"Talk. Now," he demanded as he shoved him against the wall.

Velius grinned, eyeing Gaultier. "You have finally surrendered to your anger."

"The only words I want to hear from you are Karaine's location."

"I take it Hanileh wasn't dead when you found her," Velius said. "You didn't give him long enough."

Gaultier balled his fist and smacked it into Velius's jaw. The older man fell to the ground, lifting a hand to his cheek. Gaultier shook out his fingers, then grabbed Velius's tunic once more to hold him to the wall.

"Where is my boy?"

"Did you really leave her a second time...to come back here to interrogate me?"

Gaultier pulled Velius close to him, inches from his face. "She has nothing to do with this. Where is Karaine?"

"I told you, you won't find him."

Gaultier thrust Velius back against the hard stone. "Tell me."

Velius cackled. "I can't tell you what I don't know."

"You do know!"

"Do I?" Velius challenged. "Fuse with me. I'll show you."

Gaultier dropped him on the floor, stepping back. He glanced over his shoulder to Almus. Ostium had joined the acting athaer.

"Hold him," Gaultier ordered, rolling up the sleeves of his tunic.

"He wants this, Gaultier. He's luring you to hostility." Almus stared at Velius. "It's part of his diabolical plan."

"Diabolical," Velius repeated with a chuckle, shaking his head.

Gaultier ignored him. "Castus prepared me for this. I know what to do. Just hold him. Make sure he doesn't escape."

Almus and Ostium moved to Velius's side, pulling him up by his arms. They held him fast as Gaultier stared at his brother.

"One thing first," Gaultier murmured.

"What's that?" Velius asked, the taunting grin curling his lips.

With all his might, Gaultier slammed his fist into Velius's gut. It was wrong, but he justified it by acknowledging it would distract and weaken Velius. Gaultier would have the upper hand as he entered Velius's mind.

Velius doubled over in pain, but Almus and Ostium kept him from sinking to his knees. Gaultier stepped close, catching Almus's gaze as he pressed his hand to Velius's forehead.

"Violence isn't the way to the Crown, Gaultier," Velius teased in a groan. "You've overstepped sacred boundaries."

"Thankfully, I serve a forgiving God," Gaultier countered.

"Be careful," Almus whispered.

"Be watchful. He's tricky," Gaultier advised before murmuring a prayer to allow him to slip into a higher state of consciousness within Velius's mind.

Torrential chaos slammed into Gaultier, threatening to drown him in madness and confusion. The barrage was overwhelming at first, but as Gaultier gained footing, he was able to tame the wild rage within the recesses of Velius's mind. He placated Velius with an image of their childhood home. The kitchen where their mother often spent her days cooking and baking delicious food. The table where the family would gather to talk and share their lives.

Velius stood in the imagined doorframe. "This is not a place of consolation to me."

"I'm not here to make you comfortable." Gaultier pulled out a chair at the table.

"This is where you find solace?" Velius asked, stepping into the kitchen.

Gaultier lifted his chin and glanced around the stone kitchen. "One of the places, yes."

"I can change that for you in a heartbeat," Velius said with a grin.

HERALDS OF THE CROWN: POISON

Instantly, the warm, inviting kitchen turned dark. Frightening flashes of white lightning flickered through the windows as wind and rain raged outside. Gaultier leapt to his feet. His father lay on the floor near the table. Obvious signs of torture and torment lined the dead man's face. His eyes were wide with horror, and Gaultier's stomach flipped as he noticed the dagger sticking up from between the stiff shoulders.

Another flash of light revealed his mother, hanging in a far corner of the kitchen. Her limp body spun in a lazy circle as the rope that held her unraveled. Her wrists and ankles were bound together. Her face carried the same terror Gaultier recognized on his father's lifeless features.

Gaultier stepped back, only to feel Velius grip his shoulders. "No, don't run away. Welcome to my nightmare, younger brother. Take it in. See what haunts me every day. See what the Crown has refused to take from me."

"You did this, Velius," Gaultier whispered in accusation. "It only serves as a reminder of your betrayal."

"I didn't do this," Velius insisted. "Raum did. He knew how I felt about Mother and Father. He did it to free me of them."

"You killed them long before Raum did," Gaultier said. "Father couldn't get over the idea you would forsake the Logia to run with that crowd. Mother cried herself to sleep every night. Raum may have committed the physical act, but you destroyed their hearts."

"You yourself said we serve a forgiving god."

"No." Gaultier turned to his brother. "I said I serve a forgiving God. I don't know what you think you serve, but it is most certainly not the Crown."

"I have served the Crown, Gaultier. And He did nothing for me."

"He's done everything for you—"

"Raum has shown me greater power can be achieved in Carnifex's service."

"It's all a lie, Velius," Gaultier whispered. "I can't believe you don't see that."

Velius stepped in to Gaultier, closing the distance between them. "And yet, look at the power I hold over you, great servant of the Crown."

Gaultier met Velius's gaze evenly. "All power, including that of Raum, or Thaed, or even this imagined Carnifex, comes from the Crown. Any power you may have has been granted only by the Creator King."

"Quote your Creed verses all you want, Gaultier. If that's the case, then it means the Crown has placed you in this situation. The Crown is the one who has taken your son. The Crown is the one who nearly killed your wife. The Crown is the one who killed your parents."

A deep sense of calm eased Gaultier as he looked into Velius's eyes. "Your logic is faulty, brother. The Crown may have granted the power, but

He gives us the choice to do with that power what we will. Instead of being a good steward with what He gave you, you corrupted the gift and allowed outside influences to overtake you."

Velius stared at Gaultier, an expression of deep hatred and rage exploding from within. Popping his hands into Gaultier's chest, Velius knocked him back. "Always so perfect. So right."

Gaultier looked up at his brother. "I'm not," he whispered.

The image of the kitchen fell away, dissolving into a vague misty landscape. Velius turned away, his shoulders slumped.

"You came here for a specific reason."

"To find out where Karaine is." Gaultier pushed up to his feet.

Velius spun around, opening his hands as he looked at Gaultier. "I don't know."

"You're only saying that."

"Am I?" Velius asked. "I allowed Raum entry to your chambers. He took the child. From there, I don't know where they took him. They wouldn't tell me, nor did I want to know."

Gaultier fought the rising panic that threatened to choke off his air supply. "You have to know something."

With a shrug, Velius lifted his arms. "You're welcome to search my very soul, Gaultier. I don't know where the boy is."

Slipping from Velius's mind, Gaultier opened his eyes, looking at Almus. He shook his head, alerting the athaer to his lack of results.

"He doesn't know," Gaultier whispered.

"I can authorize a round of concentrated questioning," Almus offered.

"It wouldn't do any good," Gaultier answered, dropping his gaze to Velius. "Call together the Council. The sooner Velius is banished, the better."

Velius chuckled, his eyes on Gaultier. "This isn't the end, brother. Thaed won't let Marcella go. She will die at his hands, and there is nothing you can do to stop that."

Gaultier stepped toward the door, glancing over his shoulder at his brother. "You're quite mistaken, Vel. This is the end. If we ever hear from you or your band of manipulators again, you will regret it."

Velius's laugh escalated to a maniacal level. Gaultier shook his head and left the room. Almus and Ostium followed, pulling the door closed behind them. Gaultier didn't know how much more grief he could stand. Not only had he lost his son, but he had been forced to experience the scene of his parents' murder, and had once again been betrayed by his brother.

"The council will meet in thirty minutes, Gaultier. We will escort Velius," Almus said.

The impending meeting of the Council of Elders was sure to be difficult, but for now, Gaultier could find a bit of comfort in his wife's presence.

"I will meet you in the council chamber," he said, stepping in front of the other seclusion room where Hanileh awaited him.

CHAPTER TWENTY SIX

Gaultier stared at his brother as Ostium brought him into the lower level of the Council chamber. The elders had gathered moments before and milled about, taking their seats on the tiered platforms at the north end of the room. Gaultier remained standing, ready to accuse his brother of his foul deeds.

Almus brought the meeting to order by lifting his arms and calling out, "Council members, let us go to prayer."

Everyone stood and quieted. Gaultier kept his eyes on Velius as the athaer spoke the petition for wisdom and guidance in the upcoming proceedings. Velius trembled with rage and discomfort. It was such a sudden—and drastic—change. When had it happened? And why had Gaultier been blind to it?

A murmuring of *assentior* wrangled Gaultier's attention back to focus. Robes rustled as the elders sat. Almus shared a glance with Gaultier before he looked down at Velius.

"Before us stands the accused, the former athaer of Kapelle, Velius Lassiter. His multiple crimes against the Logia have forever sullied his reputation among us."

"Where's that grace you preach to the masses, Almus?" Velius challenged, glaring with venomous eyes.

Almus ignored him. "Witnesses have come forth, claiming he was involved in the kidnapping of Karaine Lassiter."

"Claiming. It's all speculation!"

"We also have reason to believe he had something to do with Athaer Castus and Sopor's murders."

"More speculation. Is this Logia justice?"

"You will be quiet!" Gaultier shouted, raising his voice above Velius. He'd spoken out of turn, but Velius's heckling was more than he could stand. "You have forfeited all rights with your actions, brother."

Velius stared hard at Gaultier. "I am the athaer of Kapelle."

Gaultier pulled Velius's journal from his jacket. He held it up as he turned to the elders. "Revoke the title. A servant of Carnifex is not fit to represent the Crown."

The elder closest to Gaultier reached for the journal. He opened it and skimmed it with disgust before passing it on to the elder next to him. Gaultier met Velius's hateful stare as Almus continued, "If the Council agrees, by sign of *assentior*, the title of athaer of Kapelle shall henceforth be removed from Velius Lassiter."

In unison, ten of the elders said, "*Assentior.*"

"Gaultier?" Almus asked.

Continuing the stare-down with Velius, Gaultier nodded. "*Assentior.*"

"Then it is unanimous. The title of athaer is now vacant," Almus announced. "We will convene at another time to appoint a new athaer."

"In a formal move, I recommend Almus continue to act as interim athaer until our new athaer is appointed," one of the elders said.

"I second."

"*Assentior*," came another unanimous vote.

"Thank you for your confidence in me, my brothers." Almus bowed his head. "I accept the charge."

"Oh, isn't this sweet?" Velius said. "I hope we all feel so very good about ourselves now."

Gaultier leapt over the partition that divided the floor from the elders' seats. Marching to his brother's side, he gripped his tunic and jerked him from Ostium. "I told you to be quiet. You are on trial here."

"I don't see a court. Or a jury. Just a bunch of biased judges," Velius snapped.

"It is our way, Velius. You know that. We are called to a higher standing."

Almus cleared his throat. "Gaultier, I advise you to listen to your own words."

Gaultier froze, staring at his fists. After a long moment, the realization struck him. He released Velius and bowed his head.

Ostium moved back to Velius's side. "It's understandable, Gaultier. You're emotionally involved here."

Ostium was right. Gaultier stumbled back toward the elders' box. He was emotionally involved. Too much so. He couldn't be objective.

"And that is something we need to consider," Almus said. "Gaultier, you and your family have fallen victim to Velius's hatred. What do you wish to see happen here?"

Gaultier shook his head. "Don't make me choose."

"Some of us would see him hanged, Gaultier. Others of us wish to be sympathetic. Perhaps because you are closest to him, you will find a most suitable solution."

Bowing his head, Gaultier closed his eyes and prayed silently. *Don't make me do this. I don't want to be his judge.* With all Velius had done in the past and now, losing his newborn son, hadn't he been through enough? Why would the Crown put this on him?

Because Almus is right. You think you cannot be objective. But because of your love for your brother, you will impart graceful justice.

"Send him away," Gaultier finally said. "He is no longer welcome at Kapelle. Warn the other domiciles. If he's so comfortable in the presence of Carnifex, let him dwell among the enemy's people."

Velius chuckled, shaking his head. "You don't know what you're doing, brother."

Gaultier lifted his eyes to Velius. "If you come near my family again, I will not hesitate to end your life. You have been given chance after chance. Grace beyond measure. From this moment on, any further harm of the Logia will justify righteous anger resulting in your death."

"Kapelle is in agreement with Gaultier. You are banned from the domicile, as well as the Logia domiciles across the system. You are also banned from any form of communication with the Lassiter family. Should you violate our orders, you will face the repercussions," Almus said.

"The Challenge is coming. There's nothing you can do to stop it," Velius vowed.

"This has nothing to do with the Challenge. This is about you and you only. The Protectors will handle the Challenge when it happens." Almus signaled to Janua who stood at the entrance to the chamber. Almus handed off the journal to his assistant, then instructed Ostium, "Escort Velius from the premises. Janua will join you."

"Yes, sir," Ostium said as Janua descended the staircase to the lower level.

"Gaultier, you are dismissed. The Council and I have some further business to discuss. I would prefer you keep watch over Hanileh."

Gaultier knew Almus wished to talk with the elders about the search for Karaine. And as much as he wanted to be part of it, he was drained. He'd hit rock bottom earlier this morning and had nothing more to offer. He watched as Ostium and Janua led Velius out of the chamber, then crossed the lower level to the opposite door.

"Don't forget, Gaultier," Velius called out over his shoulder. "You did this. You separated me from the Crown. You condemned me!"

Gaultier closed his eyes as he slipped from the room. He felt the full burden of Velius's fall on his shoulders. It was because of him his brother originally chose the path of the Strages. Now, Velius had returned to them once again, and Gaultier had no choice but to shun him. Could Velius ever

HERALDS OF THE CROWN: POISON

be reconciled to the Crown? Did the Crown's mercy have a limit?

If so, perhaps Gaultier himself had reached it.

Shaking his head, Gaultier staggered back toward the private quarters he shared with Hanileh. He needed time with her. He needed time with the Crown. The Creed would provide comfort. It had been too long since he'd read and studied. Shame that something so tragic had to happen to call him back. But in the calling, the Crown's grace was evident.

At the door to their quarters, Gaultier lifted his eyes and murmured, "Thank You. As hard as it is to say right now, thank You. 'In all things, I will praise Your name, for You are merciful and mighty. You walk beside me in contentment, and You carry me in catastrophe. You are a loving King—a kind, gentle Ruler of Your people. Praise, praise be to Your name.'"

$$\spadesuit$$

"We have much to discuss, Gaultier." Almus sat next to Gaultier.

Gaultier had sought refuge in the chapel. He wasn't sure how much more he could take. Hanileh wept non-stop, and he could offer her no comfort. He was as inconsolable as she was. Even his relationship with the Crown remained strained, despite his efforts to seek the King.

"We need to take security measures," Gaultier mumbled, staring at the wood grain of the pew ahead of him.

"I've already asked Ostium to select several residents to act as guards. The Dignitaries ordered domiciles across the system to do the same. This Thaed person has proved himself quite the adversary," Almus said.

"It is the time of the Challenge," Gaultier said, dropping his gaze to his clasped hands as he leaned upon his knees.

"Castus said it would be some time before the Challenge was issued. No, I don't think we're there quite yet." Almus glanced toward Gaultier. "Your burden is heavy, Gaultier."

Squeezing his eyes closed, Gaultier rocked back, lifting his chin toward the ceiling of the chapel. "Something I've tried to avoid."

"You thought by passing up the role of Protector, or even the athaer title, you could escape struggle?" Almus chuckled, shaking his head. "It doesn't work that way, son."

"I did as the Crown asked, Almus," Gaultier whispered. "I heeded His call."

Shifting slightly to turn toward Gaultier, Almus met him with a questioning gaze. "You really don't realize how important you are?"

"What are you talking about?"

"Look at all that has happened, Gaultier. Significant events that could only be orchestrated by the Crown. You circumvented the responsibility to

173

become Protector or an athaer, but our King had a much higher intention for you. He brought Hanileh to you in a most glorious manner you could not deny. Had you seen her on the streets of Bellemort, you probably would have paid her no mind. But He put you in a situation that established and cemented your relationship with her.

"And beyond extraordinary circumstances, you were able to spend time with the Queen of Sagesse."

"That didn't turn out so well," Gaultier grumbled.

"In the Crown's eyes, it turned out exactly as it should. He is waiting to use the Queen in a very different way than any of us suspected. We cannot know everything this side of Eternity, my friend."

"That is certain," Gaultier said with a sigh.

"This situation with Karaine...I know it's grievous and painful, but you must remember our King is merciful and mighty. He has a plan for this as well. He is the Victor, no matter how bleak things may appear."

"You're just saying that because the Council named you athaer," Gaultier said, a hint of a smile on his lips to let Almus know he was joking.

Almus smiled. "If I didn't believe it, I wouldn't be the athaer."

"What do I do, Almus? Do I keep searching?"

"You and Hanileh are tired. Exhausted. I think you should take her back home to Serenata. Being here is a constant reminder of the hole in your lives. Let us continue searching, and when you have started to heal, if we've not found him, come back."

"It is more than just Karaine," Gaultier admitted, a frown darkening his brow. "We're fractured. Our marriage is crumbling."

"It's understandable. Allow Hanileh to be there for you. Let her in, Gaultier. She has an ingrained mothering instinct," Almus paused, lowering his voice to inflect sensitivity, "and the focus of that was just ripped from her. Allow her to care for you. And reciprocate that."

"There's so much more to do, Almus," Gaultier said.

Almus shook his head. "It's overwhelming you. Don't let it. You're not alone. You have all of us, but more importantly, you have the Crown."

Raising his chest in another sigh, Gaultier nodded, his eyes falling on the symbols at the altar. Almus provided him the reassurance he needed. Of course, that was Almus's job now, but Gaultier almost felt like his old friend Castus sat next to him. They were words he needed to hear. Words he would cling to.

"Thank you, Almus," he said, scooting forward to rise. "I will inform Hanileh of our plans to recuperate."

"She will more than likely fight you on them, Gaultier, but it is what you both need right now. Each other."

Gaultier nodded, slipping from the pews. Of course, Hanileh would put

HERALDS OF THE CROWN: POISON

up a fight. It seemed crazy, allowing the search for Karaine to go on without them. But Almus was right. They had to allow the Crown to run His course. He was in control, and ultimately, His plan would unfold. Trusting Him was the true challenge.

———————◆———————

Serenata: 4 months later

Hanileh stared at the blank page before her. Gaultier sat on the other side of the room, scanning computer files for information leading to Karaine. He wasn't supposed to be looking. He'd promised Almus he would allow the Kapelle domicile to search. He would spend time with both Hanileh and the Crown. That lasted only a couple of days. Too many weeks had already slipped by, and both of them were so agitated with worry and fear that something had to be done. So Gaultier activated his computer and left Hanileh to her own devices.

She hadn't attempted to draw anything since the Continuum restored her and she and Gaultier laid the Queen to rest. She wasn't even certain if she still carried the gift. Lifting the pencil, she closed her eyes.

"My King, You know my despair. Help me. Speak to me through this, and allow us to find our son," she whispered under her breath, not wishing Gaultier to hear her. "Help me see where he lives."

Without opening her eyes, Hanileh pressed the pencil to the paper. The tip danced across the page in grand, glorious strokes. As she drew, she thought of something Queen Nyssa had said long ago about being a conduit. She could almost feel the power of the Crown surging through her.

Expectation welled in her heart as she pulled the pencil into her lap. The paper before her held the answer to Karaine's whereabouts. She was one glance away from knowing where the Strages kept him.

Every muscle stiffened as she took a breath, held it, and opened her eyes. The sketch was nothing more than a hastily rendered version of their bedroom in the Kapelle domicile. The place where Karaine had disappeared.

Hanileh cried in frustration, hurling the pencil onto the table.

"Hey," Gaultier murmured, crossing the room to place his hands on her shoulders. "What is it? What's wrong?"

He reached over her to lift the drawing into his hands. "You've started drawing again," he said softly.

"Pointless," Hanileh muttered. "Just like before."

"No. Before led us to the Continuum, and they were able to help you," Gaultier reminded her.

"I prayed for a vision."

"Hmm." Gaultier paused in thought. "And how did you word your prayer?"

"To see where Karaine lives."

Gaultier sighed heavily, spreading the paper before Hanileh, his arms around either side of her. He spoke softly into her ear. "My love, this speaks to us yet, even if it's not the answer we want."

Hanileh leaned back into his embrace as he folded his arms over her. He continued. "Karaine still lives in that room in our hearts. It was the last place we saw him. And we've never let go."

"I can't let go, Gaultier." Hanileh squeezed her eyes closed again.

She felt him brush her hair back before he kissed her cheek. "I didn't say let him go, Hanileh. We have to let go of the pain and hurt before we can move on. I am as guilty of clinging to that as you are. In fact, as much as I hate to admit it, the injury has almost taken my focus away from the Crown. We have to get our hearts in the right place."

"And a single prayer won't do it," she murmured, looking at him.

"It's not that easy. I wish it worked that way." Gaultier smiled. "I imagine it will take a long time to walk the path of contrition. But we have each other and the promise of being led to restoration in the Crown." He kissed her shoulder.

"Does He know our pain, Gaultier?" she asked softly. She knew the answer, but it felt good to voice the doubt.

"That and immeasurably more, my love," he answered. "And beyond knowing it, He seeks to heal it. 'In the storm, it is difficult to see His hand, but before long, the clouds break and sunlight imparts the touch of the King.'"

Hanileh relaxed against him, taking comfort from his words. He always lifted reassurances from the verses of the Creed, and every time, the message spoke directly to her heart. It was as if the Crown Himself spoke through Gaultier. If only He'd reveal through Gaultier where Karaine was...

Placing her pencil to the page once again, she started moving it about lazily. She wasn't trying to draw anything in particular, but soon another image appeared to them. Gaultier cradled a baby, walking back and forth before their large window. Hanileh joined the two, smiling as she peeled back the blanket. The baby's face was different from Karaine's. The blanket had the name *Dacke* embroidered along the edge.

Dacke?

Looking up at Gaultier, Hanileh frowned in puzzlement. Gaultier's eyes welled up as he smiled down at the paper.

"You see, Hanileh? Through this drawing, the Crown has given us hope. We are to have a second son."

CHAPTER TWENTY SEVEN

Serenata: 425 CT

Gaultier woke Hanileh with the gentle whispering of her name. He brushed her hair back from her forehead. Her eyes fluttered open as her mind took a quick survey of where she was and what was happening. *Oh, yes. The baby.* She had delivered the baby. Marita had taken him so that she could rest.

"Dacke..." Hanileh murmured as panic rose through her drowsiness, fearful that Gaultier was about to reveal the unthinkable: Lucian had taken her second child.

"...is perfect. He's in Marita's care, sleeping soundly. It's all right, my love," Gaultier said softly. "I must speak with you, otherwise I would allow you to continue to rest."

"What is it?" Hanileh propped herself up on her elbows.

Gaultier moved to adjust the pillows behind her for better support. He then sat next to her on the bed and took her hand.

"I've been in contact with the Kapelle Council. They've had a long discussion about Dacke. Being the second son of a Logia, they wanted to measure us against the Creed's prophecy of the Third Son."

Hanileh sank back against the pillows. "How did we fare?"

Gaultier shook his head. "The Ruler Prince must come first and take His throne among His people. His death and the Reconciliation Prophecy must take place before that of the Third Son."

Lifting a hand to rub her eyes, Hanileh sighed softly. "This all has to do with Karaine, doesn't it?"

"They still believe Karaine to be the Divine Warrior, Hanileh. The Dignitaries confirmed it, but they've asked us to keep it among ourselves and those who already know." Gaultier let out a heavy breath. "They feel we, the Logia as a whole, failed him. We should have taken measures beyond ourselves to protect him. And because of that, they want to hold a ceremony, dedicating Dacke to the Crown and His sovereign protection, as well as a special time of prayer for Karaine."

"I cannot take this much emotion, Gaultier," Hanileh whispered as tears threatened her eyes. "They are scratching at wounds that have yet to heal."

Gaultier shook his head, again moving closer to Hanileh. "My love, it's not about us. I understand what you're feeling. You weren't the only one to lose Karaine. We merely want to bring both Karaine and Dacke before the grace of the Crown."

"'We?' You've already agreed to this?" Hanileh asked, sitting up. Gaultier always put his Logia friends before her and made decisions without her.

"I have, Hanileh. Dacke is my son. As is Karaine. I believe the Crown will care for them, no matter if they are in my arms or in the arms of an enemy. It certainly cannot hurt to place them before the Crown."

Hanileh bowed her head, turning away from Gaultier. He reached up and touched her cheek.

"You knew having Dacke could not make the hurt go away," he whispered.

"The worst part is the Dignitaries have opened themselves up for the blame in Karaine's kidnapping, but I cannot lay it there," Hanileh cried. "The blame lies only in myself."

"No, Hanileh," Gaultier said, taking hold of her shoulders as he craned his neck to capture her attention. "You did nothing wrong. Velius invited evil into the heart of the domicile. He allowed it. You were walking in trust."

"And I haven't since that day." Hanileh looked into Gaultier's eyes. "Don't you see? I cannot trust the Crown to watch over my son."

"Sons," Gaultier corrected softly.

Hanileh squeezed her eyes closed. *It's too much to deal with.*

"Oh, Hanileh," Gaultier said, pulling her into his arms. "There's a much bigger plan at work here. And our first order of business is to restore you to the Crown. You've blamed yourself for far too long. And you've blamed the King for foul deeds done by others."

"The King allowed it, Gaultier." She sobbed into his chest.

"For His purpose, Hanileh. And perhaps we will not see it until we pass to Eternity, but He will do mighty and glorious things with this."

She sniffled, pulling back from him. "And what do we do with Dacke in the meantime?"

"Love him." Gaultier smiled. "Love him enough to cover both him and Karaine. Give him over to the Crown and help him learn our ways."

Hanileh collapsed against Gaultier once more. "When does the

HERALDS OF THE CROWN: POISON

Council wish to perform the ceremony?"

"As soon as we can make it to Crenet. We will leave this evening. The Council will call the entire domicile as well as the Logia and Lumen residents of Kapelle to gather in the chapel. Once we get there, we will take Dacke to the sanctuary. Almus will guide the people while his assistant Munio leads us. The Dignitaries will join us via vid-link."

Hanileh nodded, allowing Gaultier's love to soak into her heart. "I would like to hold Dacke now," she murmured.

"I'll link Marita to bring him to us." Gaultier kissed the top of Hanileh's head.

◆

Gaultier cradled his sleeping baby as he stood in the sanctuary at the Kapelle domicile. The ceremony hadn't taken very long, but the hushed prayers murmured around Dacke were enough to lull the child into a peaceful slumber. Gaultier smiled as he admired Dacke's tiny face, a perfect blend of Hanileh and himself.

"My King," Gaultier whispered to the Crown, "You know we have seen far more than our share of troubles. And through it, I have tried to remain faithful. Forgive me where I have failed you.

"This ceremony, my King, has been overwhelming. So many people crying out to You on our behalf...I am humbled. You hear not only their cries, but my softest plea. Please, my King. Please keep this child within Your care. Cover him with Your hand. Allow us to be Your instruments of charge, protecting him and defending him as necessary. But even without us, my King, I pray for Your mighty protection. In the all-powerful name of the Ruler Prince, *assentior.*"

Pulling the baby closer, Gaultier landed a gentle kiss on Dacke's forehead. He closed his eyes, focusing praise and adoration into a moment of worship toward the Crown. Despite the loss of Karaine, the hope of Dacke filled Gaultier with gratitude.

"Gaultier?" Almus's voice spoke quietly from the entrance to the sanctuary.

"Join me, Almus," Gaultier murmured. "The King is with us."

"*Soli Deo Gloria,*" Almus acknowledged. "His presence is indeed tangible."

"Thank you," Gaultier turned to look at his friend, "for all you've done."

Almus smiled as he stepped closer, his eyes on Dacke. "Don't be so quick to thank me. You may not feel the same after we're done here."

Gaultier's brows knitted together. "What do you mean?"

ASHLEY HODGES BAZER

Gesturing for Gaultier to take a seat on one of the benches, Almus cleared his throat. As Gaultier lowered to the wooden plank, he watched the older man. Almus sat next to him with a sigh. "The Council wished for me to present an idea they would like for you to consider."

"Oh?" Gaultier asked.

"We've not been the same since Velius was removed as athaer. Try as I might, I cannot bring unity to the Council. There is too much hurt and mistrust among us."

Gaultier pressed his lips together. He did not want the title and position of athaer. He hoped Almus wasn't about to ask him.

"I need your help, Gaultier," Almus whispered.

"The Council needs consistency," Gaultier advised. "You should remain as athaer."

"I took the position temporarily," Almus reminded him. "Until another was named by the Council."

"Ask them, then. I am certain they will insist you take it permanently."

"We do not have a full Council. We lack one member."

Gaultier stared down at Dacke. "Is that all you want of me?"

"Yes. The Council would like you to return to Kapelle with Hanileh and Dacke. That would resolve the issue of Dacke's security."

"We thought Karaine would be safe here, too. Look what happened."

"We have better measures in place, Gaultier."

"I don't know, Almus," Gaultier said. "We've been yanked around, moving here and there and back again. Our lives don't need any more turmoil."

Almus reached out, touching Gaultier's arm. "If you don't do this, the Dignitaries will separate you from Dacke."

"What?" Gaultier asked, drawing the baby even closer to him.

"They have demanded we keep the child in custody here."

"You can't do that. Dacke is my child."

"They will take no further chances, Gaultier," Almus replied. "I'm sorry. I've tried to offer a compromise here."

Gaultier nodded, lowering his eyes to the floor. "So we really have no choice."

"I'm sorry," Almus repeated.

"I will inform Hanileh of my decision," Gaultier murmured before looking back at Almus. "Athaer Almus, I accept the position of Council member."

"I had a feeling you would." Almus smiled, a hint of regret stirring in his eyes. "Your former quarters are available to you, and your things will be here within the week."

"I wish to keep the residence on Serenata," Gaultier said. "It will be helpful to have a place to get away."

"As you wish," Almus responded. He stood and stepped toward the door.

"Almus?"

The older man turned back, his gaze intent on Gaultier.

"Thank you for telling the Dignitaries I would not be athaer."

"How did you know that's what they wanted?" Almus asked, a look of confusion on his face.

"I could tell," Gaultier said. "That is what they wanted, right?"

"Yes."

Gaultier nodded. "Thank you for standing in the gap for me."

"Always, my friend," Almus said, stepping from the sanctuary.

Lifting his eyes to the altar, Gaultier shook his head. "Forgive me," he whispered. Both to the Crown, and to Dacke.

CHAPTER TWENTY EIGHT

Crenet: 416 CT

Hanileh stared at the link in her hands. Neither she nor Gaultier had heard from Velius since he'd been sent away from Kapelle by the Council of Elders. They didn't even know to where he had retreated. But now, he had broken the silence and contacted her.

I have crucial information for you regarding Karaine. I'm outside. ~V, the message read.

Tucking the link into her palm, Hanileh glanced around their quarters. She didn't trust Velius one bit. Dacke slept safe within the confines of the sanctuary, but then again, so had Karaine at the time he was taken. Velius no longer had inside access, though, so perhaps Dacke would be safe. After all, Gaultier was in the next room.

She couldn't say anything to Gaultier about this. He'd had a very difficult time following Velius's disappearance. His distance had created a heavy strain on their marriage, and only recently had they started to grow close again. Of course, Dacke, in his sweet, child-like manner, asking why the two of them were so sad all the time had prompted both of them to examine themselves and their relationship. The conversation that followed sprouted a new, deeper love between all of them.

Leaning against the doorframe, she watched her husband for a long moment. The heartache and trauma of losing Karaine had aged him the last few years. Dacke, now nine, was indeed a great joy to them. But there was still a void, an emptiness. It could never be filled, even perhaps if they were reunited with their first son.

She crossed the room, placing her hands on Gaultier's shoulders. "What are you looking at?"

"I'm going over census records." Gaultier leaned back in his chair and rubbed his eyes. The computer before him blazed with its unnatural blue hue. "Karaine's name is so popular, though. There must be a thousand kids

HERALDS OF THE CROWN: POISON

his age with that name. I'm just looking for anything out of the ordinary."

Hanileh sighed, her fingers massaging the tension in his muscles. "You've done that hundreds of times, Gaultier."

"And I'll do it hundreds more," he whispered, his hand resting on hers. "I can't let it go, Hanileh."

"I know," she said, squeezing her fingers. "I, um—I'm going to step outside for a few moments. To get some fresh air. Dacke is resting. Would you mind keeping an ear open for him?"

"I thought he was reading."

"He fell asleep. You wore him out this morning playing tossball."

"We had a good time." Gaultier smiled. "I don't mind at all. I know you need the break."

"Thank you. I'll be right back."

"Take your link."

"I won't need it. I'll just be a moment."

"All right." Gaultier grabbed her hand, pulled it to his lips, and kissed her fingertips. "Enjoy the sunshine."

Hanileh smiled, withdrawing from him to head for the door. She dropped her link on the little table at the entry. *I'm not really lying. I'm going out.* Her motivation may not have been exactly as she told him, but if it meant she could come up with something to prevent Gaultier from pouring over those records, it would be worth it.

The domicile had little activity this time of day, so the corridors were quiet and abandoned. Most of the residents were wrapped up in studies or prayer. The families usually retreated to their rooms to allow young ones to nap. The elders gathered in the sanctuary for corporate worship and prayer. Hanileh would often wander the halls, enjoying the quiet. But today, she had a mission.

The wide glass panes that looked out onto the courtyard revealed a day full of sunshine. Gaultier would have expected her to venture to the courtyard. Of course, she purposely didn't disclose to him that she was going beyond the confines of the domicile. She had to. Velius wasn't allowed to show his face within fifty feet of the sacred buildings.

Ostium, now the head guardian of the gate, greeted her as she approached the foyer. He usually engaged her in polite conversation.

"Afternoon, Madam Lassiter."

"Good afternoon, Ostium," she said with a smile. It was their routine.

"How is our boy, Dacke, today?"

"He is well. Napping, at the moment."

"It's a beautiful day belonging to the Crown."

"Indeed it is." Hanileh crossed through the open gate, close to the reception desk. "I will be stepping out for a few moments."

With a nod, Ostium slid a digital tablet across the countertop toward her. "I'll just need you log in with the register."

Hanileh furrowed her brow. She would be forced to lie to someone today, but again, she might be able to pull it off with only a fraction of a lie.

"I am expecting a, um...a gift for Gaultier, and I'd prefer him not know about it."

"Didn't want to go through the delivery bay, huh?"

"It's a small gift. I didn't want to bother them with something trivial."

Ostium grinned. "I wouldn't consider a gift for your husband trivial."

"Well..." Hanileh bowed her head, then peered up sheepishly at Ostium. She felt the old temptation to influence Ostium to make things go her way. "Can we skip the register today?"

"I'm not supposed to," Ostium answered. "But you'll only be a few moments?"

"Just long enough to retrieve the gift from its deliverer." Hanileh hoped the truth of the partial lie outweighed the falsehood. If Velius did have information about Karaine, as he promised, then it would be a gift to not only Gaultier, but to the entire Lassiter family and the Logia as well.

Ostium nodded, sliding the tablet back toward him. "All right. Do you want me to step out with you?"

"No need," Hanileh said. "I'll be just fine. I know the deliverer personally."

"And they are expected at the front gate?"

"Yes."

Ostium frowned, examining the tablet. "I don't show them on the front gate register."

"I already coordinated the delivery with one of your associates. I won't tell you who," Hanileh offered what she hoped was a charming smile. Her thoughts pressed into his mind, manipulating him from within. She chided herself for doing so, but her desire to reach Velius was overwhelming. "I don't wish to get anyone into any trouble."

With a smile, Ostium moved from behind the counter, keycard in hand. He crossed to a panel mounted on the wall next to the wide gates.

"You're a sly one, Madam Lassiter. I won't press the issue."

Placing the keycard to the panel, Ostium entered his personal access code to release the lock. "I would leave the gates open, but with the heightened security requirements, I cannot. When you're ready to come back in, just position yourself before the camera and sound the bell."

The heavy stone doors scraped along the marble flooring, the sound reverberating across the open foyer. Hanileh smiled her thanks to Ostium before slipping through the crack between the doors. As soon as she was through, the doors reversed and slid closed once more.

HERALDS OF THE CROWN: POISON

Despite the sunshine, Hanileh felt a chill nip at her. She pulled her wrap around her and crossed her arms over her middle as she tripped lightly down the steps. It had been some time since she had left the safety of the domicile. She'd nearly forgotten what the outer world was like.

Kapelle was a fairly quiet city. Of course, it helped that the domicile had several acres of land surrounding it, enclosed with a sturdy iron barrier. The Logia had even secured the air traffic overhead, so the domicile could remain removed from distraction.

Hanileh crossed the vast green lawn and followed the graveled ground transport path to the gatehouse that separated the domicile lands from the outside world. Ostium normally kept the gatehouse manned, and Hanileh wondered who might be on duty today. She prayed she could talk her way past whoever it might be without him contacting Ostium.

Her chain of lies and deceit grew.

"Forgive me, my King. I only wish to find answers to questions we've been facing for too many years. We must bring Karaine home." She lifted her eyes for a moment as she skirted the trees that lined the drive.

Janua, Ostium's second-in-command, stood in the gatehouse. Hanileh knew him as a man of tremendous discipline. He stood ever watchful, using more than just his eyes to keep watch on the entrance. His gifting included a deeply rooted sense of all that went on around him...

...which was why he turned quickly as Hanileh drew near.

"Madam Lassiter?"

Hanileh smiled, stepping from the shadow of the trees. "Good afternoon, Janua."

"Is everything all right?"

"Yes," Hanileh said. "Why wouldn't it be?"

Janua stepped from the gatehouse, watching her closely. "You are on the grounds unescorted. And I didn't get word from Ostium you were coming."

"He is helping me keep a secret from Gaultier. I'm here to retrieve a gift from a private deliverer."

Janua's blond eyebrows dipped into a frown. "Ostium wouldn't break from procedure like that."

Hanileh dropped her gaze, feeling her cheeks flush. "He's just looking out for me, Janua."

"I'm going to link him. Find out what's going on."

As Janua started back for the gatehouse, a black cloud leapt upon him from the trees above. Hanileh screamed, stumbling back onto the gravel. The gnarled black figure callously threw Janua's body to the ground and proceeded toward her.

Scrambling to her feet, Hanileh's survival instinct kicked in. She snatched up a handful of rocks and threw them toward the attacker before turning to run. She screamed again, hoping to get someone's attention or perhaps even rouse Janua if he hadn't been killed.

Hanileh risked a glance over her shoulder. The gatehouse and Janua were in plain sight...and there was no sign of—

A force slammed against Hanileh, knocking her flat onto her back. She blinked in the sunlight, groaning as pain crackled fire through her spine. *Gaultier. Please let him hear me*, she begged silently as she reached into her mind to call to Gaultier.

"Marcella," a rough male voice said as a brawny silhouette loomed over her, blocking the sun.

"I'm not—"

"Hush," the man ordered, pressing a folded cloth over her mouth and nose.

Hanileh squirmed, trying to cry out, but the cloth muffled her efforts, as did an oppressive weight that settled upon her. A sickly sweet smell filled her nose as she fought against him. *Oh, by the Crown, he's put something on the cloth.* He was drugging her.

Please, my King, please protect—

All at once, a heavy stupor swept all lucid thought from her brain. She couldn't remember what she was fighting, or even what she was doing. Disorientation spun her head a million different ways, and it seemed best to close her eyes. She was so sleepy, after all. She should just...

Just...

———————◆———————

Gaultier stroked his son's hair as he hummed the old lullaby that Hanileh often sang to him. Dacke had awakened shortly after Hanileh left, crying inconsolably from a vicious nightmare. It was uncharacteristic for the nine-year-old. After nearly an hour, Gaultier had managed to calm him back into a somewhat fitful sleep. He glanced toward the doors of their quarters, wondering where Hanileh might be. She was never away this long.

Drawing the curtain around Dacke's bed, Gaultier slipped from the room and back to his computer. His eyes wandered to his link, and he chided himself for not insisting Hanileh take hers. But she had said she'd be back in only a few moments.

The knock on the door relieved his worry. Not sure why she'd knock, but...

Gaultier moved to the door to allow Hanileh entrance. "Dacke's been crying for—"

Almus and Ostium stood where Hanileh should have been. Ostium

HERALDS OF THE CROWN: POISON

bowed his head, while Almus, his face full of frown, looked at Gaultier. "We need to speak with you, son."

This can't be good.

Gaultier stepped back to invite them in. "What's going on? Is it Hanileh? Did something happen?" He sounded nervous, but he couldn't help it. Losing Karaine changed his entire sense of security.

Ostium glanced to Almus, who gestured for Gaultier to take a seat. Gaultier closed the door and crossed to a hard chair across from a plush loveseat. The two men followed him and sat on the small couch. Ostium wrung his hands, staring at the floor.

"Tell me," Gaultier said. "Don't sugar coat it, please."

With a nod from Almus, Ostium scooted forward to look at Gaultier. "Your wife came to the entry, saying she was retrieving a gift for you from an unspecified deliverer."

Listening to his every word, Gaultier nodded and urged Ostium to continue. He obviously had some important information.

"I expected her to be gone only a few moments. But when Cordus went down to the gatehouse to relieve Janua..." Ostium dipped his head again, closing his eyes. Distress rolled off him in somber waves.

"What happened?" Gaultier asked, looking to Almus.

"Janua is dead," Almus said solemnly.

Had she finally lost it? All the stress and heartache leading her to kill an innocent—

Why would you think like that, Gaultier? Things are much better now. She has Dacke. She has...

"Hanileh wouldn't..." Gaultier tried to keep his breathing even.

"We're not accusing her," Ostium said. "Our surveillance footage shows an outside assailant. But Gaultier...Hanileh is no longer on our grounds."

Gaultier leapt to his feet. "She's gone?"

Almus stood, touching Gaultier's arm. "Panic isn't going to help the situation, son. We have to proceed with reason and forethought."

"Dacke..." Gaultier sank back onto his chair. "Dacke knew. I didn't listen to him."

"What do you mean?" Almus asked, kneeling at Gaultier's side.

Gaultier lifted his eyes to the entrance to the sleeping rooms. "He was napping and woke up with a terrifying nightmare. It was the attack, I'm sure of it." He looked at Almus. "Thaed is behind this."

"Let Ostium and his men handle this, Gaultier. Dacke can't risk losing you, too."

"We've already got a presence scouring Kapelle. We'll find her."

Gaultier shook his head with a sarcastic chuckle. "Just like you found

ASHLEY HODGES BAZER

Karaine."

Almus frowned. "It's because of Karaine these security measures are now in place. You have no grounds to fault Ostium."

Gaultier waved Almus away, shaking his head again. "I have to go after her."

"You don't know where they may have taken her," Ostium said. "Or if she's even..."

"...alive." Gaultier dropped his face in his hands to hide the rising tears pooling in his eyes. He felt Almus's hand on his shoulder. "Why does the Crown wish to strip me of my every joy?"

"It is all too easy to blame the Crown," Almus murmured. "But He is instead where we should place our trust and our hope. I realize that is easier said than done, son, but you must believe He is using these crises for His benefit."

"I used to believe that," Gaultier whispered. "Until He began taking the ones I love."

Almus nodded, glancing back to Ostium. "You are dismissed, Ostium. See what you can come up with, and let me know."

Ostium stood stiffly, looking at Gaultier. "I do extend my apologies, Gaultier. And I covet your prayers. My men lost a powerful leader in Janua, and I, a friend. You have my assurance we will do all we can to find Hanileh and bring the assailant to justice."

Gaultier met Ostium's gaze. "I am sorry, Os."

"I know." Ostium offered a sympathetic smile. "As am I."

They clasped hands as Ostium stepped past him and exited the room. Gaultier leaned over his knees, hanging his shoulders. "I had not expected this, Almus."

"We never do. The best thing you can do at this point is be there for Dacke. No doubt he will be frightened and worried. He will look to you as an example," Almus advised.

Gaultier nodded. "I cannot just wait, though, Almus. I am a man of action. It nearly destroyed me when Velius ordered us to allow others to search for Karaine."

"That was to protect you and Hanileh."

"That was to allow his plan to unfold," Gaultier growled. "It bought him enough time to hide Karaine."

"Nothing I say will bring you comfort, Gaultier," Almus said, shaking his head. "But I ask you to remember who you are. That you hold on to and trust the Crown."

Gaultier stared at his boots. Who he was? He was a crusader. He was a man who passionately followed his faith. He was a man who cared beyond measure for those closest to him. And he was a man who had had too many

HERALDS OF THE CROWN: POISON

of those taken from him. He would not stand for another.

"Have the bay technicians prepare my ship." Gaultier rose from his chair. "Dacke and I leave within an hour."

"I cannot allow that, Gaultier. Not until we know more."

"You can't stop me."

"I can, Gaultier. I will seek a ruling from the Council if I have to."

Gaultier stared at Almus. "Why would you do that? Why would you keep me from going after Hanileh?"

Almus pointed behind him toward the sleeping rooms. "For that boy in there. If you go after Hanileh, you put your life at risk. I watched you grow up without parents. Do you wish to sentence him to the same fate?"

An intense anger boiled in Gaultier's stomach. Almus was right. And at the very center of all these events was Velius. It was always Velius. He—

"Her link," Gaultier said, darting about the room in search of the tiny device.

"What are you talking about?" Almus asked.

"Velius had something to do with this. I want to check her link to see if there's any evidence of such."

"Gaultier..." Almus followed behind him. "You're under a great deal of stress, son. There's nothing connecting Velius to this."

Gaultier shoved a pile of papers off the desk. No link. He moved to an end table near the loveseat and squatted down to rifle through the drawers. "There has to be, Almus."

"You're basing your accusations on his past."

"Since when are you on his side?"

Almus folded his arms over his chest. "I'm on the Crown's side, Gaultier."

Crossing the room to the entry, Gaultier spotted Hanileh's link on the table. He gripped it, taking a breath. "I asked her to take this with her."

Almus moved to his side. He spoke softly, "Anything?"

Gaultier activated the link, watching as the screen revealed exactly what he had theorized. He closed his eyes, passing the link to Almus.

"He lured her outside." He pressed his fingertips to his forehead.

"I'll give this to Ostium," Almus said quietly.

"I'm going to link Alton and Jax. I want their help. I'll ask Alton to bring Marita to care for Dacke," Gaultier said, gripping the chair at his desk.

"We work together on this, Gaultier," Almus reminded him.

"Of course," Gaultier replied. "I'd like to be alone now, please."

Almus sighed. "All right. Would you like for me to arrange for someone to watch Dacke until Marita arrives?"

Gaultier shook his head. "No. I want him near."

"If there's anything I can do—"

ASHLEY HODGES BAZER

"Just get that to Ostium. Have him alert me with any news on the investigation."

"All right," Almus said again. "I'll be standing by."

"Thank you, my friend." Gaultier glanced over his shoulder. "And keep us all in your prayers."

Almus bowed his head as he eased from the room. He pulled the door closed behind him. Gaultier dug his fingernails into the chair, looking up at the ceiling. "Keep her safe. And keep me sane. I am losing my faith, and I need every ounce of strength to continue to hold on. Give me a reason to hold on," Gaultier whispered in prayer.

Pulling out the chair, Gaultier sat down and immediately set to work. He had much to do. Contacting his friends was only the beginning.

CHAPTER TWENTY NINE

Hanileh swam through the dark grogginess that drowned her. Grasping for some sort of hold on reality, she broke through the surface, her eyes opening to a single green flame. Her chest rose and fell in panicked breaths as she tried to calm herself. She couldn't move.

"Good. You're awake. We can proceed." The words belonged to the grating voice that had haunted her dreams only moments before.

"Where am I?" she asked, fighting off the dizzying sensation that spun her thoughts into horrific scenarios. "Who are you?"

"We've never met," the man answered. "But you know me."

A powerful wind whipped across her body as the green flame extinguished. She couldn't help but whimper. In a blinding flash, everything around her became ablaze with the terrible fire. She immediately recognized the rugged, cavernous terrain of Ferus. They must have been deep inside a cave system. Jagged red rocks lurked behind the cruel green glow, forming the pillars that she remembered from a time long ago. It was a sacred place to the Strages. It was where Lucian had bestowed her with her first markings. He'd placed her hands on the altar...

This time, it was she that lay upon the altar.

"Where is he? Where is Lucian?" she demanded.

The man chuckled. "You're still referring to him by that old name? He'll find that amusing. Or repulsive. Either way, it won't matter, because when I leave here, I carry with me your heart. The rest of you will rot among the rocks."

Hanileh tried to move, but her limbs wouldn't respond. A crushing mass bore down on her. Even her chest felt compressed. The man had some sort of hold over her.

"Who are you?" she asked again. Perhaps if she kept him talking, she could delay her end a little while longer. Or convince him to show mercy.

At her right, he stepped into view. "Remember me now, Marcella?" he asked as he began to pace around the altar. "I captured your Logia friend—

Criswell, was it? I took your place when you were banished. I killed the athaer of Kapelle."

He leaned close, whispering into her ear, "And I made Karaine disappear from your lives."

Hanileh screamed in anger, once again tugging on her invisible bindings. Her effort earned nothing more than a mocking laugh.

"That thrashing around won't do you any good," he said. "I do Thaed's dirty work, and I'm good at what I do."

"Raum," Hanileh whispered. "Raum Carrick."

Raum tipped his head, smiling at her. "I have to share with you a little tidbit. Really. It's this wonderful morsel of news that will send you reeling. And then perhaps you'll understand how we're going to be able to conquer the Logia and the Crown. You see, your husband...is my cousin."

Hanileh released a heavy breath, staring at him. "It's not true."

"Oh, but it is." Raum stood to his full height, reversing the circle he'd walked around her. "He and I share the same blood."

"And Velius..."

"Velius was just easier to manipulate than Gaultier. Gaultier had too strong a sense of duty."

"Why did you take Karaine?" she asked.

"We're not here to answer your questions," Raum said severely. "I have my orders."

"What? Are you to kill me?" Hanileh followed him with her eyes. "Lucian is too cowardly to do it himself?"

Raum pounced on her, his face inches from hers. His breath stank of decay and made Hanileh gag. "He let you live once before. He realizes what a foolish mistake that was. But you see, he loved you."

"He is incapable of love. It's not in his nature," Hanileh said evenly.

Shrugging, Raum stepped back, his fingers toying with several strands of her hair. "He sent me to ensure he would not fall for your wiles."

Hanileh closed her eyes, fighting off a second gag. The familiarity Raum assumed between them made her ill. She wanted no part of him. If it were not for Dacke and Gaultier, she would invite death.

Dacke. She had to get back to him. She couldn't allow Thaed or Raum or anyone else to separate them. Gaultier would be worried sick. She could nearly sense his heartache.

"How are you going to do it?" Hanileh forced courage into her words.

Raum chuckled, drawing his rough, calloused hand along her arm. "Slowly, Marcella. Very slowly."

"I am not Marcella," she said, looking up at him.

"You will always be Marcella. The stain of blood cannot be washed away," Raum replied as the weight upon her grew heavier.

HERALDS OF THE CROWN: POISON

"It can," she gasped, "by the Creator King."

Raum cracked his hand across her cheek. "This is a sacred location to the Strages. You will not defile it with mention of the Crown."

"'Deliver us from that which does us harm. For your kingdom is perfect,'" Hanileh began to recite from the Creed. It's what Gaultier would have done.

With a growl, Raum gripped her throat, cutting off her breath. She closed her eyes and prayed for strength, but found a void. She felt no connection with the Crown at all. Raum's hold on her throat tightened with a cruel cackle.

"The flames isolate you, Marcella. I told you this was a sacred location."

Hanileh struggled under him. She couldn't breathe at all now. And she had no other way to fight. Perhaps the Crown would be merciful.

Reaching into a part of her mind she had avoided for a long time, Hanileh darkened her thoughts. Flashes of memories seared into her vision—the markings, the pain, the crafting. She saw the blood on her hands and the faces of the Logia she had slain. She had cast all that aside, believing the Crown loved her and had intended her for a higher purpose. But now, she allowed the darkness to fill her, to take control, to...

A ring of bright white energy pulsed from her. The force blasted against Raum, knocking him back on the floor. Hanileh instantly felt the release of weight from her body. She curled onto her side, coughing and panting for air. She had to move, but she allowed herself a moment to recover.

She sat up, looking down at Raum. He had information she needed. He knew where Karaine was. He knew how to escape the maze of caves and where his ship was. But she couldn't risk trying to wake him. Long ago, Lucian had taught her how to invade a person's thoughts. She'd already sinned against the Crown. What was one more?

Slipping off the altar, Hanileh knelt at Raum's side. She now saw the physical similarities between him and Gaultier. The height and stature. The dark hair and tanned skin. The strong line of the jaw. How two related people could be so different was beyond her. But then again, Gaultier was also related to Velius.

She splayed her fingers along his temple and closed her eyes. With a deep breath, she concentrated on her desire, willing herself into the mind of the monster at her fingertips. Bracing herself for what was to come, she pushed deeper and deeper into—

Powerful fingers gripped hers, twisting her wrist into an unnatural position. Hanileh's mind snapped back into her own. The shock was disconcerting. Raum's wild eyes met hers.

193

"You should know better, Marcella," Raum scolded.

Hanileh didn't answer. Instead, she slammed her knee into Raum's side. He shouted in pain and released her. She leapt to her feet, shaking out her wrist as she started to run.

Raum's reflexes were quick, though. His hand flipped up, catching her toe. Hanileh fell across his legs. He grabbed for her leg, but she kicked at him and caught his shoulder. She used the momentum to scurry away from him.

"Thaed said you'd put up a fight," Raum said, crawling to his knees.

Hanileh pushed herself to her feet, trying to find her breath. The hideous green flame ringed the cavern. Long ago, she'd been able to resist its toxic effects. But now, the rocks around her spun in crazy circles, and her stomach rolled with nausea. The fire weakened her. Raum smirked, now standing as well. He stalked toward her. "You can't pass through the flames. Thaed saw to that."

"Then I will defeat you." Hanileh backed away from him.

Raum opened his palms, cocking his head in question. "How?"

He was right. Just like Gaultier, he was what seemed to be twice her size. She no longer felt the presence of the Crown. All hope seemed lost. But she had to try.

"You know, I don't appreciate you using that little trick on me. But it sullied your standing with the Crown, didn't it?" Raum laughed to himself, staring her down. "You used forbidden power. How did it taste, Marcella? Did it give you a longing for home?"

"I am not Marcella," Hanileh repeated.

"Is that denial for my benefit?" Raum asked, now within a few feet. His expression revealed his anger. "Or are you having to remind yourself of that?"

Hanileh lunged toward him, hoping the surprise of her movement would be enough to tackle him. He held fast, wrenching her around in his arms until her back was pressed to him. A sharp metal blade flicked from his wrist, and he swiftly positioned it against her neck.

"Now that you've had one last little game, let's get down to business," Raum growled into her ear. "Thaed couldn't believe you actually survived his last attempt to kill you. He is also concerned since you have now borne two sons, you might bear a third and fulfill what the Crown's book says."

"'The third son shall restore righteousness. The third son of the one of reconciliation. It is he who shall put to death the enemy of the Crown, and raise up a new realm of peace and prosperity,'" Hanileh quoted, drawing some comfort from the promise.

"Aren't you so proud of yourself?" Raum snarled. "It's now my duty to ensure that never happens."

HERALDS OF THE CROWN: POISON

"I am not the one to bear the third son," Hanileh cried, her words carrying the tone of begging. "That is prophecy for another time. Another age."

Raum dragged Hanileh back toward the altar. "Thaed doesn't want to take that risk. So before I kill you..."

Whirling her around, he captured her wrists in one hand. He pushed her back as his foot swept hers out from under her. She landed hard on the rock altar, the heavy weight returning. Withdrawing a longer half-sword, Raum stabbed it through her right shoulder. She screamed in pain as the tip cleaved the rock under her.

"I'll ask you to stay still for a moment so I can do my work," Raum said.

His hand spread across her belly. He murmured a string of unintelligible words, but Hanileh caught phrases that were forever emblazoned in her memory. He called upon the power of Carnifex to remove the capacity for life from within her.

Intense pain sliced through her mid-section. She cried, writhing under the weight and the sword that held her in place. Raum's fingers pressed firmly against her torso as the agony churned and twisted deep in her body. He muttered a few final words, then turned a gaze of awe upon her.

"It is done."

Hanileh went limp as the pain diminished. It didn't completely leave her, but it did relent a bit.

"How dare you..." she whispered through tears.

"What does it really matter, Marcella? You're about to die, anyway."

It mattered because she was a creation of the King. He had sculpted her being. He had molded her form. He had chosen how she would look, think, and act. He had allowed her to find her own path to Him. And He had rewarded her with a loving husband and two beautiful sons. It mattered because in this one destruction, the Strages seemed to triumph over the Crown.

It destroyed her hope.

"You're a monster," she breathed, closing her eyes.

"We all have those qualities within us, Marcella. To Thaed, you are the monster." Raum scraped the point of his dagger along her arm as he whispered in her ear, "He wants you to suffer."

"Tell him I already have."

Raum clucked his tongue. "Not good enough, I'm afraid."

He plunged the smaller blade into her left side. Hanileh screamed, trembling despite the weight holding her down. Raum withdrew the blade and wiped it on his tunic.

"It's going to take several hours for you to die. I'm going to prepare my ship. I'll come back in time for the grand event. Just before you slip away,

ASHLEY HODGES BAZER

I'll carve out your heart to present to Thaed." Raum's fingers caressed Hanileh's cheek. "I might even send your ring, finger and all, back to Gaultier. Just so he knows it's time to shop for a new wife. Maybe Dacke will get the mother of his dreams out of the deal."

A sob choked Hanileh as Raum slunk away. She felt the weight lift off her, but her strength was draining away quickly. She wouldn't be able to make an escape. Raum had planned for that. Death would meet her before she could find any sort of help. Lucian had finally won.

CHAPTER THIRTY

Gaultier paced the length of the library as Jax and Alton studied the logs of Kapelle's public docking bays. Nothing out of the ordinary, they both reported before Gaultier asked them to look again. He paused as he saw Alton's wife, Marita, enter with Dacke.

"Be right back, guys," Gaultier muttered as he marched across the library to his son.

"Dad," Dacke said, his eyes sparkling. "Marita just showed me how to make a tree dance in the courtyard."

Gaultier smiled at Marita as he knelt down in front of Dacke. "She did? Can you do it, too?"

Dacke nodded proudly. "I want to show you and Mom."

Tousling Dacke's hair, Gaultier took Dacke's small hand in his own. "Soon, okay? We've got a...a project we're working on right now. That's why Marita's here. Remember?"

"Does it have to do with Karaine?" Dacke asked, his tone bordering on begrudging.

Gaultier released a heavy sigh. "No, actually. It's something different." He lifted his gaze to Marita. "Look, why don't I take a little break so you can show me the tree dance, and we'll let Marita get a bite to eat or something, okay?"

Dacke's face lit up with a bright smile. "You mean it?"

"Yeah," Gaultier answered. He stood and glanced over his shoulder. "Guys, Dacke needs some Dad time. Take a little while to rest, relax. We'll get back to this in a bit."

Jax lifted an eyebrow. "You're giving up?"

Gaultier shook his head. "No. But I'm focusing on the here and now."

Alton extended his hand toward Marita, who slipped past Gaultier and Dacke. "You go on, Gaultier. Enjoy your son," she murmured.

"Thanks, Mar." Gaultier gripped Dacke's hand. "Now, show me this tree dance trick."

Hanileh pressed her hand against the wound on her side. Life slipped through her fingers in vital red droplets. She had managed to yank the sword from her shoulder and get off the altar. She crawled toward the ring of green fire. She remembered the fire being cold, but as she reached out to touch it, the flames singed her fingertips. Just as Raum had said, Lucian saw to it she couldn't leave.

Sitting up was no longer an option. She couldn't move her right arm, and in order to stay awake, she had to keep her head low. Not that she wanted to be alert when Raum returned, but every second that passed allowed her time to think through what she could do. She also turned to fervent prayer, not for herself, but for the protection of Gaultier and Dacke.

"Hanileh?"

Wonderful. Now I'm hallucinating.

She closed her eyes, repositioning her hand to cover the stab wound. "Grant me mercy and grace, my King," she whispered.

"Hanileh!" she heard again.

She knew that voice.

"Come back to me, Hanileh. Come on. Open your eyes."

"I'm...dying..." she breathed.

"No, you're not. I'm not going to let that happen. Open your eyes."

Doing as she was told, Hanileh opened her eyes to see Velius hovering over her. His expression held concern, but he forced a smile to his face.

"Hey, there."

"I can't—"

"Just relax and keep quiet. We've done this before, remember?" Velius asked, replacing her hand with his own. "I'm sorry I can't restore you in the name of the Crown, Hanileh. But I can mend you. It will hurt, but it will save your life. Hold my hand."

Hanileh slid her fingers into the offered hand. Velius mumbled something and jammed his hand under her ribs. She cried out as a sharp pain, worse than the stabbing itself, pulverized her side.

"Hold on, Hanileh," Velius whispered.

The sensation of thousands of tiny needles tingled through her insides. She gripped Velius's hand and gritted her teeth.

"Breathe, Hanileh," he urged.

She took in a lungful of air. In the midst of anguish, she'd forgotten to breathe. Velius shifted his hand slightly. Hanileh watched as his face contorted in pain, and she began to understand the true nature of the mending. He took on the pain she felt in attempt to find balance.

After several more moments, the pain dissipated. Velius fell back, out of breath. He looked at her and frowned. "We have to get you out of here. I can mend your shoulder later."

"Raum..."

"...will be waking any moment. I couldn't let him kill you, Hanileh," Velius said, pushing up to his feet. "I have to get you back to Gaultier. You need to try to walk, even though you're going to be very weak for a while due to the blood loss."

"You contacted me..." Hanileh started, confusion skewing her perception.

"That wasn't me." Velius took her arm and pulled her to her feet. "Come on."

Hanileh swayed, collapsing against him. Her feet felt like they were surrounded with clouds, lifting her right off the ground. Velius pulled her close to him, wrapping her arm over his shoulders.

"Stay awake, Hanileh. Resist the urge to sleep. Once we get to my ship, I can get you connected to medical equipment to help you recover. But stay with me, please."

Velius dragged her toward the flame. He spoke a few foreign words, and the flame died away. The ring behind them blazed a bright path through the cave. Velius pulled Hanileh along, jogging quickly through the labyrinth.

He ran up the ramp of a small shuttle that didn't seem to be in the best condition. He settled her into a chair and pulled a mesh harness over her. "I have to get us off the ground and en route to Kapelle before Raum catches on."

"He'll know," Hanileh cried. She didn't speak of Raum, though. She spoke of Lucian. He would most certainly learn of Velius's betrayal and punish him for it.

"That's for me to worry about," Velius said as he stepped to the cockpit. "I have to make things right."

Hanileh sagged in her seat as the engines roared to life. It was a tough battle to keep her eyes open. She clung to the hope she would soon see Gaultier and Dacke. Lifting up a prayer of gratitude, she begged forgiveness for her failings in the face of evil. What would Gaultier think when he learned what she had done? Tears fell from her eyes as she realized he would dismiss it as easily as their King. She only wished she could do the same.

◆

The ship's groaning and shaking settled into an extended wheeze.

Hanileh allowed her head to drop back against the seat rest. She was still in pain, but at least it was manageable. The pain of her attack against Raum was far more wounding, though.

Velius emerged from what Hanileh guessed was the cockpit. He crossed the tiny cabin in silence and opened a cabinet nestled in the bulkhead. Withdrawing a tattered blanket, he shook it open and brought it to Hanileh.

"We are on course to Kapelle," He situated the blanket over her.

"Thank you," she said in response to both the blanket and the news.

Velius took a chair at the table across from her. "I had nothing to do with this, Hanileh. Please believe me."

She stared hard at the blanket. "I have no reason to trust you,"

"I saved your life," he reminded her.

"And for that, I am grateful." She wound the blanket around her fist. "But first, you stole my life. You created this nightmare I now endure every day."

"Would you accept my apology?" Velius whispered, leaning into her. "I have changed, Hanileh. I've renounced them, as you did. I've not been in Thaed's service for many years now.

"I committed a great sin, allowing Raum into the domicile that night. I don't know what I was thinking. Perhaps Thaed's influence runs far deeper than I thought."

Hanileh looked up at him. "And that's why I don't trust you. He could be using you even now."

Velius shook his head. "'The Crown covers me. He has taken my wickedness and cleansed me. All darkness is gone, and I am a reflection of his glory.'"

Hanileh pulled the blanket up over her shoulders and folded her arms over her middle. "I see you have Gaultier's penchant for memorizing verse."

"That verse got me through my worst days. Not all of us are fortunate enough to have our memories erased," Velius replied.

Hanileh dropped her gaze again. *Fortunate?* He had no idea how difficult it had been—unable to remember, unable to communicate. Yes, it had led her to Gaultier, but she had to suffer through much to get where she was. Nightmares of the Continuum still haunted her sleep, as did what they had done to Queen Nyssa. Not to mention, it was quite a struggle reconciling Marcella with Hanileh. And the last several hours had proved she never had accomplished that fully.

"Something else is bothering you."

"It's none of your business," she snapped.

"I'm not your enemy, Hanileh," Velius said, his tone gentle and soothing. "I am taking you to safety."

HERALDS OF THE CROWN: POISON

She sighed, closing her eyes. The blanket fell across her legs as she dropped her hands into her lap. "I did a terrible thing," she admitted. "I allowed Marcella to surface during Raum's torture session."

Velius's lips tightened into a tiny smile. "Marcella is part of you, Hanileh. She's not a separate entity. If you used the powers you had as Marcella against Raum, don't you think the Crown granted you that ability to save you at that precise moment? As with the mending. I lack the spiritual strength to restore you in the name of the Crown. But He granted me the mercies and the grace I needed to perform a mending. Enough to save your life. The Crown still loves us, even if we sway now and then."

His logic was tainted with the philosophy of spiritual tolerance. Hanileh knew his reasoning was faulty, but she had other concerns on her mind.

"But will Gaultier? Will he still love me?" she whispered, unable to keep the horror from her voice. "He will be appalled when he learns I fell from the Crown."

"Gaultier stands in judgment of no one. He is a child of the King, just as you and I are. If he places himself above us, the Crown will surely remind him of who he is." Velius took her hand and looked into her eyes. "And you didn't fall from the Crown, Hanileh. He still holds you," he said, turning her hand over and tracing his fingers across her palm, "right here."

She stared at their interlocked hands for a moment, chilled by his words and actions. Lucian had said the very same thing to her shortly after Karaine's kidnapping, but in a much different context. It frightened her to hear Velius use Lucian's words.

Snatching her hand away, she hid it under the blanket. "How long until we reach Kapelle?"

"A little under three days." Velius rose from his chair. "I'll get you to Gaultier as quickly as I can."

As Velius started back for the cockpit, Hanileh asked, "What happened to Karaine, Velius?"

The man paused, bowing his head before he turned back around to look at her. "He is not with Thaed, if that's what you're asking."

"Then you know where he is?"

Velius shook his head. "I was not privileged to that information. Thaed didn't tell me because he didn't want me to slip up and give you the information. He is aware of Gaultier's ability to fuse, and he knows Gaultier will do anything to find his son. I don't think even Raum knows for certain where he is. But I've been told he was delivered to a family to be raised Crepusculum. His gifting will remain a secret until he is of age. And when the time is right, Thaed will craft him and induct him into the Strages."

Hanileh bent over herself and closed her eyes in prayer. "My King,

ASHLEY HODGES BAZER

spare him the torment. Take his life, if you must, but spare him from being crafted."

She felt Velius's hand on her knee. She looked up to see him kneeling before her.

"I have seen him," he said.

Hanileh couldn't believe the words that had just come from Velius's mouth. "You've...seen him?"

With a nod, Velius withdrew his hand. "In passing. I was not permitted to speak with him."

"Where, Velius? Where was he? Who was he with?" she demanded.

"The caves of Ferus, Hanileh," Velius answered quietly. "Exactly where I found you. It was nine years ago. One of the last times I was involved with the Strages. Thaed performed a dedication ceremony, claiming Karaine for Carnifex."

Hanileh couldn't breathe. It was hard enough to lose a child, but to lose him to the horror she had experienced herself was devastating.

"D-did they hurt him?" she spluttered.

By the Crown, did Lucian bestow my child with markings?

Velius released a sigh. "They tried. But he was strong, Hanileh. He was somehow protected. I'd like to believe although he is in the midst of the Crepusculum and the Strages, the Crown is keeping watch over him."

"I wish I could think as positively," Hanileh said. "But I know what Lucian's doing. He's toying with the Crown. He's playing a very dangerous game, and Karaine is the pawn."

"I've also had visions of Karaine lately. He's vibrant and astute. He has your eyes...and your gift."

"That's what Lucian wants," Hanileh said. "The power to destroy."

Velius gripped her hand again. "Then let me help you find the boy. Together, with the Crown, we will bring him home."

Hanileh scoffed as tears pooled in her eyes. "You must be joking, Velius. Look at us. Broken, shattered souls who fail the Crown at the first real test of our faith. And we've tried for years, unsuccessfully, to find Karaine. Perhaps the Crown is calling me to resign my hope..."

"No," Velius insisted, throwing her hand into her lap. "You're not allowed to give up. That little boy needs you. Your faith has been tested a multitude of times before this, and you've come out the other side, shining with the Crown's glory. If He cannot overlook this one infraction, then He is not the King He claims to be. He's not the King of the Creed. He's no better than Carnifex or Thaed. And in this shame you're shrouding yourself with, you take away from what He truly is. He is mercy. He is grace. And more importantly, He is love."

Hanileh stared at Velius. The words pierced her heart. How right he

HERALDS OF THE CROWN: POISON

was. And the conviction and passion with which he spoke convinced her of his sincerity.

"It will be difficult to win over Gaultier..." she murmured.

"I'll speak with him. I imagine my bringing you home will influence him a bit, too. But I'll need you to back me up," Velius said, patting her knee before he rose once more.

Hanileh nodded, clenching the blanket in her fist. While she hated to disappoint the Crown, she balked at the thought of how Gaultier would react to what she had done. But Velius was right. Gaultier had no authority to judge. Either one of them.

CHAPTER THIRTY ONE

Crenet: 3 days later

Gaultier stood in the doorway of Alton's quarters watching Marita as she lulled Dacke to sleep. It had been a long day for all of them. When Dacke asked where his mother was, Gaultier broke down. He was as honest as he needed to be with a nine-year-old.

Jax touched his shoulder from behind. Turning to look at him, Gaultier saw Alton's face. There was news.

"Ostium says a small personal shuttle has requested permission to land at the domicile. It's registered in Velius's name," Jax whispered.

Gaultier pushed off the doorframe, marching through the residential part of the domicile to Ostium's operation facility. Jax and Alton both followed close behind. Gaultier had to rein in his anger before he faced his brother. Velius certainly was bold, Gaultier had to give him that. Stupidly so, but bold nonetheless.

Before even greeting Gaultier, Ostium looked up at him from the computer screen. "He's not allowed here, Gaultier. You know that."

"Give him permission." Gaultier crossed to him, pointing at the computer console. "I will end this here and now."

"The athaer won't go for that."

"Tell Almus this is my responsibility. Whatever happens will be on my shoulders."

"I don't have enough men—"

"I've got this." Gaultier was determined to end the game with Velius personally. No outside assistance...or interference. "Give me a few moments to get down there, then seal off the docking bay. I'll keep in touch with you by link."

Ostium stared at Gaultier for a long moment. "Almus is going to remove me from my office," he said, agreeing to Gaultier's plan.

Gaultier clapped him on the shoulder. "I'll make sure that doesn't

204

happen."

Shaking his head, Ostium slid his headset back over his ears and lowered into his chair. "*Excursor*, this is Kapelle. You have permission to land. Transmitting coordinates in three-two-one."

With a grateful nod, Gaultier stepped back to Jax and Alton. "I'm not asking you to join me. He's dangerous, and this could get messy."

Jax glanced to Alton. "I think you should go back to Marita."

Alton shook his head. "She and I have already discussed this. We both support Gaultier, no matter the cost. It's for the Crown."

Gaultier blew out a breath. "You two are closer to me than my own brother," he murmured.

"Let's save the sappy stuff for later, G." Jax grinned, handing Gaultier his sword. "We've got a kidnapper to take care of."

"When did you—?"

"Grabbed it before we came to tell you about the ship," Jax answered.

Alton smiled. "We knew you'd want to confront him."

Giving them both a smile of thanks, Gaultier tore down the corridor toward the docking bay. Alton and Jax both kept up easily. *My King, thank you for the good friends You've provided through Jax and Alton. Protect them. Keep them from harm, even if it means I face Velius alone.*

The docking bay was completely silent. Several ships filled the available fields, including Gaultier's ship, the *Midnight Sun*. But there was no activity down here. Ostium had ordered the on-duty technicians to evacuate. That meant no one would be available to guide the *Excursor* in and shut it down. Velius would be on his own.

"Seal the bay, Os," Gaultier ordered into the link. "And once the ship is in, seal off that entrance as well."

"Acknowledged, Gaultier, and Crownspeed. Let me know if I can be of further assistance," Ostium replied. The door behind them bleated a gentle alarm, then lit up with red lights.

"Just have a couple of men standing by to deliver Velius to the seclusion chamber."

"Copy that."

The wide bay door on the far end of the bay opened to receive the *Excursor*. Gaultier and the others darted around the other ships to get closer as the small shuttle flew into the doorway and settled onto the floor. Without moving into a field, the engines extinguished as the bay door closed once again.

Using the tip of his sword, Gaultier pointed to strategic locations for Jax and Alton to place themselves. Gaultier dashed across the bay and waited just out of sight of the ramp. The outer hull was still hot to the touch. Gaultier crouched down to avoid the heat.

The ramp cracked open from the shuttle with a loud screech. The ship definitely needed some attention. Of course, if Gaultier had anything to do with it, Velius wouldn't be going anywhere of his own volition for a very long time. It was such a paradox—loving his brother so deeply, and hating him at the same time.

"Come on," he heard Velius say.

Gaultier gripped the ramp, yanking it down as he leapt upon it. Clutching Velius's tunic from behind, Gaultier threw him down the ramp and held the tip of his sword menacingly toward him. Through narrowed eyes, Gaultier glared at the trembling man at his feet.

"Welcome home, broth—"

"Gaultier?"

Hanileh's weak voice took him by surprise. His breath caught in his throat, choking off the compulsion to even the score with Velius. Gaultier spun around to see his wife at the top of the ramp. Her face was pale, and she looked rather ill.

Tossing a quick glance toward Alton, Gaultier lowered his sword and moved to the end of the ramp. Alton and Jax closed in on Velius, issuing the words of arrest. Hanileh watched through tearful eyes, then looked down at her husband.

Gaultier extended his hand to her as he stepped up the ramp. "I didn't think I'd see you again, my love," he murmured.

She stumbled toward him, and he caught her in his arms. He held her, stroking her hair. "Thank You, my King. Thank You for bringing Hanileh home." Easing her down the ramp, Gaultier settled her on the floor and lifted his link. "Os, we're going to need some medical attention down here. Alert Almus and the elders that Velius is in custody."

"Acknowledged, Gaultier. Teams are already on their way."

"Are you all right?" he whispered to Hanileh.

She nodded, averting her eyes.

"We'll talk later," Gaultier murmured, pressing a kiss to her forehead. He then stood to face his brother.

"I don't know whether to thank you or kill you," he growled.

"I had nothing to do with this, Gaultier."

"I don't believe you," Gaultier spat, lifting his sword as he stepped closer to Velius.

"He speaks the truth," Hanileh said, a cough taking her voice.

Gaultier looked from his wife to his brother. "Talk fast, Velius."

"Thaed ordered her execution," Velius explained. "Raum lured her out from the domicile using my name."

Jax turned quickly, slamming his fist into Velius's gut. Velius doubled over and sank to his knees. Jax shook out his hand, glancing to Gaultier.

HERALDS OF THE CROWN: POISON

"Sorry, man. My hand slipped."

"We're not supposed use violence like that, Jax," Alton said under his breath.

"Logia aren't," Jax bantered, looking down at Velius. "But I'm not Logia."

"Enough," Gaultier said. "What was your part in it, Velius?"

Velius shook his head. "I've been removed from the Strages for a long time."

"Then how did you know Thaed ordered her execution?"

"Raum came to me, asking for my help." Velius met Gaultier's gaze evenly. "I refused. He took my link, which is how he was able to make contact with Hanileh."

Gaultier knelt down before his brother. "Why should I believe you?" he whispered. "You've lied to me too many times."

"Tell him, Velius," Hanileh said, urgency penetrating her weak voice.

"I've seen Karaine," Velius answered quietly. "The boy is alive and well. I want to help you find him. I want to make things right again."

"It's all a game, isn't it, Vel?" Gaultier stepped close, his face inches from his brother. "You arrange the board to suit your victory, then invite me to play. I want nothing more to do with you."

"Then there is a limit to our King's grace?"

Gaultier stepped back to wedge the tip of his blade against Velius's throat. "He's not your King. You've denied Him over and over again."

"And He's welcomed me home each time." Velius lifted his chin, offering himself as a sacrifice. "Strike true, Gaultier. For I know where I will awaken."

"In the flames of Carnifex," Gaultier spat.

"In Eternity with my King," Velius countered. "You cannot judge my heart."

Gaultier shouted in frustration as he threw his sword aside and rose to his feet to turn away. Velius cut him to the quick by throwing Logia doctrine in his face. Gaultier's eyes fell on Hanileh, who sat hunched over, her shoulders rising and falling as she cried. He stepped to her, caressing her hair as he took a knee next to her.

"I don't know what to do, Hanileh," Gaultier confessed in a whisper.

"Velius brought me home," she murmured, her eyes meeting his. "He saved my life, and it pained him to do so. Give him a chance, Gaultier. Show him favor."

Gaultier bowed his head. Forgiving Velius went against every instinct, but it was Hanileh's wish. He nodded silently before turning back to Velius. "My apologies...for assuming the worst about you, Velius."

"And mine for past offenses," Velius said softly. "Help me to move on,

ASHLEY HODGES BAZER

Gaultier."

"I cannot promise complete reconciliation, but..." Gaultier paused, glancing at Hanileh. "...but I thank you for returning my wife to me. And I will walk with you in your journey."

"That is more than I expected," Velius whispered. "Thank you."

Jax shook his head toward Gaultier and stepped away. The doors to the domicile opened, allowing several teams of people to enter. One group surrounded the shuttle, readying it for field placement. A med team flocked to Hanileh and a third descended upon Velius. Alton moved back, allowing Gaultier to explain what to do with him.

"Take him to the seclusion chamber. Post a guard to watch over him through the night. I will appear with him before the Council in the morning. Supply his needs as he wishes."

Ostium's men nodded, flanking Velius. Gaultier looked at his brother. "Don't give me cause to doubt you again."

Velius clasped his hands before him. "You have my word."

Jax walked out with the men. He was obviously in disagreement with Gaultier's decision. Gaultier would find him later to discuss the issue. While Jax could be judgmental, he always had good reason. His opinion meant a lot to Gaultier.

But right now, Gaultier had to focus on Hanileh. Alton was already at her side, along with a couple medics that resided at the domicile. They had her lying on her back, a stiff board under her for carrying purposes. Gaultier knelt down again, taking her hand.

"How are you, my love?" he asked, pasting a smile over his concern.

"Sleepy," she murmured.

Alton met Gaultier's questioning gaze. "She's lost a lot of blood. She says it was due to stab wounds." Horrific scars on her side and shoulder lurked under her shredded clothing.

"Velius mended her," Alton said.

"Mended," Gaultier repeated.

"It was all he could do, Gaultier," Hanileh explained, a fresh round of tears starting. "I—"

"I'm not judging him." Gaultier hoped to ease Hanileh's worry.

"He's not the only one who has fallen."

Taking a steadying breath, Gaultier nodded. He knew that meant Hanileh had much more to tell him. *Please don't let that mean what I think it means.*

"Let's get her to a place she can rest," Alton advised the medics. "And we'll do a more thorough exam."

The medics lifted the board, carting Hanileh into the domicile. Alton stood, offering Gaultier a hand. "There's more."

HERALDS OF THE CROWN: POISON

Gaultier gripped his friend's hand and pulled himself up. "She faced death and survived. What more could there be?"

"With that stab wound to her shoulder, regardless of the mending, I'm fearful she may have lost the use of her right arm. And she told me Raum did more damage. Internally. That he..." Alton bowed his head, blowing out a breath. "That he robbed her of the ability to bear any more children. Thaed's command."

"Is it true?" Gaultier whispered in horror.

"From what I can tell, yes," Alton confirmed.

Gaultier covered his mouth with his hand, staring at the floor. He couldn't believe anyone, even Raum—or Thaed, for that matter—could be so cruel. The cry of his heart reached out to his King. There was no way he could endure this alone.

Give me strength and wisdom, my King. My heart is broken. My Hanileh...what she must have endured. Allow me to help her, to be there for her, and to provide the comfort and understanding we need the face of such absolute iniquity.

"Will you try restoring her?" Gaultier asked.

"Of course. But the damage is extensive, and it's had time to settle in. I'll do what I can."

"That's all I ask."

"Come on." Alton nudged Gaultier's shoulder. "Hanileh needs you."

CHAPTER THIRTY TWO

Almus moved to Gaultier's side and murmured, "This is a mistake, Gaultier."

"Perhaps." Gaultier stared straight ahead.

The athaer shook his head, moving to his place within the Council chambers. The other elders were already seated. Gaultier rose from his chair to join Velius on the floor before the elders. He thanked Ostium and Cordus with a nod. They withdrew from Velius and moved into position on either side of the chamber.

Almus sounded the bell to officially begin the called session. He cleared his throat, addressing the elders. "I will not mask my disagreement in why we are gathered here today, gentlemen. We have among us one who has betrayed the Logia and shunned the Crown. He now stands before us to dispute his banishment."

"Excuse me," Velius said, interrupting the proceedings. "I do not wish to dispute my banishment. I don't want to return to Kapelle."

"Velius," Gaultier said, turning to his brother. "But I thought—"

"My brother misunderstood my intentions in this. I know I have wronged you all. And the Crown," Velius glanced toward Gaultier. "For that, I am very sorry."

With dramatic flair, Velius looked at each of the elders in turn. "You should know I have made my peace with the Crown. I came back only to deliver my brother's wife to safety. I ask you to pardon this violation of our previous agreement and to allow me to go on my way without further punishment."

Gaultier stared at his brother in disbelief. He was under the impression Velius wanted to be welcomed back with open arms. Yet Velius seemed ever eager to say goodbye again.

Almus shared glances with the Council, then looked back at Velius. "The consensus is in your favor, Velius. We thank you for your duty to the Lassiter family. With gratitude, we will fuel your shuttle and see you off.

HERALDS OF THE CROWN: POISON

However, our previous conditions still stand firm and will go into effect once more upon your departure."

Velius bowed deeply before meeting the athaer's gaze. "Thank you, Athaer. Council."

"Ostium, please escort Velius to the docking bay. Remain in his presence until the time of lift-off."

"Athaer," Gaultier spoke up. "May I please be the one to see him off?"

Almus frowned at Gaultier. "I don't think—"

"Almus, please."

With a hesitant nod, Almus agreed. "I want Ostium stationed in the bay, though."

"Certainly," Gaultier said.

"We are dismissed," Almus declared, once more ringing the bell at his right.

The elders stood as a group, then filtered from the room. Gaultier made eye contact with Ostium, who pointed in the direction of the docking bay. With a nod, Gaultier turned to his brother. Velius stared at the athaer's chair, regret heavy on his brow.

"It's time to go," Velius whispered.

"Yes," Gaultier said. "It pains you, doesn't it?"

Velius turned his eyes to his brother. "Every day."

"You said you made your peace."

"And I have. But it doesn't mean I've forgotten what I've done." Velius started for the exit of the chamber. "Forgiving yourself is the hardest thing to do. Remember that as you speak with Hanileh."

"She bears much sorrow," Gaultier said, walking with his brother.

"She bears much guilt. When she confesses what she's done, withhold your judgment, or you will destroy her," Velius advised.

Gaultier's frustration replayed his interaction with his wife over the last ten hours. Hanileh hadn't spoken to him since she arrived home. Of course, she was resting and recovering in the medical ward. He hadn't left her side until the meeting with the elders.

"You know what happened?" Gaultier asked.

"We traveled from Ferus to Kapelle, Gaultier. Conversation was all we had to keep us sane." Velius glanced at him as they walked the corridor adjacent to the sanctuary. "I do have one request."

"Name it," Gaultier said. "Whether or not I will grant it is a different matter."

"One of the conditions of my exile is I refrain from contacting you and Hanileh." Velius paused, looking into Gaultier's eyes. "I would like to help you search for Karaine."

"It's been ten years," Gaultier whispered, "since you..."

211

ASHLEY HODGES BAZER

"Yes. Ten years since I was foolish enough to allow power to corrupt me. Ten years since I was irrationally hung up on destroying the perfect life you led. Ten years since I walked away from everything I loved and sacrificed my soul for a meaningless cause."

"It's not meaningless," Gaultier growled. "The Strages intend to obliterate the Logia."

"And it's been nine years since I turned my back on them."

"You said Raum asked for your assistance."

"He found me. I've been living in seclusion at our childhood home."

Gaultier couldn't believe his ears. "You...went back?"

"I had to face the ghosts of my past, Gaultier," Velius answered. "Only then could I find peace."

"You really have had nothing to do with the Strages for nine years?"

Velius nodded. "And in the last few months, I started retracing my steps, putting pieces together of where Karaine might be. If anyone can get you to the heart of the matter, it's me. Let me help you."

"I have to admit, I've found very little."

"Examining census records?" Velius asked, lifting an eyebrow.

"How did you know?"

With a smile, Velius nudged Gaultier's arm. "You and I are more alike than you think, Gaultier."

They resumed their journey toward the docking bay. The technicians had cleaned up the *Excursor* and had positioned it on the prep strip for take-off. As promised, the fuel tanker was disengaging and pulling back from the shuttle. Almus had wasted no time in preparing for Velius's departure.

Gaultier climbed aboard behind Velius. A technician gave him a curt nod as he exited the ship. "Pre-flights are completed. You're good to power up."

"Thank you," they both said.

Velius looked at his brother. "Consider what I've said, Gaultier. I know I've let you down before, and I really don't deserve anymore chances."

"No. You don't," Gaultier answered. "But that's not what grace is about."

Gaultier extended his hand to his brother. Velius gripped his hand as they pulled each other into an embrace.

"I will be in contact," Gaultier promised, patting Velius on the back.

"I look forward to it." Velius smiled as he withdrew.

"Thank you for bringing Hanileh home."

"Take care of her," Velius said, standing at the door to the cockpit, "and her heart."

"Safe journey, my brother. Crownspeed."

212

"*Soli Deo Gloria*," Velius murmured as Gaultier stepped back and descended the ramp.

Once Gaultier was at a safe distance, the engines ignited. Ostium joined Gaultier, and in silence, they watched the shuttle lift up and fly out of the bay. Ostium glanced at Gaultier. "Are you all right?"

"Puzzled, Os. My world is upside down right now."

"Don't expect much is ever right-side up this side of Eternity," Ostium answered and drifted back toward the domicile.

Gaultier's eyes remained on Velius's shuttle until it was out of sight. Words from the Creed slipped into his mind. "'Your ways are ordered by reason and wisdom. Chaos devastates, confusion bewilders. Such are the methods of the enemy,'" Gaultier recited aloud. "Oh, My King, help me cling to those words."

Chapter Thirty Three

Why does consciousness have to carry such pain? Hanileh's fluttering eyes took in the shocking white of the med bay, although the staff had been considerate enough to turn down the lights a bit. Her entire body ached, but that wasn't the worst of it. She still had to face Gaultier. Perhaps—

"Hey," he whispered.

Of all the luck. He was there. Waiting for her to awaken.

"Where's Velius?" Hanileh stared up at the ceiling.

"He's gone, my love."

"You sent him away?" Hanileh demanded, pushing up on her elbows. She ignored the throbbing in her right shoulder.

"I—"

She launched into Gaultier, fists first. "He wants to help us find Karaine!"

Gaultier wrapped his hands around hers, immobilizing her in a strong embrace. "Calm yourself, Hanileh," he insisted. "The elders requested he resume his exile, to which he agreed."

Hanileh squirmed in Gaultier's grip. Her thrashing resulted in several powerful poundings of fire, piercing both her side and her shoulder. She winced and collapsed in his arms.

"What is it?" Gaultier gently settled her back on the bed. "Didn't Alton restore you?"

"He tried. He couldn't."

"But—"

"He said the power behind the mending was offensive to the Crown. The damage was already done." Hanileh smiled sadly at Gaultier, dropping her voice to a whisper. "The Crown will no longer use me."

"That's not true, Hanileh. He does his best work in weakness."

"Weakness, perhaps, but not in disgrace."

Gaultier sighed, reaching for her hand again. Hanileh anticipated his move, clenching her fists to avoid his touch. Biting his lip, Gaultier stared at her hand before he spoke again.

"Why did you not tell me?" he asked.

"Tell you what?" She had so many secrets now, she wasn't sure which one he was talking about.

"That Velius had contacted you."

"You would have done nothing." Hanileh focused on the ceiling again. "You would have continued scouring your computer records, simply because it was Velius bringing the information to us."

"When did you start to deem him trustworthy?"

"When I thought it was him on the other end of that link saying he had a lead."

"So all his evil deeds have been forgiven?"

"Isn't that what Logia are called to do?" Hanileh glared at Gaultier.

Gaultier took a breath and raised his hands in surrender. "I could have protected you," he whispered, trailing a gentle finger along her arm.

"I didn't need your protection." Hanileh hoped he felt the darts from her hateful glare. "You are not the strong, stalwart guardian you think you are."

"Hanileh—" he said, shock in his voice.

"You couldn't protect Karaine," she accused, her eyes filling with tears, "and you wouldn't protect me."

"How can you say that?" Anger nipped at Gaultier's words. "I would give my life—"

"And wouldn't that make you a great hero in the stories and legends of the Logia?"

Gaultier squared his jaw and set about smoothing out Hanileh's blanket. "I am going to let this slide, as I know you are going through a difficult time—"

"Always so noble..."

"Stop it!" Gaultier slammed his fist against the bed. "What is the matter with you?"

"The Crown has forsaken me!" Hanileh threw herself onto her other side. Squeezing the sheets in her clenched fingers, she screamed internally.

"Hanileh..."

"I could not find Him. He would not answer my prayer. Marcella—no, I fell into my anger. I allowed myself to hurt Raum. I gave into weakness and temptation."

Gaultier's reassuring caress floated along her arm. "You were battling a great evil, Hanileh. I'm not so sure I wouldn't have done the same thing."

"Always about you..."

"No." His touch lifted as he walked around the bed. He knelt next to

ASHLEY HODGES BAZER

her and looked into her eyes. "I'm sorry. Continue. Please."

"I slipped into my old ways. I attacked Raum."

"He was hurting you, Hanileh."

"And the Crown allowed him to do so."

Gaultier ran a hand over his mouth.

Probably trying to come up with some verse to comfort me.

"'The Creator—'"

"Don't," Hanileh insisted, jabbing a finger into his face. "Don't quote your Creed to me now. I don't need your self-righteous—"

"Self-righteous?"

"—arrogance drilling false words into my head."

"False?" Gaultier stared at her. "Hanileh, do you hear yourself?"

"Leave me," she said, pulling the covers over her head.

"Never."

"I don't want you here. I don't want you to look at me."

Gaultier gently edged the blankets back. He started again for her hand, which she tucked under her opposite arm. As with a child, he took a hold of her arm, lifted it, and placed his hand atop hers.

She growled, shaking him off.

"Are you going to attack me now?" Gaultier asked, taking an angry breath through his nose as he stared down at her. "Will you hurt me as you did Raum?"

Hanileh had never seen him lose his patience. His words stung deeply

"How dare you!"

"Go ahead, Hanileh. Marcella. Whomever you deem yourself to be. But know this," Gaultier bent down, bridging himself over Hanileh, "I love my wife, but I am dedicated first and foremost to the Crown. He has called me to care for you, to shield you. And if that means to protect you from yourself, I will do it."

"The Crown betrayed me first."

"No." Gaultier locked his eyes on hers. "You listened to the lies of the enemy. You believed them. The Crown never will betray His children, even if they betray Him."

"Go away," Hanileh cried. "You are always so certain, so perfect. You want nothing more to do with me."

Gaultier sat back on the bed at her side. He pushed her hair back from her face. "Would I be sitting here with you if that were the case? You are rejecting me so I won't even have a chance to reject you. And I wouldn't, Hanileh. I won't. I thought you knew me better than that."

"You want to know? Go ahead. Fuse with me. You'll see."

"I will not fuse with you while you are hostile toward me."

Hanileh scoffed, rolling her eyes. "You don't trust me."

216

"No." Gaultier touched her cheek to draw her attention back to him. "Because I cannot handle the power behind your rejection. I love you."

Hanileh's tears began to fall freely as Gaultier drew her into his arms. "Please, my love," he whispered, "come back to me. Allow me in. You will find no judgment here. Only my heart, open and full of love for you."

She dropped her wall of anger, allowing Gaultier's love to fill her. She hadn't realized how far away she had pushed herself.

Settling in at her side on the bed, Gaultier pulled her close. "We are both exhausted, my love."

"I have no strength left," she cried softly.

Gaultier kissed her forehead. "Thankfully, we don't have to rely on our own strength anymore. We have each other. And..."

"Don't say it." Hanileh knew he wanted to remind her they could rely on the Crown.

"It's all right to be angry with Him, Hanileh. He can take it," Gaultier advised. "But don't reject Him."

"What? He can't take that?"

"Oh, He can. Have no doubt of that," Gaultier answered with a severe frown. "But you can't. That will destroy you."

"He doesn't want me," she said in a small voice.

"Hanileh, consider all you have been through. If He didn't want you, don't you think things would be very different?"

Hanileh closed her eyes as Gaultier's fingers trailed over her arm.

"It's a terrifying feeling—being lost. But He brought you home physically, so I could help you come home spiritually," he said gently.

"You don't know," she whispered. "You've never been lost."

"I experienced a very dark time after my parents were killed. Castus helped me put things back into perspective. Some of those feelings returned when Karaine was taken, and again, when you disappeared," Gaultier confessed. "It is less of a struggle to give those feelings over to the Crown, but nevertheless, it is still a struggle I face every day."

"You've never told me that."

"I've never needed to."

Gaultier leaned in, brushing his lips along hers. Hanileh closed her eyes again, allowing the tenderness of the moment to penetrate the feelings of devastation and despair.

"I've agreed to maintain contact with Velius," Gaultier murmured. "We'll find Karaine together."

"You are reconciled, then?"

"Not completely. But he saved your life, as you pointed out," Gaultier said. "And he brought you back to me."

Oh, by the Crown. In all this, she'd forgotten all about the one thing that was most precious to her. "Dacke—"

"—is safe. He is with Marita and Alton." Gaultier looked into her eyes. "We need to get you healthy and strong before he sees you. All right?"

Hanileh sank back into the pillow. "What have I done?" she asked.

"Exactly what I expected you to do," a cruel voice spoke through Gaultier. "Faltered in your strength. Failed the Crown at the first real test. The true source of your gifts could not be hidden, Marcella."

Defeat immobilized Hanileh, leaving surrender as her only option. "Have you come to claim me?" she asked. She had no might left to entertain fear. She only had despondency.

"I claimed you long ago, my child," Lucian took Gaultier's place in Hanileh's eyes. His hand reached out to touch her cheek. "You belong to me."

"I do not expect mercy," she murmured.

"Nor shall you receive it," Lucian answered with an eerie calm. His hand snaked along her neck and settled at the base of her skull.

Hanileh stared straight ahead, unable to meet Lucian's intense gaze. A dreadful chill whipped across her as darkness descended. The iciness was met with raging fire that licked through every vein in her body. Her pulse raced with her breath. She felt her muscles stiffen in response to Lucian's control.

From the opposite end of the spectrum, a powerful white light eradicated all traces of shadow. Hanileh felt as if she were tumbling backwards into an infinite void. She grasped for something—anything—but still she continued to fall.

"—rebuke you! In the name of the Creator King. In the name of the Ruler Prince," Gaultier's voice spanned a great distance. "You will no longer harm this woman. You no longer have the power to reach her, to touch her. Your bridle of fear and terror is lifted. She has been saved by the Creator King, and in His name, I rebuke you!"

With a jolt, she landed, falling back on the bed where the vision had started. Gaultier's presence closed around her. The intimacy was staggering, much like the times he had fused with her. This time, though, something felt different. Like puzzle pieces coming together.

Gaultier continued in fervent prayer, "My King, my Crown, I beg You to place Your seal upon this woman. She has dedicated her life to You. You know Your daughter. You love her soul as if she were the only one in existence. In Your name, O Crown, I place her under Your shield. Make Yourself known to her. Shine Your light upon her face and order her steps so that she may not know the evil that has dwelt inside her for too long."

Hanileh tried to breathe, but she felt a Presence intermingling between her and Gaultier. She could hear Gaultier's heart beating in powerful strokes, adding a natural rhythm to his words. His voice resonated through her and healed both old and more recent wounds. His thoughts aligned with hers, filling her with peace, understanding, and reassurance. Doubt and shame could no longer exist in this new realm of enlightenment. She felt secure in both Gaultier's love and the Crown's.

"He no longer holds power over you," Gaultier whispered.

He spoke of Lucian. For the Crown reigned in her heart and soul now, as He should have from the moment she first accepted His love. She understood she had held onto the old ways too tightly. But having released them, she felt like she could have a fresh start.

"We can never be worthy of him, Hanileh. But 'Behold, in Him, you have been made a new creation, and by His hands, you are redeemed and made worthy,'" Gaultier murmured. "You are redeemed, Hanileh."

"*Soli Deo Gloria*," she whispered, clinging to her husband.

◆

"Gaultier, Hanileh, thank you for coming," Almus greeted the couple as they entered the private office of the athaer. "Please, have a seat."

Gaultier held Hanileh's hand as she lowered into a chair opposite Almus's desk. They had been there many times over the years with news of promising leads on Karaine's whereabouts, only to find bitter disappointment and further sorrow. He hoped Hanileh had braced herself for such news.

"How are you feeling, Hanileh?" Almus asked.

"Better, thank you," Hanileh said with a gentle smile. "I'm not about to let a couple of Strages get me down."

Almus chuckled. "I'm glad to hear that. You're in good spirits."

Hanileh lifted her chin, blinking. "As good as can be expected, I suppose."

In an instant, Almus's joviality crashed into complete solemnity. "I hate to be the one to change that."

"What's going on, Almus?" Gaultier sat next to Hanileh. "Has there been news of Karaine?"

"No." Almus looked first at Gaultier, then Hanileh. "The Council of Elders met last evening."

"Without me?" Gaultier asked, suspicion now rising.

"Yes. It's been determined that you...how do I say this?" Almus frowned, looking at Gaultier. "You're a risk to the security of the domicile."

"They want us to leave," Hanileh whispered.

"We've exhausted our resources in searching for Karaine. There's nothing more we can do to help you. And with the recent security breach—

"There was no security breach," Gaultier replied.

"One of our men was killed."

"An isolated incident," Gaultier explained. "It won't happen again."

"Hanileh reported her assailant to be a relative of yours, Raum Carrick."

"Yes." Gaultier gritted his teeth.

"Raum Carrick has been dead for many years, Gaultier. He went missing when your mother and father were killed."

The chair seemed to collapse below Gaultier. He gripped the armrest, just to be sure it was still there. "The Strages have a way of slipping away and resurfacing when least expected."

"According to Castus's journal, Raum's body was recovered along with your parents. Avner just didn't want to add to your grief, which is why he kept that from you."

"So you're sending us away because the Strages have been clever enough to use a dead man's identity to attack us?" Gaultier massaged away the frustration from his brow.

"It's been decided, Gaultier. You and Hanileh can return to Serenata. You will always be welcome here, but we can no longer afford the risks involved in allowing you to stay with us."

"What of Dacke?"

Almus sighed, locking his gaze on Gaultier. "He is to stay here."

"Unacceptable," Gaultier replied. "He's a child. He should not be without his mother and father."

"May I remind you, Gaultier, you spent much of your childhood here? Alone?"

"I didn't have a choice."

"And right now, neither does Dacke," Almus said. "He must continue his studies."

"I will teach him," Gaultier argued.

"You're not qualified."

"I'm a Council member."

"You were a crusader, and you have a record of following your own path."

"I thought we were friends, Almus."

"We are friends, Gaultier. This has nothing to do with our friendship."

Gaultier rose to his feet, but Hanileh gripped his arm to stop him from verbally attacking the athaer. "This is my fault," she said. "I was the one to go after Velius. If I was to leave, would you allow Gaultier to stay with Dacke?"

"That's ridiculous!" Gaultier said, shaking his head. "We are husband

and wife. I'm not letting you go."

Hanileh looked up at Gaultier, tears in her eyes. "We haven't been husband and wife for a long time, Gaultier."

Almus cleared his throat. "It sounds like you two have some things to discuss. I will give you some time alone."

As the athaer stepped from the office, Gaultier dropped to his knee to focus on Hanileh. "What are you saying?" he asked in a whisper.

"Losing Karaine ripped us apart," Hanileh confessed, lowering her gaze to her knees. "We both thought Dacke would save us from that."

"That's a heavy responsibility to place on a child," Gaultier said.

"And it's not fair to him. All these years, he's not had a mother."

"You've been a good mother to him," Gaultier reassured. "I've failed as a father."

Hanileh shook her head. "It's not our fault, Gaultier. I wanted to love Dacke as much as Karaine..."

"What are you saying, Hanileh?" Gaultier asked, choking on rising tears.

"I think you and Dacke should stay here—"

"No."

She raised her voice as she finished her thought. "—and let me face Lucian."

"Absolutely not!" Gaultier answered, smacking his hand on the arm of Hanileh's chair. "You will not go in search of him."

"If I don't go, you will lose the only true home you've known," Hanileh said.

Gaultier gripped her hand and pressed it to his lips. "You are my home, Hanileh. You and Dacke."

"Our marriage is—"

"Don't you dare say it," Gaultier said. "Our marriage is salvageable. Our lives are salvageable. We owe it to Dacke."

Hanileh shook her head again. "I don't want to—"

Gaultier pressed his hand to her lips. "Please, Hanileh. You're breaking my heart. I ask you to stop before the damage is irreparable."

"Haven't we already reached that point?" she whispered under his fingers.

With a sigh, Gaultier slipped his fingers into Hanileh's hair. "Here's what's going to happen. We—you, Dacke, and me—are going to move home to Serenata. We are going to get our lives back. And you and me..." Gaultier leaned forward, pressing his forehead to hers, "...we're going to get our marriage back."

"What about Karaine?" Hanileh whispered.

"We will continue to look for him, but right now, our lives have to take priority." Gaultier stroked Hanileh's hair, looking into her eyes. "I love you. And I promise you I will pursue you as my wife. I will do everything in my power to work on our marriage. I will also dedicate myself to strengthening my relationship with Dacke. But I need you to promise you will join me in this effort. Can you do it? Will you?"

Hanileh bowed her head as tears began to fall from her eyes. Gaultier placed his hand under her chin and gently eased her gaze back to his.

"Will you?" he whispered, unable to keep the plea from his tone.

"I will," she whispered back.

With a relieved cry, he wrapped her in his arms and held her. She clung to him, something she hadn't done in months. He pressed several kisses to her head as he continued to stroke her hair. "My King, we place ourselves before You. Through our hardships, we've forgotten the true strength and wisdom You provide, if only we ask. Forgive us for failing You. Help us to find each other again. And help us to give Dacke what he needs. *Soli Deo Gloria.*"

CHAPTER THIRTY FOUR

Serenata: 412 CT

Velius sat across from Gaultier, sipping a mug of coffee. He'd arrived the night before, but there was little time to visit, as he was exhausted from his journey and both Gaultier and Hanileh were worn from their day. Dacke had already been in bed for a couple hours. Morning brought a fresh opportunity for the brothers to catch up.

"How are the boy's studies?" Velius asked.

Gaultier sighed, rocking back in his chair. "Dacke is doing well. Reporting to Kapelle is getting a little old."

"You're still reporting to them?"

"Every day," Gaultier confirmed with a nod. "After four years, I am still on probation status."

Velius chuckled, lowering his mug to the table. "I could have told you Almus would do something like this."

"Almus is my friend," Gaultier argued. "I trust his judgment. It's the Council I'm having trouble with. They're the ones who have placed this condition on us."

"Almus may not be the person you think he is, regardless of his title of athaer. He runs that Council like a bunch of puppets." Velius lifted his mug again, taking a long sip.

Gaultier leaned forward, resting an elbow on the table. "He is the reason we have Dacke. I can't fault him too much."

"Gaultier, on more than one occasion, I witnessed him manipulate people. He would tell them the Council had demanded this or that, when the Council had done no such thing."

Gaultier released a slow breath as he stared at his brother. He'd chosen to trust Velius after he had saved Hanileh. And Velius hadn't given him any reason to doubt over the subsequent years. Almus, on the other hand, had started to get to him with the daily reports. The friendship between them

ASHLEY HODGES BAZER

held an obvious strain.

Velius must have realized his words planted the seeds of suspicion. He quickly changed the subject. "How is Hanileh?"

The change didn't bother Gaultier one bit. He really didn't need his world turning upside down again. His fingers trailed around the rim of his cup. "She is well. Growing stronger in her faith every day."

"She had already conquered much the last time I saw her," Velius murmured. "Her past didn't seem to bother her as it used to."

Gaultier rubbed his eyes with his fingertips. "We've worked through a lot together. It took me a long time to earn her trust again."

"I don't think her trust in you ever faltered, Gaultier. I think she no longer trusted herself, and you were the easiest target of blame."

"None of that matters now." Gaultier smiled at his brother. He prayed Velius didn't see through its insincerity. Velius had a habit of picking at touchy matters, and Gaultier just wanted a friendly visit. "It's behind us."

"Indeed," Velius said into his coffee mug.

"Fill me in on what you have been doing, Vel," Gaultier asked, hoping to turn the tables on his brother.

"Well, I, too, have been growing in my faith." Velius stared down into his mug with a faraway expression.

"Alone?" Gaultier watched his brother, almost feeling sorry for him.

"No," Velius answered, drawing himself from his stare. "I've been serving a small...gathering."

"A domicile?"

Velius shook his head. "Just a gathering of people devoted to the faith."

"I see," Gaultier said. "And how do you serve them?"

"I'm not in a position of leadership, if that's what you mean." Velius wrapped his fingers around his mug.

"Is there...a leader?"

Lifting his eyes to Gaultier, Velius took a slow breath. "We have someone who guides us, yes."

"And you feel like you're learning from this person?"

"I don't know why you're questioning me so, Gaultier," Velius murmured. "But yes, I have become much stronger and more secure in who I am."

Gaultier raised a hand. "I'm not trying to start anything, Velius—"

"Uncle Vel!"

Dacke bounded into the room, nearly tackling Velius from the side. Amidst the gangly legs and arms of the teenage boy, Velius emerged with a chuckle.

"Hey, kid," he said.

"Oh, I'm so glad you're here!" Dacke grinned with a childlike exuberance. "I have so much to tell you! And show you! Dad's taught me some new tossball tricks. Will you play with me?"

"One thing at a time, kid," Velius laughed. "I haven't played tossball in years, but I'd love to take part in a game with you."

Hanileh stepped in, smiling at Gaultier. She moved to his side and rested her hands upon his shoulders. He lifted his fingers to touch hers.

"Dacke, let's allow your father and your uncle to finish their conversation," Hanileh said softly. "It's good to see you, Velius."

"And you, Hanileh," Velius replied, still holding the lanky boy in his lap. "I do have something I'd like to speak with you and Gaultier about."

"Have you finished your lessons today, Dacke?" Gaultier asked.

"Aw, Dad..." Dacke said. "You've been in here, and—"

"He couldn't concentrate, Gaultier," Hanileh explained. "He wanted so badly to see Velius."

"Son, you are thirteen years old. I expect you to be able to complete your lessons on your own." Gaultier gestured to the other room. "Go ahead and finish up, then we'll have that game you want to play, all right?"

Dacke heaved a dramatic sigh, looking over his shoulder at his uncle. "Do you see what I have to put up with?"

Velius laughed, playfully pushing Dacke from his lap. "I've seen worse."

"Dacke..." Gaultier said with an edge of warning.

"Yes, sir," the boy said. He crossed the room toward the door, pausing near the frame. "I'm really glad you're here, Uncle Vel."

"Me too, kid."

Gaultier took Hanileh's hand, pulling her around to the chair next to him. He leaned on the table, looking at his brother. "What do you have to tell us?"

Velius took another deep breath. "I didn't want to say this in front of Dacke, because I know how sensitive he is, but I have a lead on Karaine."

"Where?" Hanileh asked, scooting to the edge of her seat.

"Hanileh," Gaultier grabbed her arm before turning his attention back to his brother. "We're tired of unsuccessful chases, Vel."

"I understand, but this comes from a trustworthy source, Gaultier. I wouldn't bother you with it, otherwise."

"It's been too long since we've heard anything, Gaultier," Hanileh said, a wild look in her eyes, almost as if the years of empty leads had never happened. "Please, just listen to him."

Gaultier swallowed, nodding. "All right, Vel. Where?"

"Rabidus."

"Lucian would keep a child there?" Hanileh glanced toward Gaultier. "It's abandoned and hostile."

"Remember, Hanileh, Karaine is no longer a child. He's a year older than Dacke," Gaultier murmured.

"He's not there," Velius explained. "But my source assures me we will find a wealth of information about Thaed's dealings and plans, as well as Karaine's location."

"Who is this source, Vel?"

"A member of the gathering I mentioned earlier. She is committed to following Thaed's every movement."

"Rabidus is a large planet."

"She gave me coordinates that lead to somewhere in the city of Cathrach Dona. And a description of a building Thaed had been using as a place of operation."

"Could Thaed still be there?" Gaultier asked, stealing a quick glance toward Hanileh. He had promised to protect her from that animal. He would not allow Thaed anywhere near her.

"No. He's moved on," Velius assured. "But he's left behind much, according to my source."

"What do you think?" Gaultier asked of his wife.

"What have we to lose, Gaultier?" she whispered. "If it leads to finding our son..."

Gaultier nodded. "I'd like some time to think about it and pray over it. I ask you both to do the same. Let's allow Dacke the visit he's expecting to have with his uncle, then we can come together again to discuss it."

"May I ask something of you, Gaultier?" Velius said. "Don't bring this to Almus. He will only cloud your judgment."

"I agree," Gaultier replied. "No, I will say nothing to him. This is between us. And the Crown."

"Indeed." Velius lifted his mug in salutation before knocking it back.

◆

The street was vacant, just as Hanileh remembered all of Cathrach Dona to be. As Marcella, she'd been there once with the Strages. The Lassiters had scoured the city, looking for the information Velius promised. After hours of fruitless searching, they decided to split up, with Dacke accompanying Gaultier. And even though Hanileh knew Karaine wasn't here, hope flickered in her heart. All she wanted was to hold her eldest son. It had been years since she'd done so.

But would he remember her? Had Lucian changed him? So many—too many—questions were at hand. And then, there was the matter of Dacke. Hanileh had finally gotten to a point where she placed him and his needs first, although Karaine was forever present in her thoughts.

HERALDS OF THE CROWN: POISON

Shadows cast across the paved road from the crossroads above. The large stone buildings also blocked the sunlight, giving a chill to the air. *Should have brought along a wrap, Hanileh.* Her long scarlet tunic and thin black leggings couldn't defend her from the unexpected cold.

She leaned against one of the rails of the bridge on which she stood. Bridge was a little generous. A wide metal plank covered the gap between the docking bay and some sort of deserted building. The rail she gripped gave her a little sense of security, although she couldn't shake the fear she was in the wrong place. Gaultier never kept her waiting, in all the years she'd known him. Was she early?

Crossing over into the building, she looking about the corridor and imagined what the forsaken grounds might have looked like upon completion. Apartments, maybe. Or offices. Frameless doorways gave way to large square rooms. Plastic sheets covered the remaining holes where windows and walls should have been. Two strips of steel bars had been haphazardly attached from one support column to the other, perhaps in an effort to prevent an accidental fall.

The room Hanileh entered leveled out to the third floor. The plastic had torn from its anchor and whipped in the bitter wind, cracking and whistling all around her. A few tools and supplies lined one of the walls, and the acrid smell of rotten paint burned her nose. She sauntered to the edge of the room, looking out over the city to see if she could catch a glimpse of Gaultier and Dacke. Or even Velius. Her fingers clung to the bars that were still attached to the columns. The metal had given way completely to rust.

Glancing down at the timepiece on her wrist, a sense of alarm tore through her. She shivered, lifting her gaze again, only to see a figure drop from the story above her. His elbow slammed against her jaw, sending her to the hard cement floor with a cry.

"Greetings, Marcella," the man spat, standing over her. He reeked of a darker sense. Without looking, she knew it was Raum.

"What do you—" Hanileh started, trying to push herself up.

"No, you don't get to talk, remember?" Raum wound his fist in her tunic and yanked her from the ground. "And I'm certainly not answering your questions."

With one hand, he threw her against the wall. She crashed into the load of supplies. As her body connected with the drywall and stone floor, all breath burst from her, leaving her gasping in a heap. Raum stepped toward her, taking a fistful of her hair between his fingers to jerk her face into view.

"I have a message for your precious husband, Marcella. He's sticking his nose in business that doesn't pertain to him," the man hissed. "Your child is gone and will not be found. Gaultier should leave the rest to the Protectors. If he doesn't back off, he will meet his end, but not before he sees you and your other son writhe in the throes of death."

Hanileh cried, her hands grasping his to find some relief from the pain. Raum released her, but in doing so, he clawed his fingernails across her cheek, tearing into her skin. She fell against a wide metal bucket and prayed he would leave her now that he delivered his message.

"We're not done here, Marcella. Thaed is still angry over your betrayal. And I'm not too happy about your escape from me. You may have found ways to mask your treachery, but the stain remains." The man grabbed her shoulders and hauled her from the ground. He marched across the room to the gaping mouth that gave way to the thirty-foot drop-off.

"Please, Raum..." she gasped.

"If you're not careful, Marcella, you will fall again," he warned. With a mighty shove, the bars surrendered to their rusty captor. Hanileh sailed beyond them into nothingness. Raum's smirk loomed above her as she plummeted three stories below. The world around her halted. Her breath caught in a scream and lingered high among the clouds with Raum's smug expression. She hit the ground in utter silence, with the exception of the terrible cracking sound that seemed to resonate through her entire body.

Fire ripped through her, tingling agony into every cell, at least the parts she could feel. She squirmed in a futile effort to get away from the pain, earning even more pain. Raum laughed before he disappeared from view. A sick wheeze reached Hanileh's ears, and she realized it came from her own chest. So, this was death. Fear. Sorrow. Loneliness.

Moments later, another form appeared, hovering over Hanileh. Barely able open her eyes, she recognized Velius at her side.

"Hanileh..." he whispered, looking her over.

She gasped, fumbling to reach out to him.

"It's all right," he murmured. "You're going to be okay."

Okay? She was nothing more than a bag of broken bones.

"Gault—" she coughed, more twinges torturing her.

"No, keep quiet," he said, glancing up. "Gaultier!"

Nauseating dizziness threatened to drown Hanileh in blackness. She closed her eyes, unable to form coherent thought. A hand patted her cheek.

"Stay with me, Hanileh. Please stay with me," Velius begged.

Forcing her eyes open, she caught a severe look of worry on her brother-in-law's face. He looked up again as Gaultier scrambled to her side. Dacke stood behind his father, matching Velius's concerned expression.

"Hanileh," Gaultier said, his fingers moving over her. If only he could hold her. Make all the bad things go away. "What happened?"

Velius shook his head. "I turned the corner and saw her fall."

"R-Rau..." Hanileh stammered.

"Shh, Hanileh. It's okay," Gaultier said.

HERALDS OF THE CROWN: POISON

"I'll run back to the ship and fetch the medkit," Dacke volunteered.

"No, son," Gaultier said, brushing Hanileh's hair back from her face. "A medkit won't do. Vel, can you..."

"I am not allowed, Gaultier," Velius said, shaking his head.

"We have no choice." Tears from his eyes splashed on Hanileh's cheek. "She's in pain, and she probably doesn't have long. Please, Vel."

"I can't feel—" Hanileh coughed again. *My legs. I can't feel my legs...*

"Dad..." Dacke whispered in fright.

"It's all right, Dacke" Gaultier insisted. "Vel, please! Help her."

Velius looked down at her, terror in his eyes. "I will harm her," he said.

"Only if you do nothing!" Gaultier's pleas growled with fervor. "I am here to help you petition the Crown. Dacke will join us. Please, Vel. Try. All I'm asking is that you try!"

"Gaultier—"

"Whatever it takes, Velius. Even if it means mending her."

Velius stared at his brother before he placed his hand to Hanileh's chest. She whimpered, now lacking the strength to cry. Closing his eyes, Velius began to murmur a prayer, attempting to reach out to the Crown. Gaultier and Dacke did the same, echoing Velius's words with whispers of praise. Hanileh rested on the cold, sharp gravel, drifting between sweet velvet darkness and the whirlpool of pain that overwhelmed her with its force. It drowned her ability to care about anything in the moment other than escaping to the retreat of stillness, even if that meant surrendering her own mortality.

"Nothing is happening," Velius said. "I can't..."

Gaultier cried out an impassioned plea to the Crown. "Keep trying," he ordered his brother. "I will not give up on her."

Velius resumed the prayerful stance. Hanileh watched as Gaultier grabbed Dacke's hand and brought him to his knees. He placed their son's hand on her body. The boy's words carried the same fervor as his father's. Hanileh wanted so badly to express her gratitude, but she was tired. So tired...

Her eyes fell closed. Gaultier shook her a little, keeping her in a state between sleep and consciousness. "Pray, Hanileh. Please."

She tried to vocalize a prayer, but no words came. "My King..." she started, formalizing the internal prayer. "...help us..."

A white heat formed at her core, filling her with peace. She opened one eye to see the healing glow reflecting off the faces of the prayerful men. Velius's brow was drawn in concentration. He murmured pleas of confession, begging forgiveness for his past transgressions and asking the Crown to spare the life of his sister-in-law. Gaultier spoke words of praise, thanking the Crown for the many blessings despite the hardships. And

229

ASHLEY HODGES BAZER

Dacke hummed a gentle song of worship.

Hanileh cried as she felt her bones fuse back together. Gaultier gripped her hands, his tone growing more fervent. Velius's prayer continued in petition on her behalf. His fingers worked over her, touching each injury with a cross between energizing radiance and grueling anguish. Her back arched as her spine adjusted and set back into place. She collapsed against Gaultier, now relying on his strength to carry her. The prayers continued for several more moments before the men quieted and the warmth of the energy flow dissipated into a memory.

"I will stay here. Velius, I know you are tired from the restoration, but I don't trust these streets. Escort Dacke back to the *Sun*. Dacke, pilot her to pick us up," Gaultier said. "Hanileh needs rest."

She raised a hand to Gaultier's face. "I can walk."

"No," Gaultier said, pressing a kiss to her forehead. "You'd have to move far too slowly. And whoever you encountered might come back. You two, go on. Hurry."

Dacke and Velius moved on, leaving behind Hanileh in Gaultier's protective arms. "Are you all right, my love?" he asked.

"I'm..." she closed her eyes, allowing her head to fall toward him. She was physically restored, but the emotions caught up with her. He held her to him, shushing her with words of love.

"Raum...he wants you to stop looking for Karaine," Hanileh said, remembering the message the evil man gave to her.

"Never." Gaultier looked into Hanileh's eyes. "I will search for my son until my last breath, Hanileh. You know that."

"He spoke terrible threats," she cried, clenching her fist to grip his tunic. She couldn't get close enough to him.

"Idle threats, Hanileh. I will not allow anything else to happen to you. Nor will I allow anything to happen to Dacke. And we will find Karaine," Gaultier vowed. "Thaed will not prevail."

His embrace around her tightened. Hanileh closed her eyes as she relaxed in his arms, allowing her sense of trust to rest fully in her husband. It had been a long time since she'd trusted him. It was good to hold onto that again.

"Thank you," Gaultier murmured. He then lifted his chin and repeated his words to the Crown for answered prayer.

"I'm sorry I blamed you, Gaultier," Hanileh whispered.

"Let's not worry about that now, my love." Gaultier again kissed her forehead. "I see the *Sun*."

The whirring of the ship's engine grew closer. Hanileh could feel the vibrations as it landed within feet of them. Velius ran down the ramp, joining them again. Gaultier passed her off to Velius, only long enough to stand up. He then lifted her into his arms.

"We will return to Kapelle immediately," Gaultier said to Velius as he carried Hanileh on board.

Velius shook his head. "I will stay here and continue to search."

"You must go with us, Vel," Gaultier insisted. "You saw her assailant."

"I am not welcome at Kapelle. If Athaer Almus allows me in, surely the Council of Elders will condemn you for being with me."

Gaultier shook his head as he carefully lowered Hanileh into a passenger chair. He turned to Velius, his words full of appreciation. "Not after they hear what has occurred. You restored Hanileh through the Crown's power."

"The least I could do."

"But now, Thaed and his cohorts must be stopped. We have to tell the Council what has occurred here."

"I have a better idea," Velius said. "Let us take the information to the Protectors."

"We could just link them," Hanileh suggested quietly.

"We could. But before Hanileh was attacked, I found something." Velius held up a data card. "Karaine is being held on Maeror."

Gaultier took the disk. "Under the nose of the Protectors?"

"It's an anonymous tip, so the only way to validate it is to check it out. And the *Sun's* comsys is down," Velius said. "Dacke tried to raise Almus when we got back to the ship, but it's not working."

"You said you'd stay here to continue to search..." Question laced Gaultier's words.

"To avoid Kapelle, Gaultier." Velius pointed at the disk. "But I found this in an abandoned Strages den not far from where we stand."

Gaultier frowned. "I'll have a closer look at it. In the meantime, I'm going to have Dacke set course for Maeror. We can verify the information, and it would do us good to see our old friends."

Hanileh stared at her husband. Since Karaine's disappearance, Jett and Delia requested seclusion in order to concentrate on Strages movement. "They cannot provide hospitality or accommodations, Gaultier. Remember?"

"I know," Gaultier answered. "But I'm getting a sense we are supposed to go there. And we have all the accommodations we need here on the *Sun*. It's possible we are being led right to Karaine. It will be all right, Hanileh. Trust."

Hanileh nodded, leaning back in her seat as Gaultier crossed the cabin toward the cockpit. She locked eyes with Velius, who quickly dropped his and turned away, busying himself with something. A chill ran down her spine. Despite the valiant rescue he'd delivered, something wasn't right.

CHAPTER THIRTY FIVE

"We're approaching Maeror's orbit," Gaultier announced over the ship link. "Hanileh, will you please join me in the cockpit?"

Dacke's mother stood and excused herself, leaving him with Vel. The two had been involved in a lengthy conversation over the rules of tossball. Vel promised to show him some strategic moves when they returned to Kapelle, or even if they had time on Maeror. Gaultier had mentioned the Protectors now had children. There was supposedly a boy named Rider who was about Dacke's age. Perhaps they could enjoy a game of tossball with the Criswells.

Velius shifted in his seat as the conversation lulled. "Hey, kid, I...um...I'm going to use the fresher. Stay here, would you?"

Dacke chuckled. "Of course, Vel. You don't need my help."

"No," Velius joined in the laughter, although he seemed a little nervous. "Just...well, you're a great kid. I just want you to know."

"All right..." Dacke answered. *Boy, that's weird. What's going on with Vel?*

Velius stood, tousling Dacke's hair as he had when Dacke was little. Dacke responded with a smile before he reached for his Creed. The quiet would allow him to meditate a bit before they landed. And perhaps he'd find some chunk of wisdom to bestow upon Velius when he returned.

He heard a click behind him, chalking it up to nothing more than Velius entering the fresher. But some sort of electronic buzz followed the click.

"Stay very still," a foreign voice ordered as cold metal pressed against the back of his skull. "Don't say a word."

Dacke raised his hands, the Creed falling to the floor with a thump. Velius's voice came from behind as well. "Don't hurt him," he insisted.

"He is strong. We can't risk him trying to defend his parents."

What? They're going to hurt Mom and Dad! Dacke leapt to his feet, ready to take on whoever was there with his uncle.

HERALDS OF THE CROWN: POISON

The weapon fired, catching Dacke in the left shoulder. He cried out, but didn't let that stop him. He dove toward the man who looked remarkably like his uncle.

"Dacke! Dacke, stop!" Velius's voice said. "Raum, don't hurt him!"

Where is Vel?

"Vel!" Dacke cried out.

The brawny man, locked in a wrestling hold with Dacke, slammed his fist into Dacke's jaw. Raum, as Velius had called him, held Dacke fast, continuing to pummel him with sharp jabs. Finally releasing him, Dacke fell back on the floor, wheezing and crying.

Velius knelt next to Dacke. "I told you not to hurt him."

Dacke eyes fell closed. Vel would take care of things. As his uncle, Vel would protect him. He'd make the bad guy stop.

"He instigated it," Raum said.

Dacke coughed, touching his fingers to his split lip. Deep red stained his skin. He was in bad shape, but he'd recover. Would these men be as kind to his parents?

"Vel..." Dacke cried. "Please don't do this...Don't hurt them."

Vel looked at him with tenderness, whether real or imagined. "This isn't about them, kid. It's much bigger than all of us."

Tears stung Dacke's eyes and blurred his vision. "Please..."

"Enough with the sentiments. We have a job to do," Raum growled, his weapon once more pressed against Dacke's head. "Move on, Vel, and I'll take care of the kid."

Dacke could no longer hold his eyes open. A thick blanket of confusion pulled him into darkness. But that didn't really matter. If Raum was going to kill him, he certainly didn't wish to witness every detail.

"No," Vel insisted. "You will not harm him."

"I will not hesitate to kill you," Raum said.

"He won't interfere. Particularly if we lock him up."

"He'll report back to the Logia."

"Not if we take him to Thaed first. He can craft him. Dacke carries the blood of the Divinum Bellator. The Continuum identified Gaultier and Hanileh as the bearers," Vel begged. "Thaed will be pleased."

A lull in the conversation stirred Dacke. He had no idea what the two men had been talking about, but he really didn't care at the moment. His pulse rang in his ears, and his shoulder blazed with outrageous fever. He couldn't even lift his head. It felt so heavy after taking that beating.

"Get him up." Raum said.

Velius slid himself under Dacke and picked him up from the floor. "Just hold on, kid. We'll play that tossball game yet."

"I don't want to play with you, Vel." Dacke heard his own words slur despite his efforts to keep control. "You're as evil as my parents always said. For some reason, my dad always tried to find an inkling of hope in you..." His eyes finally cooperated, opening enough for him to lock onto Vel.

Shaking his head, Velius chuckled softly. "Yeah, Gaultier never thought much of me. It's only fitting his son would feel the same way."

"Turn back to the Crown, Vel," Dacke begged in a whisper.

"Sorry, kid. I've found a power I can't even begin to describe," Vel said, easing Dacke into the cabinet. "You'll understand once we deliver you to Thaed."

Dacke found a reserve of strength and shot back out of the cabinet toward his uncle. "Dad!" he shouted, hoping to get Gaultier's attention.

Velius rolled back onto the floor, shoving his hand against Dacke's mouth. The butt of Raum's weapon slammed into Dacke's skull. His body went slack as unconsciousness sparkled in his eyes. He fought off the darkness, only to see Velius jamming him into the cabinet. The darkness came anyway as the door closed. He heard a lock slide into place. Placing his throbbing head against the cool metal locker, Dacke closed his eyes, crying in helplessness as he slipped further and further from reality.

◆

Hanileh slid into the co-pilot's seat, smiling softly at her husband. He reached across and took her hand, pulling it to his lips.

"How are you feeling?" he asked. "Did you get any rest?"

"I did," she answered. "And I'm feeling much better, thank you."

"We're within an hour of landing."

Gaultier made some adjustment to the craft. On more than one occasion, he'd tried to explain, but she just had no interest in flying. She much preferred being on the ground.

"Good," she murmured, daring to look out the viewport. She was never comfortable sitting in this chair.

"It's all right." Gaultier smiled at her again. After so many years together, he knew exactly how she felt.

"It will be good to see Jett and Delia again after all this time. Do they know we are coming?"

Gaultier shook his head. "I was unable to repair the comsys. It seems to be in working order, but I can't get it to do anything."

"Is it plugged in?" Hanileh asked with a wink.

Chuckling, Gaultier glanced over his gauges. "First thing I checked."

She sat back, closing her eyes. "I am ready to be home."

Gaultier's fingers brushed along her arm. "I know."

Hanileh pressed her lips together. The thought of their home on

HERALDS OF THE CROWN: POISON

Serenata spurred so many different memories and dreams. Karaine. Dacke. Quiet solitude. Tranquility. She'd nearly found the peace she'd sought for way too many years. But what were she and Gaultier doing?

We're stirring it all up again by chasing after a ghost.

"It's been fourteen years, Gaultier."

"I know, my love," Gaultier repeated. "Are you giving up?"

She rolled her head, looking at him. "Do you honestly think we will find him?"

Gaultier's chest rose and fell in a sigh. "I don't know," he admitted. "Are we pursuing this for the right reasons? Is it for the Crown, as we've always claimed, or is it for us?"

"Poor Dacke has given up his entire childhood for this hunt," she added.

"Does Karaine have any idea he belongs to someone else?"

Hanileh dropped her eyes to her lap, fidgeting with her fingers. "Is he even alive?"

"Velius's lead sounds promising," Gaultier said. He touched Hanileh's head, running his fingers over her hair. "Let's check out this information. If nothing comes of it, we will return home and focus solely on Dacke."

Hanileh nodded, trying to come to grips with letting go of Karaine. She'd spent more years in search of him than she'd spent caring for him. In recent years, the search had become routine. She was just going through the motions. She'd given up in her heart long before. And despite their promises not to do so, they had overlooked Dacke for far too long. No wonder he'd grown so close to Velius.

A scuffle toward the back of the ship caught her ears. Gaultier frowned, looking over his shoulder. "What was that?"

"Vel was talking with Dacke about tossball. I imagine he's showing him some moves." Hanileh forced a smile to her lips.

"You don't trust him," Gaultier said, digging immediately into her heart.

Hanileh sighed, unable to avoid a frown. "I am grateful for what he did for me, but something didn't seem right. I—"

"Hanileh, you know I have often struggled with trusting my brother. But I owe him your life, on more than one occasion." Gaultier smiled, his fingers caressing her cheek. "If he hadn't come to your rescue..."

"It felt contrived, Gaultier. The entire incident."

"Surely, he wouldn't go to such great lengths to hurt you. Hanileh, he cares deeply for you."

Hanileh shrugged, closing her eyes again. "I can't explain my feelings, Gaultier. It's just the impression I got."

Gaultier fell silent. The ship jerked a bit as it entered Maeror's atmosphere. Hanileh gripped the arms of her chair. She hated this part of

ASHLEY HODGES BAZER

flying.

"It's all right," Gaultier murmured again.

"Dad!" Hanileh heard Dacke call out.

Concern rose in the form of panic. Hanileh glanced over her shoulder. "I'll check on him," she said.

"Sit tight," Gaultier ordered. "We've got more bumps coming."

The *Sun* rocked hard to the port side. Gaultier compensated, leveling out. Only a second later, the ship shook violently. Hanileh whimpered, clinging to her chair. Gaultier flicked every switch mounted above him, his hand still gripping the steering controls.

"Come on!" he said.

"What's going on?"

"It's not responding. It's like something is disabled."

"Something is," Velius said.

Hanileh looked up to see Velius, his hair unkempt and a scar visible over his left eye. She screamed. Velius clapped his hand over her mouth and aimed a slender gun at Gaultier.

"Get up," he demanded.

"What are you doing, Vel?" Gaultier's question was tainted with disappointment and heartbreak.

"Following my orders." To Hanileh, Velius said, "Move, and I kill him."

Locked in a silent standoff, Gaultier's expression flickered with grief and torment. Years of conflict with his brother had just collided with the understanding that Velius had never really changed. Sorrow set into Gaultier's eyes as he glanced at Hanileh, then reached across the console to the navsys.

"Don't do it," Velius warned.

He's scrambling the coordinates!

Velius produced a second smaller gun, and aimed it at Hanileh. "Reset them."

"I die first," Gaultier retorted.

Without even blinking, Velius squeezed the trigger. The blast made contact with Hanileh's right arm. She cried out and curled in on herself. White heat erupted across her skin as the fabric of her tunic melted against her burning flesh.

"I will kill her if you don't reset those coordinates."

"Don't do it, Gaultier," she whispered. A desperate trembling quaked through her limbs.

"Take me to the Protectors," Velius demanded, emphasizing his threat by shaking the gun toward Hanileh.

"Why?" Gaultier asked. "What do you want with them?"

"I said, I'm following my orders. And to show you that I mean

HERALDS OF THE CROWN: POISON

business..." Velius pulled the trigger again, this time hitting Hanileh's leg.

She screamed in pain, her body jerking in an attempt to shake off the agony. Gaultier leapt from his seat, batting the weapon trained on him from his brother's hand. Velius stumbled back against the bulkhead, while the gun landed somewhere under Gaultier's chair. Another blast from the gun that attacked Hanileh sizzled through the ceiling of the cockpit. Gaultier wrenched it from Velius's hands, but lost his grip on it. The weapon clattered to the floor.

Grunt after grunt exposed the pent-up hatred and anger between the two men as they punched and bashed each other. Gaultier slammed his fist into his brother's jaw. He lost his footing as Velius swept his legs from under him and threw him against the hard metal floor. Gaultier reached for the smaller gun, but Velius's angry foot crushed his hand. Velius bent down to retrieve the weapon.

"Gaultier, reset the coordinates," he demanded breathlessly, but with a deadly calm.

Gaultier groaned. Through clenched teeth, he asked, "What have you done with Dacke?"

"He's safe. For now," Velius answered. "But I can't promise his well-being if you don't cooperate."

"Gaultier," Hanileh whimpered. She was in such pain, and she didn't know what to do. They couldn't jeopardize the Crown and His Logia by leading Velius to the Protectors, but she couldn't bear for something terrible to happen to her other son.

The ship shuddered as it launched into a spin.

"Get control of the ship," Velius ordered Gaultier.

"Velius, think about what you're doing."

"I have thought about it." Velius moved to Hanileh's side. "You no longer win, Gaultier. I am the victor." He squeezed off another shot, taking out her left shoulder.

Her pained cry coincided with Velius saying, "I can take her out piece by piece." A sadistic smile darkened his face.

"Stop." Gaultier raised his hands in surrender. "All right, Vel. I'll do it. Just leave her alone."

"Gaultier," she gasped.

"It's all right, Hanileh." Gaultier whispered. "I love you."

In his words, she heard goodbye.

Like a lightning bolt, Gaultier dove for the weapon under his seat. But even faster, Velius circled the gun in his hand to focus on Gaultier. Blast after blast hit Gaultier, leaving him unmoving and smoldering.

"No!" Hanileh's heart cried out.

Ignoring the fire in her leg and her other wounds, she leapt to her feet.

Velius tackled her. She tried to break free from his grasp, but he was much stronger, and she had been weakened by the shooting. He pinned her to the floor next to Gaultier, a snarl contorting his face.

"Everything you've ever thought of me is true, Marcella, only much worse. I killed Castus. The fusion...if you hadn't woken up, I would have killed Gaultier and taken you for myself. I wanted you. The darkness within you called to me. Drove me crazy. And Karaine—it was almost too easy..."

"No!" Hanileh shrieked again, pushing back against Velius.

He dug his fingers into the wound on her shoulder, earning another screech of pain. "I delivered Karaine to my cousin, Raum's brother, on Serenata. They changed his name to keep the secret. He now serves the Crepusculum, but in a few years, he will be crafted by Thaed and married to one of the Gathering. The woman who took your place. Her name is Grania. She is favored by Thaed, just as you were, although he has sworn to never take a bride because of you."

Tears blinded Hanileh as Velius spoke of her son. She felt the ship spinning beneath her. The floor left them, then slammed into them. Velius landed hard on her before he rolled to the side. Hanileh gasped for breath, trying to sit up.

Velius groaned and met Hanileh's gaze. His weapon lay between the two of them. With only a second of hesitation, they both scrambled for the gun.

His fingers scratched her hand as she grasped the weapon. He wrenched her arm around painfully, pulling the firearm from her hand. He raised it, backhanding her with the handle. She fell away, landing on the floor with a cry.

"And you were right, Hanileh. I arranged the attack on you. I had to gain my brother's trust to get back on this ship. All I had to do was lie to him about Karaine being on Maeror. I knew he'd get us close to Jett and Delia. Once we land, I will slay them and earn respect and power among Thaed's Gathering. The Logia will fade from existence. If you play nice, maybe Thaed will give you a second chance."

Hanileh gripped the grate below her. The ship was completely out of control now. Or perhaps it was only her injuries.

"Never. I told Lucian long ago I gave my heart to the Crown. And I meant it. Unlike some," Hanileh said, narrowing her eyes toward Velius, "I've never turned away."

"That's a lie," Velius said, shaking his head. "You forget what you did on Ferus."

Another furious vibration shuddered through the *Sun.* Velius glanced out of the viewport before turning back on Hanileh.

"It was me, Hanileh. I was there. Raum and I are one."

"That's...that's impossible."

"When I committed to the Strages, Thaed crafted me. As part of my induction to the Gathering, I was ordered to kill. My parents were easy targets. I had hated them since Gaultier was born. It was my cousin, Raum, who tried to stop me. Ironic, though, as he was the one who introduced me to Thaed. Raum died by my hand that day, too, but he didn't pass on. His soul somehow intertwined with mine, and he's haunted me ever since."

A frightening whistle squealed through the cockpit as the *Sun* entered Maeror's atmosphere. Velius, gun in hand, sprang into the pilot's chair. Hanileh's eyes fell on her husband. Gaultier's arm flinched slightly.

He's still alive!

"Blast!" Velius slammed his fist against the console. His eyes turned on Hanileh. "You have to fix this."

"I can't—"

"It's programmed to only receive commands from you or Gaultier."

"I don't know how to fly."

"Then give me your codes!"

Hanileh shook her head. She'd never willingly assist such a monster.

Gaultier rolled over, his forehead split with a thick line of blood. With a growl, Velius scrambled from his seat and grabbed Gaultier's tunic. "You're the death of us all, my brother," Velius shouted into Gaultier's pained face. "I need a code."

"Never," Gaultier whispered.

Velius's animalistic cry shook the cockpit. He kicked open the door to the main cabin and hurled Gaultier into the table at the center. Before Hanileh could crawl to join her husband, the barrel of Velius's firearm jammed against her cheek.

"One more chance, Marcella. Give me your code."

Hanileh closed her eyes, bracing for the worst. "Do it, Velius."

The sound of metal separating from metal preluded another intense tremor. Velius staggered back into the set of chairs. Instead of returning to follow through on his threat, he slipped into the seat and shrugged the harness over his upper torso. His fingers worked frantically over the console.

Hanileh edged toward Velius, her grip closing around his weapon that had been forgotten under the pilot's chair. Her hands shook as violently as the ship. Slowly, carefully, she forced herself to her feet. The gun's sight rocked back and forth, but somehow she steadied it in alignment with the back of Velius's head.

Forgive me, my King.

A single shot. Velius slumped forward across the instrument panels.

Hanileh scurried to her chair. How she wished she had paid attention all those times Gaultier had tried to teach her to fly. She was able to access the main controls, but beyond that she had no idea. Something about lift. Thrusters.

What was it?

Closing her eyes, Hanileh prayed. *Help me.*

Without looking, she allowed her fingers to dance over the panel. Their lives would be in the hands of the Creator King, where they always had been.

Hanileh rose from the chair, but a sudden bump threw her to the floor. She crawled into the main cabin to Gaultier's side. Blood soaked his clothing where it surrounded his charred flesh. She gently touched his cheek. He opened one eye to look up at her.

"The ship is going down," he said quietly.

"Yes." A cry slipped from her as she pressed her head to his chest. She could feel him strain to place an arm around her.

"M-my King," Gaultier prayed in an strained whisper, "I beg Your hand to be on Jett and Delia. Protect them and their family from what is about to happen."

The ship shuddered again, setting into another spin. Gaultier gurgled, his breathing ragged and uneven. He was not far from joining the Crown. He continued, "Remember our sacrifice, my King. Be merciful."

She clung to her husband. *Please, my King, spare Dacke*, she begged silently. *Keep him safe to deliver the Logia from those who seek to harm your people...*

Gaultier's chest fell for a final time. A sob ripped from Hanileh as his arm slackened around her. She held onto him, preparing herself for the moments to come. A loud scream came from the ship as it slipped into a nosedive. Hanileh filled her lungs with air and wound her fist into Gaultier's tunic. She closed her eyes to darkness, but only seconds later, a bright white light surrounded her.

She felt Gaultier's comforting embrace...

———————◆———————

EPILOGUE

412.236 CT

Revered Dignitaries and Elders of Kapelle,

We've recovered Dacke Lassiter from the wreckage of the *Midnight Sun*. With deepest grief and unspeakable regret, I must report that both Gaultier and Hanileh were killed, along with one other. I can only assume it was Velius Lassiter.

Due to the circumstances surrounding the Lassiters, I will keep Dacke in my custody, as Almus and I have discussed on previous occasions. The boy is precious to the Logia faith, and at this juncture, must be protected to the utmost. I am exercising my authority as Protector and do not wish to be questioned or debated in this matter.

Please respect my expectations that none of you attempt to contact Dacke. He has experienced more grief and trauma than any boy of his age should have to endure, and I want to spare him further damage. I will raise him as one of my own, and I will let you know when and if he begins to show signs of the Divinum Bellator. While I realize Karaine was the chosen brother, it is quite within the Crown's power to bestow the remaining brother with the divine title. At that time, we will convene a council to determine his training and education beyond that which I intend to provide.

May the Crown bless and keep you.

Soli Deo Gloria,

Jett Criswell, Protector

Look for Book Two in the
Heralds of the Crown trilogy...

FUSION

———————◆———————

The lives of the Criswell family are disrupted when a spacecraft near their home. Amidst the wreckage, an injured boy—Dacke Lassiter—is discovered. As the only survivor of the accident, the Criswells decide to take Dacke into their home.

Ten years pass, and Raven, the youngest of the Criswells, has fallen in love with Dacke. Their plans to run away together are foiled by news of a legendary challenge. Raven learns her mother and father are the Protectors of the Logia faith and are required to defend the honor of the Crown against the Strages—evil, merciless people bent on destroying the Logia and the Crown alike. Within a few short days, they will be facing the battle of a lifetime.

Raven's brothers and Dacke prepare Raven for the battle, but when she comes face-to-face with Thaed, the leader of the Strages, she isn't ready and pays a hefty price. It is a crushing moment for Raven, driving her to the very edge of sanity and the brink of suicide. Instead of ending her life, though, Raven chooses to seek revenge. Thaed is still out there, and Raven intends to hunt him down.

FUSION EXCERPT

Raven stumbled across pieces of the ship's nose before finding the actual vessel. The dreary gray metal almost blended into the chalky green bushes and trees that served as its landing cushion. The size was impressive for a smaller class shuttle. Long, deep gashes split the top and bottom of the ship, the metal curling away from itself. The outer hull had burrowed deep into the soft ground, leveling the ship's midsection with the forest floor. A dull droning whirred from somewhere within the ship.

Rider and Griffin marched past her. Rider's eyes trained on the wreckage while Griffin puffed up his chest to wedge a barrier between her and the crash site. "Raven, go home and fetch Dad. Now," he commanded.

"No. Griffin, I want to see it, too."

"This isn't a game, Raven."

"I don't think it's a game, Griffin."

"Yeah, you won't think it's a game if this whole thing explodes!"

Rider turned and touched her shoulder gently. "Rae, there might be people on board who are hurt or even dead. Griffin is just trying to protect you. And I think he's right. It's dangerous. This is the kind of thing that stokes nightmares."

Raven lowered her eyes. Lately, frightening dreams haunted her, and Rider knew it. He also knew exactly what to say to make her obey. "All right, Rider," she mumbled in submission.

"I'll tell you all about it later." Rider charmed her further with his smile as he patted her arm.

"Not if it blows up," she muttered.

Shuffling away from him, she looked back over her shoulder to see Griffin hunting for an entrance to the ship. Her oldest brother never understood her. All she wanted was to see the inside of a real starship. Sure, she had seen the vessels in her father's collection many times, but she was never allowed to get close enough to touch anything. And oh, how she yearned to fly one...

"Rider! Help me!" Griffin called from the far side of the ship.

Rider jerked his head back toward home as a silent plea with Raven to get going, and then he dashed to Griffin's aid. Instead of obeying, Raven waited and watched, wondering what her brother had found. Maybe some kind of alien life form survived the crash and was eating him alive! Or, like he said, the ship was on the verge of exploding. She caught snippets of their conversation as the words wafted along the twilight.

"...men must have shot..."

"...died on impact..."

"...parents?"

"Oh, no..."

"Raven, go now! Get Dad! Quickly!"

Rider's insistence, mixed with her over-active imagination, grabbed her attention and sent her running. She barely felt the brambles nip at her as she sprinted back toward their large home at the edge of the trees. Her mind analyzed the few comments she had overheard and tried to piece together what her brothers must have found. She probably didn't want to know, but part of her was dying to see what was on that ship. Perhaps her father would let her return with him.

◆

ACKNOWLEDGEMENTS

My readers and fans—for the motivation to keep writing in this universe. Thank you for loving my characters and for allowing their stories to reach your hearts. I couldn't do this without you!

My Facebook friends—I'm grateful to you all for walking with me through this journey, especially those of you who helped me polish some of these pages.

My Pikes Peak Writers friends—for teaching me so much and instilling confidence in this venture.

My real-life friends—from my fifth-grade teacher to my Scottish cheerleader in purple, and many, many others, I am blessed by each of you. Thanks for being there and rooting for me.

My fabulous co-workers—for putting up with my fictional world while we strive to make the real one a better place.

My mama, Jane—for encouraging me and believing in me.

My brother, Bryan—for your multiple contributions, your listening ear, and your dedication to the success of *The Crown's Call*.

My Dingoes—for understanding whenever I say, "Give me just a few more moments." I love each of you so much.

My Gary—for supporting this crazy dream and being my biggest fan.

My Lord and Savior Jesus Christ—throughout these stories, I hope to honor You and bring glory to Your name. Thank You for the gifts and talents you've blessed me with. May Your name evermore be praised! *Soli Deo Gloria!!*

ABOUT THE AUTHOR

Ashley Hodges Bazer is the author of the sci-fi series, *The Crown's Call*. She's often decked out in bellbottoms and grooving out on the lighted dance floor. Okay, not really, but she does have a thing for the BeeGees. She lives in Colorado with her husband and three children. After earning her bachelor's degree in theatrical stage management from Arizona State University, she went on to work for Disneyland in that capacity. A love affair with books led her to work for several different bookstores. Currently a producer for an international daily radio program, she's learning to balance working, writing, and momming duties. When she's not writing, she's crocheting or belting out Broadway show tunes. And she's a real duchess! Learn more about Ashley and her upcoming books at www.AshleyBazer.com.

Made in the USA
Lexington, KY
20 April 2016